"Delany's work exists on a kind of borderline — ᴜᴄᴄ.. literary practice, between canonical and popular culture, between aᴄᴜ demic and nonacademic culture — a borderline familiar to feminist theory and cultural critique. The Nevèrÿon series is one of the most sustained meditations we have on the complex intersections of sexuality, race, and subjectivity in contemporary cultures."
— Constance Penley

"A literary creation of considerable importance . . . at once a colorful adventure yarn and an insightful philosophical meditation on the nature and requisites of civilization."   — *San Jose Mercury News*

"I consider Delany not only one of the most important SF writers of the present generation, but a fascinating writer in general who has invented a new style."   — Umberto Eco

"The tales of Nevèrÿon are postmodern sword-and-sorcery . . . Delany subverts the formulaic elements of sword-and-sorcery and around their empty husks constructs self-conscious metafictions about social and sexual behavior, the play of language and power, and — above all — the possibilities and limitations of narrative. Immensely sophisticated as literature . . . eminently readable and gorgeously entertaining."   — *Washington Post Book World*

"Delany continues to surprise and delight . . . [his] playfulness is the kind that involves you in the flow, forces you to see details in a larger context, yet never lets you forget that what you are reading is, after all, nothing but artifice, a series of signs."
— *New York Times Book Review*

"Complex and carefully crafted . . . his language is lovely, often approaching the poetic."   — *Publishers Weekly*

"This is fantasy that challenges the intellect . . . semiotic sword and sorcery, a very high level of literary gamesmanship. It's as if Umberto Eco had written about Conan the Barbarian."   — *USA Today*

"Instead of dishing out the usual, tired mix of improbable magic and bloody mayhem, Delany weaves an intricate meditation on the nature of freedom and slavery, on the beguiling differences between love and lust . . . the prose has been so polished by wit and intellect that it fairly gleams."   — *San Francisco Chronicle*

Return to Nevèrÿon

Samuel R. Delany

Return to Nevèrÿon

WESLEYAN UNIVERSITY PRESS

Middletown, Connecticut

Wesleyan University Press
Middletown, CT 06459
www.wesleyan.edu/wespress

Printed in the United States of America   5   4   3
ISBN: 978-0-8195-6278-4

"The Tale of Rumor and Desire" first appeared in *Callaloo, a Tri-Annual Journal of Black South Arts and Letters*, Spring–Summer 1987, Johns Hopkins University Press. Reprinted by permission of the author and his agent, Henry Morrison, Inc.

"The Tale of Gorgik" first appeared, in a somewhat shorter form, in *Asimov's SF Adventure Magazine*, Vol. 1, No. 3, Summer 1979, and is reprinted by permission of the author and his agent, Henry Morrison, Inc.

LIBRARY OF CONGRESS CATALOGING-IN-PUBLICATION DATA

Delany, Samuel R.
    [Bridge of lost desire]
    Return to Nevèrÿon / Samuel R. Delany.
        p.   cm. — (Return to Nevèrÿon)

    Originally published: Bridge of lost desire. New York : Arbor House, c1987.
    ISBN 0–8195–6278–5
    1. Fantastic fiction, American.   I. Title.   II. Series: Delany,
Samuel R. Return to Nevèrÿon.
PS3554.E437B75   1994
813'.54—dc20   93-31051
♾

For
John P. Mueller,
with thanks to
Susan Palwick,
Robert S. Bravard, &
R. Keith Courtney.

A NOTE: The book-bound order of these stories reverses the chronology of many of their internal events, so that someone more concerned with plot than structure might be more comfortable reading the three tales here from last to first. Also there's an appendix that might do as an introduction for those only intermittently acquainted with some of the series' other stories. Then again one can simply open the book and start at the beginning . . .

But it's my hope that Nevèrÿon can be explored from many directions.   — Samuel R. Delany, New York, 1987

Contents

The Game of Time and Pain

It is at this point, Lacan writes, that the analyst will do his work not by responding sympathetically, nor by failing to respond (the apathetic listener). He has to replace the mode of the voice and the ear with the image, becoming, as he puts it, a 'pure unruffled mirror'. Coupled with his description of the ego as 'opaque to reflection', the use of the term 'mirror' cannot be overlooked. It is in the mirror that the ego is first born as an idea, and it is in the echo of the symbolic voice that it gains its identity: the analytic mirror must displace — 'subduce' — these 'archaic imagos'.   JULIET FLOWER McCANNELL, *Figuring Lacan*

'No one is in the castle.' Barefoot, the old woman squatted before her loom. (Someone had told the pig girl the pattern the woman wove was magic — though she didn't remember who or when. Perhaps it was just a tale that went from yard to yard in the afternoon.) 'Never has been. Never will be.'

'I *saw* him,' repeated the tall woman. With one hand she propped a full water jar on her shoulder. (Swinging by her knee, the jar hooked to her forefinger *had* to be empty.) 'He was a big man. He rode a wonderfully high-stepping horse with trappings of beaten brass and braided leather. His armor was more elaborate than that of any soldier you've ever seen pass through this part of Nevèrÿon. He was no ordinary Imperial officer. His cloak was embroidered like the richest of lords'. He rode into the overgrown courtyard, dismounted, and went inside. I watched him from the trees.' The jar's shadow moved from the grass to the crumbled earth around the loom's foot to the half-finished fabric and back. 'You can be sure, he's a great personage, who'll stay up there overnight so that he can join Lord Krodar's funeral cortege that passes here tomorrow. Why he's not with a whole retinue, I don't know. Someone who rides such a horse and dresses in such armor and stops at the local castle shouldn't be traveling alone. He should have servants and guards and fine-fringed wagons — don't you think? That's what I'd expect — at least of someone like him, stopping there for the night.'

'There's no one in the castle.' The old woman pulled up swinging shuttles, pushed one down among the threads, hooked another through with her forefinger, completing one line to start in on the next. 'You played among those walls and corridors when you were a girl. It was empty then. I played there when I was a child, too. No one

was there. Those rooms, those halls, those stairs, those towers . . .'
She wrapped two threads around each other and thrust one through
the warp, then tamped it with the tamping stick. 'And you say there's
someone living in the castle . . . Ridiculous!'

'Not living there. Just stopping there. For the night, no more. Why
do I stand here arguing with you, old lady!' (The pig girl saw the
shuttles' shadows dance off on the grass far faster than the swinging
jar's.) 'There's a man in the castle this evening — a strong, great, powerful man, who rides a fine horse and sports rich armor and wears a
wonderfully worked cloak. Lord Krodar's funeral procession will pass
along the north-south highway before midday tomorrow. You just
watch. The man will stay in the castle tonight, and in the morning
he'll ride down to join the procession and pay his respects to that
greatest minister of Nevèrÿon. He'll travel with them all the way to
the High Court of Eagles at Kolhari. And when he rides down to meet
them, he'll pass along here. If you can look up from your work for a
moment, you'll see him!'

'I played in the castle,' the pig girl said. She was eleven, very serious,
somewhat gawky, and held a cat in her dirty arms. 'Castles are full of
wonderful women in beautiful clothes who dance and dance with
wonderful men. You give orders for impossible things to be done; and,
in the castle, people run right off to do them. That's what *every*body
plays in the castle. I bet that's what he'll play. When you play in the
castle like that, it doesn't *feel* empty.' She looked at the old woman,
then at the tall one. She wanted them to approve of her, but they
seemed unaware she was there.

'The castle's empty.' The old woman shifted her squat. 'There's
never been anyone in it. There wasn't anyone before. And there isn't
now.'

'This is silly!' The tall woman raised her chin beside the jar on her
shoulder. 'I only came to tell you a bit of gossip — ' the one by her
knee swung faster — 'and here you sit, arguing with me about something *you* didn't see and *I* did. I mean it's just too — '

'The castle's *not* empty!' the pig girl blurted. 'It's full of lords and
ladies and wet, dark dungeons where they lock their enemies up in
chains and beat them and torture them and kill them horribly and
they come back as monsters who run hooting through the upper
halls, so that the children who followed you in all turn around and
chase each other out, shrieking and scared to death!' She giggled.

'Look down over the banister, watch them run outside, and you can
laugh yourself sick — then sneak around and hoot some more! The
castle's full of beautiful queens and handsome warriors and monsters
and sorcerers — ' Here she must have squeezed the cat, for she was a
strong, friendly, clumsy girl. It meowed hideously, twisting in her
arms, dropped to the grass, ran from the yard and up the slope, stopped
to stare back, then fled.

'Of course it's empty! That's not what I mean.' The tall woman
frowned at the pig girl. 'Really, you're as bad as she is. I only said
there's a man there this evening. And I'm sure he'll stay till the funeral procession passes the village tomorrow.'

'And I say there's no one.' The old woman pushed her shuttles
through the strings. 'You know it as well as I do. I think it's always
been empty. Who would ever live in those drafty halls? Who would
ever stay in those cramped little rooms? Think of the cleaning. Think
of the furniture. Think of the work!'

'And I have work to do!' The tall woman shook her head. 'I certainly haven't time to stand here arguing with someone who can't
follow two words in a row (how do you keep your weaving straight!)
and a dirty creature — ' this last was to the pig girl — 'who dreams of
queens, when she has work to do too!' But there was a smile in
with it.

The old woman, however, looked up crossly. 'I'm doing *my* work!'
she declared. Strings quivered. Shuttles swung. 'You're the ones standing about, with your silly lies and your chatter!'

The tall woman shook her head again and, with her full and her
empty pitchers, started across the yard.

The pig girl wondered if she should go after the cat, who, for all its
meowing and occasional scratches, was better company than grown-
ups. But she lingered by the loom for minutes, watching the pattern,
with its greens, its beiges, its blues, extend itself, fixed and stable, line
after line, behind quivering strings, aged fingers, shaking shuttles . . .

2

His breath locked on what burned in his throat: the air he dragged
in through the heat, past whatever scalding constriction, woke him,
rasping, choking, roaring. He opened his eyes on blackness, while a

clutch in his stomach muscles jerked him to sit — which hurt! He thrust a hand down, grasped wet fur. Astonishingly warm, the air slid *so* slowly into his loud lungs. Water dribbled his cheek, his back, his forearm.

It was incredibly hot in the dark. At his breath's painful height, he tried to push the air out; it leaked loudly from his gaping mouth, only a little faster than it had come in; only a little quieter.

Seconds later (it seemed minutes), he began to drag in the next chestful, dreading it even as he felt the constriction loosen. In his sleep, he'd urped some little stomach juices that, rolling into the wrong pipe, had stung his throat to spasm.

He tasted the acids at the back of his tongue, felt them burning deep down.

What ran on him was sweat.

And the small stone room in which he'd chosen to sleep (there'd been a bed, for one thing) had grown hugely hot.

He moved one leg over the fur throw he'd spread on the boards: the fur was drenched. Momentarily he wondered whether, in his infernal sleep, he'd spilled his urine. But no. It was only perspiration. As he stood up, bare feet on stone, it trickled his flank, his buttock. He rasped out one more breath, got in another, loud as a dying man's gargle: the air came a little more easily . . .

He took a lurching step in darkness toward where he remembered the window. Pushing out, he felt rock. He moved over, pushed again, felt rock again; moved and pushed once more; wood swung —

The sliver of moonlight at the plank's edge became a slab of silver: the shutter banged back.

He blinked.

(When he'd gone to sleep, it had been open, the moon down. Some breeze at moonrise must have blown it to.)

The air — from what was probably the warmest summer night — hit like springwater. It made him cough. For moments, he thought he would choke again. But in another minute his breath, though still labored, made only the normal roar between his lips, the usual whisper in his nasal cave.

Leaning naked on beveled rock, he looked down.

From its greenery (olive under the moon) a tree thrust out a dead branch. Below it lay a pool, rimmed with bricks whose pattern had been obscured here and warped there by grass tufts and roots. Above scummed water, a single owl (or bat) darted down and up and down, so that ripples rilled among the leaves and algae. Sweat on his lashes tickled into his eyes: he blinked. And twigs, ripples, and the lines between bricks seemed a tangled loom, with the mad shuttle of a bat (or owl) swooping through.

He turned to the sweltering room. Either side of his shadow, moonlight dusted the stone. Heat again was against his face. Air from the window chilled his back. How *had* the room gotten so hot?

In the corner lay his pack (from which he'd taken the fur), open, spilling the funeral gifts. His sword in its sheath lay on the floor. There was his helmet, his gauntlets, his grieves.

On the rumpled fur was a black blotch where his sweat, neck to knee, had soaked it.

Another drop trickled his calf.

Taking one more breath of stifling air, he crossed the chamber, stopping to feel the fur. To lie on that again would be like crawling into wet rags. Besides, though he was a vital man, he was no longer a young one: he was of an age when to interrupt a night's sleep was to end it.

At the door, he lifted the locking plank and leaned it on the wall. The rock was hot — almost too hot to touch! As he pulled one and another doorplank free, again he wondered how the little tower room he'd picked to sleep in could, on a summer night, become such a furnace.

As the third came loose, a cross breeze started. He shivered, naked, leaning the board against the wall; the heat warmed his knuckles. Taking another long breath, he stepped into the hall.

Not cold, he tried to tell his body. Just a summer's night in an abandoned ruin. He rubbed the heel of his hand down his temple: sweat came away oily on his palm. He ran his other hand over his head: his rough hair, thin on top, was usually braided in the club-like military manner at the side of his head. But it had come largely loose. His fingers, catching in it, pulled the rest free.

Starting down the steps, he put his fingers against the rock. Yes, the wall even here was warm, despite the stairwell's cool.

He descended in darkness. Beneath his bare feet the steps were dusty and irregularly spaced. Under his hand the stones were gritty.

Once he crossed a landing he vaguely remembered, before doubling around on more stairs. For the third, the fifth, the seventh time he wondered if he should return to the little room for a weapon — just a knife. Then he saw the flicker.

Something crackled.

He moved to the arch and looked around the wall.

Across the hall, in the long fireplace, flames lapped the logs. On the floor, ten feet from the hearth, a young man lay, stomach down, head on his bent arm. The hair was yellow. The face was hidden in sleep and shadow.

The big man frowned.

Again he thought of returning for a knife — though this youngster, some barbarian who'd made his way into the castle much as he had, was as naked as he. The man looked around. Why, he wondered, build such a fire in high summer? Could the night outside have grown that chill? Along the balcony the arches were dark caves. Staring as far into the corners as the firelight reached, he could see no pack.

But certainly these summer flames had started some convection in the castle's flues, vents, and conduits that, with the rising heat, had turned the room above into an oven.

No, he decided, he did not need a weapon with this naked barbarian — unless the boy slept with a dagger beneath his belly. But, while desert men sometimes did that, it was not the barbarians' style. As if answering the man's thoughts, the boy snorted and rocked to his side, trying to turn on his back. (No, there was nothing under his stomach but stone.) In his sleep he scrubbed at his sparse beard, then settled on his belly again, one leg drawn up.

Among the fire's crackles, the man heard the boy's breath. If I had my blade, he thought, I'd only frighten him if he woke. Stepping out into the hall, he walked toward the barbarian, dropped to a squat to watch —

The hooting began high in the dark and soared up under the ceiling, to warble out within its own echo.

The man twisted to look, lost balance, and went down on one knee, catching himself on the rock floor with a fist. And the boy came awake, pushing himself up, blinking about, staring at the ceiling, at the man.

Man and boy — for the barbarian, despite his scraggly beard, was
no more than sixteen — looked at each other, then at the dark.

The boy said: 'What was that? Who are you? What are you doing
here?' and kept looking up and back; when his face came down, the
fire lit one blond cheek, one blinking eye, leaving one side of his face
near black.

For the length of three of the man's slow breaths (and seven of the
boy's quick ones), flames snapped.

'I suppose,' the man said, after a while, 'it was one of the local gods,
ghosts, or demons that haunt these old piles.' He regained his squat.
'My name is Gorgik.' (At that the boy looked over sharply.) 'What am I
doing here?' Gorgik shrugged in the flicker. 'Much the same as you, I'd
guess. I stopped to spend the night because it was more protected than
the forest; these villages are not that friendly to strangers. There's a
funeral procession due by the town tomorrow. I must ride out and join
them, to go with them on to Kolhari. Since you asked, I've been a state
minister ten years, now at the Court of Eagles, now abroad in the land.
You look like you've heard my name . . . ? Many have, especially
among the barbarians: because many barbarians have been slaves.
And I lead the council on the Child Empress Ynelgo (whose reign is
just and generous) to end slavery in Nevèrÿon.' Gorgik chuckled.
'Some even consider me a hero for it. In parts of the land, I am known
as Gorgik the Liberator.'

'Are you?' The boy frowned even harder.

The big man shrugged. 'It's a clumsy title — not one an evening's
companion should use. I thought I'd come in where I could enjoy
your fire a bit more than I could back up there.' He reached out, took
the boy's chin in his rough hand, and turned the face full to the light.
Both the boy's eyes blinked now, close set, brown, and long-lashed.
(On the man's face, the fire lit a scar that wormed down the brown
cheek into the rough beard, salted here and there.) Gorgik let the
boy's jaw go. His hand dropped back to his knee. 'Now, you tell me
who *you* are.'

'Why do you look at me like that?'

The man shrugged again. 'I was having dreams, I think. That's
what woke me. I wanted to see . . . But I've told you enough about
me. Who are you? What's your name?'

'I'm Udrog,' the boy said. 'Udrog, the barbarian. Why did you build a fire here?' He sat up now. 'The summer night's warm. Did it turn cold outside?'

'I didn't build it,' Gorgik said. 'You built it, Udrog — before you went to sleep. Didn't you?'

'No . . .' Again the boy looked around the hall, then back at the flames. 'Didn't *you* light this fire, while I slept . . .'

Gorgik shook his head. 'When I came in and settled down to watch you, it was already burning.' He narrowed green eyes.

'I have no flint for making fire,' Udrog said. 'Besides, it's summer.' The boy drew his legs under him. 'What kind of castle is this? It has strange sounds, strange fires . . .'

'There're many strange things in the world.' Gorgik shrugged. 'You learn to live with them.'

The boy looked at the dark-skinned man. 'You're not scared?'

'Nothing has hurt us yet. If someone wanted to harm us, it would have been easier when we both slept alone than now, when we're both awake together.'

There was a long, long silence. Some might have called it embarrassed. During it, the man watched the boy; and the boy began to watch the way in which the man watched him. (The man saw him see.) At last, after having looked around the hall, grinned at a few things, growled at a few others, dug in his ear with his little finger, scratched at his belly with his thumb, stood up, sat down, stood up, and sat down again, Udrog let his eyes return to the man's . . . and stay. 'You just came to crouch here,' he asked, 'and look at me . . . ? You're strong.' He let his head fall to the side. 'Do you like to watch me . . . when I sleep, maybe?'

Gorgik pursed his lips a moment. 'Yes.'

The boy blinked. Then, with the smallest smile, he said: 'You like to do anything besides watch, now I'm awake?'

After a moment, Gorgik asked: 'Such as?'

'You know,' the boy said. 'Things together, you and me. Like we could have some fun with each other.'

'Sometimes.' Gorgik chuckled. 'What things do you like?'

'Anything. Anything you want. To have a good time, together. The two of us. You're a big man. You're not afraid. If we were together, you'd protect me from any monsters. Or ghosts. Or gods. I don't mind old men, if they're still strong and masterful. Perhaps, afterwards, you might give me a coin?'

Gorgik snorted. 'Perhaps.'

'And you're not *that* old. I like to do it with strong men, big men. You ever fuck real rough?'

'I have . . .' Gorgik paused. Then he said: 'Sometimes I do it so rough most men and women wouldn't think of it as fucking.' He smiled; and the smile became a laugh. 'Is that what you want?'

'Sure!' The barbarian grinned broadly.

'All right.'

'In these old castles — ' Udrog leaned forward — 'you look around; simetimes, in the cellars, you find old, broken collars that they used to chain the slaves in. I always look for them when I come to these places. Sometimes I put them on, you know? The broken ones, that you can take off again. But I didn't find any here.'

'Do you want to be my slave?' Gorgik asked. 'Would you like me to be your master?'

'Yes!' Udrog grinned hugely in the firelight. 'That's what I like to do!'

Once more Gorgik hesitated. Then, in a motion, he stood. 'Wait here.' He turned and started for the arch. 'I'll be back.'

'Where are you going?'

'Just wait.'

'Don't go away too long!' Udrog called. 'It's scary here!'

But Gorgik was out into the corridor and, a moment later, climbing the black stair. Again in the dark, he wondered at this encounter. He'd had them before. But this barbaric directness was both uncommon and intriguing. Besides, such meetings were rare with someone this young; when they happened, they both surprised and pleased.

Now and again his hand touched the wall — yes, and here, where he was almost certainly just behind the fireplace, the stones were hot. It must have been the oddly unauthored fire, working through the castle's conduits (set up to warm the room in winter . . . ?) that, now it was summer, had caused the overheating.

When he reached the door, the warmth came out to brush his belly, his chin, his knees.

Moonlight still lay on the floor. But the moon itself had moved so that it took him a minute to be sure nothing had been touched. Though the shadows had all shifted, helmet, grieves, sword, and sack were where he'd left them.

He stepped into the hot chamber, went to squat before his pack, reached in, pulled back this, moved aside that. Yes, his own flint was still wedged toward the bag's bottom, wrapped in oily wadding. Gorgik drew out the hinged metal semicircles — the slave collar Udrog had described. Holding it in one hand, he stood, turned, and, with his free hand, pulled the fur throw from the bed — yes, the intense heat had almost dried it.

The rug over his shoulder, he started for the door, then glanced at his sword.

No. What he had was enough. But, when he was outside (he'd begun to sweat; already the corridor that, before, had been warm seemed chill), he put the fur and the slave collar down to pull one plank, then the other, into the doorframe — not evenly and tightly: he lay one diagonally across the entrance and another loosely the other way. A third he barely balanced against them so that, if any but the most careful person moved it, all would topple loudly.

He picked up the fur and the collar and went back down the steps.

'You were gone so long.' Udrog sat on the hearth's edge at the side where the flames were lowest, holding one foot and rubbing the other. 'I was frightened. Where did you — ?'

'There.' Gorgik tossed the rug down. 'We can lie on that. You are my slave now. Come here.'

The boy gazed at the iron Gorgik held out. The boy's lips parted slightly; his eyelids closed — slightly. He came forward, on his knees, raised his chin, and rested one hand on Gorgik's naked thigh. 'Yes, master . . . !'

Gorgik closed the collar around his neck.

'Tie me up if you want,' Udrog said. 'I like that, too. Maybe if you go looking again, you can find some rope. Sometimes they even have chains in these places — '

'You're my slave,' Gorgik said. 'You do what *I* say now. At least for a while.' He sat down on the rug and put his arm around the boy's shoulder, pulling him, first gently, then roughly over. 'What I want you to do is be quiet.'

'What are you going to do?' the boy asked.

'Tell you a story.'

Udrog frowned. 'I think it would be good if you tied me up. Then you could beat me. Hard. I don't mind if it's hard . . . I'll let you know if it hurts *too* much. Though sometimes I even pretend it's too hard when it's not. So you don't even have to stop then . . .' When Gorgik was silent, the boy suddenly pushed away over the rug. He put his hand up to feel the iron. 'This is really bad, isn't it? This stuff we do.' He sucked his teeth, shook his head, looked around. 'I don't know why I do it. But you like it too, don't you? I just wish it wasn't so scary, here. But maybe that will make it better? This fur, it smells like you sweated in it a lot.' He lowered his face to plow his chin through, then sat up again. 'I like that. You *didn't* build the fire — ?'

'Be quiet, slave!' Gorgik's voice was loud enough to make the boy start. 'Come here. And listen! I want to tell you something. So lie against me here and be still.'

3

We pause before this tale within a tale within a tale — to tell another tale.

We'll talk awhile of Udrog.

The young barbarian was confused, you see, about certain things — although he was clear enough about certain others.

Economic upheavals in Nevèrÿon, of which the abolition of slavery by proclamation of the Child Empress Ynelgo half a dozen years before was only the most recent, had commenced much movement in the land.

Once fear of slavers was gone from the highways and backroads of Nevèrÿon, more and more folk from the southern forests and the northern mountains and the western deserts had begun to make their way to the cities. And those in the cities with money, imagination, and industry had begun to take their primitive industrial knowledge out into the country to see what profit and speculation were to be had. Motion from margin to center, from center to margin was constant — till, in a handful of years, it had altered Nevèrÿon's whole notion of margin and center. New margins had been created, which, today, like cracks between the more stable parts of the social engine, worked from the back alleys of the great port cities, such as Vinelet and Kolhari, to the waterfront refuse pits of fishing villages on the coast and quarrying towns off the river, such as Enoch and Ka'hesh. Now and again a margin passed right through some ancient castle abandoned to its demons, ghosts, and gods by an aristocracy who had moved on to be absorbed by the more lively, more energetic, and finally more profitable middle classes.

These margins were often left to those like Udrog.

Udrog's personal history was common enough for such a boy. When he was six, his father had died in a hunting accident. Always sickly, his mother had passed away a year later from a fever. For most of the next year he was a ward of his small barbarian tribe — a possible but not a pleasant life for a child.

The man who'd provided most of Udrog's (very irregular) material care had beat the boy and cuffed him and had generally abused him far too much and been far too sparing with the affections which are all that, at last, can heal such abuse. The man had been ailing and, himself, finally died. The woman who next took Udrog into her family was kind and caring enough, even if she'd had too many brats from various relatives already foisted off on her. There were two older children who liked to take Udrog off into the woods, where the three of them would play games in which they tied each other up and pretended to beat each other and cuffed each other, games that now and again had an overtly sexual side — perhaps the older children's early lives had been similar to Udrog's. But reducing to play what once had been true torture gave them — the two girls and the younger boy — a power over the mists of pain that was all memory had left (at least to Udrog) of childhood. After the first time, he never objected — indeed, now and again he nagged the girls to go off with him and do it again. Perhaps they could even bring some of the older boys . . . ? By the time he was ten, the tribe was only a third the size it had been four years before — because a village fifty stades to the east had grown, with northern monies, into a sizable town. The woman was living with another man now, kind enough in his way, but who had brought with him children of his own.

Too many children altogether, certainly.

Some of them must go out to work.

Some must go off to one town.

Some must go off to another.

There was still another, where a friend of a friend had said there was at least a promise of a job.

Could the boy travel the way alone? Well, whether he could or not, there was nothing else for it.

By the time he was twelve, spending more time between towns than in them, Udrog had entered those margins along which he was to travel for, really, the rest of his life.

In many ways they provided quite an adventure; they spanned far more of Nevèrÿon than most of his people ever saw.

They took him from country to city. They took him from desert to forest. They took him from great breweries to share-cropping combines to tanning troughs to construction sites — seldom as a worker, at least for more than a day or so, but as someone who lived off what spilled into the marginal track — now in the fields and woods, now in the cities and villages.

Among the sexual encounters with adults (almost all of them men) that plague, pleasure, and — perhaps — heal as many such lost children as they harm (for it is not hard to be kind to those who provide pleasure; and kindness must often do for those who lack all love), there were, now and again, those who wanted to collar and chain him.

'No *way!*' Udrog had protested.

And was surprised when his protests were, generally, heeded.

Then, of course, there was the man who suggested as an alternative: 'Well, will you chain and collar me!'

That was certainly more feasible.

Only thirteen, Udrog had done it — and had recognized in the shaking, moaning body beneath his juvenile assault a naked pleasure, which made the boy (as he hit and cursed and labored) pant, sweat, burn toward an astonishing release that left him, in dazed identification, as drained as his adult 'slave.' For three days Udrog tried to tell himself what he'd experienced was the pleasure of the born, sexual master.

But desire, looked on that closely, even by a child, shows too clearly its obsessive outlines.

He had recognized what he'd seen.

When men asked to abuse him, he still said no — sometimes.

But when he met some man who, to his sexual interest, projected a certain calm and ease, a certain reassurance, a certain solidity and common sense, it was Udrog who now asked, more and more frequently, more and more quickly, to be bound and beaten.

Often they said yes.

Often Udrog enjoyed it.

It was only a game, he told himself. But in his limited lane of petty
thefts and minor pillagings, of irregular hunger and regular isolation,
of surprising kindnesses from a woman hoeing an orchard or a man
driving a chicken cart (kindnesses he quickly learned he must always
demand from everyone he met, yet never expect from anyone he asked
of — because as easily he might receive a blow, or a hurled stone, or
shouts and curses from people who wished to drive him away), it was
the only game that gave him intense, if inconstant, pleasure, over
which, by asking, he had at least *some* power.

A young person who lives his or her life within such margins soon
seems astonishingly, even tragically — or (depending how much we
value, or desire, innocence) immorally — precocious to the more socially central of us. Yet the children who have amazed us with their
precocity often turn out, at the same time, to be wholly incapable of
taking advantage of the simplest social forms or institutions — at
least if those institutions lie or lead anywhere outside the marginal.

We need no more detail how, by age fourteen, Udrog had learned
that the root of his passions thrust directly through what was, after
all, one of the more common perversions in a Nevèrÿon so recently
awakened from a troubling dream of slaves. We need not specify all
the encounters over the next year that familiarized him with acts and
activities that remain incomprehensible to many of us much older.

But standing among cool trees with his mouth wide so that nothing might hear him breathing and his body bent along the same curve
as the trunk he leaned on so that few would even see him if they
passed, or ambling diagonally across a foul alley near some city market, with a bumptious lope that, as much as his light skin and yellow
hair, marked him an outsider, country bred and uncivilized, a true,
common, and most ordinary barbarian of the most socially unaccept-
able sort, the boy achieved a certain invisibility, both sylvan and urban, that protected him from the reprisals of just such people as his
preferred sexual activities, now in the country, now in the town,
might most have shocked.

What, most specifically and most recently, had confused Udrog
was, however, this:

Days before, wandering west in the vicinity of the High Hold of
fabled Ellamon, the boy had come across a campfire off the road
where he'd found himself in the bushes watching, then sitting across

from, finally talking to, and at last eating with, a big-bellied bandit. The man's flank was scarred like a criminal's or slave's, he wore a carved peg through one ear, and one hand was missing a finger. One blind eye was a red ruin between half-closed lids, wrecked by a double scar that rose over his cheek and went on to split his brow as if the point of some uncanny blade had once lifted through his features, marking him not only with ropy lines of flesh but also with a bewildered amazement that, even as the ruptured ball had sunk away in the healing, had still not quit his face. The bandit's talk had been distracted, full of violences that both frightened Udrog and entertained him, even as the man offered him more food, jokes, and tales of derring-do. Then, in the middle of it, the one-eyed man had begun to call himself Gorgik the Liberator, the Greatest of Her Majesty's Ministers, and the Savior of the People.

And did the boy have anything he might wish to spare for the Liberator's great and noble cause of helping ex-slaves establish themselves in the land?

Udrog had certainly heard of that fabled Minister, who, some years before at the time of the empress's proclamation, had been for a while the most famous man in Nevèrÿon. Indeed, there'd even been some tale connected with Gorgik the Liberator, that the boy only half remembered, about someone with a scar — or *was* it a single eye?

Not that Udrog was particularly disposed to believe the bandit: he had the distinct feeling that, after only a sentence or two, the man might even set on him . . . or would have, had Udrog been traveling with any pouch or purse or cart. (The young barbarian, like so many of Nevèrÿon's marginals, went naked and without possessions: it was the best protection against someone's wanting to rob you.) Nor was he disposed to contradict the one-eyed man: there was something about this bandit/Liberator's distracted tale of soldiers spying on them from off in the woods, or troops which with a single call could be marshaled from over the hill, that spoke of madness as much as villainy.

While he finished up the piece of meat on the roasting stick the bandit had given him, Udrog *thought* about propositioning the gruff, ugly fellow — but decided he was too crazy.

So, suddenly, Udrog was up and off into the woods, tossing the stick behind him ('Where are you going? to leak in the trees, 'ey?

Well, then, hurry back. I have more to say to you, boy . . . !), swiping a jar from beside the bandit's cart that, perhaps because it was on the man's blind side, the bandit didn't see.

In the woods he cracked open the seal.

The jar contained some highly fermented beer. Udrog drank as much as he could, threw the rest away, then, on a pleasingly drunken whim, snuck back to crouch in the shadows, to see what the bandit was doing: perhaps there was something more he could steal.

While, from behind leaves, twigs, and darkness, Udrog watched the scruffy madman mumbling by his fire, another cart pulled up to the clearing; some men walked along with it. They hailed the bandit and (they looked like bandits themselves) asked if they could use his flame. In the course of the monosyllabic exchanges, somehow an argument broke out.

Then the one-eyed man was up and rushing for his mule cart, doubtless for some weapon — whereupon he was stabbed and stabbed and stabbed again by one of the quietest men waiting just behind him, knife already drawn.

A real murder! thought Udrog with great gravity and some fear. Occasionally he'd come across the traces of one, so that he might say he'd seen it, boasting to other youngsters he met later in the city. But the act itself? That was rare to catch!

The murderers began to rifle the bandit's cart, while Udrog, his drunkenness gone and a sickishness left, was torn, in his hiding place, between waiting for them to finish so he might pick over the leavings and getting out of there — when he heard another wagon!

The murderers stopped their search and fled.

From their clothes, their manners, and the caravan guards with them, the new arrivals seemed merchants or traveling businessmen. They climbed down to look at the corpse sprawled on bloody leaves in the firelight. They expressed grave shock at the heinous slaughter. They walked around and around the fire. They stared off anxiously into the trees. (One stood for a while with his worried face, unblinking and unseeing, not much farther from Udrog's, unbreathing and unmoving, only a few leaves hanging between them, than your nose is now from your knee.) They talked with their guards and one another of the violence lingering in all the margins of Nevèrÿon today. Finally, they ordered the guards to lift the body and strap it to their wagon's back.

But they did not kick the corpse; or beat it with a stick a few times to see if it was really dead; or immediately search the cart for anything salable; or try to flee the place as fast as possible — in short, they seemed to Udrog madder than the one-eyed man.

One merchant, who finally went to look through the bandit's wagon, found, first, some well-wrought weapons and, a moment later, an embroidered belt. 'I guess we have a thief here, murdered by more of the same for his booty. It must have been the men we heard moving so quickly away.'

'Or,' said another, stepping over to see, 'we could have a man more important than he looks, but with the good sense not to travel these back roads wearing such ostentatious finery — much good the deception did him.' (The next remark stayed with Udrog:) 'For all we know, he might be some minister of state in disguise. It would be just our luck, too, to fall in on an assassination. We'll take his body back to Ellamon and see if anyone there can identify him.'

They took the corpse, the mule, and much of what was in the cart away, to leave Udrog, still in the bushes (the moon had just come up), staring at the fireplace, while silver smoke rippled and raddled over the ashes.

Now, unknown to Udrog (or, indeed, to the merchants), within the walls of the High Hold of fabled Ellamon that same day, Lord Krodar, minister to the Child Empress, come to the mountain hold on the most delicate of Imperial missions, finally succumbed to a fever, which had come on the aging archon three days before. When, by nightfall, that most powerful lord was declared by his distraught doctors to be at last and truly dead, riders galloped out from the Vanar Hold toward all points of empire with the news, while, through the dark hours, servants and hired men and women worked by lamp and candle to ready six black carriages for the funeral cortege, which, with twenty-four drummers, twelve either side, would return the body first to Kolhari and the High Court of Eagles, where the Child Empress Ynelgo would join the procession, then go on to the south and Lord Krodar's birthplace in the Garth Peninsula for the interment.

Before sunrise, the drums began to pound.

The six wagons pulled out of the Vanar Hold.

Half an hour later they rolled from the High Hold of fabled Ellamon itself.

About an hour after Udrog woke next day, he was walking at the

edge of the north-south highway, hitting at the weeds leaning from
the shoulder with a bit of branch and feeling very hungry, when he
heard an ominous beating, growing louder and louder, like the heart
of a giant about to burst from its own strength. Minutes later, the
wagons and the drummers and the attendant guards moved slowly
and thunderously into the slant light that, here and there, cut the
violet shadows under the branches. Dawnlight caught on beaten
brass ornaments set in black-lacquered wood, still showing green in
the crevices from the night's over-quick polishing.

Clearly this was the funeral procession of a great lord of state!

Thunderously, it rolled away.

Half an hour later, after taking some plums from an orchard and
eating them, Udrog came back to the same orchard to ask the farmer
he'd sneaked past (down at the other end of the field, fifteen minutes
before) what recent news there'd been. He'd picked the poorest looking and most destitute of the three farms he'd passed from which to
get both his breakfast and his information. The farmer was a man
almost as marginal as Udrog: but it was the only farm at which the
barbarian felt at ease.

'Some state minister,' the skinny man said. 'Did you hear his funeral wagons go by? I don't know much about it, save that he died up
near Ellamon. Probably murdered by assassins on the road — that's
how they always did it in *my* youth. They're taking him south to
Kolhari, I guess. Now get off from here. I don't have anything for you,
boy!'

A richer farmer might have known more, might have said more,
might have been more generous with food and facts. But that was the
margin Udrog traveled in, felt most comfortable in.

Remembering the merchant's remark last night about the corpse's
possible identity, what Udrog thought about it all was: the one-eyed
man he'd met had *not* been lying! He *had* been a minister to the empress! The murderers *had* been assassins! What Udrog had taken as
signs of grandiose madness in the one-eyed man had been signs of the
grand itself.

And Gorgik the Liberator, Minister to Her Majesty and Savior of
the People, was dead.

Last night Udrog had seen him slaughtered beside his campfire.

Today he'd seen his funeral procession pass by on the road.

Oh, certainly, Udrog was not so stupid as to *tell* anyone he'd seen

Gorgik the Liberator (traveling in his bandit's disguise) killed — or that he could probably identify the killers if it came to that. In times like these, such information could get you thrown into a dungeon somewhere. Still, the whole incident rather pleased him, as if he'd had a private and privileged experience that allied him to the larger world's controlling scheme.

Later that morning Udrog was lucky enough to beg a ride on a fast horse at the back of the saddle of a private messenger, galloping along certain back roads with information a wealthy Ellamon importer needed to send hurriedly to one of his suppliers in the south. A good-hearted, hard-riding fellow, the messenger might have dispelled Udrog's confusion. But it never occurred to the boy to ask. And the man did not offer much in the way of conversation to the scruffy, itinerant barbarian. Still, the day's gallop was fun, if tiring. The messenger gave him an iron coin at the end of it (with which the boy bought a meal one village over) and sent him on. And they'd passed ahead of the funeral procession, anyway — though they hadn't actually seen it, for they were not taking the main highway. And the funeral caravan went slowly, stopping at each small town for a respectful hour or two while the more curious inhabitants came out to stare at the milling soldiers, at the sweating drummers, at the entourage of red-robed aristocrats who traveled with them, while whatever lingering aristocracy (or just the very rich) who wished to join them came down on their horses or in their closed funeral wagons to ride on with the procession to Kolhari and into the Garth.

These mangled facts, then, were what the naked Udrog had carried with him into the ruined castle that evening when he decided to rest.

When he awoke in the ancient hall, it was not only the sounds and the fire and the naked man, squatting by him, watching, that were strange. The strangest thing was that the naked man claimed to be someone Udrog himself had seen murdered beside a campfire a night back; and, that morning, the boy had seen his drumming funeral cortege roll past. Udrog was sure the big man was lying to him. Everyone lied in sexual situations. (Certainly Udrog did, whenever possible.) But, so far, the lie, if strange, seemed harmless — since Udrog knew the truth.

This more or less marks the extent of Udrog's confusion. But there are still things to say of that about which the boy was clear.

When, by the roadside campfire, the one-eyed bandit had claimed to be Gorgik the Liberator, from the first exchanges between them Udrog had observed signs of madness, deceit, and danger numerous enough to make him wary and watchful for the rest of the night — however he'd later re-read them beside the loud procession of the dead as signs of greatness, nobility, and power. Those signs, indeed, were why he had not propositioned the bandit. And the night's violence had only confirmed the rightness of his intuition.

When, by the castle fire, *this* man claimed to be Gorgik the Liberator, from the first exchanges between them Udrog had observed no such signs at all. He'd heard no halts, over-excitements, and sudden uncertainties. The strangenesses, the oddities, the blatant contradictions with what Udrog believed to be the case all seemed, somehow, within the firelit summer stones, too abstract to act on — although Udrog was quite ready to dismiss the entire ruling class of Nevèrÿon as mad, or at least very different from himself. These oddities puzzled him, yes, as, finally, so much in the world puzzled; but they were not decipherable signs with clear warnings of danger he could read, comprehend, and respond to with proper care and precaution.

So, in the way a child will accept a judgment of the unknown from an adult who at least seems sane, Udrog tried to accept these.

In the same way that, had something about this man caused Udrog to feel wary and suspicious, no abstract reassurance or intellectual explanation could have swayed the boy's action and observation from what he felt was the right concern for such a case, so, as this man's manner and bearing made Udrog feel safe and protected despite all contradictions with the world around, nothing moved the boy toward the poise-for-flight, the suspension of desire that might have seemed, given his confusion, more appropriate.

Udrog had already followed his sexual whims through many situations that would have been more than strange enough to deter, with our greater age and wisdom, you and me.

Thus he followed them here.

The desired collar had been produced.

But with the impatience of a child before his own lusts, he wished the deed begun and done quickly. The prospect of more talk introduced only another contradiction.

Udrog lay beside the big man, listening impatiently, quiet through the tale, but only because Gorgik was bigger and stronger than he, if not, for the moment, his master.

4

They lay on the fur rug, the boy in the slave collar, the man beside him, watching the ceiling beams, which the fire, flickering lower and lower, lit less and less.

'Odd, even tonight: the man whose corpse comes toward this town, whose funeral I go tomorrow to join with full honor and respect, was once my greatest enemy. How many times, in the early years, when I was abroad in the land, not much better than a bandit, when my tactics and campaigns and strategies were about to fall before the impossibility of my enterprise, was it his face I dreamed of striking, his heart I hoped to hack out, his body I tingled to torture, till, mewling and weeping, he went down, down, down into death! For he was already a minister, with all the weight of birth and tradition behind him, in support of Nevèrÿon's most conservative policy as regards the institution I'd sworn to destroy. By the time I was called to court as a minister myself, we'd already had a dozen encounters, some of them cool and reasoned — some of them near mortal. But now, as I came within the walls of the council room with a voice and a vote and at last the title of equal, my enemy was suddenly my teacher, my critic, my exemplar. He was the mirror I had to look into to learn what I was to do. Only by searching among his could I find what had to become my strategies; for he was a man — I admit it — far more skilled in the ways of state, diplomacy, and government than I. It was he I had to imitate if I would win the day. I was now a minister, a man sworn to end, by political means, what I had not been able to end by military might:

'I would make the Court of Eagles, with the Child Empress speaking for it, end slavery in Nevèrÿon. I knew it could be done. But doing it? In the real world of hunger and thirst, sorrow and joy, labor and leisure, it's hard to imagine the intricacies of power that make the law move, that make its enforcement possible, that make a mandate from the empress — "Slavery is now ended in Nevèrÿon!" — more than words muttered by a madwoman on a foggy field.

'To learn, then, I had to turn to a man, a minister, and a politician, dead today, who, for all his skill, was then still nameless to half the country — whose anonymity, in fact, was half his might.

'He hated me.

'I hated him . . .

'It's strange, Udrog, to feel the clear and cloven boundary between you and all you've ever stood against break away. But to win what I wanted *from* him, I had to become more and more *like* him.

'Maybe you know it, Udrog. I was once a slave. When the Child Empress Ynelgo seized power, my parents were slaughtered; I was taken captive and sold to the empress's obsidian mines at the foot of the Faltha Mountains. I was not far from your age now when I was left there — when the collar you wear willingly tonight was clapped and locked around my most unwilling neck. Certainly I can tell you: my first sexual interests in the collar were fixed years before that when I was perhaps — oh, five or six. In the back room of a warehouse where my father worked, once, as a child I'd come upon some two dozen slaves in their collars toward whom I'm sure I felt . . . ? But the pause holds desire as much as it holds all my uncertainties about it. Yes, I have such memories. You have, too. We both return to them, now and again, to weave, unweave, and reweave the stories that make our lives comprehensible to us. But whatever fascination, or even partial truth, such memories hold, how useful *can* they be to someone who wishes to understand how his or her freedom works? How can you define the self from a time when the self was too young to understand definition? Let me speak instead of the stunned, wary, and very frightened boy who, a decade later, *was* a slave.

'Who was he?

'How did he become something other?

'My father began as a common sailor on the Nevèrÿon coast and ended as an importer's dispatcher at the Kolhari docks. My mother began as a porter in a market of the Spur and ended as a woman in her own house with no other work than caring for her family and supervising the barbarian girl she paid to help with cooking and cleaning. Both of them, in affluent times, took their lives far beyond childhood expectations. And since they had, they expected me to. As they had done better than their parents, they wished me to do better than they. Believe me, little man from whom, I suspect, no one has ever expected anything, such expectations — like such suspicions — are a burden.

'I didn't carry it. Better say I set it down each day I crossed our dockside doorstep to saunter the city's alleys or run the Kolhari waterfront; say that I kept as far from it as I could: I befriended bad company, became a sneak thief one day and a daredevil the next. Say I hid it behind every smiling lie I told whenever a lie would suit me. Youth hurled me through a life never set, in its greater form, by anything other than laziness. Oh, I was friendly and good-natured enough; but only because friendliness and good nature were the easiest way to win the worthless goals that were all I'd set myself as I tried to avoid everything that might be called responsibility. I was only a grin and a joke and a gratuitous kindness (the only sort I'd let myself indulge) from becoming a scoundrel who, in another decade, would have inserted his scurrilities into some business venture, likely with success, but only through the adult form of the laziness that had formed the boy. Yet, by one of those chances that, searching out the inevitabilities they call history, Nevèrÿon's masters mull over and explore for years afterward, till the exploration becomes a distortion we who lived through it can no longer recognize at all, when I was fifteen my life swerved.

'The Dragon was struck down.

'The Eagle was raised up.

'My parents were slain. My father's death I saw. My mother's, in the other room, I heard.

'And I was taken as a slave to those dripping, noxious pits at the Falthas' foot, beyond all expectations now.

'My first weeks at the mines I was shattered, numbed, even a little mad. As far as I could think at all, all I thought of was escape. But the only escapes I could imagine were magical, mystical — impractical and impossible: while we sat outside, hunched over our suppers by the barracks, one of the fabled dragons supposed to live wild on the Falthas' upper ledges would swoop down; and, as the rest screamed and fell in terror, I'd leap on the beast's green neck to be carried off and up to new heights of light and glory. Or, one morning when I got up from our dirty straw, everyone I looked at, slave, guard, or free farmer in the neighboring field, would cringe and crumple, unable to bear my eyes, which, in the night, had grown fatal with power, so that, simply and suddenly, I would walk away to an inanely volcanic and sunlit leisure and delight. Or, again, while I toiled in the mud and slippery rock, the air fouled by the red flares set in iron on the walls, I would start to crawl forward, down some dank, hip-high passageway, into the dark, while the space narrowed and narrowed; yet somehow it never ended or became too low to wriggle forward; and, after hours, days, weeks of inching through sweaty black, I'd emerge in a wide and wondershot meadow where the sun was cool as autumn and the stars as warm as summer, a land of wholly inverted values where the very sign of my servitude, the iron at my neck, would be taken by all I met as a symbol of transcendent freedom.

'But the extravagance of these fancies was balanced — overweighted, bowed, and bound down — by what had been numbed, deadened, all but killed in me by capture. Everything that allowed thought to become word, idea to become act, or plan to become practice had been shocked, stunned, petrified. I was no more capable of fixing a real plan toward freedom, or of making a move to implement it, than I was of flying into the sky, killing with a glance, or crawling under a mountain. All possibility of praxis had, thanks to that random seizure, died. What did those around me see, guards, foremen, and my fellow slaves, when they looked over? After the first months, when the shock of my circumstances had settled, what they saw was a good-natured fellow just sixteen, moving on toward seventeen, who now or again would lie or steal to better some side of his indenture, who now and again might indulge a gratuitous kindness equally to slave or guard. (One such — food I swiped from an overfat foreman to give to a boy only months newer to the mines than I and harassed by the guards for his jokes and high spirits — precipitated a riot and gained me this scar. In the confusion, a guard flung a pickax at me; the point caught my forehead and tore on down my cheek. I'd wanted to help the boy because he amused me in a place where very little made you grin. I was mauled because the guards had already decided such spirit as his might be a point around which rebellion could gather; and all who took to him were marked. The lesson was that, when you are oppressed, your acts, even if gratuitous, must not only be, but must seem, aimless, random, purposeless — so that reprisals don't fall on whomever you'd help: afterward the boy was transferred to the worst and most murderous mining division.) But all my actions, however they were interpreted, were only done to alleviate the tension and discomfort of the moment; I was to cowed even to consider the linkage moment makes with moment to create the history that, despite our masters, is never inevitable, only more or less negotiable. Through it all, though now and then I had hours of equally gratuitous anger, there was no bit of rebellion. What rebels had been all but slain in me; and all my labor, all my jokes, all my banter with those around me, in the pits, at the barracks, or in the journey between, were simple — even mechanical — habit, left over from my life before; habit that only aped a certain liveliness, while the self which gives life meaning had been banished from my body. What they saw, I'm telling you, Udrog, was the perfect slave. They saw it because, during the height of my freedom, loose among Kolhari's docks and at large among her side streets, I had been already so near the debased creation all political power yearns to turn its subjects into that my new condition made (my masters wanted me to believe in order to control me; and I wanted to believe in order to survive their control) no difference.

'What did I think at the time?

'I was intact. Only circumstances had changed.

'Ha!

'I think it was three months above a year after my capture that the lords came to the mines. But it could have been six months more — or six months less.

'What I remember, at any rate, is this:

'One afternoon rain brought us back from the flooded pits an hour early. Ivory clouds were piled around the ragged Falthas. The piney escarpments in the late light were black as the heaped chips we hauled from the obsidian tunnels after we cut the larger blocks and slabs. Copper smeared the west with red, as evening scratched the sky to blood. Crossing the leaf-strewn barracks yard, I'd stopped to look down at myself in one of the puddles that joined another with a silver ribbon across black earth while the water threw back the burning day — when the foreman bawled: "You there! I want you over at the south barracks! And you too — yes, and you!"

'Confused, I started toward where I'd been directed, along with half a dozen others who'd been picked from among the tired men returning from the pit to our quarters.

'Beside the south barracks, the seven of us milled: two wore leather clouts; the rest were naked. All were filthy — dirt to the hair and eyebrows. All of us were in our iron collars. But it was clear we'd been chosen, from among the hundred fifty miners, because we were the biggest, the strongest, the most strapping fellows in the place. And it should tell you something about the others of us that so many of the

seven were as young as we were. A guard came, cursing, in among us;
and, a moment later, four strange soldiers with spears and shields
stepped up. (We glanced at them, then stared into other puddles and
did not whisper.) One gave the order forward, and — with the soldiers
at the corners of our group — we started through trees and brush to
turn down a slope of tall grass, which beat wet whips against our
thighs to make the dirt there mud.

'We'd gone half a mile when I saw, beside a grove ahead, horses
tethered among several wagons, while more soldiers led four or five
others, stepping high at the end of their lead lines. With spears and
shields another dozen Imperial guards ambled about. By one closed
carriage men were raising a blue pavilion with braided fringe. Once I
glimpsed some rich red cloak (passing between the common leather
ones) set with so much metal and so many glittering stones my first
thought was that at the center of this military show must be some
mummers' troupe, like those I'd sometimes watched as they mimicked
the doings of earls and baronines back in the Kolhari market.

'Someone shouted for us to halt.

'Standing there on grass already muddied and worn down, I'd forgotten the guard with us, nor did I see the tall man who'd stepped up
on the other side, till one called to the other, voice carrying over us as
if we were not there: "All right. We can handle them from here. We
don't need you. Leave them and go back to your barracks." The man
who spoke was tall, brown, and stood easily on the wet slope. I looked
at his sandals, his worked metal belt, and the half-dozen neck chains
from various government orders hanging, bronze and copper, over his
blouse. Edged with fur, his cloak had fallen forward over one shoulder.
This was no mummer miming with theatrical exaggeration the image our debased populace carries of Nevèrÿon's nobility. Here was a
noble himself! "Thank you, my man — in the name of the empress,
whose reign is grand and gracious." The lord raised his hand to touch
the back of his fist to his forehead in that traditional gesture of respect, which, as he performed it, became the merest relief of the tiniest
irritation, practically unfelt — he brushed it away that quickly!

" 'Yes, sir!" The guard looked astonished and uncomfortable and
dumb at once. He was squat and strong, with a heavy lower lip, a
leather clout sewn up with thongs, and a club hanging at his hip. He
had stolen my supper three times, had nearly broken that club across

my calves twice, and had stood laughing over me when I'd lain bleeding from that pickax flung by another guard he counted as his friend. He was almost as dirty as we were. "Of course — yes. You'll be all right with them, My Lord? Well, sure, if you say so, sir. Right, sir. Right." Then, as if struck by gross memory, he smashed the back of his fist against his forehead. "The empress . . . !" bowing, backing, barefoot, up the slope, he beat his head again. "Yes, the empress, whose reign — " He almost tripped. And fisted his forehead once more. "Whose reign is just and generous . . . !"

'The tall lord smiled. "Come on, men. I'll put you to work in a moment. You'll be serving me, also Lord Anuron, and Count Jeu-Forsi — Anuron, is the big one running around in the red. You see him, down there? And the Lesser Lady Esulla rides with us. I doubt you'll see too much of her. But she's the reason you're here. If she tells you to do something, jump to it. You hear me, now?" He laughed and led us into the encampment to turn us over to the caravan steward, who put some of us to work hauling tent ropes and staking down the pavilion, while others of us were told to unload the provision wagons, and still others sent to help with the horses — though they had quite enough soldiers and servants for the work. But we did as we were instructed and tried to stay as unnoticed as possible among those around us who knew so much better what they were doing than we. Bewildered by our momentary transition, we had no way to question it.

'Not till years later did I begin to learn the mix of guilt and fascination with which Nevèrÿon's lords regarded their slaves — though it manifested itself about me for the whole of the afternoon and evening. What I did learn that day, however, was a myriad of separate facts about the nobility, whom, during the time of my freedom, I'd never seen from so close.

'That day was the first I heard the preposterous nicknames they call one another, in parody or denial of their power: the red-cloaked Lord Anuron was Piffles to his face — and Acorn Head behind his back, even when his fellow lords were addressing his own servants. Count Jeu-Forsi was called Toad by his companions. And Fluffy, a name I overheard from time to time, now as I carried someone's trunk across the yard, now as I came back with an armload of rope (the three young lords had stopped to talk beside two soldiers staking down the last pavilion guy), I assumed was the unseen Lesser Lady.

'In ten minutes, I was treated to one of those tantrums all too frequent among the very, very rich: within some group of his own guards and servants Lord Anuron began to turn about, left and right, his red cloak waving, shouting in a shriller and shriller voice: "All right! You think you can dominate me? You think you run everything? Well, you don't, you know! It's uncivilized! I could have every one of you replaced by *real* slaves! Oh, and don't you think I wouldn't for one *second*! You see, I've already called seven of them here! So you all just better watch yourselves! I should have every single one of you whipped, whipped, whipped within an inch of your shitty little lives! No, I will not tolerate it! I will *not*, I tell you!" Then, quivering — between the shoulders of two soldiers, I could see the thick, strapping young man was on the verge of tears! — he turned and stalked from the encampment.

' "I'm afraid Piffles — " the tall lord who'd met us spoke right at my ear; it startled me — "is under quite a bit of strain through here. You mustn't mind him when he gets like that. You'll get all *too* used to it in a while. Sorry." Then, while I blinked after him, he walked away. I don't know if I was more surprised by Lord Anuron's outburst or by my being spoken to by another lord as if I were someone whose judgment of it mattered!

'Over the next hour, now overhearing the guards, now the servants, now daring to exchange a quick grin and some whispers with another miner, now through some chance comment from the lords themselves, I pieced together a story as romantic as any mummers' skit.

'The three lords had been traveling from the western desert to the eastern shore. Stopping at a baron's estate a few days back, they'd learned that the baron's daughter, the Lesser Lady Esulla, was to journey in the same direction. In these days of bandits and the general dangers of travel, the baron wished to know, would the lords consent to let her wagon join their caravan? Lady Esulla had been recently widowed. The purpose of her trip was to seek a new husband. Indeed, either Lord Anuron or Count Jeu-Forsi might find an alliance with her family both honorable and profitable.

'Most certainly they would. They'd be honored, they said. It was their privilege to ride with and offer their protection to the baron's daughter.

'The first three days of travel had seen a rising competitiveness between the two lords whose family connections made them acceptable husbands — Jeu-Forsi and Anuron — with more and more daring deeds of a more and more outrageous sort, now perpetrated by one, now by the other. That, in fact, was why seven strong slaves had been ordered up from the mines, as part of some entertainment for her ladyship, though the day before, when it had become clear to the lady that this stranger and stranger behavior on the part of her traveling companions was really some manic courtship rite, her response had simply been to remain within her traveling wagon throughout the day. Though that wagon, the one at the side of the clearing with the woven curtains drawn tightly across its windows, had stopped with theirs, and one or two of her servants had been in and out of it briefly ("Yes, her ladyship was well . . . no, she did not wish to be disturbed"), the Lesser Lady herself had not appeared — which only made the young blades that much more irritable.

'I was wholly unclear about *what* entertainment we had been called to provide. But as we were set now to this job, now to that, I just assumed, whatever it was, it had been put by because of the lady's lack of cooperation. I became as curious as anybody in the camp (as curious as I might have been had I been observing it all in a skit of countesses and thanes on the mummers' market platform): what *was* going on within that silent wagon, with its drawn curtains, its red and orange designs, its closed carriage door?

'Yet now and again, something or other would bend that interest:

'First, I happened to step behind one of the other wagons and saw Count Jeu-Forsi, sitting on an overturned chest, knee to knee with a miner called Namyuk, who'd been captured three years before by slavers on some back road in the south. The count was drinking from a cider jug and was already drunk. "You must let me touch it. Let me. Let me, I say. There! No, no, you can't protest. If you do, I shall order it cut off. I can do that, you know. I just don't understand why all of you have such *big* ones — even those of you who weren't born to servitude. When the slavers go out on capturing raids, is that the first thing they look for? Now tell me, doesn't that feel good? You must say yes. Say 'Yes' to me. It feels good enough when I do it to my own. 'Yes.' Now." The irony is that, I'd long ago noted back at the mines, Namyuk was completely repelled by, and uninterested in, the various sexual adjustments any large group of men denied women make among themselves almost immediately. Perhaps because he *was* such a strong boy, he'd managed to keep almost wholly away from them. (As soon as I'd realized they were flourishing about me, I was at their center.) Often that takes a show of violence. But there was no violence possible here. Namyuk glanced up at me with a dull, opened-mouth look neither of surprise nor horror nor outrage nor disgust. (He was missing some teeth.) It was simply the blank stare of the stunned. The drunken count did not see me. I'm afraid I grinned — before I stepped back out of sight. Did I have a moment of sympathy? Sadly and savagely I think I found Namyuk's plight funny. And my real thoughts were all of the lord: so, this was the noble sot who was wooing the mysterious Lesser Lady. It seemed a bit of comic relief to heighten the drama going on in the clearing.

'The second incident was only minutes later, when I paused to overhear the tall lord in the fur-edged cloak, leaning against one of the pavilion poles and talking to his body servant, who squatted before him, busy searching for something in a small casket open on the ground. "Frankly, I find it disgusting the way they're carrying on — both Piffles and Toad competing to see who can act the perfect mule turd. And all for that skinny twit shut up in her wagon — though, really, with the two of them acting the way they are, I don't blame her. If I were in Fluffy's position, I'd probably do the same." I listened, sure I was as unnoticed here as I'd been behind the carriage. But the lord turned to gesture at me, though his eyes swept by me as his fist had swept his forehead when he'd saluted the empress. "Now, of course, we've got *these* loathsome fools to deal with. It's disgusting — disgusting! Not Her Majesty's policy at all; and both of them know it. Come here, my man."

'I stepped up, surprised all over again.

' "You seem to have finished the last thing you had to do. Let me give you another job, before Toad gets his moist little fingers on you. Really, though, with that wound on your face — " for the pickax injury, if from time to time I forgot it, had not yet settled to this single scar, but was still a ravine of red flesh and dried scab that cascaded my brow and cheek — "if the dirt doesn't stop him, that, at least, should keep you safe from his sloppy attentions. Now you go on and . . ."

'He gave me another job.

'And I, who'd been telling myself how *I* would have exploited the

interest of that most noble besotted lord, went off to perform it —
with the same stunned expression Namyuk had worn: a man who'd
welcomed us so cordially, whose natural nobility had so flustered my
guard, and who had passed a comment to me like an equal, had just
dismissed me, on some whim that *was* the incomprehensibly random
itself, as a disgusting ugly fool.

'In the middle of my work, I heard a call for the slaves to come to
the clearing. Were we to be sent back to the mines now? Confused, I
trotted out, into the space among the wagons.

' "That's right. Come here, the lot of you!" Lord Anuron had taken
off his cloak. In his red tunic, he waved an arm about in its long, loose
sleeve. He was a great, brown, bear of a man, with nappy black hair,
thick arms, and furry thighs showing below his red hem. "We're going
to have a little contest, now. We're going to see what you're made of.
We called for the seven strongest slaves in the mine — though they
seem to have sent us the seven youngest, instead." All those standing
around laughed. "But no matter. We've been watching you, you see.
Now you." He beckoned me to step forward. "You look like a strong
boy. Though not quite so strong as" — here he turned to survey the
line of us — "you there!" The one he pointed to was a miner called
Vrach. "What's your name, my man?"

' "Eh . . . Vrach, sir." Looking about warily, Vrach stepped out. "My
name's Vrach."

' "Are you ready to wrestle for your freedom, Vrach?"

' "My Lord . . . ?"

' "You heard me. A fair fight to a single fall — yes, between you and
me. How do you like that? If you win, I'll buy you from the mines, take
that collar from your neck, and give it to you as a present in honor of
your new-won liberty. That is, *if* you can beat me . . . ?"

'Vrach was one of some half-dozen miners whom I'd already decided
that, because of their strength (or because they were simply half-
mad), I would *never* fight. He was about twenty-four and had been in
the mines a decade — though before that he'd been born into servitude somewhere in the west and had only been sold here when the
estate he'd worked on was broken up. His hip-heavy body was all
knots and blocks and angles, balanced on big, cracked feet. Some of
his beard was already white; though, with the dirt, it looked mostly
no color at all. He'd always been quiet. I'd tried a few times to befriend
him. It hadn't particularly worked. As I stood in the clearing, watch-

ing Vrach blink his wrinkled lids over reddened eyes, Namyuk came from behind the wagon. (I guess because he was clearly not the strongest of us, nobody did more than glance.) Moments later, Count Jeu-Forsi came out, too. He folded his arms and stood on the sidelines.

' "And . . . if I lose, sir?"

'Who, I wondered, in these last hours had stunned Vrach?

' "Oh, why then — " Anuron turned up his large hands and laughed. He was taller than Vrach, darker, and broader; but though Anuron was strong, foot to forehead Vrach was clearly harder — "it's back to the mines with you. That's all. Nothing to lose, certainly. What do you say?"

' "Then why must I fight you sir? Why not just send me back now?"

' "But my man, we want some sport here!" The lord laughed, broadly, nervously. "A little entertainment. A fair fight, one fall, with freedom as the prize. Now don't tell me you're frightened?"

' "Yes, sir!"

' "But of what?" demanded Lord Anuron; the others around us, guards and servants, were starting to smile.

' "You'll kill me if I raise a hand to you!" Vrach blurted. "You're the lord. I'm only a slave, sir. I'm not allowed to fight with you; and you'll kill me if I dare!" Vrach, I realized, was terrified. And so, it struck me, was I! In his iron collar, Vrach went on: "You want to fight me to show off to the Lady inside." The clearing we stood in was directly before the closed wagon; posts had been set at the four corners of a wide space and an attempt had been made to clear the ground of stones and fallen branches, though it was just as puddled and ribboned as our barracks yard. "You want her to see you win. Then why should you let yourself lose? If I come near to hurting you, or even to getting the upper hand, you or one of your guards will strike me dead! I know it, sir!"

' "No, no, no!" The lord was becoming flustered. Still wearing his sword, he reached down to unstrap it. "There — " He flung it, with its belt and scabbard, to the sidelines, then hauled his red tunic over his head, to toss it off to the other side of the clearing. "Now, you see, my man? We're equals. I'm as naked as you are!"

'And though Vrach was a slave who went naked, the iron was still at his neck. "No, sir. Please, sir! Don't make me fight you! Don't — "

'Crouching a little, Lord Anuron stepped forward and swung his hand against Vrach's beard. "Come, now, my man! Fight, I say! A coward?" He slapped Vrach's other cheek. "Protect yourself. Come on. I thought our slaves were made of better stuff!"

'Vrach put a hand up to his face, turning almost wholly away. He mumbled back over his shoulder: "Please, sir — !"

' "I say fight!" and here Lord Anuron closed with Vrach.

'Vrach tried to twist away and almost fell, so that he had to turn back to catch the bigger man; and held him — only to keep from slipping. And, after a fashion, they fought: I'd seen Vrach level any number of miners in the brawls that had broken out in our barracks. But here the slave fought the way, two or three times in Kolhari, I'd seen well-bred merchants fight when set on by a street vandal: since fighting was something they simply never did, and thus the encounter was, for them, outside all known law, and since they were also completely ignorant of what hidden weapons their assailant had (usually none — though, of course, not always) or what levels of violence the battle might, in a moment, rise to (again, usually none — though, yet again, not always), they fought not to injure the assailant or even to defend themselves. All their effort went into immobilizing the attacker, trying only to hold him still, hoping vaguely that, if they could only go *on* holding him long enough, he would come to his senses and cease his rowdiness. And since, thus, they fought in a dream, they always lost — usually sustaining injuries as well as theft. Vrach tried to hold on to the bear-like Anuron, just to keep the nobleman from hitting him.

'Standing beside me, the tall lord began to cheer. The circle of servants and caravan guards (how many swords and spears and shields could I see among them!) took it up. I didn't.

'Neither did Namyuk.

'Nor did the other slaves at the sidelines. Though some servants and soldiers were shouting for Vrach and some were shouting for Anuron, I believe that, even if the promised prize had been freedom for all seven of us, I could not have cheered Vrach on. Rather, I — and I think it was true for the rest of us — was *with* him, slipping and struggling in the mud; we were as terrified as he that, at the least display of strength, someone — a soldier if not the lord he fought — would just step out and slay him.

'With a great grin, Lord Anuron shoved staggering Vrach away, and the two stood panting, Vrach looking around, perhaps for somewhere to run — when Anuron barreled into him, toppling with him in a puddle. The mirror broke. The two flailed, splattering first water, then mud, now this one rolling on top, now the other. But, through the whole thing, Vrach only tried to hold the lord off or to pull himself away, while the muddy Anuron pummeled and struck with fist, elbow, or knee.

'The soldiers and servants went on shouting. (What, I wondered, constituted a single fall? Anuron was still fighting.) Though I had begun the day observing as if this were some mummer's skit of the lives and loves of hereditary nobility, what I saw here was something no mummer would ever show on the platform: these nobles were free, free to do anything, anything to us. They were free to summon us or send us away. They were free to speak to us as equals one moment, and free to call us disgusting fools the next. They were free to caress us in any way they wished, and free to strike or maim us in any other. They were free to promise us freedom, and free to thrust a blade in our livers as we looked up in joy. That's what had stunned Vrach; and it stunned the six of us as we watched Vrach get his feet under him, as we watched Lord Anuron grab Vrach's leg and yank him back down for a second fall. And I knew that whether the tale was that of a slave's winning his freedom in a single fall or of the lord's proving his manliness to a noble lesser lady, neither story was for my benefit nor the benefit of anyone else in the collar.

'The two struggled.

'And for all the ripples around them in that muddied mirror, I could no longer make out in it any turn of cloud, nor any branch of tree.

'Then the door to the Lady Esulla's wagon opened. Crouching down, a servant woman looked out, ducked back in, then pushed something forward: an elaborate box splatted onto the mud. She disappeared. (The cheers and cries increased at the contest, but I was watching the wagon.) A thin, dark woman with short black hair, wide-spaced eyes, and wearing a white ankle-length shift stepped carefully out to stand on the pedestal.

'She looked at the fighters.

'Lord Anuron must have seen her. Perhaps he relaxed his grip, because Vrach pulled away from him, splashing on all fours, and, three yards off, staggered to his feet. Vrach turned to her too, mud from sole to crown. Blinking, he took a step back.

'Lord Anuron reeled upright, made a clumsy bow to the Lady, and grinned through the slop. He turned in the torn-up clearing to face Vrach, who stood, looking between the lady and the lord. Anuron took a breath. Then, again, he barreled forward. What he did next was to bring his knee up, hard, between Vrach's legs and, at the same time, bring both fists down, like dropped rocks, on Vrach's shoulders. The miner rose enough for his feet to suck clear from the mud, gave out an "*Ugggggggg* . . ." and fell, splattering, both hands thrust between his legs. He lay there, the "*Ugggggggggggggg* . . ." going on. And on.

'Guards and servants applauded.

' " . . . *ggggggggggg* . . ."

'And on.'

5

'Panting, grinning, Lord Anuron looked around at his audience. That must have been the fall he was waiting for: he gave another small bow, then turned to Lady Esulla. "See?" he called, over the applause, between gasped breaths. "I won, Fluffy . . . ! That last was a trick my father taught me . . . Does it every time! I could even teach it to you too, if you'd like . . . ? I tell you, it's not a bad idea for women to know how to fight in these strange and terrible times!"

'As guards and servants moved off, Count Jeu-Forsi came forward to stand over Vrach. Slowly, he stooped, took the miner's shoulder, and peered at him.

'The Lesser Lady stepped from her pedestal, to make her way across the mud and squat, beside them, the hem of her shift in seconds soaked and soiled.

'In his fur-edged cloak, the tall lord walked out to join them. Vrach's moan came from among them. I couldn't hear what they were saying, but from their whispers and consultations, they were talking about the fallen miner.

'I was surprised.

'So was Lord Anuron.

'Still buoyed by his victory, he went over to see what they were do-

ing and said genially: "I knew if we got started, Fluffy, that would
bring you out. Come on, now. You must tell me: what did you think
of that last one — the one I dropped him with?"

'Lady Esulla looked up from where she knelt on the muddy ground.
"Piffles — " her voice was both breathy and chill — "will you, if only
for my sake and the honor you bear my father, put some effort into
being a *little* less tiresome? Otherwise, I don't know what I'm going to
do!"

' "Tiresome . . . ?" Lord Anuron stepped back. "Tiresome . . . !"
His face contorted toward the same flustered petulance with which
he'd raged at his servants. But he turned and, with the mud still on
him (some blood in with it, too, on his shoulder and his thigh), once
more stalked, this time naked, from the encampment toward the far
pines.

'The three nobles turned again to Vrach. Now they called the six
of us over — what, they wanted to know, did *we* think of his condition? I have no idea what we mumbled. Lady Esulla sent for towels
and a basin, and stooped there, washing mud from Vrach's face and
chest. Now over his drunkenness (perhaps that had only been for
Namyuk), Count Jeu-Forsi called someone to run to his tent and
fetch the stoppered bronze pitcher — it was a powerful, even dangerous, potion; but he never traveled without it. At least it would ease
the miner's pain. (Though it took almost half an hour to take effect, it
did.) They had a stretcher brought. Count Jeu-Forsi took one end and
ordered a soldier to carry the other. (I didn't think the little lord was
strong enough for it and stepped up to take it from him. But, though
he still smelled of drink, he waved me back; and managed very well.)
As the stretcher went past us, the tall lord stood with his hand on
Lady Esulla's shoulder, the two talking softly, now with concern for
Vrach, now with barely controlled outrage at Acorn Head.

'Lady Esulla sent three servants to set up a bed of benches for Vrach
by the side entrance to the pavilion. We kept glancing over where
they were bringing out mats and pillows and rugs — none of us, you
understand, slept on anything but straw and earth in our barracks.
Yes, it was best for the others to go back to the mines this evening.
Really, the lords could not apologize enough — to *all* of us! Namyuk
and I were chosen to stay over at the caravan site and help Vrach back
in the morning, since he was in no condition to return that night. A

soldier would go with the other miners and explain our absence. We two mustn't worry. It would all be taken care of. The others went off, while Namyuk and I were told to make ourselves as comfortable as we could, there beside the pavilion, where Vrach was stretched, dazed from the drug. Supper hour had arrived at the caravan, and servants began to come out to Namyuk and me with a dozen (it seemed) astonishing dishes, more than half of which we were afraid to eat because we didn't know what they were. Still, the remainder made a meal more sumptuous than anything I'd ever known, not only at the mines but, indeed, at my home in Kolhari. Vrach's occasional moan behind us joined the sound of our eating and the soldiers' and servants' chatter coming and going inside.

'As the sky's blue deepened, the tall lord came out to us.

'He'd come to look at Vrach.

'He'd also brought out his own plate and, after once more examining the injured slave (who now at least was conscious and able to mutter a few words), sat down to finish his meal with us. He called for a small bowl of broth to be brought and held Vrach's head in his lap to spoon a few sips past the miner's beard. For the first time since the fight Vrach managed a smile — then threw up all over the lord's lap and leg.

'Always squeamish, Namyuk bolted from the bed's edge at that one. But the lord only called for more towels to clean Vrach and himself. Then, when he'd made the miner as comfortable as possible with more pillows and rugs, he sat down beside me again on the bed to continue his supper. (Namyuk finished his, squatting on the ground, his plate between his toes.) My mother's care for me during some childhood sickness played at my memory. In the mines, no one received such treatment. There, a sick or injured slave was simply put to work on a less demanding job. If his ailment was such that he would be indisposed for more than two or three days, he was often taken off somewhere and left to starve — that is, if a guard didn't grow tired of his calls for food and kill him in the night with a knife across the throat.

'The tall lord — I didn't know his name nor can I remember what Toad or Fluffy had called him — stayed on to talk to us, to ask about our lives at the mines, about our lives before. He told us that, while his own parents had once owned many, many slaves, though he remembered seeing them in the fields when he was ten or twelve, the empress did not relish the institution, and, though buying or owning slaves was still legal, when his family had moved to the north their slaves had been freed or sold. For all four of the nobles together in the caravan, including Lord Anuron, mastery such as we had seen abused today was a childhood memory, not an adult reality. (That night I first learned, while the empress still owned various slave-worked institutions such as the mines there in the north and the quarries off in the south, no slaves were used at court.) His curiosity about us and our lives was as sincere as his concern for Vrach, and as we talked there, through the evening, all of us, despite our discomfort, despite our distrust, became more and more open, more and more honest —no doubt he as much as we. That evening, I learned things of Namyuk and Vrach (who was, after a while, able to talk a little) I'd never have learned at the mines — if only because I'd never have thought to ask such questions as that tall lord asked. Doubtless they learned similar things of me. And all three slaves learned things about the life of a Nevèrÿon noble that bewildered, that astonished, that seemed as unbelievable to us as any night dream reconsidered in the day. Oh, not all we learned was pleasant. When Vrach fell silent awhile, Namyuk and I were soon talking of our freedom, our capture, our life before the mines. The tall lord listened. The tall lord smiled. But now from a momentarily noble frown, now from a lordly blink of incomprehension, now from a look of truly imperial blankness, soon Namyuk, Vrach, and I — and, finally, the lord himself — began to suspect that the life we were describing to him was *so* far below his in comfort, privilege, and power, that both Namyuk's forest village and my dockside home were *so* chained about in what for him was just pettiness and poverty . . . well, as he finally admitted to us, leaning forward on his knees with a small smile of apology, he was just not sure he could see the difference between such freedom and actual slavery; nor was he clear why one state was really preferable to the other and accepted it (if indeed he did) only on our say-so.

'And so we talked of that awhile.

'There's a tale newly freed, or presently rebelling, slaves often tell, of how, when speaking with a master, there is always something held back, always an inner core kept in reserve no master ever sees, a secret self no slave will ever show to any lord. Yes, there're many moments of conflict, rebellion, hostility, of injurious or insulting ignorance where such reserve is real. But as a universal, I suspect, like almost any other, that is just another mummer's tale, however and whomever it aids. True, in the course of the day these nobles had violated me and Naymuk and Vrach in just about every way they could. Yet now, when one turned to offer his humanity, grown generous and complex in a field of privilege we could not even conceive of, you must tell me, Udrog: what did we *have* to hold back? I cannot speak for Vrach or Namyuk. But certainly *I* had nothing; it had all been taken from me with my capture. So the four of us, three slaves and a lord, talked on, innocently and honestly, out of our ignorance of the chains that held us together, of the chains that held us apart, while the sky blackened and the night's chill came on.

'We'd been speaking there over an hour, when Lord Anuron stepped from the pavilion, holding up a smoking brand. He was clean now. (Under his torch's light his new tunic was blue. So was his cloak.) "You know," he said, "it's not right, your spending all this time out here with them. It really isn't. Fluffy and I have had a *long* conversation, and we've come to an understanding; I must say, it's lifted quite a burden. All three of you have been acting beastly. Believe me, it hasn't been fun at all. But since my discussion with Fluffy I understand a *little* of the 'Why,' now. Well, you must try to understand me, too. I've only done *any* of the things that have put you all so out of sorts with me in the last three days because I thought they would amuse you. I just didn't know you felt that way about it. Really, it's that simple. Fluffy doesn't approve of slaves, either; and, I confess, I finally see her point. But for *just* the reasons she's been outlining to me for the past hour, I *don't* see how you can spend your whole night sitting out here, talking to people in . . . collars! You're only doing it to make *me* feel guilty, anyway. (There now, you *do* look a little better, don't you? Yes, my man: I'm glad you're feeling more on top of things. Really, even if you didn't win, I thought you put up quite a fight. And you did give me one or two good ones. You should be proud of yourself! You really should. There? See? You're smiling!) But on that front, at any rate, Fluffy's been a little more human about the whole thing than you have. She, at least, has spent her hour this evening trying to talk some sense — as she sees it — about the whole matter with *me*. But to think someone I've always respected, someone who was a childhood friend, someone I've always looked up to would just throw over all social responsibility to come out here and chatter on with these poor collared creatures only to slight me . . . well, it's childish and small-minded. It really is. You've done what you can for them. (Toad has said it right out, three times now: *he* thinks at this point you're just being silly!) Why don't you come inside and let us all tell you what a real prince we think you are for it. I'm not fooling. I want you to leave them alone and come back in and join the rest of us. Honestly, your sitting out here like this with these . . . well, I just can't countenance it. And I don't think, if you came out and asked her, Fluffy would either."

'I sat there, my cheeks heating, grateful for the darkness, for the scabs on my face, for anything that would conceal me: I could not tell you if I were embarrassed for myself or for the lord.

'He listened through Anuron's speech. Then he reached around into his cloak, brought out something that, in the torchlight, I didn't recognize — I had not seen one in over a year. He turned to Vrach, reached down for the blinking miner's neck, and inserted the metal bar into the locking mechanism that held the collar closed, twisted, then pulled open the hinged iron. With one hand again under Vrach's head, he pulled away the metal, turned forward again and, with a gesture of astonishing violence, hurled the collar in among the hangings over the pavilion's entrance. It disappeared inside with such a billowing of cloth I expected all sounds inside to cease. When they didn't, I imagined the collar itself, somehow, vanishing from the world before such power!

'He reached for me, took my scarred face in his hand to lift my chin. He shook a little as he touched me. I felt the iron at my neck pulled free. Again he hurled the collar within the hangings. Now he reached for open-mouthed Namyuk and, in a moment, hurled his collar after the other two. The key still in one, both hands again on his knees, he looked up at Anuron. When he spoke, a tremor touched his voice that made my flesh glitter, as the tingles already about my neck, free of iron for the first time in a year, went on down my body.

' "Now I am no longer speaking to men in collars. When I'm ready, Piffles, I shall come in. But *not* before!"

'Lord Anuron batted his shallow eyes below the torch. "Oh, inside, when I tell them this, they're *just* not going to *believe* . . . !" He breathed. He blinked. He searched for more to say. What he finally came out with, a nervous halt in it, had all the chill the Lesser Lady Esulla had summoned with him hours earlier. "I wish you'd just . . . try to be . . . well a *little* less tiresome!" Then he dashed the torch to the ground, where the yellow flame joined its rising reflection in a puddle and, after it rolled over and the fires for moments flickered with the oil that spread the surface, went out. He stalked back into the pavilion.

'Perhaps what the mummer's tale of the reticent slave speaks of is what now we all found ourselves withholding from one another. Though the lord made his attempt to continue from where we'd been interrupted, he was clearly upset. But it was Vrach, now, who made the greatest effort to "save the evening" (as one of the nobles themselves might have put it). He wanted to tell of the cruel behavior of a guard no longer at the barracks; and he wanted to speak of something a sister of his had never gotten a chance to say to him because she was sold away too soon; and he wanted to tell us of the riotously comic revenge he'd once gotten on an overseer, years before Namyuk or I had come to the mines, who'd tried to arrange a fight between two other miners, which the match today had put him in mind of.

'Really, Vrach went on there like a man arguing for his life. But it may have been the potion.

'The tall lord listened, nodded, smiled when it was appropriate. (Namyuk and I listened but were too uncomfortable to smile.) And when at last his lordship stood up, excusing himself — really, it was time for him to go back inside; he hoped we understood . . . ?

'He was back out only a few minutes later, of course, with more pillows and rugs. Namyuk and I must bed down and make ourselves comfortable under the stars. It was higher and drier over here. Why not use this spot? The night was clear. Rain, for now, was over. He stood for a while looking down at Vrach, who'd drifted off immediately and was snoring irregularly.

'We must come wake him, he told us, if there was any change in the miner's condition.

'He pointed off toward a tent through whose corner lacings we could see lamplight. That was where he would be sleeping. If there was any change at all, we must not hesitate to come.

'All the lamps in the pavilion were out. The sky was starry. Namyuk and I bedded down in our rugs and furs beside the snoring Vrach, glancing at the tall man, who strolled toward his light-stitched tent. (Did either of us think that because we were to spend a night without collars, we might bolt for freedom? Perhaps it was because we had been entrusted with Vrach's care, but I don't believe we did.) I remember I slept.

'And, I remember, when hours later I woke in the starry dark, for moments I was not sure if I'd only been dozing a few breaths' time.

'Up on his bed, Vrach was moaning. The covers had fallen off, and it was chilly. Vrach was making the dull, insistent groan I'd heard when Lord Anuron had first felled him. I listened for minutes. The sound halted only at the end of the breath, then began all over again:

' "U*ggggggggggg* . . ."

'Then he would thrash some. But when I asked him — three times — if he were all right, he didn't answer.

' "U*gggggggggggggggggg* . . ."

'And Namyuk was snoring.

'I sat up.

'Across the dark clearing, lamplight still prickled the tent seams. He had *told* us to come . . . Wondering if I should disturb him, I pushed from my covering, stood, and put a rug back over Vrach (who, without waking, immediately twisted so it fell off), and stepped onto cold ground. I started, naked, across the grass. Should I say something outside, first? Should I look in, to see if he was asleep? Since a lamp still burned, he was still awake . . . Unless he'd drifted off without extinguishing it. Would he really want me to disturb him? Certainly there was nothing he could do that hadn't been done already. But he'd said . . .

'At the tent's front hanging, I pulled the flap a little aside to peer in.

'What I saw within that drab canvas, lit by the lamp on its low table, stays with a vividness I doubt I can convey to you, Udrog. The tall lord stood beside his rumpled bed; he was turned a bit away, so that he did not see me. He was naked — as naked as you, Udrog, or as I. He held something, which he stared down at with a fascination that, over the seconds I watched, was clear as much from his stillness as from the fragment of his expression I could see in the shadowy light. He held one of the iron collars, a semicircle of it in each fist. Did I watch there a full minute? (It could have been longer!) What I

learned over the course of it was how long *he* must have been standing there when I looked. Then — and when he began the gesture I felt
my body overcome with an excitement that meant I had already
realized, had already recognized, had already known what you, certainly, would have seen as clearly had you stood in my place — he
raised the collar to his neck and closed the semicircles on it, without
taking his hands away, as if afraid, once having donned it, he might
not be able to doff it again. I recognized it as a sexual gesture with an
intensity enough to stun me and make all my joints go weak. I have
already told you, Udrog, my own sexual interest in the collar was as
precocious, in its way, as yours; have I already spoken of the
pause . . . ? Which, I suppose, is all we can cite of desire.

'I was wholly at, if not within, it.

'Tale tellers talk of lust as a fire that makes the body shiver as
though cased in ice. But it's not the fire or the ice that characterizes
desire, but the contradiction between them. Perhaps, then, we should
go on calling it a pause, a split, a gap — a silence that, on either side,
though it seems impassable, is one that, while we are in it and it
threatens to shake us apart, it seems we will never escape.

'Suddenly he turned (perhaps my breath became hoarse), saw me
(perhaps my hand on the tent flap shook the canvas), and started.
"What are you — why are you . . . ?"

'Shocked at his shock, I started as much as he. (Now I did shake
the tent. I'm only surprised it didn't fall down about the two of us!)
"The miner . . ." I blurted, letting the canvas drop behind me. "Vrach
— he's making that sound . . . and I didn't know what was wrong
with — "

' "Well, what am *I* supposed to do about it!" he blurted back, pulling the collar from his neck. "Oh yes — of course. I told you to come
and . . ." That's when, first, I guess, he really saw me.

'We were both naked.

'We were both male.

'I had seen him; and he knew I had seen him. Now he saw; and
from what he saw he knew of me just what I knew of him.

'He looked a moment longer. I could not have denied my reaction
to him any more than he could have denied his to the iron.

'After a while, I said, again: "Vrach, he's making that sound. Again.
You said . . . Perhaps you should come and look at him."

'He took a breath. "Very well. Perhaps I should." He took another.

And looked down at the collar in his hand. "But I think it's time to have these on again — for tomorrow. So they'll let you back in the mines." He gave a small laugh. It was a poor joke, but though I very much wanted to laugh with him, I didn't. He came over to me, raised the iron, and closed it about my throat. The lock snapped to. And just as I had recognized the sexual in his placing of it about his own neck, I knew that, though lust still reeled in his body and still staggered in mine, this gesture was as empty of the sexual as it is possible for a human gesture to be. He was only a frightened man, recollaring a slave whom he had let, briefly and unwisely, pretend awhile to be free.

'I have called the conversation between the four of us earlier "honest." I believe it was. Still, there'd been no words about any of this, while we were among the others, from either him or me. But though I'd snickered to myself over Jeu-Forsi's violation of Namyuk, I was wholly surprised at the sudden knowledge of this shared perversion that, tonight, we would not share.

' "Now," he said, "let's go see how our man is doing." He picked up the lamp. Both the other collars were on the bed. He picked them up, too. Then without cloak, clout, or tunic, he stepped by me to the flap.

'I followed him from the tent over the cold ground.

'Beside the pavilion, under the raised light, I saw Vrach had curled up, uncovered, in a kind of ball, forearms thrust down between knees drawn almost to his chest. His eyes were closed. His breaths were short and sharp.

' "Here, hold the lamp."

'While I took it, the naked lord bent over to secure Vrach's collar. The miner made a choking sound — again I started. But, as if answering my thoughts, the tall lord said: "He's . . . still breathing." He stood up. "Put a cover over him, will you?" And while, again, I covered Vrach with one of the rugs, he went to where Namyuk snored, stooped down, and fastened the third collar on the sleeping boy — who uttered three incomprehensible words, turned in his blankets, and snored on.

'Again he came to me. For a moment he hesitated; and while he looked at me, I felt us slip again toward the sexual. We stood, naked, before each other, the way Anuron, naked, had stood before naked Vrach. But I knew then that if he had said something, even collared I would have said yes. I suspect, now, that had I spoken, despite my dirt, despite my scar, despite anything and everything that made him think me hideous, he would have said, however hesitantly and with whatever downcast eyes, the same.

'I did not speak.

'He did not speak.

'What we saw — what we had recognized — was still outside of language.

'He took the lamp from me, glanced again at Vrach — "We'll see how he's doing in the morning. Good night, now." — and turned back to his tent. But I must tell you this: it was a very different boy who bedded down now to sleep from the boy who had bedded down on the same rugs hours back. Now I was full of schemes, plans, ideas. Should I go back when he slept and steal his key? But then, I didn't know where he kept it. Should I get up and start out on my own, the collar still on me? But there were both soldiers and slaves on the road. How indeed, once I was back, *could* I escape the mines? If I acted on none of those thoughts that night, or even in the days or months afterward, it was only because of the fear of real reprisals — as real as the plans themselves. But somehow, in that moment when the two of us, slave and master, looked on each other, I was given back my self. Oh, not, certainly, by that poor, frightened man. What had returned it to me was no more than a chance configuration of fog on a morning meadow that lets us recognize, momentarily, the shape of some imagined dragon, so that, ever afterwards in imagination, we can ride her where we wish.

'But I had now seen one further aspect to the play of freedom and power that allowed me, in a way I had not been able to for a year, to want, to wish, to dream. I had known that the masters of Nevèrÿon could unlock the collar from my neck or lock it on again. What I had not known was that they could place it on their own necks and remove it. Now I coveted that future freedom, that further power I had witnessed in the master's tent: however vaguely, however foggily, as I drifted off to sleep, I knew I would not be content till I had seized that freedom and power for myself, even though I knew I had to seize the former for every slave in Nevèrÿon — before I could truly hold the latter.

'The next morning when we woke, all four nobles, with their servants, were up to see to us.

'How was Vrach doing today?

'By the morning light, it was evident: his testicles were bruised black and purple and hugely swollen — as was his whole lower abdomen. Anuron's torch lay on the grass, burned wadding at its end. Though Vrach could support himself on one leg, the other could bear almost no weight at all. He hurt, and was obviously concerned about it, however well he bore it.

'It was Fluffy's suggestion: perhaps another dose of Toad's painkiller? So they let Vrach swig down a good bit. Then there was nothing to do but send us back. The caravan had to move on. With Vrach's arms around our shoulders, Namyuk and I supported him between us. Lord Anuron sent a soldier along.

'The tall lord wished us well.

'In the course of our concern, none of us even mentioned that, once more, our collars were in place.

'To go even half a mile with a man who can only use one leg is not easy. A few times the soldier switched off with us, when Namyuk or I needed a rest. Three times Vrach asked us to leave him alone awhile in the bushes. The third time, when he called us in to get him, he was breathing hard and looked up at us with a worried smile, grimacing as we got his arms again around us. "You see it feels in the *worst* way like I've got to piss." He grunted as he came up between us. "But I can hardly get it to trickle."

'At the barracks, Namyuk and I were sent straight off to the pit for our dirty work, while guards took over Vrach. Because he'd been there ten years, I guess, and because he'd always been a good miner, he was allowed to lie in sick.

'That evening, through supper and into the night, we heard his groans — shouts, some of them, finally — coming from the next barracks over.

'Even the trickle had stopped.

'They didn't have to kill him.

'Two nights later he died.

'In the morning I saw them carry him out. Though he'd only been dead those hours, gut and belly were big as a corpse's left to bloat a month.

'I've thought about it often. It might even make a better story — another mummer's tale — to say it was my anger, my rage at Vrach's murder that spurred me to freedom, to my own liberation, to the liber-

ation of all Neverÿon's slaves. It's a tale I've sometimes told, sometimes to others, sometimes to myself. Like any slave, I've many more
than this one. I've told some often enough to know the truth that's in
them. There's certainly lots of reality. But a tale I've told much more
rarely, though I've found myself thinking of it again and again, is the
story of the night when none of us knew (or, at least, I didn't) Vrach
would die; when, through my chance observation at the flap of that
lamp-lit tent, I gained my self, the self that seeks the truth, the self
that, now and again in seeking it, becomes entangled in falsehood,
error, and delusion, as well as outrage and pride — the self that tells
the tales.

'But more and more, now that my purpose is so largely won, I
reflect on the paradox that one cannot reach *for* something till one
has something to reach *with*. That night at the tent, when I recognized my own lusts in the lord, I knew that I was different from other
slaves: and with that knowledge it began to flood upon me the endless ways in which I and all the slaves I knew were, for all our differences, subject to one oppression. That night at the tent, when I
recognized that I, a slave, and he, a lord, could see in each other one
form to desire, it began to flood upon me, as I rehearsed the night's
talk on which I'd grounded the oneness of master and slave, the endless ways in which that lord and I were different in every aspect of
our class, history, condition — and every other social category im-
posed to form us.

'I wanted his power, Udrog. I wanted it desperately. And by recognizing that want, I woke to my self: what I wanted was the power to
remove the collar from the necks of the oppressed, including my
own. But I knew, at least for me, that the power to remove the collar
was wholly involved with the freedom to place it there when I wished.
And, wanting it, I knew, for the first time since I'd been brought to
the mines — indeed, for the first time in my life — the self that want
defined.'

The fire crackled awhile.

Udrog, who'd attended this tale with stretches of interest and
stretches of boredom, had again become alert when addressed by his
name. Still and silent for so long, now he ventured a comment: 'That
lord, when he put the collar on his own neck, he freed you to put it
around your own — '

'In no way did he, or his gesture, free me!' Gorgik glanced sharply at the boy, who wriggled against him, sighed, and lay back, though from a twitch in his shoulder here or a movement of his mouth there, it was possible the boy was going on with some other story to himself, even as Gorgik declared: 'How could *he* have freed *me*?

'That man was not free to put the collar on and wear the sign of his desire openly among both intimates and strangers. When he started at my presence that night, what *I* saw was a man as terrified of discovery as, no doubt, I'd have been had I been in his place.

'That man was not free to give me my freedom: even as we recognized our own lusts in each other — even if the notion to buy and free a slave had suddenly struck him — because of our mutual recognition I was now the *last* slave he would have chosen to free. (Wasn't I the first he chose to recollar?) With my recognition, which, believe me, he recognized as well, I'd already gained too much power for him to tolerate in me any equality.

'I'm talking, understand, Udrog, of an incident almost wholly outside the chain of language that holds us to the social world, as far outside those chains as a true, observed, and social incident can be. But real as the incident was, had someone chosen to question me about it, I certainly would have lied — with full knowledge I was lying — to protect my lord, to protect myself. And I suspect he would have lied, too, to protect himself, to protect his slave. But the reason I'd have lied, far more than for the protection, is because, at that moment, I had no notion of how the truth might be articulated. And I'm willing to grant him the same.

'But he, *free* me?

'How could you, Udrog — or I — even think it, once he relocked my collar? Say rather the gesture with which he placed the collar on his own neck, when he thought himself unseen, was a mirror in which I saw — or in which I could anticipate — the form of my own freedom. Say rather that when he placed the collar again on me and locked it, he broke that mirror — but without in any way obscuring what I'd already seen in it.

'Well, all that was a long time back. I'm telling you of things that took place in another world, Udrog. There're no slaves now. There haven't been since you were a child. And some like us, at least in the larger cities, wear their collars openly — which is why you, here, can be as forward as you are. Can you, with your freedom, understand that? But now you have heard the beginning, understanding what you have, lie here a little longer and let me tell the end. It'll only take a bit more time. For many years later, when I — '

But Udrog, about to protest that this was not the particular type of torture he'd had in mind for the evening, pushed suddenly to his knees, pointed off from the rug, and cried out: 'What's that?'

The big man frowned, raised up on one elbow, and looked behind them. 'What, Udrog?'

'There, look! Do you see it?'

'See what . . . ? Oh, there, you mean?'

'But what is it?'

Frowning, Gorgik turned over on the rug. 'A cat — at least that's what it looks like.'

The animal had run from the shadow to pass silently within inches, and now stood, some feet off, looking back, firelight luminous in one eye and moving in and out of the other as its head moved left, then right.

'What's it doing here?' Udrog demanded.

'Whatever cats do when they wander around empty castles at night.' Gorgik shrugged. 'Come, boy. Lie back down while I finish my tale.'

But Udrog reached up, pulled his collar open, and turned to Gorgik. 'Maybe it would be better if *you* were the slave. For a while. Here — ' He pushed the collar about Gorgik's neck. 'This way I can show you, first, how I like it done. You'd like that, too; I know it. I'll show you — '

'Be still, boy!' Though he wore the collar now, Gorgik spoke in the same commanding voice as before: but there was a smile in with it. And Udrog, caught among fear, lust, impatience, and, yes, interest, looked around again — the cat had gone — then settled himself on the rug against the big man, who'd already started speaking.

6

'Freedom fell to me at twenty-one as much by chance as servitude had fallen to me at fifteen. Another caravan stopped at the fields near the mines. This one belonged to the empress's Vizerine. She bought me on a whim as capricious as that of any noble's I've talked of. When she tired of me, she gave me my freedom — and a three-year officer's commission in the Imperial guards. But, because of that night when I was seventeen, freedom came to a man who could want, who could wish, who could dream. Under the reality of freedom, I learned to act.

'Once, during the last year of my Imperial service, when I was returning with my cart to rejoin my troops at Ka'hesh, as I passed through some southern market in the daytime heat, suddenly I halted my ox, turned to the slaver who'd parked there by the tomato stall with his six charges — both he and his wares were scrawny and slow-moving — and purchased them all from him.

'I ran my forefinger over their gums (bony here, spongy there), blinked at their wide-spaced teeth (this one broken, that one rotten), stared into their pimply ears (full of flakes and discharges), an examination the slaver insisted I make, coughing the while as he urged me to it. Even as I did it, I tried to tell him I did not need it, but my voice, hoarse, snagged and snared on my outrage, so that the five or nine words I muttered came out as incomprehensible grunts or whispers. Finally, silently, I thumbed iron and gold from my palm into his grimy, crisscrossed fingers, re-roped their arms behind them at his instructions, and at last secreted the iron key in the leather military purse on one of my belts. The man must have thought me mad or near mute. Was my partial paralysis — not only of voice but of hand and foot, for stepping up to bind one old woman, I stumbled, and in paying I dropped three coins in the dirt — desire for some barbarian boy, like you, among the six, Udrog, his hair thinned out by ringworm? Was it fury at the institution that had smashed my childhood out of existence and had strewn these half-dozen broken, sunburned creatures at the shore of what was left me of my life? Or was it just fear that something — huge, unnamable, and incomprehensibly greater than I — would, for my transgression, crack the clouds, reach down, and crush me on the dust?

'All three were there to mute me, to halt my hands, to shake my feet. Yet, mumbling, halt, shaking, I did it. Then I took my six slaves, behind my cart, outside the town, removed their collars, and, with embarrassed curtness, told them: "You're free, now. All of you. So go on."

Two thanked me effusively. One just stared. And, after faint smiles at me, guarded frowns at one another, and a great deal of blinking in the sun, three more — including the barbarian with the scabby scalp — turned with the same so-human persistence that had, doubtless, let them walk to that town in chains and, free, walked away from it, as inarticulate as I.

'When I rolled on to rejoin my men, the collars were deep in my provision cart.

'Another time, Udrog, perhaps a year beyond my Imperial service, I walked down a road where only occasional moonlight through this or that tear in the clouds let me identify in the dirt the dozens of lapping prints of what had to be a band of chained and collared chattel. Then I saw a campfire off to the side of the road and heard, not a tired, drunken slaver haranguing his property to move, to get their crusty bodies here or there, to let this one or that one have his share of food, but, rather, I swear it, an exaggerated and comic parody of the slaver you used to see in the mummers' skits that mocked those same overseers: he was shouting, blustering, shrieking, beating at them with some kind of club, now at this crippled woman, now at that old man, while some were crying, and some, afraid to cry, only whimpered . . . the part the mummers so judiciously leave out.

'I had a sword. I had a knife. And the expression on my face, there in the darkness, was the same grin I'd given so readily both to guard or slave back at the mines.

'One weapon in each hand, I crept through the brush, like a bandit sneaking up for a roadside murder. Did I hesitate, watching him beating and screaming, as long as I did at the edge of the firelight to observe exactly the nature of his crime? Was it fear — even as I grinned — that held me? Did I wait as long as I did so that I could see how many men he had with him? Did I tarry those ten, fifteen, twenty seconds to judge my chances better, better to plan my one-man attack in the dark? No, Udrog: for one second after the other, I kept wondering if the man were, somehow, in the midst of some ill-conceived joke — that this was some foolishness I was watching that had just gotten out of hand.

'After all, standing a little way off, one of the three armed overseers with him was laughing as hard as he could, even as blood splattered from the slaver's stick.

'Did I finally start from desire, rage, fear? What I felt, Udrog, was the same tingling that had rolled through my body the night the tall lord had removed my neck iron. Why not call it freedom? I pushed to my feet, sprinted forward, swung my sword — in one hack, I think I severed his arm, and, in another, cut through his slaver's apron to slice open both his thighs. As he fell, I turned on one of the other men, who was not laughing. It was quick and bloody and very noisy. Everyone shouted, including me. Once I yanked a chain free from its peg links and cried, "Run! Run! you're free . . . !" though only two slaves ran. (I'm sure they thought their liberator quite as crazed as their overseers — two of whom, by now, I'd killed and one more of whom I'd badly wounded.) As I was opening the locks, one slave blundered into my knife and cut an arm — how deeply I never learned — because she fled shrieking.

'I whirled, and the remaining guard danced back, whispering, "No, no — ! All right! No . . . !" then turned and barreled into the forest as if he too were a fleeing slave.

'There were twenty-seven captives. I stalked through firelight with salt in my mouth (once, when I'd turned to swing at someone, I'd bitten my inner cheek to blood), unlocking collar after collar after collar.

' "Go on, now . . . ! Go on . . . ! Get out of here!"

'Those two incidents tell you of the day and night of my struggle, Udrog; but let me talk of its evenings and dawns. For, more than a year later, in the late afternoon, while gold light glittered in the higher leaves and, to the east, fragments of blue between branches began to deepen, I was talking and laughing with some dozen of us who had stopped to enjoy the belonging, the protection, the temporary community around some forest campsite, when it somehow came out that, among this particular group of travelers who'd happened to come together at the camp, almost half of us had, at one time or another, been slaves. First one had told his story; then another had told hers. Oh, believe me, they were no less incensed at the injustice of servitude than I was. When it came my turn to talk, I made one joke and another about my clumsiness, my haltness, my inarticulateness while I had stumbled through that mute manumission in the market sunlight; now I derided the tingling procrastination I'd felt before that grinning night attack — a delay that had only allowed a dozen more of the slaver's blows to fall.

'A heavy woman standing at the group's edge sipped from a water mug she held in both hands and said: "I remember you, Gorgik. I was a slave you freed." And while all were silent, two men, one cross-legged and close to the fire with flames a-glimmer on his brown knees and one squatting off in blue-black shadow from a wide branch fanning to within inches of his balding head, now explained, first one, then the other, that *they* were slaves the woman had freed — though, for all she chewed her mug rim and twisted at her coarse green sleeve, she remembered them individually no better than I remembered her.

'I've often tried to recall whether it was an ex-slave or merely a free barbarian at the evening fire, appalled at what the rest of us had been saying of slavery, who first made the suggestion: "Even if only ten of us banded together to work for the end of slavery in Nevèrÿon, we could accomplish a hundred times what the same ten in isolated anger, could do. Lead us, Gorgik."

' "How can I lead you?" And I laughed. "I cannot tell rage, fear, or desire from the love of freedom itself. Nor am I at all sure they aren't, finally, the same."

'A black man with a shaved head and whip marks on both flanks said from the group's middle: "But you can grin at the confusions; you can dismiss the distinctions — they do not stop you. You can act. Lead us, Gorgik."

'And, yes, I wondered whether he were slave, criminal, or both. But I bent to my pack, wedged below my knee against the log I sat on, tugged it apart, and pawed through to pull out a metal collar — the two hinged semicircles of iron. I sat up, lifted it, and closed it on my neck. "What does this mean to you?" I asked, putting my hands back on my knees. Yes, I felt fear. Yes, I felt desire. Both had roughened my voice — though, perhaps, to them, it only made me sound the more authoritative. But I knew I had to give them a sign — to perform an act — that would show them who I was.

'Someone who'd drunk a bit too much said: "Is that the sign you take to tell us you were once a slave, that you are now a leader of slaves, that you are the liberator come to set men and women free? Yes, I like it, Gorgik. Lead us."

'Now I laughed again. And got some drink myself. And as the fire grew brighter against the coming dark, conversation drifted to the more violent matters of darkness. But at dawn — not the next dawn, but a dawn maybe eight months later — I remember how I stood, checking my weapons, conferring with my aides, going over my plans with this cell leader and that one, under the larch trees in the wet grass. There were twenty with me that morning; we had come to a suburb just outside Kolhari and had slept just beyond a village wall. There were only two with me who had been among our company that former evening. My lieutenant was a barbarian not much older than you, Udrog, whom I had purchased as a slave in Ellamon and who was now my lover; and who had already learned with me the crises of the night.

'We were going to meet that morning with a slave-holding baron, to talk through the sunlit hours. But we were ready to fight if, when darkness came, our peaceful negotiations had not made suitable progress. As I readied myself, I felt the same tingling about me — the fear, the desire, the rage. But somehow we had started a kind of revolution. Dream had become deed — indeed, private act had become an entire system of public actions.

'A day, a night, an evening, a morning . . .

'But we are talking of actions that were to go on for years, Udrog, through many days, many nights, many mornings and evenings.

'Many were gloriously successful.

'Many were shot with defeat.

'And for those actions I was beaten down and raised up again; I suffered private joys and public failure, personal loss and social glory. Commitments are odd, Udrog. You have them. You live by them. And live for them. But most of us who've given our lives to them don't relish talking of them a lot. You do what you have to do to maintain them. When asked about them, you grin a little. Sometimes you grunt. For the most part, you look stony and let others figure it out.

'Rage, fear, desire — and the love of freedom?

'None of them encourages articulateness. Sometimes I wondered at this as I rehearsed for the hundredth time, alone in my tent by lamplight, what I would have to say the following day, now to a delegation of merchants, now to a meeting of farmers, now to a council of lords — or sometimes when, come through some fence in the night, I caught my breath to begin whispering to a gang of slowly waking quarry slaves. Sometimes I wondered at it even when, my throat raw with shouting, blood running from my shoulders to my fingers, I swayed in the light of some torched chateau, amidst the screams and guts, daring to hope, with my teeth tight, I might see another dawn.

'Sometimes there were hundreds of us fighting together. And often, Udrog, I looked around, breathless and blinking, to find I fought alone. But as often, when I thought despair would swallow up my more and more isolate struggle, I found friends, slave and free, men and women, willing to fight with me and for me, who wielded a hot, bright energy I'd thought lost from the land.

'Oh, it was quite a revolution we led, Udrog. And fucking? I can't imagine anyone doing it more, or more imaginatively, than we did. Some revolutions are cold, bloody, celibate businesses. Others are violent and hot. And some others, like this one, fixed within the system by the innocence of full belief, take lust's heat and raise it to levels of day-to-day excitement most good citizens simply cannot imagine — or, if they imagine it, can't remember their imaginings more than a masturbatory minute. There were boys. There were men. And, yes, there were women. You! Come to me like a dog on all fours! And you? Crawl on your belly like a worm! Bind me, beat me, and I'll piss all over your thigh! All through my life I've reached as best I could for my freedoms, my powers, and my pleasures. When I was a slave, sometimes I reached for them prematurely, sometimes cruelly, sometimes with great pain, if not bodily harm, to myself and others. When I was free, I learned that the power, the freedom, the pleasures you and I would indulge here tonight take place within the laws of a marginal society and an eccentric civility that allows us to grasp them, one and the other, with a stunning force and joy that whoever skulks after them like a slave cannot imagine. Ah, I see that perks your interest. You reach again for my collar — there! You want it back now? But I knock your hand away. You smile, waiting: for me to confirm the pleasure you, too, know can be excited by carefully planned delay to truly terrifying heights. You'd have liked our revolution, Udrog, if you'd had the heart to join it or the luck to live through it. The only problem with such excess was that I had no way to know if a new fellow passing through my bed on the way to my cause was going to debate with me till sunrise — or fuck and suck my brains out. Still, I got enough of both debate and sex so that I never wanted for either more than half a day. Oh, yes, I had my bad dreams. I had my good ones, too. Both required critique.

'That was evening work.

'Yes, I worried over the right and wrong of them, with my fellows and friends, long into many nights, through the darkness and into the next new, brilliant day. But while I let those worries guide me, I would not let them stop me. And I was lucky enough, through them all, first to have a lover who loved me but did not believe in me. Though, for all he fought by my side in the early years, his love finally turned to hate. Then he was replaced by a lover who believed in me but did not love me. And when, after a handful of years, he realized what held him to me was only enthusiasm for a dream, his belief turned to indifference. He drifted away. Though I've searched for him, in my fashion, I've never seen him since I came to power. But I'm grateful to them both for the criticisms that, in their different ways, they offered. But I've often thought that had I been cursed with one who both believed *and* loved, I'd have likely turned out the tyrant and monster the first always feared I was, and the second, half blind though he was, always saw I might become.

'But at last I was called to the High Court of Eagles by the empress, whose reign is long and leisurely, to conduct my work from within its walls. My ministry first fell on me, I tell you, Udrog, like a plague. I thought, from then on, I would be restricted to a daytime revolution. In those first months at the court, there were hours when I sat in my new offices, feeling as if I were starving amidst the splendor. But once two hundred newly freed slaves began a revolt in the Avila: I had to ride out of Kolhari by moonlight, as I was the only one they would allow to negotiate between them and the lords. Another time the report came in the middle of the night that some western earl, grown madder and madder as his holdings were whittled down by time and economics, had begun indiscriminately murdering freemen and slaves, claiming his carnage for the elder gods who'd once ruled in the south. I had to lead troops against him — and it was I, with my own sword, who, after a day's battle in the raging rain, hacked his head free so that it hung from his neck by a single sinew, and the quarts of his blood slurred the sopping sands. Oh, there was enough of the night left in my work to satisfy any adventurer. And soon I'd learned that the license at court was no different from the licentiousness outside it, at the same time as I learned that the lord I'd hated through it all was now the most specific reality I had to deal with, morning and evening, in the council chamber — if the day were to be mine. These were brave and brutal times in a brave and brutal land. I'd been called to the High Court not just as a man, but as a man with a purpose and a passion. How I carried them out was my own affair. And so, a slave at seventeen, I was a respected minister at forty-seven, in pursuit of my political goals with all the energy and commitment I could muster (one with those I began to conceive that long-ago night) — till finally, by this and that, I managed to triumph over the man whom death has just brought down: the council finally agreed officially to abolish slavery from Nevèrÿon — to lend the task not only silent tolerance, but Imperial edict, might, and organization.

'*His* protests were marked only by silences and dark looks from his corner of the council table.

'But the High Court was at last prepared to enforce emancipation to the extent of empire.

'The decree would go out from Her Majesty, the Child Empress.

'Six years ago, when that happened, Udrog, though you might not remember it so well, there was quite a celebration. Among all my memories of the man whose funeral journey I go to join with tomorrow, the one that returns most often is from that morning in the Council room, when, the decisive meeting done, the others came up to laugh and clap me on the shoulder.

'The old man walked over, smiling.

'Many grew silent before him; they knew my success was his defeat. "Congratulations to you," he said. "I know how hard you've fought for this. And I respect you for it, Gorgik. It's only a notion," he went on, "but such a decision as you've led us to today requires a certain . . . sign. It's well known, nor have you ever made a secret of it: you spent some years as a slave in the empress's obsidian mines at the foot of the Faltha Mountains. Through you as much as anyone, slavery is hardly a shadow of what it once was. The mines are all but closed down. My researches tell me only three slaves are left there, among a dozen guards and paid maintenance men, to oversee the property in the empress's name. To think, once more than three hundred of my — " he dropped his eyes in a moment's self-correction — "three hundred men once labored there. But what better way to celebrate your achievement? Why not return to the site of your youthful indenture and, with your own hands, take the collars from the necks of the last slaves there, while, here in the capital, on the same day, the empress will make her proclamation? We will celebrate your victory both here and in the new, thriving towns that have grown up between Kolhari and Ellamon, between the Argini and Kolhari. They'll all send delegates to see you perform your terminal manumission. I can think of no better way to make a gesture to the people more in keeping with this day and decision, both of which are yours."

'When your opponent speaks smilingly, you listen warily. But if this were capitulation, I wanted to receive it graciously. The intricacies of bringing the council around had made me aware that neither my life nor his nor both of ours together were over in the hive-like halls of the High Court. My feelings about his suggestion? Though I can be fascinated by ritual and repetition, I've never sought out pomp and ceremony — though as much as anyone I know the value of a successful public sign. I thought his notion childish, presumptuous, and stupid. But if the only price I were asked for my success was this, then for the time ahead we still would have to work together I thought I'd best pay it.

'I looked at him.

'I mulled this over with the speed he'd managed to teach me.

'I said: "In a week then, My Lord, I'll ride to the foot of the Falthas, where I shall carry out your wish as you have expressed it." And, fist to my forehead, I bowed.

'Three or four observing read my obeisance as a mark of my triumph. But that is the way with the exchange of signs among the suggestions and suspicions, the implication and innuendoes surrounding the play of power in the halls of the High Court.

'There at the capital, a caravan of closed wagons was made ready; I oversaw some of the preparation and cursed that I had to take time from important matters to do it; then managed to delegate the rest to others. Messengers were dispatched north and south to prepare the day. Somehow by the night I was to leave for the mines, I and my secretaries and my assistants and my aides had actually done all we had to in order for the ceremony itself (including the empress's proclamation in Kolhari) to be more than words.

'The ceremony?

'Because I had done the work around it, because messages had been sent, alliances secured, commitments confirmed, promises elicited, and pressures put to see that certain other promises were quickly carried out, the celebration can be dismissed as the empty sign it was. The bored musicians, the official delegates, the curious locals, the interminable speeches, the lateness that began it, the rain that interrupted it, the banquet that concluded it all made it the mirror image of any number of like provincial functions. But what I want to tell of tonight, Udrog, the incidents that complete my story, happened in the margins of that ritual vacuousness.

'Because I'd done my work well, I'd brought no significant worries with me. What would it be like, I wondered as I rode in my closed wagon, to return to the barracks, the mines, the fields about them I had not seen, save to ride by when traveling hastily between north and south with my mind on other things, after twenty-six years? I threw my thoughts ahead to the pit.

'I am a man who, where his thoughts go, his body follows.

'During a morning stop, I climbed from the wagon and told my caravan steward I would take an extra horse and ride ahead: I wanted to spend some time, if only a little hour, along among the scenes of my servitude.

'I'm glad I did.

'As my horse finally trotted through what a farmer and two women carrying some calves in a high-sided cart had assured me, under the overcast sky, were the grounds of the old obsidian mines, I found roads where no roads had been; I found trees and underbrush in places that had been open fields; I found both a hill and a pond I had no memory of at all; I saw huts and houses off where there should have been empty bogs. And the single mine tunnel I came on was one that, back when I'd been there, surely had already been shut down, while the ones in which I and my companions once sweated had either been filled in or swallowed up by the encroaching forest — *I* certainly couldn't find them! When I rode out from among the trees and saw the long wall of a slave barracks, nothing about it looked familiar. A caretaker was just coming out, an old barbarian woman in a collar — one of the slaves, I realized, I'd come to free.

'When I rode up to speak, though I tried to be friendly, she was taciturn. But once I told her who I was, she became all welcome and solicitude. Gorgik the Liberator? Yes, she knew all about the ceremony to take place later that day. There'd been talk of nothing else here for a week. She grew terribly excited, knocking the back of her fist against her forehead, with a slew of praises for our empress, whose reign partook of every alliteration she could call up. And would I come inside? Did I wish to meet the others? She would take my horse, would find refreshments for me, would indeed, serve me in any way she could.

'No, I told her. I'd only come to look at the place where (yes, she knew of it) I'd spent five years as a slave.

' "A lot must have changed," she said.

'I nodded. "Yes. I can see." I asked her to tell me what she could. Of course she would. Yes, these were the slave quarters of the old Imperial obsidian mines. She'd been here fifteen years. There was a man, another of the three slaves in residence whom I'd be freeing along with her that day, who'd been here for twenty. He'd even worked as a miner in the last years of obsidian production. But he was off right now on an errand. The third slave, she said, was a youngster of twenty-two, who hadn't been here a full ten years yet. A good-for-nothing, she assured me. But, really, when the older man came back I should speak to him. The guards and free caretakers who had the actual responsibility for overseeing the Imperial property? Well, these days they came and went every two or three years. None of them had any firsthand knowledge of the place. But she would tell me everything, anything I wanted to know, if, indeed, she knew it. As best I could make out from what she said, the barrack buildings I had lived in — as well as the one Vrach had died in — had been pulled down long ago. Ill-built, slat-walled structures, today there was not a mark on the earth to show where they'd stood. No, she'd never seen them. The demolition had occurred before she'd come: she pointed where she thought she remembered hearing they'd once been — amidst the briars and waving sumac on the slant there. (If she were right or wrong, I could not say. But I didn't remember the clearing our barracks had been ranged around as particularly slanted.) The long building she'd just stepped from, she assured me, was, however, the oldest barracks at the mines. True, it was about barracks size, as I remembered them. Certainly it must have been here when I was a boy, she declared to my frown, for though some work had been done on it ten years back (and she led me over to point out the newer planks), as clearly the rest of it dated from fifty, if not sixty, years before that. Looking at the walls with her, I had to agree.

'Along the foundation (and none of the barracks I remembered had had foundations at all), every few inches a stub of metal was sunk into the stone. In two places an iron staple remained: once staples had been driven in at equal intervals all along it. Only those two were whole. The rest had rusted away or broken off so that only nubs were left. "When I first got here," the woman said, as she watched me stare down at them from my horse, "there were at least ten whole ones. We still tarred them over each season." She was wondering, I could tell, if I'd ever been chained there. "But they let that go, with so much else to do and fewer and fewer to do it, three or four years after I came. And by three or four years after that, they were down to what you see. In a way, it's a shame. Oh, I wouldn't want them *used*, any more than you would, sir. Still, I've always thought they should be preserved. Just so people won't forget. I mean, the way it used to be. When you were here." Some of the studs had come completely out, leaving only holes. Rusted stubs (or holes) extended all the way down the stone base of the fifteen-yard building. In the years since my freedom came, I'd seen many such foundations (or sometimes stone benches, or sometimes stone walls) where numberless rows of staples spoke of the hundreds of slaves once chained there, slaves who had worked the quarries or the mines or the fields in the generations before mine. The staples were signs of the oldest slave quarters, going back a century or more, of which this building was easily an example: I'd first seen them when I spent time as a soldier in the south and in the west. When they were first explained to me, I remember how I'd noted to myself that there'd been none at the mines. There we'd been chained together only when we were moved in groups from place to place, as happened when some of us were pulled out to help with a forest fire, or to pile rocks, logs, and mud against a flooding stream. Looking at this stapled stone, I wondered if I'd actually come to a wholly different mine in a wholly different place from the one I'd lived at and labored in, for though I'd presumably spent five years only a dozen yards away in what was now brush and sumac (if the woman spoke rightly), I had no memory at all of this building, these stones, or its nubs!

'My horse stepped about restlessly. I patted her neck. "Tell me." I frowned down at the woman in her brown shift. "There was an open field where caravans used to stop, behind the . . . well, behind what we then called the south barracks. Once you left the living quarters here, it was about half a mile away."

' "You mean the place where they're going to have the ceremony . . . ?" She was a barbarian, like you, Udrog. But her skin was burned so brown she already looked like a freeman, and the overcast seemed to leave it and the iron at her neck one hue below straw-colored hair. "Where you're to take off our collars."

' "Yes," I said. "I imagine so."

' "It's right through there. You take your horse around the bend, and you'll find the road swinging off to the left." (*Road*, I thought. There'd only been a footpath in my time, which, here and there, had been overgrown enough so that in parts you couldn't even call it that.) "Ride along for ten minutes at the gentlest walk — or gallop hard for two — and you'll come to it. It's right within sight of town."

'A *town*? I thanked her and reined about, starting in the direction she'd pointed. Could there have grown up a town? Still, the traveling time sounded right. I rode along, following her directions, not recognizing any tree, nor remembering any boulder; right where she'd said, I took up a double-rutted wagon path, wide enough to let two horses canter abreast. For all I knew, I could have been going in the opposite direction from the one I wanted, at a mine in a hundred stades away from the one I'd actually worked in. Riding along, I worried through possible explanations. Perhaps the building I'd just seen *had* been there when I was, but had been abandoned somewhere back in the woods, years before, as the spaces I had lived and labored in had been swallowed up since. Because the structure had stood ten or twenty (or thirty or forty) meters off in the forest, I'd simply never known it was there. Time passed, and as other buildings were torn down, the space around this one was cleared away to bring it back into use . . .

'Or perhaps it had actually been among the six, seven, eight slat-walled barrack buildings I recalled. I just didn't remember it: having not known at the time what those studs and staples were, I simply had not *seen* them. Still, for the staples to stay — and the woman had said there had been at least ten whole ones, when she'd arrived fifteen years ago — they had to be tarred every season or so. I'd been a miner there five years, first a common pit slave and finally a foreman. Who would wander off in the undergrowth to tar staples on an abandoned building swallowed by the brush? Wouldn't I have remembered someone in the barracks sent to do such work?

'Then it struck. There'd been one building, off from our barracks, I'd never entered through all my five years. I'd never stood directly before it; I'd only glimpsed its roof, now and again, over the tops of trees — many of them sumac bushes. At the same time I suddenly recalled, on those exhausted evenings when I and the others had come back from the pit, maybe three times noticing some guard making his way through our tired group with a bucket of tar. I'd never thought to ask about it. But now I knew what the building was.

'Once it might have been a slave barracks, years before I'd come there. What it had been when I'd labored at the mines was the guards' quarters.

'Slaves were not allowed near it.

"That was why I had never seen its stapled foundation. And if that *was* the guard building, then the road my horse walked along *must* be running toward the caravan site. Then, as I looked at the trees and greenery around me, the clarity vanished. Because if that was the guard building and this wagon road actually lay more or less along the old path, that would have put my barracks themselves in an entirely different direction from the one in which the old woman had pointed . . .

'I sighed and looked around. How close did this road, I wondered, lie to the path along which Namyuk, the caravan soldier, and I had helped Vrach? As I looked off at the bushes, I wondered where along it we might have paused to let Vrach try to spill his ruptured bladder. I looked up through the branches at the gray sky. How had the clouds lain on the blue that day?

'A thought returned I'd mulled on many times in past years: I had no idea where Vrach was buried. As pit slave and foreman, I could count thirty slaves who'd died here by violent or natural means. But I did not know where any of their bodies lay.

'In Kolhari, if you follow Netmenders' Row up from the waterfront past the pottery shops that cluster near the docks, all the way to where it crosses the Avenue of Refuse Carters, then on another half mile, till, after passing through the quarter of desert folks, it all but loses its name, you come to a potter's field, where, with numberless victims of that night-long massacre in the Month of the Rat, my parents, I'd been told, were interred. I'd visited it occasionally over the years, sometimes to see other surviving children of that night walking by the spare trees, pausing to stare at the unevenly sunken ground, or gazing toward a dirt mound beside which another communal pit had been opened for the beggars whose corpses had been picked up on a cold dawn from under the Bridge of Lost Desire. But at the mines, where hundreds of men had toiled for a century or more, confined the length of their lives till they died (often before age thirty), I simply did not know what field or swamp or hillside held a one of their bodies — where, indeed, my own would have been tossed had I fought with Piffles.

'As I rode, looking for a break in the clouds, I thought — not for the first time, but with an intensity that made the thought seem new — that what we'd been most denied as slaves here was our history. Oh, we'd had our jokes and tales, our accounts of heroics and glories, whispered of now and again during the day, now and again before we fell into our exhausted sleep in our weevily straw. But, as I rode, I also remembered how, no longer in the mines but abroad in the army, I'd heard soldiers tell tales they swore had happened to a friend that were identical to tales fellow slaves, a few years before, had sworn to me had happened to friends of *theirs*: I was young when I first learned that, while the incidents that can befall a man or a woman are as numberless as sunlit flashes flickering on the sea, what the same man or woman can say of them is as limited as the repertoire on the platform of some particularly uninventive mummers' troupe. Indeed, it *is* that repertoire. Our history had been denied us as systematically as we had been denied the knowledge of our burial place, or as we had been denied sight of the guards' house or any hint that, whatever its apparatus of oppression, that house had once been ours.

'What I had begun to do that night at the caravan site, in the pathetic, impoverished way allowed a single youth, without help or communal language or public tradition, was to construct the start of a personal history. What I had learned is that such a personal history must, just like impersonal ones, be founded as richly on desire as on memory.

'Would I recognize the caravan site at all? I had been in the barracks every day. The field, in my five years, I'd only visited half a dozen times. And yet, if only from what had happened there, I felt I *must* know it. Among some trees, I came out on a slope.

'Was this it . . . ?

'Across the grass and under dark pines, mountains rose into morning mist — though the trees didn't come as far down as I remembered.

'And there *were* dwellings off at the foot. *They* hadn't been there thirty years ago. The wagon path I rode on continued down and across some two hundred yards of grass to disappear among the huts and hovels — more than a path, really, but not yet a road. Along its middle ran a rib of small stones, weeds thrusting up among them. On either side of its dusty ruts (gray rather than tan beneath the overcast), tall grasses swayed like ship masts along an endless, double dockside.

'I don't think I can explain how uncomfortable that new track across the field made me. But looking along it, I found myself thinking: that path, clearly grown up in the last few years, could sink back into the grass in just about the same time it had taken to wear its way in, so that no one might ever know it had been there. Indeed, the clustered huts at its far end looked no more permanent. But, if it proved particularly useful, and if the huts thrived, some bunch of farmers and fieldhands might eventually cart out loads of sand and gravel, to scatter along it, to even out the low points that yearly sank beneath summer puddles, and finally to pave it with large flags, mud, and tar — so that it might hold contour for a hundred years. But now it lay poised before some moment of material choice that I would have nothing to do with, however meaningful or meaningless the ceremony I conducted beside it should be. Mine was simply another set of feet to walk on it, contributing only their minuscule amount to its usefulness, an amount no greater for a minister than for a slave. But neither it nor, really, the tiny town it led to was more fixed than my own evanescent memories — though thirty families might now consider the village at its end their home and twice that many children, born here since I'd left, might believe their field the whole human universe, and that this path was the ultimate lane connecting *here* to *there*. But my analysis only made them — village and road — in their newness and their ephemerality, that much more annoying.

'No, this *couldn't* be the meadow I remembered . . .

'But if it was, just over the rise to my left should lie the north-south highway, along which respectable travelers and footsore wanderers and farmers in their carts and many-wagoned caravans moved back and forth from the High Hold of fabled Ellamon to Kolhari. (From that highway, in minutes or hours, my own caravan should turn in to make camp — and raise its ceremonial pavilion.) Turning from the town, I trotted my horse off to see. What should I do if, when I topped the ridge, there was only more grass? Could the highway have been in a wholly other direction? Could I have misremembered things as completely as now and again I suspected I had — ?

'But there it was:

'The north-south road, the Royal Highway, the Dragon's Way!

'I wheeled my horse back and forth and around in breathless joy. Yes, if one blotted out that excuse for a town struggling on over there, this had to be it — the place where, one night thirty years ago, I became myself.

'I walked my horse back to the wagon path, looking at the field, the slope, the jagged Falthas. I jumped down to tie my mare to a tree and looked up the slant. I was standing within yards of the spot where, thirty years before, I'd stood with half a dozen other slaves, our guard on one side, the tall lord on the other, the two of them talking across us.

'Since then I'd known as friends name-bearing relatives to the Lesser Lady Esulla. No, she, I knew, had never married Lord Anuron. And only two years back I'd dined at a heavily piled table with the aging Count Jeu-Forsi — across from me and half a dozen guests to my left — white-haired and plump now, but still called Toad.

'No, I didn't make myself known.

'I looked across the field, trying not to see the cart track that scarred it, trying not to see the village, like a new bunion on the mountains' foot. Instead I tried to reconstruct precisely where Fluffy's wagon had been parked, where the clearing had been in which Lord Anuron had wrestled Vrach, exactly where the fringed pavilion had risen, or where the lamplit tent had stood — grinning, as I foundered among these dim speculations, because, within hours, my own wagons, tents, and pavilion would rise there, destroying any hope of an accurate image of the past with their own insistent presence.

'I *would* walk to the new village, I decided suddenly. This nostalgia was absurd. I must see what lay here *now*. I started out — directly along the road, first on one side of the weedy mound down its middle, then on the other. Although I tried to fix my thoughts on the here and now before me, still, while I walked, I pondered: Did these ruts carry me over the spot where I'd stood at the tent flap in the dark, gazing in the lamplight at the naked lord? Did they perhaps lead me along the line I'd walked between the lighted tent and the sleeping Vrach?

'To think too long on such things is to feel the gut twist, the throat constrict, and the emptiness behind all mirrors swell. And it was a long walk to that town. But I almost managed to dismiss the ache by telling myself: You have come here as a man victorious at the termination of a great battle. This must be *your* celebration . . .

'At which point again I saw the face of that mighty minister, my enemy, dead tonight but that day at the side of the empress in Kolhari, and at whose behest I'd come here. For a moment, like some ghost or god of the field, it seemed much like the face of the tall lord . . . Could either have known of this pain, I wondered? Could either have possibly and purposefully placed me here, like a piece moved on some gaming board, to make me feel precisely this? But the preposterousness of the thought finally released me from it all. Again, as I walked, I grew certain of the celebratory present I was moving toward. To gain it, the past was what I must *not* think of anymore today. Yet when I was ten meters from the first thatched and hide-walled hovel, I stopped. I watched a few folk amble between the huts. One glanced at me. I wondered if she knew who I was.

'Then I turned and walked back toward the part of the field with which — how else can I put it? — I was more familiar.

'I'd almost recrossed the whole of it when I saw, up beyond where my horse was tied, the four on foot coming down the cart track.

'In front was the old slave woman, in her brown shift and iron collar.

'Three men were with her. One was a rangy, elderly man, also in brown, also in iron. He must be the long-term slave she'd told of. She and he were smiling broadly. And there was a younger one, a muscular, well-knit fellow, with matted hair, a leather clout around his hips, and iron at his neck. He was not smiling: but he walked with his mouth half open.

'He was missing some teeth.

'Have I mentioned it, Udrog? Namyuk had also had that dull habit of wandering about with his lips apart. A moment's confusion: the young slave *was* Namyuk. The old woman and the old man were bringing him to me! Illusion, yes; but it was strong enough so that I waved my hand, quickened my step, and grinned like a madman. It lasted only seconds, but when the thought shook clear from my mind, what replaced it was: no, it wasn't the young slave who was my old friend, but the older one! *How* long had the woman said he'd been here? She'd only kept it from me as a surprise —

'That illusion cleared too, of course. And I felt myself an ass. (She'd said the older slave had been here twenty years, which would mean he had come six years after I'd left. For a moment though, I'd thought it had been only two, rather than three, decades!) And I was standing before the old, leather-necked fellow, who, there in his collar, was smiling as broadly as I had been, his long teeth yellow and sound, while I tried to salvage the fragments of my own smile.

'The youngster watched me with his gray-eyed, gap-toothed gaze.

'But neither the young man nor the old was any more Namyuk than I.

'The woman stepped forward, gesturing at her companions. The man was Mirmid, she said. Her own name was Har'Ortrin. The youngster here was Feyev. (Feyev's dull face only let the faintest of smiles pass around his dark, dark lashes, his light, light eyes.) But she'd told me of them before . . . ? I looked at the fourth, a man with no collar, standing back and to the side. He was dressed in a leather clout sewn up with thongs, the same sort as Feyev. A simple and brutish fellow, he looked wary, uncomfortable, squat, strong — and as dirty as Feyev, too. With surprise, I realized he was a guard, as he blurted: "And I'm Iryg, sir." He threw his hand up to knock the back of his fist on his forehead. "A free servant of the empress — the empress . . . whose reign is loose and liberal!" Even now, every few seconds, Namyuk's face in memory seemed to join Feyev's before me; and though it defied all sense, I was sure Iryg was not just similar to, but the physical twin of, the guard who'd once walked us here to the caravan site — though it was only because I carried such an unclear image of the old one that this new one replaced it so easily.

'In honor of my coming, of the coming ceremony, of the freedom that was to come to them, this was, of course, a holiday. There was no real work; so Har'Ortrin had brought them here to meet me. ". . . If you don't mind, sir. You seemed such a kind sort, for one so great. And you've come here on our behalf, anyway. So I just thought, if it wasn't any bother — and you'd *said* you wanted to talk to Mirmid

. . . who's been here so much longer than I have. And maybe if the boy'll listen — " she nodded toward Feyev, who wasn't paying much attention —"he might learn something meaningful of this place he'll leave tomorrow forever!"

' "Come, then." I smiled at them. A heavy tree had pulled up by the roots and fallen a bit away; another trunk, this one cut, had been laid one end across it. I told them: "Let's sit and talk."

'The five of us went and sat. It all began very well.

' "Yes, that's right, sir. Har'Ortrin told me where she'd pointed out the old barracks to you. But *that* wasn't where they were at all!" Mirmid explained. "She wasn't here for any of that. The barracks you were in were on the *other* side of the building that's there now . . . yes, sir. The guards used to use it for their own, though we all live in it today. At any rate, *your* old barracks burned down in the fire — a year before I came. Everybody said what a terrible night that was! No one ever really got the number of slaves burned up. Among the thirty or forty left, they were always mumbling that it was negligence, or even done on purpose; or at least could have been prevented — all those creatures roasted alive in their straw-filled coops! When I was brought here, you could see burnt bits and pieces, still scattered about — it hadn't grown up fully. But what *she's* talking about over on the slope were the temporary shacks they put up right afterwards when they first tried to run the place on a reduced scale — where I stayed when I first came. That's when they closed up the three big tunnels — the ones you must have worked in. And opened up a smaller one, closed down years before, that was still supposed to have some good lodes in it. But that didn't go so well . . . finally they decided more or less to shut the whole place down: down came the temporary shacks. Most of us were sold off to the west. But there were only twenty-five or so of us by then, anyway. They brought some women in, to cook and clean, since it was only maintenance going on by then. That's when Har'Ortrin came. Today, of course, there's just the three of us . . .'

'While he talked on, my thoughts were abroil.

'When Mirmid mentioned the fire, I was thrown back to a breezy evening on a river's rocky bank, where, as an officer in the Imperial guards, I'd stopped to question a band of desert men in their heavy robes, with copper wires sewn up the backs of their ears, who'd first told me of the holocaust at the mines. So, of course I'd known of it, known at least in vague report how bad it had been. But since it was so long ago, at the prospect of returning somehow I'd blotted it out.

'And if *my* barracks had once, in fact, stood on the *other* side of the guard house, then finally I had a sense of the physical place I'd been — indeed, in a place I'd never been before because back then it had been all grown up with trees.

'I kept glancing at the youngster: did this slack-lipped young man, who sat with his knees wide, pulling at a piece of bark with dirty, work-thickened fingers, really look so much like Namyuk? (He was closer to Vrach's age. Still . . .) I thought to ask Mirmid and Har'Ortrin — or Iryg, if it came to that — whether they knew what had happened to Namyuk. Had he escaped the fire to be sold? Had he been burned to death? Perhaps one of *them* knew where we slaves had been carted off to be buried? But as I'd halted before the incipient city of the present, I hesitated now before the accomplished city of the past.

'I asked nothing about either.

'Feyev frowned at me: I was staring at him again. No, this wouldn't do. I began to ask them questions about their lives, who they were, where they'd come from, what they did at the mines these days. Slowly, very slowly, all five of us, guard and slaves and Minister of State, began to relax with one another.

'While I listened, I tried to remember the questions the tall lord had asked of Vrach and Namyuk and me. And do you know, those were the questions that, when *I* asked them now, drew from them the warmest answers, even from dull Feyev, even from sullen Iryg. I tried to remember which of that tall lord's tales about his own life had struck me most vividly: and I tried to find like things from my own recent time (tales of the opulence and affluence of court; certainly nothing more of my memories of my time in the mines!) to entertain them. And do you know: those were the tales that made Feyev stop fiddling with his bark to look at me and grin, that made Mirmid and Har'Ortrin chuckle and shake their heads, that even made Iryg nod with dogged interest. As we talked more and more easily, I began to wonder: Though I'd never thought much about it, I'd just assumed the conversation with the tall lord that night thirty years ago had been the first he'd ever had with slaves such as Namyuk and I. But now I remembered how quickly all three nobles had gone to Vrach once he was down. Perhaps the tall lord had had several such encounters. Perhaps he'd known what to ask to put us at our ease. Perhaps he'd known the tales that would most entertain us. Perhaps he'd known, from other such talks with others, what questions would intimidate and discommode us, what topics would baffle and defeat us — and so had avoided them. (After all, I'd had many such conversations with many such myself. That talk with him was not the only one that had taught me what to say here.) Perhaps, with the best intentions, he'd only been playing us, as a game master deploys his pieces on the board to call up the most pleasing pattern, as I found myself, with just as good intentions, playing them.

'My intentions *were* good, you understand. I only wanted them to be at ease — and they were! I only wanted them to avoid misunderstanding me, to hold off upset, and stay away from what was beyond them — and they had!

'Still, for a moment, the suspicion that what I'd once thought so spontaneous might, as it had occurred on this meadow thirty years ago, have been wholly calculated struck me as an ugly — and palpable — probability. In many ways they were very limited people; and I knew their limits very well.

'How could the tall lord *not* have known ours?

'The three slaves had begun to talk of their coming freedom, where they would go, what they would do. Har'Ortrin had free family in the south, who she was sure would take her in. But while she told me about that good man, her uncle, and her many cousins there, silently I reviewed a report (that had taken five days of council meetings to present!) on the situation of newly freed slaves returning to families for help: a synopsis of that torrent of catastrophic evidence? The majority of such families would have nothing to do with the returned, unwanted, bewildered, new and often angry freemen — though Har'Ortrin clasped her hands at the prospect, now and again unable to speak for joy, hope, and anticipation.

'Mirmid explained that he'd once been promised by a former master, who'd valued him highly but had been forced, nevertheless, to sell him, that, should he ever gain his freedom, he should return —whereupon he would be given a bit of land, the materials for a shack, and tools, with which he could work as a free farmer. Well, at least three other council meetings had been devoted directly to the cases and complaints of slaves who, given like promises, had returned to take them up, only to find that the promises could not be fulfilled — in many cases the estates they had worked on bore as little resemblance to what they remembered and were as reduced in circumstances as the mines were to what they had once been, the masters themselves having long since gone — though Mirmid went on in awed respect for the great thane who, though he had once been the owner of a hundred slaves, had made *him* such a promise!

'And Feyev? Well, he was going to the city. What city? He wasn't sure. But once there he would get a good-paying job. (What job? Well, that was unclear.) And he would work hard and buy a house and become a rich man with servants and fine clothes and lots and lots of money! He blinked his light gray eyes.

'I listened. I smiled.

'Back in Kolhari, the palpable problem of freed slaves had occupied *so* many council meetings — many more than the five and three just come to mind. But difficulties these here had not yet even envisioned had been distressingly familiar to me now for years!

'I made what I thought was a practical suggestion. Should any of them have problems with their plans, here were the names of some organizations they might turn to for help, set up by the empress several years back for just such contingencies . . . But (and this itself was already so familiar to me) I could see little of it was taken in.

'Inwardly, I only hoped they would remember what I'd said when the time came they would need it.

'Outwardly, I smiled at their enthusiasm, at their naïvete, at their joy over their coming release (contenting myself with the private conviction that there would be time later for the practical), but I was sharply aware: the riches, the privileges, the power all three of them saw lying only weeks, days, hours before them, for all my sympathy with the knowledge of what impelled their vision, were no more realistic than the belief that one of them might burrow through the mountain before us or that another might fly up into the air. And I wondered:

'Speaking of the more than wonderful, the near mystical, the glorious freedom we'd been snatched from by slavers and Imperial guards, had Namyuk and I, thirty years ago, sounded anywhere near as naïve, romantic, and simply out of touch as these three talking about their freedom to come? I made another suggestion — again, only of the most hard-headed sort, telling them the names of more plans and programs the council had already instituted to help the newly freed. But even with that, as they talked on, one or the other would glance at me with the tolerant smile of someone who realizes he or she is simply speaking to a man who, if only through the happenstance of history and experience, *cannot* understand what is *really* being said. They held nothing back. They didn't have to. The gap was already too large: Because I *was* free, I could not understand what *their* freedom would mean.

'Suddenly I wanted to end the conversation.

'I suggested abruptly that I had to leave them: I needed to walk about a bit, to see where it might be best to have my caravan arrange itself once it arrived. ". . . Please understand, but once the wagons come, there'll be so much to do!" (It was an asinine excuse any lord or lady would have recognized instantly for what it was — acceding to it immediately if only because its idiocy revealed so clearly the distress it hid.) But now it was stolid Iryg who took the part of garrulous Vrach under drugs. The brutish fellow leaned forward on the log to erupt with incidents that had to be told, and nothing would do but that I heard them. They started and ended with the difficulties he'd had disciplining his charges, the nasty temper of that one, the thief-like cunning of this one (Oh, he hated to think of that woman, free to connive and steal, out in decent society!), the perverse depravity of another. Not that some of the guards were much better! Even at this place, with six guards for only three slaves . . . ? Why, within the week he'd seen — but perhaps he'd best not mention names. Nor indeed say anything else. A day like today wasn't the time for it. And certainly *I* would know what went on in a place like this . . . ? There was no reason for him to start in. But slaves, now. You just couldn't trust them. Always scheming to get something out of you. Oh, no; not these three here. They were good slaves. Even Feyev — who, with lowered lashes, was picking at his bark again. No, Feyev wasn't so bad. He was a good sort. Most of the time.

'But he remembered one . . .

'And he remembered one other . . .

'And he remembered still one more . . .

'Iryg had been a guard for twelve years, here and at four other institutions, and he'd known every kind of slave, the good and the bad. And the bad were a low and despicable breed the free folk of Nevèrÿon couldn't imagine! "But I'm sure you've thought of all that, sir. I mean, when you were running around setting them free. After all, you used to *be* one!"

' "And I was one of the worst, too, my man!" Then I wished I'd remained silent. But my comment didn't seem to affect him. He was still going on. His point was, if he could be said to have had one, that my coming was probably a great and glorious thing, because once slavery was officially done with, he would no longer have to be responsible for the kind of scum — oh, not these, here, no, certainly not these — but the kind that, in the past, he'd been lumbered with.

'I nodded where I felt I had to. Once or twice I smiled.

'The others did not nod or smile. Feyev looked dull and bored. Har'Ortrin and Mirmid looked old and quiet. They must have felt hugely uncomfortable — unless they were so inured to Iryg's complaint, repeated so often to one or another, that none of it registered.

'It went on till Feyev turned to blink across the field, then pointed with uncharacteristic interest: "Hey, look — !"

'Having pulled off the north-south highway, the first of my caravan wagons breasted the ridge.'

7

'The next three hours, Udrog, were servants and soldiers, tents and tarpaulins, secretaries and stewards, hurry and harassment. More carts and wagons arrived, with delegates and visitors from a dozen towns. The population of the village I'd decided not to enter came out, entire, to gawk at us — just as the chief cook began a ten-minute tantrum: Where were the *other* six helpers? And just look at the sky! *If* we were to eat, the provision tent *must* be taken down from where it was now and set up over *there* — so that the few wretches she had would not be running back and forth in the rain that was sure to come. Did we think they were all slaves? This was insufferable! And she would *not* tolerate it! Really, it sounds reasonable enough now — and seemed wholly preposterous then: she tore off her apron and stalked from the encampment, only to come back half an hour later, sullen, silent, and busy.

'I was rushing from one problem to another, when old Mirmid stepped in front of me — I nearly bumped him; but he grabbed my shoulder. Please, was there *any* work he and the others might do to help?

'I kept my balance. No. No, that wasn't necessary.

'But they *wanted* to work, Mirmid insisted. After all, this confusion was for them, wasn't it? It seemed only right they lend a hand.

'They could help most, I explained, by keeping out of the way as much as possible; but if they'd just stay near enough so that once the ceremony itself began, and we needed them to —

' "Oh, go on, sir!" Iryg stood with a hand on his hip and one foot on a log. "Make 'em work!"

'I wonder if he thought that made things easier.

' "They're state property another few hours yet." He put his foot down and came over. "And put me to work with 'em! When there's all this stuff to do — " he gestured around at the frenetic caravan: the pavilion was being raised behind him and wagons were being reparked to his left (and the provision tent was being moved) — "there's no excuse for anyone standing around idle."

'Har'Ortrin hung behind Iryg's shoulder, all pleased and expectant. Even Feyev, at the other end of his log, leaned forward on his knees, beating a fist into his palm, the look in his gray eyes clearly that of a young man who'd have been happier hauling something.

'Just then a steward came up to ask me about the platform that was being erected across the way, half of which had not arrived, and also about six musicians who had — above the dozen expected. (When I checked, I discovered they'd been supposed to be the cook's helpers. But in Kolhari there'd been a slip of the stylus.) I turned Mirmid, Har'Ortrin, Feyev, and Iryg over to another steward, who took them off and gave them something to do. Soon I was surrounded by people I knew; and people whom people I knew wanted me to know.

'I said I was glad I came early?

'The field looked like nothing I'd ever seen before. If I'd arrived expecting the familiar and had gone through my disorientation in such confusion, I'd have been far unhappier with the tenor of the day than I was.

'The ceremony itself?

'Of course it began an hour late, while, overhead, clouds thickened. During some lull when everything remained to be done and, because of circumstances, nothing could be, I wondered if, when I called the three slaves to me to unlock their collars before the crowd, I should hurl the iron from the platform against the pavilion hangings as the tall lord had once done. (Didn't I owe him *some* little sign for all this?) But when one speech and another was actually ending and I turned to see the master of protocol herding Mirmid, Har'Ortrin, and Feyev onto the stage — I smiled at them, but, by then, as they came forward, they looked only stunned — as I inserted the key in the lock under Mirmid's sparse, tight-curled beard, the first drops pelted my shoulders, my arms, my face; and the old man closed his eyes and bared his yellow teeth while his runneled cheeks grew wet.

'Everyone had to crowd into the pavilion, where, somehow, we completed the ceremony.

'The downpour went on twenty minutes, then slowed to a steady spattering. Between tufts of wet grasses, puddles and silvery ribbons across the field were raddled, pocked, and peppered. Though I heard a few complaints about the banquet service, by my judgment the cook did a spectacular job. Later I went to tell her so in her sweltering tent; she sweated, beamed, and nodded, rubbing her dark cheeks with her palms and thumbing perspiration from her eyes.

'Because of the rain, most people left early. It stopped, with another rumble of thunder, just about the time another canopied visitors' cart pulled off for the highway.

'An evening celebration had been planned. But there were not many people left to celebrate. Everyone, I think, felt it was just as well. The cart road that had split the unified field of my memory was itself two lines of mud, split by the wet rocks and weeds between — and as familiar to me by now as any line across my palm, so that it was hard to remember why, hours before, it had seemed so egregious. As I've said, it was like any number of other public functions.

'But as I stood there pondering it, I could not help thinking that for all its halts and hitches, it had had its moments of impressive, even moving, display, filled with silent meaning — like all empty signs.

'The sky was deep gray. Repeated thunder said the rain might start again — probably to fall through the night. (We were due to leave for

Kolhari in the morning.) A small tent had been set up for me. Tired by the day's formalities, I'd just started back to rest when I saw Feyev walking ahead of me. He was making for my quarters, carrying something; but it was in front of him, so I couldn't see. He glanced left and right a lot more than someone like him usually does. He didn't look back, or he'd have seen me. At my tent, he stopped. (I stopped too.) Feyev lifted the flap. (Only minutes before, a servant had come to tell me she'd lit a lamp and left it for me, burning on a table.) He peered into the light, then stepped inside.

'What, I wondered, did he think he would find! I tried to recall what few objects, belts and their buckles, chains of office, parchments, rules, or writing implements he might, in fact, walk off with. (*Had* I been so silly as to leave coins in the casket beside the bed?) Walking up, I lifted the flap.

'He stood in the lamp glow, turned a little from me. He had just pulled free his leather clout and tossed it now to the rug. It had been bound tight by its thong, which left a line low on his naked flank. A semicircle of it in each hand, he held an iron collar . . . which he raised now to his neck. With both hands he began to push it closed —

'Till he saw me. And started.

'I started, too. "What are you — " I blurted: "Why are you . . . ?"

'Feyev turned to me, his openmouthed gaze, his gray-eyed stare absorbing his surprise. He closed the collar, leaving at his neck awkwardly his heavy hands. "I came here — " he . . . did not blurt back; rather he moved one and another thick finger on the metal — ". . . for you. I mean, if you wanted me to . . ." He frowned, perhaps because of my own frown. "I mean, I thought . . . they say you — you like . . ."

' "What are you talking about?"

'Feyev looked around, finally shrugged, let go the metal with one hand, and dropped his fingers to his leg to scratch himself.

' "Go on, tell me," I said. "Why are you here?"

'Embarrassment — or just uncertainty — made him glance up again. "You know . . . I mean, everybody knows. About you. And the collar." He said: "It used to be your sign."

' "Yes, Feyev. That's right. But," I said, "what is it *you've* come here to do?"

'He blinked. "Some of the others . . . they said I — "

' "They'?" I asked. "Not Mirmid . . . ? Not Har'Ortrin . . . ?"

' "No. Not them. The guards."

' "Which guards?"

'He shrugged again, again looking vaguely around, as if his attention were wandering. But I knew it was a kind of mime. "*You* know," he said. "Some of the men who like to do it . . . that way — real rough; they get jobs as guards here. So I do it with them. Some of them, anyway. And one of them said — "

' "Iryg?" I asked.

'Feyev's icy eyes came back, bright and narrow. "No! Not him!" He was actually angry. I felt a kind of tingle. "Iryg's a fool! He only laughs about the ones who do; and makes jokes about us. About me. He tells you about my 'perverse depravity,' without saying my name . . . then goes on and says I'm really a *good* slave — that's the kind of game *he* likes to play! But I don't care. Not about him." (I did not even ask if Mirmid was Iryg's nasty-tempered one; or Har'Ortrin his woman thief. I knew these games, too. They're all part of a single one where the winner deals out humiliation to the losers.) "But some of the guards . . . well, like I said, they like to fuck rough. So I do it with them. That's all. Like you. Sometimes they give me money. They say I should save it for when I'm free. But I don't save very much. And I *am* free — now!" In his collar, he gave his gappy grin. "Well, some of them were talking about how . . ." The grin began to break up. I saw worry beneath it. "I don't mean they put me up to it. Oh, no. *I'm* not getting anybody in trouble. It was my idea, me coming here like this . . . afterwards." (While he spoke, while I watched his dull face that at least I knew could be angry, could worry, could smile, it was still hard to believe he'd ever had *any* idea on his own.) "You're a powerful man, sir. A strong man. We saw you . . . *I* saw you staring at me; before. And since they say you like it that way, too, I thought maybe, if you liked it with me, you might . . . Maybe you could help me some. I mean, afterwards. With some money."

' "Tell me," I said. "Do *you* like doing it? That way, I mean?"

'Feyev shrugged again. "I don't mind."

' "Here," I said, suddenly. "What are you doing with that thing on?"

'Feyev lifted his chin above the collar. "My teeth," he said. "I suppose I'm not as good-looking as some you've had. Because my teeth fell out. Someone like you, you could get anyone, I guess. But some of the guards say it makes it better, though; they say I look like such a low-down fool . . . I have a whip mark on my shoulder — it's not a real one. But some of them like it — " He started to turn and show me. "And you looked at me — "

' "My poor, poor man," I said, "this is not right. You can't just come in here like this and think someone might — ' Though, as I said it, I wondered what would make him think otherwise. "But you . . . tell me, now that you're free — " I asked the question mechanically (as, I realized with embarrassment, I'd asked it of them all when we sat on the log before the ceremony: but from so many conversations with so many slaves, I'd learned there was no other question more likely to produce a happy answer. Again I wished I had stayed silent) — "where are you going? What are you going to do now?"

' "I'll go to the city — to Kolhari." Though his face brightened as it had before, it was not the answer he'd given before. "Some of them told me there's a bridge there, outside an old marketplace, where I could hang out. Maybe make a few coins . . . you know, doing what I do with them."

' "The Bridge of Lost Desire," I said. "To be sure." I felt some relief that what he'd spoken of out on the log with Mirmid and Har'Ortrin had been, for him, a kind of mummer's tale. But I was unprepared, in the midst of the day's formalities, speeches, and ideals, to encounter the simple sadness of a dull young man whose every thought was of another way to prostitute himself. "I've known my share who've gone there. Had I not been locked away here, I might have gone there myself. But it's not an easy life on the streets of Kolhari."

' "Then I'll just have to work hard at it." He gave me another half-toothed grin. "If I get stuck, then I'll try some of the things you said, before."

'My practical suggestions. "You'll work *very* hard." I thought of offering him some witless work on my own. (But what, I wondered while I thought it, could such a youth do *besides* stalk the walkways of the bridge?) I thought of accepting his offer and giving him a handful of coins. Or just the coins — and sending him away. Yet any choice seemed a trap I'd somehow set myself. I'd wanted to legislate his freedom, not ensnare myself in his survival. "Give that thing here." I reached out.

'Questioningly, he handed me the collar. "*You* want to put it on?"

'The only reason it surprised me, I guess, was because it had been so far from my mind. "No," I said. "No, I don't want to . . . not now." I took it in both hands, looked at it, looked at him.

'As though there were only one other choice, he stepped toward me and raised his chin.

'I took a breath. And raised it. Why? Perhaps to see what would happen if I did. I closed the collar again on his neck. My hands stayed on the iron.

'He looked at me with his light eyes. Then, slowly, he smiled: "You *do* want to, don't you . . . ?"

'If that pause is desire, while he may well have been within it, I was wholly outside it. Oh, there was some physical response — most definitely — and as a younger man, I might have pursued it, seeing what I could work it into. But it was of the sort that, I knew from experience, if I tried to follow it in even the simplest way, it would only die against this unpleasant reality. And because I stood outside desire's pause, I was incapable of any clear reading of what might or might not be occurring within it, either in Feyev, or in myself. And that was the ambiguity that had killed — would kill — its physical detritus.

' "Let me tell you what I think is going on, Feyev." With my hands on his neck, looking down at a face that had already turned to look away from mine, I was aware how much taller I was than he. "Think of it just as a story. But listen: because I'm not a stupid man. Someone — maybe one of the guards, one I haven't met — told you to come and give yourself to me. You've done it before. You'll do it again, no doubt. You'll want a lot of money for it. And if I give it to you, because he gave you the idea and maybe loaned you the collar — you're supposed to give him some, or half, or most of it. The two of you wouldn't try to do me out of money by violence. There're too many of my own soldiers around in the caravan for that. He's probably waiting for you back at the barracks. Maybe you're even a little afraid of him — especially if you go back empty-handed. But you're just going to have to tell him that it fell through. After all, you *are* free now. Certainly I understand why he — or you — thought up the idea. I mean, if it's a guard, he's also out of a job. And so are you. Now. What do you think of my tale?"

'Feyev stood there awhile. Then he looked up. "So what? We could still have fun." He looked away again. "If I was your slave, you could make me do it. But I'm free now. So you have to pay me. Something. For it. That's all. You set me free. Why don't you do it, then?"

'I shook my head. "Not if you want money." I managed half a grin; and took my hands away. "And maybe not even if you didn't. You go on your way now, Feyev."

' "Is the reason you won't do anything with me because there's somebody else in with the plan? Because you think that's the story. Because it *isn't* all like that — I mean not *all* of it. Sure, some of it is. But not all."

' "Right now," I said, "if I heard the full tale, I'm sure it'd just be worse. I'm complimented you want to please me. I don't blame you for going along with it. You're going to have a very hard time — harder than you have any idea. Perhaps another day I might even have gone along with it, too, and said, 'So what.' But with all that's been happening today, I'm just too tired," though it was the silences from another night entirely that loaned meanings to this evening's words. "Besides, I want to give you the benefit of the doubt. Perhaps I'll run into you in Kolhari. But right now I want to rest. By myself."

'He blinked up at me, nodded a little, his mouth still open.

' "Go on, now. Get out."

' "You're sure . . . you're tired?"

'I nodded.

' "All right." He stepped by me and pushed open the tent flap. "Because I couldn't do it for nothing. That would be like I was still a slave. And free men get paid for what they do. That's what they told me." He started out. Then, at once, he looked back, with his bright, bright eyes. "You're right, you know. My story's not as good as yours. It *is* Iryg — the one back at the barracks, waiting for his cut. He told me I had to get paid. And I don't like him any more than I said I did . . . He knocked out some of my teeth, once, when he thought I was trying to steal something I didn't even know was there. But he broke the lock for me. So he has to get paid, too. I guess it would be better if it *was* one of the guards who at least *liked* to do it the way you do. Or maybe it wouldn't be." Feyev shrugged. "I don't know. Thank you, master," though the nameless gods know what it was he thanked me for. "Good-bye." He walked out.

'I went to the flap and pulled it open. Standing there, I watched him walk, heavy-footed and a little stooped, off beneath gray and indigo. Lightning flared. The soaked field glistened. As he crossed the puddled road in the flicker, foot to foot with his reflection, he reached up, pulled the collar from his neck (I thought I heard the broken lock click), and let it swing down by his thigh. On his shoulder, I saw a whip mark — that was not real. More lightning overtook the evening. Thunder overtook the lightning. I turned back and let the tent flap fall.

'Feyev's leather clout lay on the rug, so like the one I'd worn — sometimes — at the mines. Thunder rolled away outside. Drops began to thud the canvas.

'I sat on the bed and thought: I'm too tired?

'I snorted.

'That one was not even worthy of a mummer.

'I felt numb, yes. But there was a tingling through it that tightened my muscles and defeated all rest. Rage? Fear? The love of freedom? Iryg was a perfect . . . mule turd; I simply could not pay him through Feyev; and Feyev was a perfect fool to think I might! Still, couldn't the real reason for my refusal have been as simple as age or aphanasis? Perhaps it was only Feyev's resemblance to Namyuk: for him such sex had been so outside the question, I couldn't believe any of Feyev's gestures were other than a game without a prize. As I sat on the bed by the lamp, listening to the rain, the whole of that other day and night rushed back. What would have happened, I wondered, if, thirty years ago, I *had* been able to speak, move, acknowledge, or initiate the sexual actuality in which I and the tall lord had found ourselves? Had I just been given another chance to find out — a chance which, once more, I had not taken? There, when I'd been bound round by real oppressions, known and unknown, every gesture had seemed readable: this one luminously sexual, that one solidly political, all showing their true form in the harsh light of power, none of them muddied by deceit, sloth, ire, or greed.

'Out of that clarity I had constructed my "self".

'But here, when power was mine and I was as close to being the lord — the perfect, freedom-bearing, benevolent lord, empowering the oppressed — as was possible, I could find nothing clear anywhere about me: not in the present, not in the past, not in my own motives, not in anyone else's. The single move that had abolished slavery and dismissed the guards had made the separation between guard and slave itself ambiguous.

'Wasn't it true, I asked myself, sitting there, that I'd paused in my hectic work one morning, only three days before, back in the city, for a moderately satisfying hour of sexual exploration with a perfect stranger I'd met on the street who no more knew I was a minister than you would have had I not told you? And I'll tell you this now, Udrog: two days after I returned from the mines to Kolhari, I passed an evening of fine sexual extravagance among three old friends. But all I could come to, as I sat there, listening to the water roar on the cloth and watching the flame at the lamp spout, was that, years before in this same field, at the flap of a tent like this one, I had looked into a mirror, recognized that mirror for what it was, and seized the image within it for my use. Now, at a sudden turn of chance, in need of an image to seize, I'd glimpsed that what I'd thought were mirrors and images and an "I" looking into and at them were really displaced, synthetic, formed of intersecting images in still other mirrors I'd never noticed before — mirrors whose angle, tactility, and location, because there were so many of them, because they were visible only through what was reflected of them in other mirrors, I couldn't hope to determine (much less determine a coherent pattern in which to place them), much less determine which, if any, were real and which were merely intersections in others.

'You understand, Udrog, my glimpse was not of the world around me. I speak of nothing so simple or cynical as disillusion: nothing had happened that day I had not been acquainted with long before. (Of what else was the revelation made *but* of such past acquaintances?) It was of the self that encompasses both folly and wisdom, enthusiasm and cynicism, illusion and disillusion, the self I had seized from the world, the self that had managed, after thirty years' effort, only a week before to seize the world back — when, with my victory in the council room, I'd actually won the game of time and pain. Oh, it would be too much of a mummers' tale to say that as I had once, on that field, found my self, there on the same field I lost it. I was trying to find, rather, the order in an asymmetric difference in the middle of which I was off balance each time I turned to grasp it; and you could dismiss me as a very silly man who'd learned nothing in his fifty years if you thought I was talking about some simple and singular reversal in the position of slave and lord, or that I set some equivalence between Feyev's involvement in a corrupt guard's failed scheme to win a handful of coins — and Piffles's mindless murder.'

Udrog had been patient. He'd even extended that patience, when the core of it ran out, by telling himself (rather than listening) exactly how patient he was being. But now he pushed up, bunched his fingers, and thumped them on Gorgik's chest, interrupting ('I was searching, Udrog, you see for — ') Gorgik's next sentence:

'But the story just goes on and on. Does this difference make you want to *fuck* more? That's what *I* want to know!'

Gorgik looked down at the barbarian, surprised. 'Well, it positioned me more and more outside of desire — again, I don't mean in any way that could make you say sex no longer interested me. Still, I found myself — '

But the first part of the answer was what Udrog had expected; and, beginning to fear for any satisfaction at all, he was just not interested in the second.

Udrog sat up. 'I told you, *I* know what you want. You want someone to be the master, to take over for you, to tell *you* what to do, to cut off this stupid talking with an act. That slave, Feyev, you couldn't tell whether *he* really wanted to do it then. So it didn't excite you, that's all. Here — ' Udrog jumped up before the fire; his shadow fell over the big man still on the rug. 'I know all about that. I'll show you what you need. No — move your hand, slave! *You're* wearing the collar now!' Naked above him, Udrog gave Gorgik a barefoot kick in the side. 'You'll see what I want. Turn over! I'll beat you within an inch of your life, you piece of dragon dung!' Udrog raised his hand in the firelight, prepared to bring it down in some violent and violating blow —

The hooting began up behind the colonnade. At the same time, there was a great rattling: someone was banging something back and forth between the columns. The noise came on, moved; the rattling moved with it.

Udrog stared around, his hand still high — and jumped away from Gorgik as, from back in the shadow, the cat ran straight across the floor.

The creature leaped across Gorgik's belly and off the rug, right between Udrog's feet.

The barbarian stumbled, shouted, and almost fell to the stone. 'What in the . . . What's going — ?'

The hooting and the clacking careened toward the end of the columns — something was up there, moving quickly and making a great noise. Something flew from the darkness, to fall, clattering, on the floor: a stick, some two feet long. It rolled a few inches, while the noise traveled off into a corridor, growing quieter . . . and, finally, stopped.

'What *was* that . . . ?' Udrog demanded.

'I think . . .' Gorgik had sat up himself. The stick, he could see by the firelight, had blackened wadding at one end. Looking up again, he began to laugh. 'I think it was some local field lad or milking lass in the balcony. Ten years old? Twelve? Somewhere around that age, from the glimpse I got. Well, we gave them a start. They decided to repay us in kind.'

Udrog turned sharply, looking up, and backed onto the fur. 'You mean somebody was *watching* what we were doing?'

'We didn't do very much.' Gorgik stretched out again, moving over on the rug.

'Hey — ' Udrog frowned down at the big man. 'You *can't* do that kind of stuff when you have people hanging around, spying on you! They don't understand that kind of thing. You — !' He shouted up into the dark. 'You get out of here, now! Get *out!*' There followed some curses that combined terms for women's genitals, men's excreta, and cooking implements in truly novel ways. Finishing, Udrog shook his head and looked back at Gorgik. 'How are we going to do anything with somebody up there, watching?'

'They're not watching now,' Gorgik said.

'I know.' Udrog squatted on the rug.

Gorgik put his hand on the boy's knee.

Udrog pushed it off. 'No, you can't do things if people are hanging around. Up there. That's not right. Not our kind of thing. Or even if they might come back to watch you, you know?'

Gorgik was silent.

Udrog started to stretch out, then looked again at the columns running about the room's upper tier. 'You think they'll come back?'

Gorgik shook his head. 'No.'

'But they might,' Udrog said.

'Yes.'

Udrog took a breath. 'No, I don't want to do anything if somebody I don't know can see me.' He stretched out, facing away from the man.

Gorgik put his hand on Udrog's shoulder.

Udrog shrugged it away once more. 'No. Don't fool around now. All right?'

Again Gorgik was silent.

'And you'd better take that off your neck, too. You don't want anybody to see you wearing that. They might think all sorts of things.'

'They might.' The man put his hand on Udrog's hip and slid his fingers forward.

Udrog said: 'You know about the plague — in the big cities? In Kolhari? The one they say men mostly give to men? Though I knew a woman who had it — '

'Yes.' Gorgik's hand stopped.

The barbarian grunted. 'Well, I've been in the cities. That's probably why we shouldn't do anything. You've been there, too. I might give it to you. You might give it to me. At least that's the rumor.'

'The rumor is,' Gorgik said, behind him, 'that the things you and I would most likely do tonight are the ones least likely to pass it on.'

The barbarian grunted again. 'I've heard that, too.' Then he said (for, as we have written, there were some things Udrog was clear about): 'Sometimes, though, I don't think about that. And just go on and do what I want anyway.'

'Sometimes — ' Gorgik made a sound the boy recognized as a yawn; and his hand fell away — 'I do too.'

Udrog lay still on the rug. He had not listened to all the story. Much of what he'd heard he only half understood. What he was left with, as the firelight dimmed, were only contradictions. The man, who was so very much alive, had claimed to be someone Udrog knew was dead — and claimed to be off to his own funeral! (Was *he* perhaps some demon, ghost, or god . . . ?) He'd said he was a famous minister, then talked of being a slave. He had his own fur rug to sleep on and carried a collar for play, but spoke of being outside sex and what seemed to be the death of desire. And when gods, ghosts, or demons went hooting around them, he'd just laughed. But the greatest contradiction about him was that he was so calm, so sure of himself, so relaxed in the strange and terrible hall. Udrog was tired, and his time for unraveling these riddles, as well as for sex, was over — though now the man's arm fell on his shoulder to slide around the boy's chest. Perhaps since the flame was low, it wouldn't matter if anyone peered. Udrog moved back, because the hall *was* cooler, and the man was big and warm — hard, too, across Udrog's upper buttock. Well, even if no one was up there now, the boy had passed beyond desire into the vestibule of sleep. And with this sort, Udrog knew, if he did nothing to respond, the man would not do much.

Behind the boy, the slow breaths sounded rougher, irregular, as if something might at a moment catch in the big man's throat.

But Udrog breathed quickly and easily; and slept.

8

And another tale.

We'll write now of a noblewoman near death.

When news of Lord Krodar's passing reached the castle of the retired Handmaid and Vizerine Myrgot, there was some consternation among the servants. Should the old lady, up in her chambers, be told now? or later? or not at all?

The question was finally put to the Vizerine's aging eunuch, Jahor, who'd recently been ailing himself. In his tapestried rooms, full of lamps and caged birds, with overstuffed cushions strewn among carved wooden caryatids and delicate chimes dangling above intricate candelabras so that the resultant breezes tinkled them incessantly, the ceilings draped with intricately woven stuffs, the air scented by braziers burning spices and aromatic woods, some glowing on carved tables, others smoking on high-hung shelves, and mirrors, mirrors, many mirrors, some small as a thumbnail in scrolled wire frames, some large as a big man's belly, hung on the walls, jagged at the edges and polished to a gloss, in his half dozen shawls Jahor looked up with paint-winged eyes from his delicate labor over gold wire, tiny shells, and precious stones. 'Lord Krodar . . . dead? Up at Ellamon, you say? And you want my opinion whether to tell the Vizerine?' Under the gorgeous cloths he shrugged. 'Why not?'

So the news was carried up the steps and through the corridors to the small rooms of bare stone. Here and there a wooden chest sat against a rock wall. In one chamber — not the largest — a desk had a few writing implements on it, dusted but not used. There wasn't even a proper rug; a rush mat lay near the bed. The Vizerine was napping when they came in. It took them awhile to bring her fully awake. But they had learned to be patient, and once she fully understood she sat on the bed's edge in her loose shift and breathed quietly awhile. 'The irony,' she said at last. 'That the Eagle should die among the corrals of the Dragon . . . !' She shook her head. 'Well, there's nothing to do but get ready. Do we have a full day before the procession passes south along the Royal Way? Fix a closed carriage for me. Hang it about with black and purple — whatever funeral ornaments we have. Order nothing special. I will make do. We'll join the cortege to accompany my departed colleague to Kolhari and then to his funeral in the Garth.'

The servants glanced at each other. Did the Vizerine feel that was necessary? She wasn't well. Certainly her relatives and younger colleagues would understand and take no offense if, in this case, she —

But Myrgot sat straight at the bed's edge. 'I have never pampered myself. I will not start now. There will be people at this funeral I shall probably never have another chance to see in my life. Besides, I wouldn't miss it for the world!'

Well, perhaps . . . said the servants. Would she require her eunuch to accompany her?

'Jahor? No, I won't need Jahor. Besides, the poor thing has been sick unto death. I shall take only a driver and a maid. Perhaps the new girl . . .? Yes, I think she should come with me. She has a pleasant way. A good companion for a funeral.'

The 'new girl' was a woman of forty, called Larla. She'd been at the castle almost five years now. The last she'd worked for nobility had been half a dozen years before that, when for six months she'd been employed at the home of Lord Vanar, during his final illness. The other servants found her rather strange, somewhat shrill, and often a bit temperamental. But she was good-hearted. And since she was the last servant Myrgot had personally interviewed before hiring, her mistress made excuses for her.

The servants left, distraught over the Vizerine's decision, both to go and to leave Jahor behind. For the eunuch's endless self-ministrations tended to be of the preventative sort, and the actual ailments he vigorously complained of were, if one listened closely, only to justify this or that medicinal, dietary, or exercise regimen — whose long-term effects were what he was after. But the Vizerine, who would never admit to any failure of health, had taken half a dozen falls in the last year. Several times for two or three days she would not, or could not, eat. Both her coming awake and going to sleep had become longer (and more and more confused) processes. While her mind was generally clear, sometimes she suffered from . . . well, it was hard to say if it were a surge of melancholy or a lapse of memory: it had characteristics of both. Then the whole castle went into confusion, since ordinarily the old woman insisted on organizing everything from her small, spare rooms; and now nothing could be done. (From these occasions the alternative of consulting Jahor had grown up. About the running of castles, the eunuch knew a great deal.) One time or another all the servants had seen her, usually early in the morning, in an old robe, hobbling along some hallway, halting between steps, now holding the wall, now both hands pressed to one hip, while she took one coarse breath and another.

Before sunup the next day, the Vizerine was bundled into her wagon, with traveling rugs and funeral gifts and hampers of provisions. Larla pushed in another brocaded sack and climbed in after it. The driver shouted to the horses.

Holding their torches high, the servants watched the wagon go. (Jahor had not come out to see her off. But though the old lady had commented on it, she hadn't seemed surprised.) Still, as the servants lowered their brands to reënter the castle, they wondered if the Vizerine were not confused about certain things, for now and again she had turned to address some comment or other to someone who simply . . . wasn't there.

Well, it would be up to the new girl now.

The timing of the departure had been propitious. The wagon joined the funeral procession half an hour after a glorious sunrise. The Vizerine jostled along while the hangings swung together and apart — but at another rhythm than the drummers outside, with their loud, slow thunder.

The drumming, the Vizerine thought, was the difficult part of funerals. She sat straight in the corner seat, which, despite the cushion, hurt her hip — she had given up trying to find a comfortable position for her leg under the dark red wool. Had she told the new girl to ride in one of the other carriages? She really wanted to be alone. But no, Larla was right there — directly across from her, dozing. Of course if she *weren't* there, Myrgot pondered, I'd probably miss her, for all her heavy arms and over-blunt opinions — not that the girl was much to talk to. If she were here in the carriage, she'd probably be asleep in the corner, her clothes in disarray, her head against the window jamb and her mouth faintly open as the hangings swayed, her lips ajar with the jarring of the wagon.

The Vizerine blinked.

Who *was* that sitting across from her in the shadow?

It *was* Larla . . . wasn't it? Or did someone else sit in the corner? Really, it was difficult to tell. And if there *was* someone else, who? Perhaps if she closed her eyes for a time . . . ? (That was, she knew, often a better way to see.) In her red funeral robe, the Vizerine sat straight, and was very tired. But she wouldn't sleep. No, this was not a time for sleep . . .

She said to the big man sitting across from her:

'I knew you would be here, my little slave, my great minister, my liberator. Really, Gorgik, you are the only reason I came myself. So, Krodar is dead. Though in different ways, it's a relief to us both. Tell me, are you now the most powerful man in Nevèrÿon? Or is that just an illusion, a momentary shape I've glimpsed this morning out on some foggy meadow? Of course for so long I was one of those whose illusions, however cruel or benevolent, were the very constitution of power. What you have done, my Gorgik, by ending slavery, is to reduce the distance between the highest and the lowest by an entire social class. Thus we, who were the highest, are, thanks to you, nowhere near as high as we were. Sometimes, you know, I feel I created you. Have you really freed *all* the slaves? Lord Aldamir and I could not have approved more had you been a favored son who'd taken up our task and program and played it out with perfect dispatch. Consider. Once two of the strictest prohibitions on slaves were those on drinking and reading. Neither was ever allowed in the south. The first time the latter was relaxed in the north was on that shameful night in the Month of the Rat when my little cousin, whose reign is rich and resplendent, came to power. "There's no time for trials! We're killing all the Dragon's supporters! Everyone knows who they are! We're taking everyone in their families your age and below as slaves for the new regime!" I stood beside her as she heard Lord Krodar declare it, there in the bloody throne room. The terrified little thing, for whom it had been corpses up to the eyebrows three days now since we'd left the Garth, looked around for her hulking blond bodyguard who'd come slashing and hacking with us all the way from the south, to slip behind his hip or grab his wrist. But, not finding him, she cried out: "All of them, you hear! *All* of the children! You mustn't harm any, not for *any* reason!"

'Her first order from the Halls of Court.

'I've always thought my little brown cousin was much younger at fifteen than most. Given her cloistered upbringing, it was understandable. Not that it protected her from much. The bodyguard she'd been looking for, we'd discovered just that morning, was a spy for the Dragon, and, with only minutes to spare, to stop a plot that would have lost both her life and mine, she'd had to run in to him, laughing delightedly, throw her arms around him — and, with the knife hidden in the folds of her skirt, slit his throat! She'd done it. Six hours later, though, her gown was still a mess. I say she was young, but in many ways we were all very old. We'd been through scenes as bloody four times in the last three years.

'The nameless gods alone know which Imperial captain, slipping on strewn entrails and sliding on bloody tiles, carried her command outside. And on the waterfront, because of it, you, Gorgik, who had spent enough time in the warehouses where your father worked to pick up the rudiments of that old, crude, commercial script, were not tested, drugged, and slaughtered an hour after your parents, as you would have been in the south. You were never led into a room among a dozen others, where various legends had been scrawled over the walls, among them, "Freedom only to those who linger, silent, in this room when the others have gone on to their labors." Nor were all told to leave through the door, and the ones who stayed congratulated with a celebratory drink (heavily drugged), then killed.

'You were simply made a slave.

'So now in Nevèrÿon, a *very* few slaves existed who knew how to read and write. (The first night I knew you, you yourself explained to me that is how you became a foreman.) The beginning of the end of slavery. It's an explanation I know you would enjoy. How many like it have I heard you offer over the years for this or that social phenomenon? Yet, how many times have I heard you tell your own story — in so many different versions, I might add. Your literacy — certainly one of the first things I noticed about you when I decided to buy you from the mines — is not usually what you mention, unless asked. And more than once, my friend, my creation, my mirror, I have thought your suppression of that fact from the general narrative you tell and retell of your life is the sign of its indubitable core import.

'Telling you this tale, while you sit here, smiling at an old lady whom you once thought not so old as all that, I expect at any moment you will take it up, but with emphases reversed, points and periods displaced, the whole re-read, re-written, clarified, you will say, but all to your own ends. How interesting, you will comment, that, from the beginning, the empress's power was wholly supplementary, correctionary, cautionary, strategic, exhortatory. Hasn't it remained so ever since? What intrigues me, from my own time at court (you will go on), is that this is the model for all political power any individual — empress, minister, Vizerine, councilor, courtier, radical rebel or petitioning merchant — holds. The most difficult lesson *I* had to learn at Court was that (you will explain) the sort of power the Child Empress wielded that night, as you have described it, was the only power there is. The illusory model of force, which distracts, dissuades, and finally destroys us all at play in the game of power and time, is modeled equally well, in your tale, by Lord Krodar, who is able to command, with a set of sentences, let these be killed or those cast down, let those be raised up or these seated beside me: the whole preposterous notion that power is limited only to that which mediates between language and action. That is why he — or his image as a blood-soaked tyrant — is our enemy to be analyzed, dismantled, dismissed in a move that, for us, must finally be one of vigilant self-correction and protection. That is why she — or her image as a bloody, frightened child — is our friend. It is simply a matter of which one is closer to the real.

'And somehow, like any man talking to a woman, you will have taken it away from me again. And gone on smiling. How am I to tell you, now that you've deprived me of my point, that it was *not* an order Krodar gave that night. He had merely run in to report a fact — which is to say your model for political power is righter than you know. His power, compared to that of the greater engine, was as supplementary as the little empress's. His brilliance — his own power, if you will — was only in his knowledge, practice, and exploitation of those supplementary strategies. For, as you also know, I have never been able to use Krodar — or his image — as you have.

'But I suppose that is why I do not enjoy stories of court any more.

'We have had so many times, over the years, you and I, for you to tell me your life. What has intrigued me, Gorgik, is that every time you've sat down to tell it, it has always come out differently. Do you recall, at our second meeting, how quick you were to confess so many things you'd told me in our first were lies — or, as you put it, "tales appropriated from other slaves"? Years later, when more and more of Nevèrÿon seemed to choose you to speak for her, I wondered if the reason wasn't that you had appropriated still more and more tales into your narrative, so that more and more people recognized themselves in it — even as some of us recognized in *that* the strategy of a man who has no tale at all.

'The temptation with such a man is, of course, for the rest of us to turn and tell your tale ourselves — or what we suspect that tale to be. Certainly I have my own version.

'Do you remember when last you came to see me? Oh, how pleased and frightened I was when I heard of your elevation to minister. It seemed only fitting that I, who first brought you into the High Court of Eagles, should invite you, once your installation was done, to my home for some rest and relaxation before your arduous duties began. I sent my messenger to Kolhari. By that time our histories were intricately intertwined, even as our lives had separated. Retired now, I was largely out of the game that you had just taken on for your own. I hoped you would visit me as an old friend to whom you once used to write the most marvelous letters. (Ah, in those early years, the wonders you used to write of, at first hiring a scribe for the modern and up-to-date Ulvayn system that set down words — then, from time to time, as time went on, writing in your own hand, using the older commercial glyphs your father taught you, where signs for things and feelings and whole complexes of ideas, which might be spoken by the reader in many different ways, were marked directly down. Toward the end, as you used a scribe less and less, your letters began to mix the two forms — as presumably, like all in our land, you began to master the modern mode yourself. Indeed, I noticed that as more and more *words* crept into your letters and as the signs for ready-made ideas became fewer and fewer, the letters themselves became rarer. And as our correspondence fell away, I wondered if you were, after all, a man more comfortable with abstract ideas and physical things than you were with the vagaries of perlocution and illocution.) But I also knew you might come as the grimmest accuser with listed reasons as to exactly why you had stopped writing. Really, I hoped you would be my mirror: once I had gazed at you long enough to discover how you felt toward me, I would, among the endless ambiguities of my own actions over the years, learn who it was I had at last become.

'We had all heard much, over the years, of your new little one-eyed lover. Some said he was a vile, low creature, once the basest of slaves, bandits, and murderers, now your fool and your clown, for whom you had developed an obsessive fondness the way, so often, the very high will become enamored of the very low. Others said he was a sorcerer who had bound you to a pact within which your past successes and your future triumphs were inscribed with equal legibility and for which, as each occurred, you paid with the blood of your body and the humiliation of your soul, the transaction carried out in the darkest hours with rituals of such a violent, painful, and demeaning intensity ordinary men and women could not conceive them. Others saw between you a more humane relation: the one-eyed creature was a brilliant military and political strategist whose advice you had once sought out and whose companionship you now clung to. He was to the army and politics what the great Belham once was to architecture and mathematics. The worst these folks could say was that your own greatness in Nevèrÿon was something of an illusion, that the real power attributed to you did not exist, that you were, in fact, only the one-eyed creature's gaming piece, an emblem of power he deployed wholly for his own ends — ends which were, of course, nowhere near as high-minded as the ones you'd been putting forward so docilely at his behest a dozen years. The least human version was simply that the one-eyed man did not exist! *You* were the sorcerer whose program of liberation masked unscriable depths and complexities, within which good and evil were so entangled there was no extricating them. The one-eyed demon, appearing in the collar that once you'd worn as your personal sign, was only the most frequent of the many illusions you could call up to manifest a strength and a will for which words like adamantine and indomitable were inadequate.

'I had known you too well — or liked to believe I had — to be taken in by any of these tales. Yet because I could believe none of the explanations I had been offered, I was that much more anxious to meet your companion myself — possibly (I can say it to you after all this time) even more anxious than I was to take up your own acquaintance again. Perhaps I suspected you had somehow found something with this odd asymmetric person who'd fascinated so many that

I had overlooked as I'd sifted the world's dust for the accoutrements to greatness. How carefully I framed my message: "You and any of your household you are inclined toward are cordially welcomed as my guests for the season." How distressing, then, that before I had even received your acceptance, the rumor reached me that you had not even brought the legendary Noyeed, with his single eye, to Court. I had it from the Princess Elyne, who stopped with me for three days on her way back from your installation to her own drear family halls: though the diminutive creature, who all agreed was your bedmate (some said as well he was your master and others that he was your slave), had started out with you on your journey to Kolhari, brown as our empress and less than her in height, he had vanished just before your party arrived for the ceremony, as if the Kolhari carnival declared in your honor had swallowed him up in its festivities.

'He had not been seen again.

'A week later, you arrived at my home, singular, alone, impressive. You swept into the hall, wearing your ministerial robes, looking both older and stronger than when I'd last seen you maybe six years before. You laughed, seizing both my hands in yours, entreating my forgiveness, as you had come without servants, guards, or retinue. Would it inconvenience me if my own people took over your care? I felt joy and delight, at the same time as I listed to myself my disappointments. Remain here for the season? It was generosity itself of me to offer it, you said.

'But it was impossible!

'Certainly I would understand that, as one who knew the engines of court much better than you. You could pass a fortnight with me. Then, it was back to Kolhari. As we stood gazing at each other, dust still on your shoulders from your ride, I realized you might as well have come to me as naked as you were the night I first possessed you, twenty years before. Without entourage, you gave me no way to judge your material strength . . . as an ordinary aristocrat would have! It was only when I was unexpectedly deprived of the information that I learned how used I was to receiving it from my other noble guests; and how much more than pleasures of the flesh or the intellect I desired it.

' "Where is Jahor?" you asked.

'I called our old friend in.

'He came, prattling and preening himself, monstrous flirt that he can be, heaping on you monstrous flatteries and appropriate praises inextricably mixed, the way, over the years, I've seen him do with anyone who terrifies him. I smiled at it, because it only confirmed for me how comfortable I felt within the arc of your friendship. Whatever past bitternesses there might have been between us, while I did not think they were forgotten, I could believe now they'd been forgiven. And that gave me much delight about my past actions, your future career, and the world sharing them.

'It was three days later that the servants called me to tell of the tale a wagoner had been bruiting about in our village market. Oh, yes, all and sundry were stopping by his cart to hear. Well, I declared, if his tale is as interesting as that, have him brought up to the castle so that he can tell it to us. Thus that dirty, dazzled man, smelling of the chickens he'd hauled along, was brought into the receiving hall and served bread, cider, cheese, and fruit, while I sat on one couch and you sat on another so that we could hear him out.

'His tale was simply this: In the town where he had begun his journey, just three to the west of ours, some dozen hungry, haggard men and women had wandered into the village together, destitute, disheveled, and dazed. They'd seemed peaceful enough. But when the elders came to question them, their answers were incoherent and fragmentary. Finally, one of the town's elder-women remembered: years before, a party of rich merchants, minor nobles, and several bright sons and daughters of wealthy farmers had passed through the village with their caravan, journeying on, so they'd claimed, to Nevèrÿon's very border, seeking to travel across it, defiant of the named gods and protected by the nameless, to explore the world beyond. Clearly these were the remnants of that expedition, stricken, shaken, shattered by the adventure, returned to Nevèrÿon at last.

'You leaned forward then, your face gone hard about its scar: "Tell me," you demanded, "was there a one-eyed man among them? A little man, no bigger than a boy, with the lids of his right eye sealed deep within the socket? He was called Noyeed!"

'That was when our driver confessed he had only seen the returning men and women from a distance, over the heads of the crowd. He'd come no closer to them than a third the width of his village square, with its purchasers and vendors of turkey eggs and squash and goat's milk crowded in between. No, he had talked to none of them. Nor had he really seen any from less than civil distance.

'That was the first time your one-eyed companion had been named in my home since your arrival. It struck me, even as I recoiled from the intensity of your demand, that had *I* been the first to mention him, any further questions I might have had would have gone so much more easily. But as you had initially named him, and named him with such urgency, I felt excluded from further articulate query. I could not mention him again simply because you had.

'The wagoner rode away.

'But with that, the one-eyed man seemed to enter my castle himself, like some hazily clinging dream that will not leave in the morning. Over the next days, a third of my thoughts were about him: who could he have been, where might he have gone, and why might you suspect that he'd returned to Nevèrÿon with this demented party?

'Three days later, another cart pulled up in my courtyard. The servants came in. A Kolhari relative of mine had stopped by on his journey home, an unassuming prince from a fine but fragmented family, who'd long ago dropped his title and turned to teaching at an academy in the capital, of which he was now Master. He wished to know if he might stay the night before continuing on tomorrow. By all means, I said. Tell him I will see him and welcome him to my house. I went to your rooms. "Come," I told you. "I want you to meet my little cousin. I am terribly proud of you both and wish to show you off to one another. Now that I am retired, such is the only pleasure I have." Again we found ourselves in the receiving hall with cider, salads, hot biscuits, and the kitchen's best meats brought out for the afternoon.

'As with so many who have turned their pursuits to the abstract, the presence of real power seemed to leave the Master of Sallese pleased, flattered, even flustered in the way that always compliments the truly strong. We talked, the three of us; and while the Master seemed to compete with Jahor in his praises of your program and your progress, you, in the face of it, were supremely cool — also, I could tell, supremely pleased. It was then I thought to bring up the tale we'd heard only a few days before: had the Master heard of the strange group, only a few towns off, who'd returned to Nevèrÿon after their mysterious exploration?

'Oh, yes. Indeed, he had. His trip had taken him right through the village. But they were *not* the returned expedition at all, he assured us. He himself, when he'd heard of the visitors, had stopped for the afternoon to conduct a personal examination. We must believe him, this was no egalitarian collection of brave wanderers, with ideals and commitments, snared in the ends of some ragged and raveled venture. Rather, they were a clutch of madmen and madwomen who'd accidentally come together and had taken solace with one another, stumbling and staggering through the Nevèrÿon countryside, for the simple protection numbers gave so sad and vulnerable a lot.

'As he said it, again I saw your attention rise as your eyebrows lowered. "You say you made your own examination of them? Tell me," you demanded, "was there a one-eyed man with them, a little one, Noyeed? I want him! Was he among them?"

'Taken aback by the intensity of your question, the Master now admitted, somewhat flustered, that he had not examined the men and women themselves. For a number of reasons, that had not been practical. But he had spent several hours personally questioning the village elders who had stopped, detained, and finally, themselves, interrogated the strangers. Surely, had such an eccentric creature as you described been in their number, he would have been mentioned. Therefore, though the Master could make no certain statement, he could certainly offer as highly probable: the one-eyed man was not with them.

'As he said it, however, I could tell — as I'm sure could he (for he certainly knew what man you inquired after, though, in the face of your intensity, he was as reticent about asking more details as I was) — that you would take no such assurances. And I pondered: Was it love you were feeling? Was it the desire for revenge? But you've always had a difficult face to read.

'The next day the Master was off.

'Later, when I looked from my high window to see you, with my two good eyes, strolling outside on the sunny grounds, I wondered what varied darknesses you carried within you that only a one-eyed man might look at and see into.

'Three days more and summer sun gave over to summer rain. And the servants came in to say that the redheaded tale teller, who now and again passed by, had called with her cart at my courtyard, asking if I would enjoy her entertainments on this drizzly day. Yes, most certainly! Tell her to come into the main hall! Again, I went to get you. As we walked downstairs together, you seemed as enthusiastic as I.

'Sure enough, when we met her in the receiving room and she stood up to greet us, it seemed you, too, knew the wandering fictioneer, at least slightly, the way one knows those wondrous creatures only a breath from true sorcerers, whom one meets and remeets about the land. It was like a reconciliation among old friends, one of whom now would introduce us to new wonders.

'Cider, beer, wine? I had all three brought out. This was certainly worth a full feast. And a full feast I had my servants set out through the day. Even Jahor came from his musty chambers to listen. Now and again, this or that kitchen boy or cleaning girl, finished serving, would linger in the room. And, oh, what tales she told that afternoon! She told old ones, with which we were all familiar, that pulled from us all the old emotions, the more intense as the ruts along which they rolled into view were the more familiar, the more deeply worn they were! She told new ones, which puzzled us and prodded us to seek out all their similarities with, and differences from, the old! There were clever ones that were all wordplay and silliness, at which we howled and clutched our sides. There were high, solemn, serious ones, to which we paid all of our highest and most serious attention, only glancing — solemnly — from time to time at some of the others to see if they'd, perhaps, fallen asleep. And which of her stories were not all sparkling artifact and invention were wicked and incisive gossip.

'Oh, while the rain pelted the rocky roof and walls, we had a *wonderful* day!

'But it was you who brought up what for me had become at once the obsessive and the forbidden. Between stories, you said, sighing: "If you could only tell us some tale of those creatures in . . ." and you mentioned the name of that town.

'The tale teller paused. Oh, yes. Her own travels had taken her through the place only days before. When she had heard about the strangers, she had presumed on her privileges as a wise and storied woman and asked to see them, to spend time in the hut where they'd been confined, to question them and listen carefully to their answers.

After all, they were rumored to have been to distant lands and locations. They were rumored to be mad. Perhaps they had tales to tell that she might add to her store.

' "You saw them yourself?" you demanded. "You did not simply glimpse them across some crowded public space? You talked to them yourself? You did not simply prattle with those who claimed to have talked to them?"

'Oh, most definitely she had seen them. And spoken with them. And listened to them. She had eaten with them in the house where they'd stayed, sat up with them through much of the evening, and slept among them as they'd slept. And in the morning, she had left them. No, she was quite sure they were not natives of Nevèrÿon who had departed and then returned. Nor were they, she assured us, mad. As far as she could tell, they were from some other land entirely, with language, habits, and customs simply different from our own, which explained why they had at first seemed insane; for they had fared hard and suffered much. Where they had come from she was not sure. She herself was from the outlying Ulvayn Islands and had been both north and south, and she'd recognized neither their language nor their manner. But they were peaceful and, in their demeanor, civilized. Yes, they had their own tales. She had listened long and hard to one man, who must have been consoling the others with one of their own stories. But it was in an unknown language and though she could enjoy its loll and lilt, and could even read a gesture or two which accompanied it, the narrative itself was opaque to her. Though she'd sat, fascinated, through it all, she'd no more idea what it had been about than she had of the tale the leaves whisper to the wind or the one the brook hisses at the bank.

'But you leaned forward with your dark look. I heard the question that hesitated, half-formed, among jaw and tongue and lip. And for a moment it was as if the one-eyed man himself stood there, his hand on your shoulder, leaning with you, waiting for her answer even as you asked: "Tell me, was there a small man among them, called Noyeed, with only one eye?"

'She was as troubled by the strength of your question as the others had been. "No," she answered, puzzled. There was none whom she had seen. There'd been a woman who was lame and who had been quiet most of the time. There'd been a fat man who was ill and had difficulty both breathing and hearing. Most of them, indeed, had sustained this or that injury in the journey which had brought them to our land. But was there a small one-eyed man? No, definitely not. She concluded by telling us that, when she'd left their hut, she'd returned to the village elders and suggested that, after letting the group have a day or so more rest, they send them on with new provisions, in the name of the empress, whose reign is grand and gracious; the elders had only to hear it from an outside author to declare that they had been only an hour from the same decision. It would be done. (Also, she suspected, the novelty of keeping the foreigners was wearing thin.) That is what she was sure they had done. And she had ridden on to the next town.

'You settled back on your couch. Soon we were all lost in other stories, other tales. But now and again I glanced over. What I saw, however, almost more clearly than I saw you, was a little man squatting on the end of your couch, clutching his knees and listening as intently as any of us to the red-headed island woman, his head turned just so, that he might, with his good eye, observe her more directly. I tell you, this one-eyed creature was oppressive in his absence!

'That night I begged the tale teller to sleep in the castle and ordered blankets and rugs to be brought for her to the hall. The rain had ceased, and, with the full moon, there rose about the stones of my house, pearled through with moonlight, a summer fog.

'You yawned, you stretched, you stood — you would like to go walking for a while. Did I and the tale teller wish to go with you among the night's mists?

'The tale teller declined, with fatigue as her excuse.

'Myself? Well, I was simply too old and too stiff to enjoy such nighttime rambles in the chill and damp. I was, in fact, exhausted.

'Jahor attempted to dissuade you, I remember. Such damps were bad for the lungs and the liver. But you laughed at him and went out. I retired upstairs. But before I lay down, I pushed back the shutters to look out on the glowing air. I could not see the ground or make out an entire tree.

'The castle seemed to bob about in moon-soaked vapor. I remembered how, days before, from the same window, I had watched you stroll in the sun where, more than likely, you now strolled in the fog. I smiled. For as you had brought your vanished friend's oppressive absence into the castle, it seemed you had at last taken it out with you. Standing there, looking for you and wholly unable to see you, I felt, for the first time since you'd come, at peace. What might you be saying to the little creature who haunted you like a dream? During all the years that have passed since then, I have just assumed it was central to your being, the articulation of some secret on which your very self was founded, the origin and end between which was organized all you despaired of, all you hoped for. Perhaps it was only because, while I looked out at the inconstant mist, I could assume you had such a center that put me at such peace that night. Feeling that such a center existed for you, I could assume there was one — however out of touch with it I was — for me.

'The next day the tale teller went off, with a reward of coins from us both. And a little later, you rode from my courtyard, back to Kolhari and glory. Am I only a woman who wishes to see love, even so demonic a love as yours, at the core of things? But I have often wondered since — I have often longed to ask you in the years that have passed — if, indeed, were you to tell your tale some night, in enough detail and at great enough length, would the secrets you and your one-eyed demon, ghost, or god uttered to each other that evening out in the fog be solid and central to it? Or would they only flicker at the corners of our attention, like marginal remarks that might as well be elided because, in fact, the whole tale was only the intersection of so many margins?

'Is it perhaps that your true story, my liberator, as you pass from the lowest to the highest, simply goes on and on, like so many others', only hinting at forms and figures and overall patterns in passing? Do you *really* repeat yourself so often and at such variance? Perhaps *we* cannot fathom the stories' unity. Perhaps *we* cannot interpret the strategies of their diversifications. (Are both failures, finally, one?) Or is it only that we, hearing you tell it, are sundered by it and so, split and shaken, must ask you, from our various and several positions, to repeat it: whereupon you, sundered by our demands, shaken and split, retell what always seems, because of the violence done you and us in the request, another tale. Well, there are some tales that may never be told in this strange and terrible land: the tale of a revolutionary's success, through loss, gain, and glory, within and without the High Halls of Court, is doubtless one. The story of one powerful woman's advice and administrations to another over the years on the basis of greater age and experience, such as my service to our empress, whose reign is proud and proven (if only by your story, Gorgik), is doubtless another.

'As Vizerine to the Empress, as Liberator to the land, you and I have lived those tales — yet even we, in these basic and barbaric times, would be hard put to tell them: we were too busy living them to attend to their narrative form. And neither of us thought to keep a mummer or a tale teller about to narrate them for ourselves and others, to give them a classic mold. We must satisfy ourselves, then, with empty signs, marginal mutterings, attending rather to the celebratory engine of someone else's distant and speculative art.

'Will someone someday ever essay their rich specificity? No, I will never hear mine related. I doubt you will ever hear yours. However laudable our actions, as tales neither aids enough men now in power.

'Gorgik, I look around me at the strong men and women of Nevèrÿon. I have always tried to seize their images for my own. But I know I am not a strong woman any longer. It doesn't frighten me. It doesn't worry me. I still retain enough strength to face my death. Still, every time I leave my castle, I wonder if I shall come back to it. When, I ponder, will it join the vacant ruins, scattered like bug husks on the land, which, more than any one else's, are now yours?'

The drumming had put Larla to sleep. And, at once, it woke her. She started in the corner of the carriage. The hanging had fallen back from the window. Sunlight blazed over the Vizerine, turning her white braids silver, making the red wool folds seem waves of blood. She was sleeping, head back in the corner, wrinkled lips apart . . .

She *was* sleeping, wasn't she? Larla peered forward. But, yes. It was more than just the wagon's shake. She could see the dark jaw moving. She reached out to hook the hanging again to the upper sill, so that the sun did not fall directly in the old brown face. She was muttering on in her sleep (as usual), though about what the serving woman had no idea. More and more confused about more and more things these days, the Vizerine still seemed to Larla in many ways (the women felt it deeply) an extremely clear-minded old thing. She only wished Jahor had come. Not only did the eunuch know just how to deal with the Vizerine, but he himself was a witty creature and, if the mood was on him, could be as amusing as any traveling tale teller — though, as had been muttered in the castle for the last year, the mood had fallen on him less and less. These days he seemed more given to brooding than anything else. Well, it was getting on in the morning. Should she take out some fruit from the hamper? Oh, perhaps in a while. Why, there, for a moment she'd almost ignored the drums! Larla moved about enough to get comfortable — then sat forward again to make sure her mistress was all right. Satisfied, she leaned back in the jogging wagon.

9

Waking, Gorgik coughed into fur, felt stone beneath . . . He lifted his head, rubbed his mouth, and, pushing himself up, opened his eyes. From the windows along the higher tier, light — shadowed with leaves — flickered in the hall. He looked back. In the recess behind the hearth, the fire was dead.

Yes, he was alone.

One shoulder and one leg were stiff. But that was every morning now. They would loosen. He cleared his throat. (Someday, he thought, this nighttime choking will kill me . . .) Was Udrog up and wandering? Or had the barbarian — far more likely — already run off? Gorgik put his hand on his chest and slid it to his shoulder. Moving his thumb against his neck, he frowned.

Then, on the rug, he sat up fully, looking to see where the collar had fallen.

The extinguished torch, thrown on the floor last night, lay a few feet away.

But there was no iron on the rug or on the stone around it. He lifted the edge of the fur three places to look under, then let it drop. Pursing his lips, he rubbed his naked neck. So, he had met a little barbarian thief! Suddenly, he started up frowning. On his feet, he dragged up the fur behind him and walked to the arch. He turned behind the wall, hurried up the steps, the rug over his shoulder, crossed the level landing, and went up the next flight:

The boards still leaned at intricate angles across the tower room's doorway. He dropped the fur (it fell against his ankle) to remove one carefully. As he lifted the second, the rest toppled to the stone, loudly — as they'd been meant to. Still, it startled. He stepped across them, looking around:

Helmet, grieves, sword, pack, the bed's bare boards . . .

Neither the barbarian nor last night's local prowler had thought to come up here. But that had been why he'd chosen it. And the room was cool.

He liked the morning's smell. Leaves moved outside the shutter. To see what would happen, he called loudly, 'Udrog!' three times down the stairs, and twice out the window. The scummed pool was still. He called once more. His mare neighed from where she was chained in one of the remaining garden sheds. Yes, the key was still in the bottom of his pack. Udrog and the collar were gone.

He sat on the bed's edge, listening to morning birds, watching leaf shadow the sun shook out on the wall. After some minutes, he went again to his pack, squatted before it (his bladder burned with the night's collected water), and pulled out his clothes for the day's ride. Standing, he began to dress. When he was in his military undergarments, suddenly he loaded everything into his sack, dragged it downstairs and out to the horse. Still looking for the boy, he smiled at the discrepancy between experience (the barbarian *was* gone) and desire (if I look for him, *maybe* he'll be here).

At the shed, he urinated by rotting planks, in a longtime coming, longtime lingering trickle that seemed, in the past year, always to fall as weakly as the urge rose strongly. Pondering age's daily disappointments, he turned back to his sack to don armor, robe, and ornament. He pulled a heavily medallioned width of canvas about his belly. Ah — just to put the stuff on was to sweat!

The horse's silken flank twitched a fly off into the shed — and a memory he'd been dipping into and drifting away from since waking cleared:

Opening his eyes in the dimmest light, he'd seen the barbarian boy, kneeling with his back to him, rise to stand.

(He'd turned over and gone to sleep again.)

Pausing at one wide shoulder strap and buckle, Gorgik laughed out loud. (The horse stepped about in her chain.) He'd been assuming it was some image from years ago. But it had happened that morning! He'd woken long enough to *see* Udrog get up to leave. Why was it so difficult to weave together the strands of the present, without having one or another of them slide into the past?

There: the strap was set.

Food for the horse? He could take care of that down in town. He hoisted up the sack, its contents divided in two halves with loose cloth in the middle, and shoved it over the animal's back. He looked down at himself again, hip and haunch heavy with metal. Well, it went along with formal affairs — births and funerals and the artificial occasions those in a position to might momentarily declare as important as one of the others.

The key was in his hand. He bent to unlock the iron, with its coiling chain, closed on the mare's foreleg. Then, hesitating, he straightened again, and walked a bit away to look for a while among the trees.

Once he glanced back at the castle. He tried to picture the branches and shrubs, which had already taken over the courtyard and blurred all articulation in the grounds, coming closer and closer to those sloping walls till the building, sunken in soil and piled around with leaves, a few trunks thrusting from it, grew indistinguishable from forest boulders.

The picture completed, he turned from it.

He tossed the key up and caught it.

And grinned. And thought how little he felt like grinning.

To tell a tale, he'd often felt, was to take as much as you gave — for he'd always had an anecdotal turn. (Had it been getting out of hand in the past year?) But because the scamp had made off with his collar, he felt bested in the exchange.

The trees stood quietly, waiting with him, while he pondered.

He'd defined himself so long by his opposition to this dead lord, it was as if — at the death — he'd been pushing against a mountain to have it collapse into a field over which he'd gone staggering and reeling; as if, running across a plain, he'd gone over a cliff, into the air, flying, flailing, falling; as if he'd woken with an unspeakable power that felled all he looked at so that even as he gazed around to assess the damages, he'd only wrecked more.

When the old definitions are gone, he thought, how we grasp about for new ones!

What am I, then?

And what is this 'I' that asks?

Despite their separation, the questions seemed one.

Yet to articulate them was to be aware of the split between them, between the mystical that asked them and the historical they asked of, between the unknowable hearing them and the determinable prompting them, so that finally he came to this most primitive proposition: only when such a split opened among the variegated responses to a variegated world *was* there any self.

But, on such a morning, where do I turn to find it (he wondered), to limit it, to seize it and secure it? Where do I look for a model, a mirror, an image of the questing self seeking self-knowledge? Do I turn to the corpse I'm out to meet who'll dominate my day? Or to the live and lusty youngster that slipped away in the night? Should I search in the ever-rising, ever-encroaching green and gray stuff of nature, or in the ever-falling, ever-failing stone and metal works of hand? Will I find it in my own body, which, though it is the register of all pleasure, whether of head or heart or flesh, is nevertheless a site of increasing ache and ailment; which grows more anesthetized to sex as it grows more sensitive to pain; which, no matter how bad it looks, always looks better than it feels?

No, he couldn't see the north-south road from here. And, anyway, there was no exact timing to these things. All he could do was ride down, wait for the funeral to pass, and take his place in the procession.

He *was* annoyed about the collar! All the way here, he'd debated whether he should put it on today, as a sign of the past, perhaps some sign for the future, or maybe a mark of the division between. Well, the blond thief had solved that one, however unhappily. Oh, he probably wouldn't have worn it. Still, he'd have liked the choice.

Despite the annoyance, or even because of it, the brush and rock around, the breeze overhead, the loam below, the bird above the bush, the bug down on the bough, all seemed exhaustingly alive — no, not with youth's unified wonder, but with the tension between small pleasures and small pains that were the life of middle age. (It had not been twenty minutes: he had to urinate again!) For pain as much as pleasure was a sign of life. And I, he thought, am off to a funeral, where we shall ride quietly, on our horses or in our wagons, dazed by drums and deeming all in order, while we pretend that stomachs are not rumbling, that morning quince and honey do not linger by the tongue, that gas does not shift in the gut, that a shadow passing on a bare calf or a raised arm does not recall at least the memory of desire for the most sedate — *that* will be our obeisance to death.

Down the slope Gorgik could just see the nearest village huts. He stood on slant rock, gazing away from the sun, with leaves combing the breeze to his right and a lapwing darting on his left. Mounded and raddled at the horizon, yellow clouds looked for the world like buildings and walls and avenues: narrow your eyes a little, and you couldn't tell if they were rock or lingering fog. Heat lay on one arm, like a warm palm. Shadow cooled the other where the moisture under his armor dried in the crevice between arm and flank, or beneath the brocade and hide that belted hip and belly. (Really, he was too old for boys like that!) How long he'd been away from people. Seeking a sign of the social, the civilized, the artifactual, he raised a hard hand to his neck, feeling for some decoration, mechanical, metal, consecrated to an elided function, so that, on such a man in such fine armor, another such ornament would have had almost no meaning.

But nothing was there.

After a while, he went back for his horse.

10

'*I* was in the castle!' In the yard the pig girl stood with the cat in her arms, looking down at the barefoot old woman squatting by her loom. 'Last night, after dark! Kitty went with me. I took a torch up. But you didn't really need it because of the moon. The bigger boys had left long logs in the receiving hall fireplace last winter. Back then, they were damp, and you could never get them going. But the wood must have dried out since, because when I went and put my fire to them, they flared right up, and . . . then I put my torch out and went up on the balcony . . .' Here she paused, stroking with one finger behind the cat's ear.

The old woman shifted the strings on her loom, thrust one shuttle of light-colored yarn halfway through, then pulled up another dark one to complete the row. 'And no one was there . . . nobody at all. Not even in the dead of the dark. Am I right?'

'I played that lords and ladies were walking and talking.' The pig girl stroked the cat's back. 'Lord Anuron . . . and the Lesser Lady Esulla — did they ever live at the castle?'

The old woman looked up for the first time that morning. 'No . . . those weren't the names of the lord and lady of *our* castle. There was no one there, was there . . .' It was not inflected like a question. But she frowned. 'Earlier, when I was coming out to start on my work, I saw a scraggly bearded barbarian boy sauntering down the path. Perhaps he'd stopped in the castle for the night. But there was no one else. You didn't see him, did you? I certainly haven't seen anyone but him who *could* have been up there. And *he* wasn't the one she was talking about yesterday, with all that fine horse and rich armor.'

'Oh, no!' The pig girl hugged the cat tighter. 'There was no one at all. There were lords and ladies, who wore beautiful dresses and wonderful cloaks. They held a contest, there in the great hall, and they made slaves fight against free men . . . and when the slaves won, they took the collars from their necks and gave them to them as prizes. Then they had a great celebration, with musicians and a beautiful pavilion out in the grounds, and a banquet with foods even finer than at our holiday meals!'

The old woman frowned harder at the girl.

This was a new story!

The pig girl rocked the cat:

'Then, in the middle of it, a dragon flew in and began to screech and hoot through the upper corridors, and made a great rattling along the columns; then I threw my torch down, because I'd already put it out anyway — and everyone was terrified and ran off. Only I sneaked back in, later, because it was dark and no one could see me . . .' In the morning sun, the girl and the woman blinked at each other. Birds chirruped from within the bushes across the path. With over-deep deliberation, the pig girl said: 'I don't *think* anyone was there . . . ?'

The old woman looked back at her work. 'I didn't think so either.'

Just then the tall woman walked into the yard. She had a dish of dried apricots and pears at one hip, its edge against her brown skirt. From the fingers of her other hand, she dangled an empty basket. 'Well,' she said, 'has the great man ridden by yet, to join his funeral? He's got to come right along here, if he wants to reach the north-south road. Even you would have to see him.'

'I haven't seen anyone,' the old woman said shortly. She looked down at her shuttles. 'I haven't seen anyone and I'm not going to. I told you there was no one up there. This girl here went up last night. She said it was empty, too.'

'Oh, now — ' The tall woman turned to look at the pig girl hugging the cat.

The pig girl concentrated very hard on the warm ridges behind the cat's ears and did not look at either woman. She wondered if the old woman would at least admit to the barbarian — though she didn't seem inclined to. The cat purred, moved its head, then twisted a little.

'Morning.'

The pig girl looked up.

'What are you three gossiping about at the start of a working day?' Laughing, the man came into the yard. He was thickset, not so tall as the tall woman, but quite as brown as the pig girl. For the last half dozen years, he'd been the tall woman's husband, though, in his way, he was related to all three — not that all three of them knew it. As a boy of nine, he'd lived at the old woman's house for more than a year (when she was not so old). He'd even taken to calling her mother awhile — though, today, neither of them mentioned that long-ago distant time. Thanks to his wilder years, over a decade back, there was a good chance he was the pig girl's father. But neither the pig girl nor the tall woman suspected that. And the pig girl's mother had been a sad, ignorant, gangling woman who'd died some years before. But many nights (in those wilder years) he'd spent out behind the shack in which the old woman, back then, lived, so that she, among the three, had her suspicions. Indeed, this heavy-armed, thick-thighed man had always had a penchant for women taller than he, which, when he'd been younger and thinner, had made him the brunt of much teasing by the other village boys. Since he had been married to the tall woman, however, by and large he'd lived the quieter and quieter life of a good and honest laborer. 'I just saw someone at the market, down from the Avila — ' he fingered one ear — 'who tells me the funeral procession's no more than an hour away.' Then he frowned. 'What's that you've got there?'

For the cat had just jumped down from the pig girl's arms to run across the grass.

'Yes,' said the tall woman, 'what *is* that nasty thing?' which was unusual, for mostly when her husband was about she was very quiet.

'I don't know.' The pig girl shrugged. 'It's nothing. I found it in the castle.' But there was no hiding it under the animal any longer.

'Give it here.' The man reached out a broad, workhardened hand for the collar. As he took it, the lock, which was broken, clicked. The iron semicircles swung apart on their hinge.

'See,' the pig girl said, 'it doesn't even work.'

'Where did you get this?' the man asked.

'I told you,' the pig girl said. 'I found it. When I was playing. Up at the castle.'

'There're none of these in the castle,' the man said.

With her full dish and her empty basket, the tall woman watched her husband.

The old woman finished another line and, with her stick, tamped the threads.

'We cleaned them out years ago.' The man frowned harder. 'A whole bunch of us went up there, when I was a boy. The ones who went up were men, of course and we — well, they — hunted out all these old things — the broken slave collars, the funny swords with double blades, the sacks of gaming balls no one knew where they'd come from, the astrolabes showing no recognizable stars. They — we — went through the whole place, from the basement dungeons to the littlest tower room; we looked all over the roof and around the foundation besides. We cleared out all of those things. We threw them away, too. We threw them *way* away, much too far for you to go finding them up there. Believe me, there shouldn't be any of them in the castle at all.'

'Well — ' the old woman did not look up from her loom — 'you could have missed one. And she found it. You, or they, could have overlooked one. It would have been very easy, back then, the way you all used to carry on.'

'No,' the man said firmly, 'we didn't overlook any. We got them all.' He looked seriously at the pig girl. 'Now you must leave these things — and all things like them — alone, young woman. They're dangerous; and they can get you into real trouble!'

'But it's broken,' the pig girl protested. 'It doesn't mean anything anymore — !'

'And it's all those strange things with no meaning that any meaning at all can rush in to fill.' The man lowered thick brows. 'You leave them alone, now.' He turned and, with a gesture of astonishing violence, hurled the collar in among the leaves on the other side of the path. Just then, a breeze chose to shake and rustle those and all the leaves around them.

It made the pig girl start.

'He's right,' the tall woman said, quietly. 'Those aren't things to play with, especially not for children. I know you've got work to do. So do we all. Now why don't you just run along and — '

The hooves' cloppings came to them down the path. The tall woman looked up. So did the man. Seconds later, a fine, high-stepping mare, with trappings of beaten brass and braided leather, came down the slope. The man astride her was no ordinary Imperial officer. His armor was more elaborate than any soldier that might pass through this part of Nevèryon. A packsack, in two halves, hung over the mare's haunches behind the saddle; and his cloak was embroidered like the richest of lords'. From within the helmet, the scarred face glanced at them as they stood in the yard.

With dazed excitement, the thick man and the tall woman raised the backs of their right fists to their foreheads, dropped their heads, and backed up three steps. It was very awkward for the woman, too, because she still had the dish of fruit on her hip and the empty basket hung from the hand she saluted with.

The old woman went on weaving.

The pig girl watched the rider on his horse, but she was thinking about the leaves across the road beyond. If she went in there (when *would* be the best time . . . ?), she might recover the collar. But the gesture? As she'd never been taught it, she did not make it now.

The great man rode down the path, which, three quarters of a mile on, would join the Royal Road.

'There, did you see . . . ?' The tall woman stepped back again. 'You see, I told you!' — for, once the horse had passed, her husband, with the excitement of a boy, had run a dozen steps after the rider: even that much distance between them let the tall woman become her other self.

'See what?' the old woman said.

'Oh, don't be — !' The tall woman turned so sharply she almost spilled pears and apricots.

But the old woman, busy with her shuttles, was smiling.

The tall woman began to laugh. 'That's the man I *told* you about — yesterday! The one who was at the castle. And now, just as I said, he's going to the funeral!'

'You hear those drums . . . ?' her husband called back. But it was only a boy's expectation. They'd not begun to sound.

The pig girl looked down to see a shuttle pulled from between the strings, ending another multicolored line.

'Well — ' the old woman reached for the tamping stick, still grinning, but at her work — 'no one is in the castle *now*.'

— New York
October 1985

The Tale of Rumor and Desire

. . . reflection is the structure and the process of an operation that, in addition to designating the action of a mirror reproducing an object, implies that mirror's mirroring itself, by which process the mirror is made to see itself. [But] Such a minimal definition, apart from the formal problems it poses, can hardly explain all the different theories or philosophies of reflection throughout the history of philosophy, although they may share a common optic metaphor predominant in the concept of reflection.   — RODOLPHE GASCHÉ, *The Tain of the Mirror*

Chronologically, in the greater Nevèrÿon series, 'The Tale of Rumor and Desire' comes after *Neverýona, or: The Tale of Signs and Cities* and before 'The Tale of Fog and Granite.'

0.1 on the tables the corpses lay out in the cool dark, scattered over with sweetened leaves, here and there a tripod *the lamp in the man's hand ahead spilled red light on the porter's barkish face. 'You've brought a friend with you, sir?' The glow pooled under the ceiling beams. Nodding, the man walked* the pool flowed

0.2 at the Bridge of Lost Desire, he

0.3 by the restaurant the tall poles either side the door *the red and blue hangings* the terrace near the pool under yellowing cloud

1. He had more good humor about him than most who might have followed him along such a path, often intricate in its individual turnings, wholly predictable in its grosser direction, would have expected.

It had not been a happy life.

In a village by low scrub, set among tangled ravines that flattened into desert, Clodon had spent a childhood in which he'd been mostly hungry or angry. Often he said (not that it was true) the only day he'd been really happy was the one, three years after his mother died, when he'd stolen the roast goat — and the rum cask and the leather purse in which there were nine iron coins someone had left on the stone bench — from the yard of the tax collector who'd just been appointed one of the Empress's customs inspectors. They'd caught him, with three of his friends, out by the sunken oasis under the sparse palms as the first stars pierced the evening like knife points through blue cloth. By then he and his friends were sick drunk. They took the coins back too: in the tiny town, there'd been nothing he could have spent them on anyway without revealing the theft.

His cousin, the bailiff, tied him up by his wrists to the metal ring at the corner of the grain storage building and left him standing — sometimes hanging — three nights. At dawn, he came back and, while a dozen dirty boys stood gawking, flogged Clodon six strokes with a knotted horsehide whip. The welts came out on his back and flanks like gutted garter snakes left to bleed. Then his cousin cut him down. Clodon fell on the blood speckled dirt, clamping his teeth in rage, pain, and exhaustion. The boys ran away then, leaving two girls, as young and as dirty, watching from a dozen feet further off.

Several times in the next week, while he walked slowly through the village, Clodon would start to cry — it always happened while some urchin stared. But what struck him at these moments, with the totality of its unfairness (Clodon was only a month beyond his sixteenth year), was that the reason he'd been flogged — and his friends let free — the reason the trial before the elders had gone so summarily, the reason his own excuses had been dismissed with an immediacy only a step away from a violation of village custom and law, was all the other things in town it was an open secret that he'd done, from his repeated near-rape of the half-witted hare-lipped girl who lived at the village edge with her aunt, no better than a prostitute and who was even now having his, or somebody's, baby, to a string of petty (and some not so petty) thefts, at least one of which he hadn't been responsible for at all.

Imrog the smith's apprentice had done that one but had said nothing when everyone in the village thought it was Clodon.

As well, there were various assaults on various youngsters — all infractions that, till then, he'd felt supremely smug about having gotten away with.

Clodon boasted to a few of his friends he was going to run away to the city, to Kolhari, to the capital port of Nevèrÿon, to the source of all advance and adventure, to the node from which all wondrous tales wound out to every village in the nation. His friends said it was a good idea. But no one wanted to come with him. That night, Clodon crawled from under the straw and the old leather robe he'd been sleeping in, blinked at a sliver of moon caught in cloud and branches, then started for the road. But he stopped at his cousin's first, stood outside the hut awhile, at last picked up a clod, and hurled it — hard — at the wall. Then he turned and ran.

For the highway.

Stupid! he thought. He will know it was me. He will know I've left! (Hours later Clodon sat by the road, while the sky went smoky copper beyond the birches. He wanted to cry, but he held it in with his teeth set and his eyes blinking.) And he will not care.

A week later Clodon was in Kolhari.

He did not like the city.

A cynical observer might say that, while the boy was always in some minor scrape — now fleeing an angry cart driver from whose wagon he'd snatched a cabbage to eat, later, raw, in an alley, now in a fight with another gamin over a piece of fruit fallen beside a market stall both had spotted at the same time — it was simply too hard, there in the city, for Clodon to get into serious trouble. The bailiffs and guards who patrolled Kolhari's squares and alleys were too concerned with crimes that grew out of planning as well as hunger, of felonies that came from intricate connivance as well as mute anger before a system in which a few had so much while so many had nothing. They simply could not bother with what was, after all, the largely unpremeditated mischief of a boy. Soon Clodon was anxious to get back to a place where people paid some attention to him when he fell down drunk in the street or went yowling through the night, flinging broken pottery at window shutters edged with lamplight.

A more careful observer, however, might tell a tale such as ours.

Clodon left after three months, catching a ride with a market driver to an outlying village, where things were on a more familiar scale and life's intricacies were easier to negotiate: people were more trusting, doors were less likely to be barred, folk were less wary about mine and thine, and more inclined to leave both lying about unguarded. Clodon was able to make his way a little better there than he had in the port — not that he stayed at the town long, either.

It says something about his time at Kolhari, however, that a few years later Clodon had convinced himself his three months in the city had been nearly a full twelve. And sometimes, if the anecdote he was telling to this village simpleton or that town drunk or some other local ne'er-do-well warranted it, he'd refer to his 'years' in the great port, back when he was young.

But the flogging and the flight to the capital were more than twenty years past. For the last five weeks, Clodon had been staying in a village called Narnis over fifty miles from the one he'd been born at. Lush pines grew to the west, and an hour's walk up the crumbling rocks beyond the cypresses a waterfall crashed down a stony gorge.

Once Clodon had been a lean-hipped youth. Now he was a ponderous man with a permanent thirst and a bad stomach.

2. And Clodon was dreaming (*pole, pool, bridge* . . .), cloud, metal, water, or . . . *something* into which he peered, squinting, at an unclear figure. *A black tendril raddled and resolved into rising thread above the lamp flame.* He turned: straw stuck his shoulder. There were flies under the lean-to's edge. In his sleep he kept trying to see . . .

He opened his eyes in the heat, moving his head back and forth in straw. Sunlight made little knife cuts in the thatching over him.

3. Because of the dream, Clodon was not sure where he was. The dream, you see, had not been vivid with voices and colors, with faces and passions, with actions and artifacts you could haul back through sleep's black currents into wakeful sun, then to ponder them like a full story, smiling over its absurdities, wondering at its glories, now and again this part or that falling away as you recognized what had been loaned it by past adventure or future hope. Rather it had been a gray, lazy, hazy froth of recall and fancy just under the film of consciousness, so that waking was like that thinnest of surface's parting, at which drowsing and waking merged. For moments Clodon could not tell if the straw under his neck and the light through the chinks and the smell of the thatching were distortions of the dream's limpid foam, or if the drift and shift in gray had merely been an extension of this clarity. The confusion was very similar to a feeling he'd had several mornings about this village in which he'd been only five weeks and the town in which he'd been born and lived sixteen years: save one was at the desert's edge and one was in the mountains, both, in so many ways, were so much alike, it was easier sometimes to think the two sets of hide hovels, thatched shacks, with the stone buildings down by the highway end (in one of which lived *another* customs inspector) were really one, so that the questioning in his mind, whose banal expression was, 'Where *am* I . . . ?' came from an awareness that though this was, indeed, not the town of his birth, for seconds he could not remember why.

4. 'Hey — ' Something tickled Clodon's side and something chattered on wood. 'Wake up, old bandit!'

'Why are you . . . ? Who do . . . ?' Clodon shifted; gas shifted inside him. So he let it out. 'That's for you, Funig.'

Outside, Funig laughed — '*Hey* — !' and threw more gravel. 'Wake up, old man! You want to work today?'

Clodon sat up, scrubbing his forehead with the heel of his hand. 'I want to get some money.' He brushed at his belly and flank, where the hard welts felt as familiar as your finger held in your fist. (Clodon was missing a finger now. It had gone ten years ago in a job as a quarryman.) 'But I don't want to work for it — unless I have to. Does Teren want me to head his digging crew and foreman them through that foundation?' He pushed himself up to a squat with burning bladder, then crawled from under the lean-to thatch, standing and narrowing his eyes against bright overcast. 'Was I drunk again last night, Funig — no, more's the pity. I wasn't! Sometimes, boy, it's easier to wake up the morning after a drunk than it is from unassisted sleep. Your eyes open early, and though you shake a little, you're still alert and have your mind about you.'

'A drunk?' Funig was tall and hard. 'The last time you were drunk, you didn't get up out of your own piss and vomit for two days! You're a pig, old man.'

'And what are you?' Clodon snuffled, then spat.

But Funig's shoulders were not the same size. Half of Funig's face was flattened; one of Funig's eyes never looked at anything. And without really limping Funig always lurched to one side and favored one arm. Sometimes he said it hurt him.

'If you get drunk again,' Funig said, who wasn't sure if he were nineteen, twenty, or twenty-one, '*I* won't come to wake you any more. You're dirty when you're drunk. At least I go in my shack and sleep till I'm better.'

'An honest laborer can always get up after an honest drunk. That's as true in Narnis as it is in any other town.' Clodon went over to the oak to pee. 'How did I get this fat, Funig? You know, I was once as lean a boy as you.'

'What's honest about you, you old thief?'

Clodon's water hit the bark, dribbled to the dirt, to separate in dusty worms that crawled beside the roots to run away between his bare feet. Clodon scratched his side. Besides those from his flogging at sixteen, another half dozen welts had been laid on top of them not eight years back, when he'd been caught again near Sarness for banditry. Why he hadn't been sentenced to death, he'd never been sure, for in working the back roads with a mule wagon and a dozen knives, clubs, and swords hidden beneath the tooled leather cart cover, he'd killed a handful of men — and at least three women. But the Sarness trial had been as ludicrous as the one back in his own village. Again, he'd been taken drunk; again he'd been too sick through it to say anything or be sure excatly what was going on. Only this time, it seemed, the elders thought he'd done much less than he had, rather than much more — which was why he'd gotten off with *only* a flogging: the second in his life. There were a dozen welts on him now.

But he had half a dozen other scars today — one through his lower lip and one across an eyebrow — he never thought about.

Five weeks ago, when he'd come here to this mountain town, looking for the local outcast or the imbecile who might befriend him, he'd found Funig in the first afternoon. Drinking with Funig out behind the refuse dump, in the moonlight, he'd told the boy the story of those more timely scars, in a grave voice, interspersed with many wise nods and much shaking of his forefinger and somber warnings to keep free of real crime: such welts or worse were *always* the result.

Now how could a man who gave you such advice be *truly* bad?

And hadn't Teren himself, when, next morning, Funig and Clodon had gone to hire on at the work site, rubbed his beard with his thumb and said: 'Flogging marks on a man only mean he once took out a debt he's paid back since. Work hard, Clodon, and they won't stand against you here.' Clodon had heard it before and knew how far it went. Still, the boy was impressed. Born in the town, and living there all his life, Funig had already amassed a sizable reputation on his own as a village drunk and ne'er-do-well. But he'd managed to avoid being whipped. In the weeks since Clodon had come, though, Funig had been Clodon's accomplice in a handful of thefts Narnis seemed able to absorb. Half of them had been the sort Funig might well have done by himself — though he'd probably have spaced them more widely. But a few had made the boy sniff and blink and swallow at their daring. Once they were done, of course, Funig was all grins and delight and slapping his thigh, ready to run boast to everyone.

'The best thing to do once you've done something like that is put it out of mind, Funig. You forget it; they'll forget it.'

Such advice was useless, though. The boy would rather glory in his misdemeanors: he had too many of his own resentments against the town. (Clodon stood before the oak, shaking his head.) Funig just wasn't sharp enough — and Clodon knew it — to do much more than beg. But since Clodon had told him the story of his unexplained good luck at Sarness, now Funig saw only the welts that lay there for high banditry. It was true irony: while Clodon might have used them to make a rum-sodden point to a rum-sodden fool, he himself spent far more time dwelling on the original indignities committed against him when he was a boy than he did on that second flogging. As for the rest? Well, forget it!

Clodon shook himself free of water.

Maybe it *was* time to quit this village sumphole, leave Narnis, and return to that more profitable — if more dangerous — life.

'Come on. Let's go down and see if Teren can use us to dig with the foundation crew,' Funig said. 'Last night when he came by the tavern, he said he could use as many men to help as would show up sober in the morning. We should hurry. He said he was going off early and he wasn't going to wait around.'

'You mean he's gone already? Why did you come and wake me then — ?'

'Oh, no! He'll still be in the yard there — '

'And if he is, he'll just say, "Why are you wasting your time with Clodon? You're a fool, Funig, but you're an honest fool. Clodon's a bad man. All he can do is get you in trouble; the only thing anyone in this town is waiting for him to do is to leave it." ' For since the initial homily about debts paid, Teren had said that too — as soon as Clodon and Funig had come back drunk and an hour late from the second mid-day break.

'And I'll tell him I can be friends with who I want!'

Clodon and Funig started across the worn grass beside the three old huts that had been abandoned up here and filled with so much junk you couldn't even crawl in to use whatever shelter the half-fallen roofs might give.

'That's *just* what I'll say to him!' Funig's lurch took his head away and back, away and back. They turned beside the bark fence, beyond which stood the first inhabited shacks. 'See if I don't. Haven't I told him before? Teren has money: and he's building his big, new, stone house — '

' — you mean the likes of *us* are building it for him!'

' — but he doesn't have the right to tell me who I can talk to and who I can't. And he'd be surprised how honest I am, wouldn't he?' Funig's grin swung at Clodon and away. 'We could tell him a thing or two!'

'You probably already have.' But Clodon grinned back. 'You are a fool to hang out with me, you know?'

'You think you're the first to say it?' Still grinning, still lurching, Funig shrugged. 'Then, I'm a fool.'

'And I'm hungry.'

They passed under a tree bough that threw its shadow on the dust. 'Pull me down an apple. You're tall enough for that.'

Funig stopped, reached up among the green arrow heads that were the leaves, jumped — and came down with the fruit in his hand: the irregular globe was mottled red, a third of it green. 'Here, old pig.' He made a gesture to toss it, laughed again, then handed it to Clodon.

Who snatched it away with a *humph*. 'You *are* a fool, boy. Just like everyone says. What would you do if you had no one to tell you how to do things?'

'I'd do all right.' Funig looked up again among the overhead green, started to reach again, to jump — but thought better. He looked at Clodon's apple, for all the world as if he might ask for it back.

'Ha!' Clodon bit into the sour-sweet flesh.

They turned down between the houses. 'Even if Teren's already gone off, maybe I can get something to eat from Jara.' Jara was Funig's fat, sullen half-sister, who worked at the tavern.

'You mean you *know* you woke me for nothing? If we *don't* work today, boy, I'm going to *whip* you — ' On *whip* Clodon swung out to smack the back of Funig's ill-shaped head.

But Funig lurched away. 'We can get some food — ' he protested.

'*You* can get some.' Clodon took another bite. 'Jara's not going to give *me* anything.' For the first week Clodon had shown up with Funig at the tavern's back door, Jara had been ready enough to sneak them a tray of this or a bowl of that. But now, when they came together, she'd curtly say there was nothing left and rush back in.

'But she'll give it to *me*,' Funig said. 'Then we can share it. Once it's in my hands, it's mine. She can't say who I can share my own food with now, can she?'

'You're always saying now that one can't make you do this, and this one can't say that to you. But they do, don't they, boy.' He let more rumbling gas.

It may have been too much for Funig to reason out. So, like most that was beyond him, he ignored it. 'You know,' Funig said, 'Last night at the tavern, after you'd gone — ' (Clodon had been put out, actually, in an argument with the owner, Krator — which was why he'd gone to sleep sober; since Teren, fond of beer himself, in an expansive mood, and less and less eager as his new house went on to return to his old thatched cottage, had been buying drink for his workers) ' — a man came in, from Minogra. He was with an actress. She says she works with a mummers troupe. But she's not with them now.'

'Minogra, was it?' Clodon had been at the cliffside village just before he'd come to Narnis. Like so much else in his life, Minogra was something he didn't like to think about. (Certainly it was easier to dwell on the indignities of twenty-two years ago than on what had happened at Minogra!) But Funig was going on:

'He was talking in the tavern about that man — the one they call Gorgik the Liberator, the one who's fighting to free the slaves, all over Nevèrÿon . . . ?'

'And what did they say?'

'Mostly the same things they always do. They say he led a raid on some slave pens to the east. They say someone saw him with a band of freed followers in the west. Dimit said he was a great man for it, and Puron stuttered out that he was only a t-t-t-trouble maker and should be p-p-p-put down or l-l-l-locked up!' Funig laughed: there were not that many folk in the village he could make fun of. Then a memory came: 'The man from Minogra said the Liberator fights alongside a barbarian, and the two of them have been all over the country, freeing slaves together.'

'Lazy, dirty sorts, barbarians. I'm glad we don't have any around here — though I knew some when I lived in Kolhari. Oh, a few of them could be just as nice as you or me. They're the ones who *are* the slaves — at least in the south. Well, we have no slaves here, thank the nameless gods. So we don't need any Liberator. It's just tavern talk.'

'*Mmm,*' Funig said. 'If they did have slaves, it would be my luck to be one. You know what else I heard?'

Clodon took another bite of apple. 'What?'

'They said he wears an iron slave collar himself — even though he's not a slave, now. He won't take it off till he's finished his task.'

Clodon laughed. 'Oh, he won't, won't he — a slave collar?' He shook his head. 'So *that's* the sort he is! I met a few of that kind, too, when I was in the city.' He snorted. 'Well, I suppose a man can be that and be a Liberator too. Though it makes you wonder.'

'What do you mean?' Funig asked. 'Be what? What kind?'

'No, you'd have to have lived a year or so in a big city like Kolhari to know what I'm talking about.' Clodon chuckled. 'They don't have ones like that out here — at least not out where you can *see* them!'

'One what?' Funig asked.

'Like . . . well, in Kolhari there used to be this bridge, and on it — no, it's too complicated. You be happy you're a fool, Funig.'

'He's a brave man, this Gorgik, this Liberator. And a great one. Everybody talks about him, all the time. At the tavern, anyone who has a story about him can always get people to listen. Even in Narnis. I bet a lot of the stories are just made up, too. About him and his barbarian. They go about freeing slaves, punishing slave owners, righting wrongs, doing what they want. It's almost like being a bandit, out in the land . . . and doing what you want? You can do that in the city. Or you can do that on the road.' Funig shook his ungainly head. 'But you can't do your shit in a town like this, without someone coming along to tell you to get back and wipe it up. It must be a fine life, don't you think?'

'I think it's stupid and crazy.'

'We could do something like that — leave Narnis and go out and live off what we could get on the road . . . like you said you used to?'

'Ha!' Clodon said. 'And will again — but not with a fool like you. Don't take on about it, boy. I'm doing you a favor.' Snorting another laugh, Clodon finished the apple and held the core in his big fist, wet and crumbling. 'You wouldn't last a month outside of town. You need a few brains for that, and brains is not your strong point. Better honest work — at least for the likes of you. Probably me too, at least awhile. Where were the men to meet Teren? *We'll* show him how to dig his cursed foundation!

When they got to the tavern and went into the yard, of course Teren and the others had left for work site an hour ago, Krator told them — then tossed a bucket of slop to the side so that it splattered over their feet. Funig protested: 'Hey, now, you don't have to — '

'Go on up to the site,' Krator said. 'You know where it is.' He reached back in the door, pulled out another bucket and tossed it.

Funig danced away from the splatter. 'You mean he's gone already — ?' he said for the third time.

So Clodon sucked his teeth and cursed and shook his fist and called Funig every kind of fool for waking him.

'Well, if you go on up to the site,' Krator repeated, preparing to take the buckets in, 'maybe he'll put you to work when you get there. And maybe,' he added, 'he'll say that if you're too lazy to show up with the others, then you must not need the pay.' With an impatient breath, Krator ducked back beyond the leather flap that was the doorway. A moment later he called out, 'And Funig, don't you go in the back bothering Jara. She's busy now.'

'Funig,' Clodon went on, 'you get me up and down here all for nothing! What do you call that? You've got a rock between your ears! Why'd you wait so long to get me — ?'

While Funig was saying, 'Well, if he can't wait for us, we've got other things we can do, don't we, Clodon? Don't we?'

'You're a fool, Funig!'

From inside Krator called: *Why* don't the two of you just go on up — '

Which is when Clodon saw the actress.

She came to the window in the tavern's sandy wall, and her skin was the color of a dark pear and her irises were startlingly black between two little almonds of ivory each. And the skin around them was darker. She smiled out on the inn yard like someone enchanted with the morning, who found this altercation between the village men intriguing and amusing and delightful and earthy; and the movement with which she stepped, in a moment, over in the window, with its shutters back for morning, was as graceful as any branch rising before a winter sun. She leaned an arm on the sill with her hand just visible, looking straight at him. Her fingertips ended in clean, cared-for nails. And, when Clodon stared back, her smile fragmented into laughter, and he found himself not speaking while his own stare became a smile. He nodded tentatively to her, feeling awkward about being a fat, loud, dirty man, with slop on his feet and an apple core in his fist, but smiling more broadly for it, because he also felt, looking at her looking at him —

5. At sixteen, when Clodon ran away to Kolhari, he'd lived as best he could on the city's crowded streets, loitering around the edge of the market, sleeping in this alley, or under that set of stairs, ambling across the bridge, or seeking out some neighborhood festival, where, with the music and the laughing and the drink and the food, it was almost possible to feel a part of the street life around him. He moved through the city, a lean youth, with a suspicious, or sometimes simply a stunned, expression, bearing the marks on his back and flanks of his provincial crimes.

Within days of arriving, he discovered how to make a few coins on the Bridge of Lost Desire; but taking money from men who wanted to do what, a few times back in his village, he and his friends had forced the weakest and most cowardly boy among them to do only for degradation and humiliation's sake seemed a slippage in values that was simply too uncomfortable. So while he spent a good deal of time in that most nefarious of neighborhoods in the city, he did not patrol the bridge's walkways to search out money, food, or shelter with friendly glances to all who passed as frequently as some others. He didn't relish begging, but the lies he often told to get a coin or a meal from this or that reluctant benefactor he could enjoy, especially when they worked.

Once a barbarian, about his own age and living on the street as he was, told him: 'Go down to the alley behind the market, to the second warehouse there. A grain merchant's always standing about in the yard: he's looking for smugglers to drive carts of illegal goods into the south. Bet he'll give you a job.'

'Why don't *you* go?' Clodon asked.

The barbarian ran a hand through his bronze hair and grinned over a gap in his teeth. 'I'm the wrong color. He doesn't want fellows who look like me. He wants respectable looking drivers. You'll get the job — if you wash and wear a shirt.'

Clodon did neither. But he did stroll down to look for the merchant. He found him, standing in the second warehouse's yard and talking to a secretary. The merchant wore lots of leather and frayed fabric laced up tight around his neck, so that sweat beads stood out across his dark forehead under whitening hair. The secretary left, but Clodon still lingered at the building's corner, wondering what he would say. Finally, he walked up, stopped in front of the man, and said: 'Hey. You're looking for drivers to take carts into the south? I can do that. I don't mind smuggling, either.'

The merchant looked at him with a bemused expression. The silence between them grew uncomfortable. Finally Clodon wondered if he should just grunt some curse, spit on the ground, turn, and walk off. (Perhaps this was the wrong merchant . . . ?) But even that seemed awkward now.

Then the man said: 'I can't hire you.'

'Why not?' Clodon rubbed his thigh with a knuckle. A rash had started there that itched him, though you couldn't see anything unless you looked closely at it in full sunlight. 'I can handle mules. I've worked with oxen,' both of which happened to be true. 'Which do you want me to — '

'There.' The merchant pointed to Clodon's side. 'There — you see?'

Clodon looked down, where the welts crawled around his flank. They made him uncomfortable and he chewed over another curse.

But the merchant said: 'You've already gotten yourself in trouble in whatever huddle of hovels you hail from — so I can't take you on. Oh, you don't have to tell me. It was an unfair trial. No one paid attention to your side of the story when it was presented to the elders. They'd had it in for you a year before they caught you and had you whipped. That's why you've come to Kolhari, where an honest laborer has a chance. I've heard it before. But I still can't use you. Not for this job. I can't have a man driving for me who brings attention to himself every time the clouds clear and the sunlight falls on his back.'

Clodon remembered what the barbarian had said about the shirt.

'You look like a good country lad — the kind I'd need,' the grain merchant went on — 'if it were another sort of job. Oh, someday, in six months or so, if you're still around, and I have some honest carts to send out — and sometimes I do — I might consider taking you. For *that* sort of work, it wouldn't matter, you see? But — ' He shrugged — 'now I have things I must get to.' Two loutish young men had come up to linger by the building's corner, impatient for Clodon to go.

'Oh.' Clodon nodded. 'Yeah. I see.' And without even a curse, he turned and walked back to the bridge.

Hoisting himself up to sit on the wall beside the walkway, heels against the stone, shoulders forward, elbows on his knees, Clodon watched the women lounging or strolling across from him, while fruit carts and men with baskets of fabric held by straps to their foreheads and a boy dragging a sledge on which were roped a dozen musical instruments went to or from the market. His scars, he now knew, marked him as someone no better than a slave — or a barbarian.

At which point the barbarian who'd told him about the grain merchant sauntered by on the far side, sucking on a drinking skin bloated with beer.

Clodon looked away, because he did not want to ask for any, though certainly he wanted some.

Then the man who'd slowed to a stop beside him said: 'You're looking glum.'

Clodon frowned back. 'Why should I be?'

In his thirties, the man wore a green tunic, belted at the waist with metal, which probably meant he was well off. 'You'd know that better than I. What are you looking for anyway, out here on the bridge?' The man wore sandals and a metal band on one wrist.

'To make some money.' Maybe, Clodon thought, I might be able to go with him and snag his purse, before — or, if necessary, after — we get down to anything.

'I wouldn't think you'd have much trouble doing that, unless you're particularly squeamish about how you make it.'

Well, Clodon was; and he knew it. But he said, 'Ha!' Did the man, he asked, want to go somewhere and have sex?

'No. At least not now. Maybe another time — '

Clodon grunted and looked away. 'People tell me that a lot.'

The man laughed. 'I was looking for conversation, actually. There's a place not far from here we might get a drink. If you come in with me, I don't think your flogging marks will make any problems.' (Clodon started to say something. But then, he was not sure what there was to say in such a situation. And the man seemed friendly.) 'I'll buy you a drink. Even two or three.'

'What about something to eat?'

'That too, if you're hungry.'

'And you don't want to do anything?'

'I've answered that once,' the man said. 'I bought an evening of sex here with a man last week — usually I'm not interested in boys, except in highly marked circumstances. I may buy another in three or four days. But not this afternoon. What a lot of questions you have for someone sitting out on the bridge. But *I'd* rather do the asking and listening. Will you be my guest, or not?'

'I'll come with you,' Clodon said. 'Sure. You just want to talk? I'll come!' He jumped from the wall.

Clodon had been in Kolhari long enough to learn that to walk in it with a new acquaintance was to turn down streets he'd never seen before, to enter neighborhoods he had not known existed, to discover whole new cities enfolded within and around the one in which, till then, he'd been living. It had already happened with the barbarian: he'd assumed their destination was some dirty, tolerant shack where they could get a mug of beer and a bowl of cinnamon-rich stew or a piece of over-hot sausage. But soon they were walking down streets with fine carriages and buildings with yards and trees. Finally, they turned in at a place with carved poles either side the door.

The antechamber was hung with scarlet and azure tapestries shot through with metallic threads. A man dressed like a nobleman, but who was some sort of waiter, led them into a hall with intricately carved columns, where many men and a few women ate and drank at small tables with little lamps burning on them — though it was the middle of the day. They were taken outside onto an open terrace, with several other tables and great pots of flowers and plants sitting beside a pool with fountains in it and rough statues of beasts half in and half out of the ripples. When they were seated, the man gave his order, the waiter nodded, then, with a sweep of his arm, pulled a cloth divider, hissing on its rings along the wooden pole overhead, to separate them from the others. 'Now you'll have your privacy.' He bowed, backing between the folds of green and blue; and all Clodon could see were yellowing clouds and their ivory reflections between floating froth.

A minute later another waiter stepped through with one pitcher of beer and another of cider, which he placed, dripping, on the table. A moment on, he was back with an earthenware bowl of sausages, fruits, and breads — which the man explained to Clodon was not part of the promised meal but just something the establishment put out with the drink.

Clodon should help himself.

He tried the cider but didn't like it. Beer, however, was what he'd been hoping for. With a sausage and piece of bread in one hand, his mug in the other, and his mouth full, Clodon said: 'The curtain . . . ?' He twisted around in his seat, still chewing, to nod at the hanging drawn behind. 'That's so . . .' He swallowed and began again. 'That's so the others won't see my — flogging marks, isn't it?' In the month he'd borne them, it was the first time Clodon had put a word to his scars.

The man raised his mug and an eyebrow. 'So many questions you've got. Well, consider this. You come in here, wearing only a rag of leather about your loins and the signs of a country felon on your back. Most of the clientele you see here arrives in tunics, robes, and capes. Perhaps you never asked yourself why. But if, by some whim of the nameless god of count and accounting, all were suddenly struck naked here, you might be surprised who among us was marked and who was not — not to mention the nature of the marks we bear.' He leaned forward. 'And I'm sure you're already aware that the biggest criminals are specifically marked by the fact that they have no marks at all!'

Trying to picture the people at the tables beyond the curtain carrying scars like his beneath their cloaks, Clodon grinned. 'Come on — that's just a story!' He wasn't sure if it was the flippant voice the man had said it in or if it was what, indeed, he'd said. But it pleased him.

'It may be. But it has its truth. And I'm sure it's a story you like. Come. Drink first; eat later. Otherwise you won't enjoy the beer anywhere near as much as you might — surely you're old enough to know *that*. Tell me, how did you get yours — the welts, I mean?'

By the bottom of another mug, Clodon was telling him, now of the goat, now of the rum (but not about the coins, for he still had a yen for the man's purse, should the opportunity come), now of the hare-lipped girl, now about his cousin the bailiff and the gawking urchins. Somehow, with enough drink, the urge to eat left. And when, three long and lazy pitchers later, the man finally paid for their fare, Clodon, stretching, yawning, missed it because he was looking from the red

clouds smearing the west to the blue over the buildings in the east —
so that he *still* wasn't sure where about him the man kept his money.

Clodon saw only a final coin — iron or gold, he wasn't sure —
pressed from the stranger's hand into the waiter's.

'Would you like to come to my place?' The man walked leisurely
from the pool's edge. Inside, the eating hall was almost empty. 'In
summer the sun stays late and fools you as to the time. It'll be dark in
a bit. I can certainly give you a more comfortable place to sleep than
you'll have down against the stones under the bridge.'

'If you want to *do* anything — ' Walking out, Clodon spoke too
loudly, searching for the belligerence he was sure he must feel at the
renewed prospect of unwanted intimacy, though its absence seemed
to be the most annoying thing about the situation — 'you still have
to give me some money. I mean, I'm not one of those you can get just
for a meal and a drink. I don't *like* that stuff. So you have to make it
worth — '

'Well, we're going to try and find some things you *do* like.' With a
hand on Clodon's shoulder, the man moved him between the poles
and into the street, laughing loudly — to cover the bumptious remarks. Outside, breathing a little heavily, he dropped his arm. 'I live
with my family, my mother and my sister — and my father. Also,
there are servants, the guards, and the porters downstairs. If I wanted
to "do" anything with you, I would not ask you to my home. I may
give you a few coins when you leave in the morning — possibly even
something more valuable. But I'm speaking of your comfort. If you
want to go back to the bridge and sleep in some alley on hard paving,
it's fine with me.' (The man, Clodon realized, was also drunk.) 'But if
you want a cushion to curl up on for the night — by yourself, believe
me — come. Understand, though: nothing obliges you to accept my
hospitality now any more than it already has.'

Somehow, between the moments when they'd gotten up from the
table on the terrace and now, as they stood, a bit unsteadily, on the
street, the sky between the buildings had slipped into indigo.

'You got anything to drink at your place?' Clodon's state was pleasant. It would be nice to maintain it.

'Of a much better quality than they do back there.' The man
nodded over his shoulder toward the place they'd left.

'Let's go then!' Clodon started up the street, till laughter made him
turn.

'This way.' The man started down the street.

At once lost and in a fine humor, Clodon ran back to catch up.

The trip from the bridge to the eating hall had been a leap to a level of luxury that, till then, Clodon had only suspected existed. And he was quite prepared for the trip from the hall to the man's house to be a similar leap. A few streets over, though, he wondered whether it was the drink — or just the darkness settling around them — that made the houses here, which were certainly large enough, look more shabby and the streets appear in worse repair than the ones they'd just been walking. The building the man finally nodded toward ('There, just ahead — '), while it took up most of the block, was, if anything, a twin of the warehouse before which, earlier that day, he'd spoken to the merchant.

Jamb and lintel were heavy beams set in yellowish stone — gone gray-blue in evening. 'My family has its business on the ground floor,' the man responded to Clodon's questioning glance. 'We live upstairs. This is the back entrance, of course. But that's how I always come in. It's nothing to do with you personally.' He pushed aside the leather hanging. Clodon ducked after him into a wooden vestibule where several lamps, two burning and three out, stood on a stained wooden shelf. 'It's not what anyone could call fashionable. But the living apartments are spacious. Mother has fixed them up quite comfortably.' On the wall, in red lamplight, set in a ceramic plaque, were three skulls. Disoriented as much by the small space as by the bony grins, Clodon backed into leather. 'This way.' The man removed a plank from the wall to reveal a black slab. He leaned the board aside and picked up a lighted lamp. 'We go down six steps.' The man walked through.

Clodon wondered if he should go forward or escape into the street.

'Come.' From the dark, the man glanced back. 'You're not afraid, are you?'

'What *is* this place?' Clodon stepped into black — and almost fell, unready for the stairs.

'Watch it.' The man glanced again. 'We have a mortuary here. A very successful one, too. It's been in the family since before I was born.'

'You mean for *dead* people?' Clodon steadied himself on the tuniced shoulder a step below — which went down another step. So Clodon did too.

'Oh, it's very *much* for the living.' The man chuckled.

The echo made the space sound vast.

Since he could see nothing ahead and down save the light over the man's arm and the glow edging his ear, Clodon looked up. The ceiling beams were not the rough irregular ones of the warehouses around the market. They crossed back and forth at even intervals. As the man descended and the red light lowered, Clodon could see painted tiles between.

'I keep threatening father to quit and get into something like import-export; or maybe real estate. But then another year goes by, and I'm still here, saying consoling things to stony lipped widows or patting the arms of blubbering uncles. I wish it wasn't so profitable. It would be easier to leave.'

As they reached the steps' bottom, the odor that had been bothering him since they'd passed the hanging finally pierced fully through Clodon's drunkenness. It was incredibly sweet, and rich, and spicy. It cloyed like too many cloves and fruits, crushed for their essence and spread about too thickly. At the same time, something sour and sharp as vinegar cut through: an intensely unpleasant smell had been masked with this most pungent and insistent scent.

A dozen feet off, blue flame rushed about the surface of a shoulder-high tripod. Some unimaginable distance away in the dark, a second blue flicker must have been another. Clodon could see, around him, what looked like mounds on tables. 'They're dead people in here?' Clodon asked. 'With *us?*'

'Some dead,' the man said, a step ahead. 'Some very much alive.'

At which point a shadow moved toward them from the man's right. Stepping into the red glow, it became a porter, with a gnarled face and a loose cloak around broadly sloped shoulders. The lamp spilled red light on the porter's barkish features. 'Oh, it's you, then.' The voice was hoarse. 'That's good. You've brought a friend with you, sir?' Above Clodon, the lamp's light pooled under the ceiling beams.

The man nodded. 'We'll be going upstairs in a moment to say hello to Mother.'

The man started forward. Clodon hurried with him. Overhead, the pool flowed. Shadow pulled across the porter.

'You'll pardon me for a moment.' They were passing a table. 'Hold this for me, will you?'

Clodon took the clay lamp, warm in the cool — no cold — dark. Flame wavered at the snout.

It looked as if it were covered with a heap of leaves and berries. But the man brushed some aside. There was a cloth beneath: he lifted it and laid it back.

For moments, even with all he knew of the place, Clodon thought the woman, with her elaborately coifed hair and gaudy necklace above and below dark lips and sunken eyes, was sleeping. When he remembered she wasn't, he almost dropped the light. As the red flame waved and wobbled, he tried to tell himself that her jaws were not clenching and clenching below her cheeks, that her eyes were not rolling and rolling under their lids, that her chest was not rising and catching between flat, wrinkled breasts. It was only shaking shadow from his shaking hand —

'Here . . .' The man glanced up. 'I'll take that.' With the lamp, he turned to call into the flame-speckled black: 'Yes, she looks much better now. This will do fine!'

They moved to another table.

That, Clodon thought, couldn't possibly be a person: it was too *big*. But when the man brushed the leaves away and turned back the cloth, Clodon looked down at a bloated, black face, with some sort of metal band across the forehead. Drool wet the chin. Under the shroud the chest swelled toward the barrel belly.

'There's not really anything we can do with this sort.' The man raised his voice to call into the dark: 'He *must* be out of here by sun-up tomorrow. Not ten minutes after!' Turning back, he shook his head. 'Even with what we do, the fat ones go off much too fast. We just can't let them stay around a moment more than necessary.'

Under the assault of the stench, the echoes, and the drink, Clodon saw movement now on all the tables. Shadows shifted and drifted between . . .

'This way.' Again the man guided Clodon by the shoulder. 'No, through here. We can go upstairs now. It astonishes me how much the business has grown, just in my lifetime. When father was your age, he was an apprentice to a man who embalmed only for the court and the nobles. Well, when his master passed away, he was sure that was the end of *his* career! Anyone else who died in this city back then was simply carted off to the potter's field up at the end of Netmenders' Row. But some of the merchant families out in Sallese decided they could use the services of a respectable gentleman — even if he had no title — who'd worked at court and knew the embalming craft.' Clodon's bare feet crushed fallen leaves. (The man's stylish sandals made a wholly different sound.) 'Well, nowadays there're even barbarians who wouldn't think of dying unless we're to be called in to eviscerate the body, pack it with drying salts, tanning ash, and sprinkle it over with herbal aromatics.'

The smell nauseated. And *this* shadow before them was another man — a big one, too. Was that a weapon at his side? The guard moved away first one plank, then another for them. At the top of the dim steps Clodon could see light . . .

'Up you go.' The man in the tunic gestured with the lamp. 'Steady there. You'll feel better when you get out of these vapors. Till you're used to them, they can get to you.'

Clodon started, one hand on the wall.

Behind, the man said: 'As you see — ' Their shadows wove ahead on the stair — 'we have any number of people here to protect us. Some are living. Some are dead. But all of them are very efficient at their jobs — in case you had any notion of misbehaving.'

Clodon looked back. 'I wasn't going to do anything.'

The man grimaced demonically. 'I didn't for a moment think you were.' The red light underlit his dark brown face.

Maybe, Clodon thought, I should wait about the purse.

At least until I feel better.

Then the leather thongs with their colored beads dragged around him.

They stepped together into an upper room.

The air was certainly fresher here — though there was still a hint of both the sour and the sweet.

'How many corpses you *got* down there?' The chamber looked like one Clodon had glimpsed through the shutters of the tax collector's window at home. There was a chest, a table, some chairs. Statues stood on pedestals in the corners. Unfamiliar implements hung on the walls. The jambs beside the arched doors were carved plaster. Heavy moldings ran around the ceilings. Rugs lay over the red tiles. An oil lamp hung in the room's center, a dozen yellow flames playing in various cups.

'Quite enough for anything anyone could want to do with them.'

Certaily there'd been more than a dozen tables down in the dark . . . ?

The man put the lamp, still burning, on a lacquered shelf and led Clodon through another door.

The light, outside, was silvery and unreal — moonlight! Clodon looked up to see there was no roof. He looked back down. On either side of the tiled path, shrubs and ivy were thick, just as though the dirt went down directly to the true earth, without the crypt between.

And there was a pool

It was smaller than the one in the eating hall, but a pool nevertheless. They were in an open air garden or inner roof court. Half a moon hung to the east, putting silver on a quarter of the water and throwing the shadows of carvings down onto ivory ripples. 'You know,' the man went on, 'years ago when this city was just a market here and the castle there, with a few fisherman's huts huddled by the edge of the sea, the nobles used to come down to hold their funerals in the great subterranean Hall of Death. It's supposed to be smack in what's now the middle of town — though it was partly filled in years back. The rumor is that recently some folks have dug it out again and are using it for the oddest purposes. There's a tavern built right on top of it today, they say. Given my profession, you'd think I'd go down and take a look — out of historical interest. But I've never been. It's as though it's not really a part of *my* city. Well, born here, raised here, I know there're still sights every tourist comes to ogle I've just never seen. But that's always the local irony, isn't it?'

Clodon had stopped again. From under one of the porches surrounding the court, a figure stepped out slowly in heavy veils.

'. . . Mother?' The man turned. 'You're still up?'

'I just wanted to see you were home safe — Oh, you have someone?' (Her voice was elderly and nasal; Clodon caught the distance of disapproval in it.) 'Good night, then.'

She walked again into the shadows.

However unpleasant they'd been, the fumes downstairs, in clearing, had cleared some of Clodon's drunkenness.

'Come.' The man sounded more affable than he had for a while. 'We've had a full and enjoyable afternoon and evening of each other's company. I have some idea of the youth you are, of the child you were, of the man you'll be.' They walked around the pool and across the garden, to another door, another heavy hanging across it. 'Almost your first words to me today were about how you wanted to make some money. My rooms are this way. Let me put a proposition to you.'

6. Though fragments from this adolescent adventure had been part of Clodon's earlier dream, it would be excessive to say he remembered it all — or that he even *could* have remembered it in such detail. Certainly while he stood in the Narnis inn yard, staring at the actress in the tavern window, we could write that such confusing and immature strayings from the centers of his own desire were precisely what he was *not* recalling then. Do the two times, therefore, present equal and opposite occurrences? Equal? No. Opposite? Well . . . But to the extent their objects mirror one another, certain instruction about what is to come may be gained if we turn from this to examine, say, the relation lust and desire had actually taken in Clodon's life.

For, in fact, we haven't mentioned the one and have only indicated the other.

7. In that age when no mechanical reproduction had standardized the beautiful, in much of his desire Clodon's wants in women were largely the usual for a male of his epoch, class, and condition. Like most men in Nevèrÿon, he wanted a woman who was young. Like most men in Nevèrÿon, he wanted a woman who was strong. Many men in Nevèrÿon would talk of wanting a woman as well who was submissive. Frequently though these same men hoped that she might have *some* spirit. Often these men's brothers would laugh and declare they wished for nothing *but* a woman with spirit — though, as often, they hoped for one who would bend a bit to masculine directive. Which is to say, as far as spirit or submission went, Clodon felt just as ambiguously as one might expect a man to in such a time, in such a place.

But there were other details to Clodon's ideal of pleasure that (Clodon was sure) set him aside from many. He could not, for example, say why or when he'd first developed his obsession with women's hands. And not *just* the hands: it was something about their nails. You must understand that, in this long-ago distant land, the amount of labor rural life required from both men and women well up into what you and I would call the middle classes was not such as to encourage long nails on either gender. But even as a child, now and again Clodon would find himself watching some woman's fingers, fascinated, when the nails simply grew forward enough to cover the crowns. Certainly the first woman whose hands had held his silent, if never-articulated, attention had been his cousin the bailiff's wife. She'd been a shy, dark, gentle thing — and often ill. Clodon had been an intractable boy. But, in his early years, neighbors often noted how she could usually get him to do what she asked, when to his other relatives and friends he was simply and insistently recalcitrant. Clodon's own treasured memory was, at age six or seven, sitting in her lap, under a tree, in the leafy shadow, playing with her fingers and touching the tips of his to the tips of hers, while she looked out over his head at the sunlight and told him stories of the nameless gods, which he paid no attention to but was happy. When puberty struck Clodon's body with the hormones none in Nevèrÿon could have named, at eleven somehow the whole process expanded to include . . . feet! No, this had nothing to do with the nails.

It was the hare-lipped girl's slatternly aunt on whom he'd first noticed it.

Clodon was loafing among some scrub on the sandy slope above the village, when he saw her come by, barefoot and a little stooped, carrying a basket on her hip with some shucks sticking up above it. As she passed, he found himself watching her naked ankles, and the way her feet, which were uncommonly narrow, with long toes and dusty at the arch, seemed to reach forward with each step, the toes spreading a little to dig into the dirt, to feel about in it, as though they could sense delicate things in the earth that would never register on her slack brown face with its rough black hair above it.

What immediately he did was look up at her hands: thick fingered, clubby, clutching the wicker. How could a woman with such uninteresting fingers have such extraordinary toes?

That was the way he thought about it — even as her heels were lifting from the sand beyond him, and she was gone.

Minutes later, and for the third time that day, Clodon masturbated — only now he tried to think of a woman (young, strong, spirited — well, maybe not too) with hands like his cousin's and feet like this woman's . . .

The experience was extraordinary.

Soon Clodon had divided all the women of his village into two groups: the first contained about two-thirds of them, with ordinary feet of no particular interest. But the second — and he was surprised by and delighted at their number, once he began to look — was a privileged group whom he smiled at when he passed, whom he contrived to watch and to be near, whom he went out of his way to walk beside or behind, and who walked through his fantasies only pausing, now and again, to turn and, gently, touch him with hands that were — mostly — not theirs. Indeed, his first complaint about his town, had anyone asked (not that any admonishing and moralizing elder or eager equal in mischief ever did), was that his cousin's wife, with her beautiful, aging fingers, simply did *not* have the feet to go with them.

Clodon's trip to Kolhari produced another addition to, revelation of, or recomplication in, desire — as well as a few educational turns to the inscription of what was already there. The first thing that surprised him on his arrival in the great port was that a quarter of the women walked the streets in one sort of shoe or another — which is to say, there was a whole class of women here, a few poor and a larger number well-off, whose toes, arches, and insteps, in the intricate mechanism of walking, were simply veiled to him in ugly leather or, sometimes (equally ugly to him), brocade, so that he could not even tell if they belonged to that group who were his central interest. As many others wore sandals, which teased him cruelly, as their straps and buckles seemed barely to withhold the freedom and motion that made a foot of concern, so that, now and again, he found himself paying more attention to these than to the feet of women who went barefoot and ill-clad, as he did. (Certainly the overwhelming majority of the city's population, female and male, was too poor for footwear.) Within a week of coming to Kolhari, he made a connection, as cruel as his initial observation, that had escaped him till now at home: the particular hands he cherished were much more likely to occur on the better-off women of the city — cruel because they were precisely the women most likely to go shod.

But the addition, revelation, or recomplication we spoke of had neither to do with women's hands or feet. Rather it involved . . . eyes! He discovered it in his first month in the city while loitering on the Bridge of Lost Desire.

The women and girls who worked the bridge as prostitutes — as well as some of the more effeminate men — wore dark wings of paint around their eyes, and affectation that, when Clodon first saw it, struck him not so much as sexual as it did a simple sign to signify what position you held in the endless chain of displacements, re-placements, and exchanges, that made up life on the bridge as much as it did life in the market beyond. The masculinity Clodon treasured and that, yes, he would admit it, seemed so subtly compromised by the homosexual encounters that, despite his basic inclination, from time to time necessity forced him to take part in, at first seemed eas-ier to secure by showing no sign at all. Yet those hustlers, usually older, whose self-presentation was a parody of that same masculinity, with great weapon belts and bits of armor worn over old rags and rude retorts to half the inquiries from potential clients and even more foul language than was customary on that most foul-tongued walkway, made themselves more masculine still by adopting a single wing of paint about a single eye: what was a sign of the womanly, when split, became a sign of the male.

That he possessed this masculinity — for, yes, he'd always liked to have some weapon, even if it was just a stone hidden in his clout: yes, he'd always worn a leather band around his upper arm, though it was not really a custom of his village: and, yes, his talk had always been blunter than was acceptable to his elders — he only realized when these parodies passed.

Several times, even as Clodon treasured his unmarked state, he adopted the single bit of eye make-up: he borrowed it from a girl who kept a small, waxy stone of blue-black tint wrapped in her waist cinch — and felt himself, at least for the day, closer to what he wanted to be by doing so. When, finally, he returned to the bare eyes that marked most of the more masculine hustlers, it was with a sense of failure and, indeed, some small but irrevocable slide toward the same ambiguity that, in this passage of sexual a-specificity, so trou-bled him.

Often there was as much human traffic under the bridge as on it. Toward the market end, stairs at either edge went down to a set of pee-troughs at both sides of the stanchion. Boys were always charging up and down them; girls were always shouting from the rocks below to some friend hanging over the upper wall.

Clodon had gone down, one afternoon, looking for the barbarian.

(The rumor along the walkway above was that a nobleman's corpse had been pulled from the water at dawn. Bodies — usually of beggars or soldiers — were sometimes thrown there in those brutal and barbaric times. But it had been carted away even before he'd arrived.) On a whim, Clodon decided to walk out over the stones that pushed above the shallows that rushed, like green smoke and froth, about a wagon wheel lying half out of the swirl, that broke on the bottom of a big, public vase wedged between uneven rocks, that flowed through some oily netting caught on a barkless branch, in which stuck some fruit rinds and a carved doll without head and one of its arms.

Somewhere a soldier and a woman were arguing, while another woman laughed at them. Clodon couldn't see where, though the echo under the arch made them sound as if they were baside or above him. He stepped across water to another rock, turning to see where the voices came from.

A woman was kneeling three stones away, where a granite slab sloped from glass-green ripples. Behind her, one bare foot was propped on spread toes, the position from which, if he could move close enough, he might note best *just* what sort of foot she had. But the way the hollow lightened behind her ankle, and the way the harder skin stretched along her wet sole told him she was one whose toes would be a true pleasure. Women always thought you were looking at their breasts or buttocks. And though he liked breasts and buttocks as well as the next, he assumed women never thought you were looking at anything else: and that gave him, he imagined, the right to move as close as he wanted, as long as he kept his eyes low.

Clodon stepped to the next rock, wondering if she were one of the women from up on the bridge. (He didn't recognize her at all from this angle.) She looked up —

She'd been washing her face. Hands and forearms, cheeks and chin were speckled with drops. Seeing him, she laughed, a smile underlying it that he recognized at once as both pleased and nervous. Had she been scrubbing make-up from her eyes?

One moment he was sure of it; the next he doubted it completely.

Shifting, she moved the foot that had been behind her in front. And Clodon saw:

Her eyes were dark: or, rather, the skin around them was naturally shadowy, almost bruised, so that, without really being set deeply in

her face, it threw white and iris into cinnamon and ivory relief. Her
foot, as the long toes moved down to hold the rock's edge, was, in all
he'd ever imagined of a foot, perfect. Still cupped under her chin, her
hands were tipped with oval nails that blushed with the blood beneath them, their ends, even on almost all, making small blades the
color of the meaty part within a pumpkin seed, and clean because of
her washing. Certainly, in terms of his own obsessions, they were the
most breath-taking hands. And more striking than both of these,
were her eyes: *they* were the most beautiful in the world.

The conviction hit him baldly, blankly, and unquestionably.

He'd never known eyes could have that effect because, he realized,
in order to have it, the face about them had to be smiling.

Or laughing.

He knew this all without words or even, really, thinking — unless
the contractions of the muscles at the back of his shoulders and the
tightening of the ligaments behind his knees were, themselves, a
kind of thought.

He also realized what natural state the make-up he'd grown so
used to on the women walking the bridge simulated — at the same
time seeing that, to him, this, when on a smiling face, was enough to
make his knees lock and the muscles above his scrotum tighten to
pain and his whole belly want to pull itself over so that he might
have collapsed, hugging himself, feeling monstrously warm and well-
cared for and wonderful.

Yet he did none of these.

What Clodon did — Clodon who was a thief, and a bully, and a
brawler in gutters, and who bore the marks of an adult criminal, and
who would be remarked for high banditry when he'd less than doubled
the age he had now — was smile.

He smiled because if someone smiles at you, and you want them
to go on smiling, you smile back; otherwise, they will frown, or look
dour, or shake their head and turn away; and Clodon wanted this
woman, kneeling on the rock, water on her face and forearms, to go
on smiling at him till the nameless gods balled up the desert with the
sea and the mountains among them, in preparation for the recrafting
of the world.

8. But while Clodon smiled, he thought — indeed, for the first time,

in a while — about the hare-lipped girl he'd brutalized again and again at home.

She had had such eyes!

They returned to him with astonishing shock.

No, she had not had his cousin's hands or even her own aunt's feet.

His initial interest in her had been because Imrog, the smith's apprentice, slept with her from time to time.

Methodically Clodon had pursued her, and, one evening, when she'd been tired enough to let him put his arm around her shoulder, violently he had brought her down, while a friend stood guard for him: through the act, he thought only of her aunt, of his cousin's wife. And the next day he discovered, with an overpowering delight, that, as he'd suspected, he'd enraged the burly, older youth, who he was sure was as great a scoundrel as himself, but who, because Imrog would work a steady job, was heir to only a third the recriminations Clodon was.

But she *had* such eyes. And they had never struck him, above her grotesque mouth, as these did: and that was because he'd never seen her laugh.

This was the closest he ever felt to guilt over his sexual outrage — and, in its way, was far more effective in keeping him from ever repeating it.

For — let *me* repeat it — we have been writing about the power of desire.

What? You thought it was lust? No.

And where does desire fit in the tale we've so far told? You must read it, as it grew and developed for Clodon to the point we've recounted, down the margin of every page we've written. It had been in his mind minutes before he stole the roast goat. It had rolled through his thoughts a dozen times as he hung from the corner of the grain building, waiting for his whipping. He'd thought about it as he went up to his cousin's hut the night he fled his village; and he'd dwelled on it as he sat by the road next dawn, wanting to cry. It would be in his mind as he sat on the wall of the bridge the moment before the Kolhari mortician spoke to him. Indeed, it lies in every pause, between every sentence, in our story so far, as it will in all to come.

With every material force and ill-known economic motive that pushed Clodon, however unaware he was of it, desire always lay ahead of him, lazy and limpid, to pull him in the same direction. Wherever profit or personal whim attracted him, desire was always behind to impel, however dimly he perceived it, maniacal and murky. If it does not glitter throughout the narrative we have so far woven, that's because its place twists through as an absence, like the space left when a thread has been pulled loose to snake from the fabric, but whose path the sophisticated weaver can still follow from the looseness and layering of the threads around.

Was it really unusual how quickly Clodon had accepted that the two, desire and lust, were not, at least for him, to go together? In his own village, the reason he'd never sought sex with the woman who was his ideal was because exhaustive searching said she wasn't there: she was something, rather, he had put together the way a village singer takes a line from one song, a refrain from another, while using a stanza from still another once heard from a carter passing through from another hamlet entirely, from the amalgam making a ballad that, a generation hence, all in town will swear began as an accurate account of something that once happened to someone else's well-remembered, if now long-dead, grandmother.

In Kolhari, though occasionally he glimpsed her or glimpsed parts of her (though seldom from so near, or so completely, as he did now beneath the bridge that afternoon), it was what some people trivialize by calling the fear of rejection that kept Clodon from her.

9. This is what Clodon did as he stood, a rock away, with water rushing between them:

He looked.

He smiled.

He thought.

But he did not breathe.

The kneeling woman may have spoken; or she may have gestured; or she may have remained perfectly still, blinking twice or thrice . . .

In about twenty seconds, Clodon began to feel unsteady. At forty, his vision began to flicker — till, with a great gasp, he turned, tried to get to the rock he'd just left, went into the water up to his knee, cut his foot on something at the bottom — he never knew what — scrambled up on the next stone, made it back to the stanchion, where, on the stair, he bumped into a heavy man coming down who cursed him, reached the walkway above, leaned on the wall, heaving in one and another roaring gasp, till he had to close his eyes, drop to a squat, and put his cheek against the stone. Breaking through a terror so complete it filled every sense with a loud ringing, the first fears came to him that someone might see, that someone might know. But as he crouched there, terror giving way to fear, he did not care.

Finally, five minutes later, with his legs shaking, he stood.

And looked around.

After trying to count ten breaths and getting lost three times, he went back down the stairs, halfway, to peer under the bridge, its arch flickering with an arc of sunlight up from the water.

She wasn't there.

He went back up to the walkway — and noticed, for the first time, the bloody footprints on the bowed stone, and, moments later, that it was his own right foot that bled. He leaned against the wall another minute. Then he went down once more, all the way to the bottom, to look again.

The shaking had reduced to a quiver in his left leg.

She must have already gone up the stairs on the other side.

He spent a lot of time, over the next three days, looking for her. He walked from end to end of the bridge. While he searched, sometimes conscientiously, sometimes just with an eye out in passing, he wondered if this were how the bridge had got its name. Clodon was a boy who valued what strength he had. As he thought back on it, the weakness, the terror, the disorientation that had assailed him before this kneeling woman — that had struck him down into the water and had drawn his blood — just seemed . . . wrong! Wasn't it closer to madness than to sex? Now he went to look for her among the stalls in the Old Market of the Spur. Now, at the other end, he searched in the alleys that cut through the business neighborhood.

One evening, six weeks later, when the moon had come up early and lingered to blue the sky till late, as Clodon returned to the bridge, he saw her — with some young people, who, from their tunics and sandals, were far better off than it had occurred to him she might be. The silver light, shining straight down, put shadows on her eyes as dark as the make-up that, on her, would have been superfluous. Nor did it light her so well that he could see the details of her hands. Or feet. But it was she. The youngsters seemed — Clodon stopped walking, stopped breathing — as if they were about to turn on to the bridge, all of them, laughing and chatting, and come right by him.

Then they sauntered off down the quay.

She did not see him.

But she still looked happy.

Slowly, slowly, his thumping heart quieted.

He never saw her again.

Certainly to seek her out further (he would think this, even as he began to search for her again, or for someone like her) was against all reason. Somehow the pursuit of lust with the girls and women available, using the images gleaned from an unknown woman's passing foot or hand or eye, while his own eyes were sealed and he hunched and sweated over this woman or that one (or, as it happened, a man who'd promised him a few coins of iron for it), seemed far safer.

And another thing: from that moment beneath the bridge, he began to find the paint on the eyes of the lazy (or sometimes unbelievably energetic) women who worked the walkways above produced in him the faintest sexual excitation. It was as if, now that he knew what it stood for, he could respond to it, if only as a sign.

10. But before we return to where Clodon, in the inn-yard, stood smiling up at the woman in the window much as he'd once smiled down at the other under the bridge, we must talk about another, equally perplexing strand weaving through his life in no less complex a pattern: lust.

The wonder of it was, just how quickly Clodon had separated it from desire — in his mind? No. But certainly in most of his material practices and in almost all of his human actions. Like most men in Nevèrÿon, Clodon had quickly located the fact that, while lust was something of the body, which, certainly, desire might provoke, still, any number of things could quench it — and quench it satisfactorily, if desire itself was only held in the mind. Lust had begun for Clodon (against Imrog) as a weapon: in its onanistic form, he used it as a tool — to relax himself, to reward himself, to indulge himself when, truly, he deserved no reward.

A weapon or tool it remained, whether he used it skillfully or poorly.

Before he left Kolhari, Clodon managed to have sex with three prostitutes: one simply got drunk with him one night and rolled with him in a doorway behind a tavern: he got away without paying. The next, he told he *would* pay but tried to run away afterwards, only to get himself punched five or six times and his arm sprained by a hulking man waiting in a doorway he hadn't even seen. A third he paid the asked-for price (with money from a purse snatched off a bald man over in the market), mainly because, for a moment when he first saw her, she had been sitting on a step, scratching with one finger between her little toe and the one next to it; and he was sure, for a moment, that those hands and feet would, when she looked at him, go with the eyes he had been seeking.

It turned out, when she frowned up through the blue-black pigment (which he himself had only ceased to wear a day before) applied unevenly and asymmetrically, he'd been wrong about her in all three aspects.

With all three women there had been real excitement. But there had been none of the swollen want that makes us all children; and to which a child's response *must* be terror.

In terms of lust, however, and its split from desire, we have now observed Clodon at sixteen.

Let us look at him at twenty-six, when Kolhari was ten years behind.

There he was, living out of a provision cart parked beside a lean-to some hundred yards from the outskirts of a village near several ravines at the edge of the desert — a village whose insistent and subtle differences from his own bothered him every time he wandered in to look at a woman weaving in her yard or tugging an ox by its bridle along an unpaved alley, to see a squatting man at work on a wooden plowhead or bending to wash himself and his three-year-old at a trough beside his hut.

He was no longer a lean-hipped youth. But he was not yet a fat man.

In his first day, walking through the town, Clodon looked for things he might steal that would not be missed. Sometimes he'd stop, try to appear friendly, and ask some man or woman if there weren't work he might do, at least for a few days, hoping they would ignore his scars — till he gave them reason not to. On his last day, he went looking for something large enough to be worth stealing that would also be worth leaving the place for. But in the evenings between, there was sex — with a woman about ten years older than he, who lived in a hovel at the town's edge: she was not pretty and was a little crazy. Clodon would visit her with a jug of beer. They would sit together before her shack, the jug between them. And Clodon would say, 'Now, have you ever seen this?'

'No — ! What's that little bit of dirt you've got?'

'It's what the fine women in the big cities wear around their eyes. I've seen them. When I lived there. In Kolhari. Now you'd be a fine looking woman if you wore it, too.'

'Wear a lump of dirt in my eye — ?'

'No. You just put a little on. It'll become you. No, no, here. Let me show you — '

'Get away! I don't want it — '

'No, here — come on, now. It won't hurt you. Let me show you how they do it!'

'Put it on yourself, then!'

'Oh, and sometimes the men do, too. But differently. Here, it won't hurt. I promise. No, I promise — let me, now! . . . Get your hand away! Be still. There — ! And . . . there! Now, see? You look like the finest and most noble lady in the great city of Kolhari, you do!'

'You can see it. *I* can't. How could I, when it's smeared all over my face!'

'But you do look like a fine woman. You *are* a fine woman — here, have a drink now.'

'*You* have one!'

'Well, I will!' And he'd lift the jug, so that the sun heated the ridges above his eyes and his chest warmed from inside and from out. Soon, he would tell her stories of this and that, and she would laugh; and he would gaze at her, with a dumb smile and slack lips. Then they would make love — sometimes in the hut, but more often in the dirt outside.

Sometimes, for inexplicable reasons, she would cry.

'Why are you weeping?'

'I don't know! I don't *know* . . . !'

He made two or three tries to get her to laugh and, when they didn't work, lost interest. Once, he even got up and left —

Only to surprise three children crouching behind a lichen-flecked boulder. He shouted. They fled. Then he stalked back to his lean-to and cart.

Usually, though, sex went more easily. Sometimes, after he had fallen heavily asleep, the woman would sit up, suddenly, while Clodon's hand fell from her shoulder to the earth, and stare at the scars on his brown flank, tracing one and another with her fingertip to his back. Then she'd try to remember why young girls and foolish women should *never* speak to a man with such scars, why you should never even look at him, and certainly never be seen with him.

Especially by staring children.

For the truth was — and does it really surprise you? — Clodon was a more considerate sexual partner than most she'd had.

At least when she wore the make-up.

At least when she smiled.

And what of Clodon at *thirty*-six?

Ten years later he was living with two other criminals. The younger one had even more flogging marks than Clodon, a lazy, foul-tempered boy, who, for all his complaining, hated above all things to be alone. With a kind of desperation, he held the others to him, even as he stole from them, lied to them, and, from time to time, got into fights with them. The other, older than Clodon, had managed to avoid whipping. He was a coward, Clodon had decided, despite his boasts of lifting this and filching that. But when they pulled a back-road robbery, he would more or less do what you told him.

For a month now the three had been sharing a filthy shack up from the shore perhaps a mile below Vinelet that had once belonged to the youngster's last partner who'd come to a bad end. From a dropped comment on their way to the stream down the slope or what once got shouted between bouts of laughter in some momentary argument when they were all drunk, Clodon suspected the boy had killed the man.

But Clodon was a good deal fatter, a good deal louder, and a good deal more of a drunk himself than he'd been ten years ago.

And there was a lot less sex in his life, too.

At this point, Clodon would probably not even have considered sex without alcohol. (He did, however, remember the woman beneath the bridge a lot. But, again, we're talking of lust now — not desire.) The problem, of course, was that too *much* alcohol made him impotent, so that it was a terribly fine line he had to walk — and the chance to walk it was now offered him less and less.

Three out of the last five times he'd bedded a woman, it was he who'd cried — though he knew no more why than the woman in the desert had known why ten years back. It was just another reason to avoid the whole business.

One morning, however, while two jays screamed at each other outside, the youngster stuck his head in by the torn hanging and said, hoarsely, 'Hey — you two! Get up. Look what I've brought! I got two women. They're hot ones, too! They do everything! They've both been fucking with me since last night. They're about to fry me with their heat!' From outside, Clodon heard laughing. 'And they want you two, now! I got some beer in the cart. We can have a good time. They'll do anything at all — anything!'

Then the women pushed in.

'Get out of the way,' the first declared, 'and let's see this nest of bandits and bad men you say you live among!' She was small, plump and shrill.

The tall one lagged a little behind and stayed almost wholly silent, except when the two of their heads would come together to whisper. Then laughter would push them apart — the plump one with her head back, turning this way and that, waving one hand wildly, the tall one with her mouth tucked behind her fists, her head low and her shoulders shaking.

Women? Clodon thought, pushing himself to sit. Neither was twenty-five, and he was that age where anything less seemed a child. The tall one whispered again to the plump one, and pointed across the clutter at Clodon. Then the plump one squealed: 'You're right! He *is!*'

The jays shrieked.

The next Clodon knew, his arms were full of both of them. (Even as he began to laugh, he wondered if he *wouldn't* have found this more enjoyable ten years ago.) 'Here, now — ' he complained, for he had something of a hangover — 'let me get a drink first. Now let me get a drink — '

Just then the older criminal with no scars came in from the back. 'Well, just look what our little friend has brought! Aren't they the two most tasty morsels in the world? Delicious, I'd say! And I haven't had my breakfast!'

'Only two of them?' the tall woman said, shortly, with a face full of Clodon's rough hair. '*I* thought there were going to be nine or ten!'

'Now you let me get a drink,' Clodon repeated, trying to hold them both, for the plump one was already starting to wriggle free, 'and I'll keep you busy enough for ten or twenty!'

Clodon would have thought that his older partner, even if he was a coward, would be the one a woman would prefer: he was the tallest, he was the most well spoken, he kept himself the cleanest, and he drank the least. (Hadn't Clodon managed to learn that sort of thing counted with women?) But though the two visitors spread their attentions all around, clearly their favorites were Clodon and the boy. And, after a little, between the two it was Clodon they seemed to prefer.

The orgy lasted three days.

Or was it four?

Beyond the first hours, Clodon retained only a few intense images.

The sharpest was when, in a rage, he swung an empty beer pitcher into the youngster's face, so that the pieces fell, bloody, to the shack floor: then, still gripping the handle and the fragment atached, he smashed it into the boy's face again, so that the boy dropped back against the wall. 'Don't you *ever* do that to me again!' Clodon bellowed, and bellowed again: 'Don' you *ever* — '

The boy went down, wiping blood from his nose and chin with one hand and swinging out drunkenly with the other, saying: 'No, no . . . that was just . . . I didn't mean . . . I was just foolin' . . . foolin' . . . ! That's — ' till Clodon hit him again and the handle crumbled in his hand, cutting his own fingers.

Another? Or was it part of the same:

On the ragged cowhide the tall girl held her arm up across her breasts, rubbing it with her other hand, while Clodon tried to help her up. But she looked at his fingers and recoiled. For a moment he stood, unsure what to do, trying to remember just what it was the younger one had done.

The pot to the face was not, however, what killed him. Clodon was sure of that. Because another of the memories *must* have come from later.

Clodon woke. A band of afternoon cut, like a copper blade, from a crack in the wall. The youngster, beside him, his face all scratched, scabbed, and deviled with his own blood, strained and grunted beside Clodon, over the plump one, while she panted. Sleepily Clodon looked to see her breast mash out and out and out again, each time the young one thrust.

So that it had to have been after the fight with the pot, and, however scratched up, by then he must have been all right.

Unless that was a dream . . .

Another? If it was early or late in the orgy, Clodon couldn't say. But the plump one leaned against him, while they sat outside under the trees, and whispered: 'You're a terrible, frightening man, with those great scars on your back. You must do terrible, frightening things to women. Like me. All the time. Don't you — ?'

Clodon giggled now, shrugged, and caressed her hair.

'Come,' she urged him, with another kiss, 'tell me the terrible things you like to do to women. Tell me. Maybe you could even show me.'

'You like a man who's rough, then?'

'Oh, very rough!' She beamed at him. And that began a silly game, out in the yard, where Clodon blindfolded her with a piece of old chamois, and sometimes hit her face with a small branch — and sometimes, when he said he was going to hit her, merely brushed the leaves across her cheek, and asked her ridiculous questions, then made her fellate him, or sometimes fingered or licked between her legs when he decided her answers, at random, were wrong. To all of which she squealed happily. Then the older one came out and got into the game. Finally the younger one, leaning drunkenly on the shoulder of the taller woman, came out. And wanted to play, too. Only, of course, *he* played too rough — though the plump girl only once seemed to mind, when he squeezed her breast too hard. Then there was another argument, mostly between the older man and the younger: and that part of it was over.

Had the boy's face carried the cuts from the pitcher at that point? Why, Clodon wondered, couldn't he remember?

After that Clodon was fairly sure he and the tall girl had taken the cart into Vinelet to get more beer. (He wanted the plump one to come, but she refused. Then the tall one said she'd go.) On the way, he kept asking her: 'You sure you want to come back? I'll let you off anywhere you like. It's all right. I'll just say you wanted to leave.'

But she shook her head, and once took his arm. 'I want to go back with you!' she declared. Not that the tall one was very talkative otherwise: still, sometime during the ride, Clodon learned that the plump one back at the shack was in some very serious trouble, which was why she didn't want to go into town. They were going to leave their home and go to the great city of Kolhari. 'Are you?' Clodon asked. 'I used to live there when I was a younger man. Stayed there almost a year. That's where I learned to play such blindfolded games.' The tall girl told him about a neighbor woman, and a boyfriend who had, consecutively, betrayed them both, and a job the plump one had had taking care of the children of the owner of some fishing boats; and Clodon had begun to suspect a complexity to the lives of both women that made the goings-on of the past days seem as out of keeping for them as it was, really, for him.

Then, an hour later, they were back.

'By all the nameless gods,' demanded the boy, when they pulled up at the shack and he leaned to look over the wagon's edge, 'how much beer did you *get*?'

'You're never satisfied with anything,' the older man said, shaking his head, 'are you? If it's not too *little* for you, then it's too much.'

Surely the only scars about him then had been across his back.

Why, Clodon wondered, did this diversion in what was actually some truly satisfactory love-making — with both the plump one, and, later, the tall one —stay so clearly? But the thing about *truly* satisfactory sex was that it tended to complete itself in its own exertion and thus left little to memory.

For the last day Clodon was too drunk and too exhausted to have an orgasm. Sunk to his pubic bone inside one and the other, he faked several — and wondered how his companions, grunting in the shadows, were doing. Still, the memory that pleased him most came from that time:

Finally, disengaging, once more, from the plump one, he'd gone to the back door to piss. His stomach felt queasy and he wondered if he were going to throw up again.

He'd stood outside under the cool moon a long time, breathing slowly, to see if his stomach would settle — or just give up what was in it. When he felt a little better, he pushed back in.

Moonlight came through a window.

The two were kneeling together. Earlier, the tall one had found Clodon's lump of make-up and put it on her eyes without his even

saying anything. Now, watching her, he thought not that it looked al-
luring on her so much as charming. It made her seem even younger,
as if she wore it, ineffectually, to make herself look older and more
worldly. Beneath the window, they touched each other, now with fingers, now with lips, while the sweat stood out on the plump one's
breasts and on the tall one's wrists.

The women, Clodon thought, were beautiful.

He pondered, a little surprised, that this beauty had nothing to do
with hands or feet or the eyes that, he already knew, when he recalled
this for private use, he would loan them.

The boy sat in a corner, head forward on his knees. As Clodon
wondered at this loveliness amidst the confusion and drunkenness,
he heard him mutter: '. . . that's not . . . two, see, not the right number . . . For us. It won't work . . . It won't. it should be *more* . . .'

This, he knew, was the one he *should* remember:

Was it dawn? Was it evening? The older man stood, holding back
the hanging, half in and half out of the shack and growling at Clodon:
'He's a pig, I tell you! Hogging the two of them, both at once! And
you're not much better! I'll kill him, if he says another word! I will!'

'Come on,' Clodon said. 'He's just a boy. He thinks he can fuck the
sun out of the sky. Weren't you like that when you were his age? I
was. Look — like last time: when the fat one comes back to me, I'll
call you in — then I'll get up and go somewhere, and you can have her
awhile.' It was a generosity he'd performed once to keep the peace,
and he did not relish having to perform it once more. Indeed, perhaps
he never got round to it. For he remembered the plump one, crawling
across the floor to him, breathing like an exhausted animal, sliding
down against him with her warm breath and her moist shoulders,
snuggling into him, so that his hard fingers were full of the soft flesh
of her breasts, and even though they were both too tired to do anything, she whispered, 'Oh, yes, lover! Yes — yes! Oh, yes . . .'

Had it been because when next they woke — the fourth day? the
fifth? — the women were gone?

So were the cart and the mule.

'Of *course* they stole it, you beshitted pair of pig's buttocks!' the
boy shouted.

Was *that* what began it — between the younger and the older?
Though Clodon had shouted too. Still, mostly, while they'd argued
he'd been looking for more beer.

There was a lot of yelling — Oh, certainly the younger one began it. He began everything. But it worried Clodon later that he couldn't remember the act itself. What he remembered was trying to leave the shack, and the older one tugging at his arm. 'No, no — you have to stay now! At least you have to help me bury him! You have to help me! What'll I do? You can't just go like that —

'Why not?' Clodon pushed the older man back against the jamb, realizing as he did so that this was the first he was sure that the boy was, this time, dead. 'It's your mess!' Till then, he'd just assumed he'd been badly hurt. 'You clean it up!'

He had the tooled leather cartcover with him. The women hadn't taken that. In the yard he threw it around his shoulders to wear against any weather that came up.

As he tied the thongs, Clodon wondered: hadn't he at least thrown a punch or two in the course of what had just happened? It had been inside the shack, certainly. But then, had he?

It *must* have been between the younger one and the older. Why else would the older have acted that way? The man had gone back inside, and Clodon had staggered off toward the road. Once he stopped to be sick among the roots of a thick tree, leaning on the trunk and heaving till only stringy mucus dripped from his beard. Then he went on. Finally, he'd rolled up in his make-shift cloak and gone to sleep. And lain sick a long time. But, over the next days, as he recovered, all reconstruction was futile. Had it been a stabbing? (He swung the empty beer pitcher into the boy's face . . .) Had it been a beating? Certainly it had been because some argument had finally erupted between the *other* two. It had to be that, didn't it?

But the truth was, had Clodon been dragged before elders and threatened with death, he could not have said who was the actual murderer; nor how the act had been committed; nor why.

Perhaps, he thought, waiting off the side road for the sound of some carter's passing, lust itself — not such a bad thing when desire was unavailable — just ran from the beauty of that moonlit moment by the window to this evil too great to recall.

Clodon had committed other murders — murders as conscientious and cold-blooded as was possible, when, on a back road in the evening, loud with crickets, where the pine needles absorbed the sound and the packed leaves soaked the blood, one person slaughtered another. (Waiting in the underbrush, he wondered if he would soon commit one more.) But none had ever troubled him like the death of this lazy, quarrelsome boy, who, in so many ways seemed almost an extreme of his younger self. That he was not even sure if he *was* the murderer only added to the irony. But whatever had happened, it made Clodon feel, at once, wise, sad, and foolish.

Better, he decided, to stick to his right hand and the memory of desire. The boy had been a fool and out to get himself killed. Hadn't Clodon said it a hundred times? No, it was too messy, too confusing, too dangerous.

Though we have written of Clodon's encounters with lust, what we have not written of here is the shifting emotional calculus in which the appetite was embedded. Whatever sort of bedmate he might have been — and we have said he was a considerate one — he was certainly no good lover. With other women entirely separate from the ones we have written of, Clodon had already fathered three children he had never seen: he believed he had fathered a fourth, who was actually not his. And he had stolen money, food, pots, and knives from all their mothers before he'd abandoned them — only the smallest of his crimes.

Though we have written of the separation between them, we have also managed to say a little, I think, of the way desire tempered lust — even in the midst of a murderous, drunken orgy. Is there any way, we might now ask, in which lust tempered desire?

Well, ten years before, after he'd left the woman who lived at the desert town, the dark-eyed laughing creature of Clodon's fantasy tended to laugh because she was a little mad. Ten years later, after the days of deadly debauchery, she laughed because she was involved in some plan and scheme beyond his intelligence to follow, though she wished to welcome him into it if only he would join her.

Though we have written of Clodon and lust at sixteen, at twenty-six, and again as a man in his thirties, what, you might reasonably ask, of lust and Clodon today?

For it was only a few years on.

In the five weeks he had been at Narnis, lust had more or less been limited to some vague speculations about Funig's half-sister, Jara. Did she, Clodon had wondered, have any of the submissiveness of the woman in the desert? Or would a little drink bring out in her any of the spirit of the two women at the shack? (Though you and I wouldn't

have, Clodon certainly thought of it in these terms.) But the answer
he'd come closer and closer to, without exactly stating it, was that
whatever the answers were, it would just be too much bother.

For over the time we've written of, the world had changed around
Clodon. One government had fallen and another taken its place; and
a man had come to challenge the institution of slavery on which the
economics of as much as a third of the nation had once been based.
His last fifteen pounds he'd put on in less than five years. Yet these
did not concern him; so we have largely elided them. Certainly, as he
stood in the inn-yard, with Funig beside him, looking at a woman
who smiled at him from the window, it was time to talk of other
things.

But we have one more strand from the past to weave into our tale
in order to reveal the smallest pattern in the present.

11. 'What do you mean?' With the roof behind them, they pushed
through the hanging —

For a moment Clodon thought the whole room was on fire.

Not only did a many-flamed lamp hang from the ceiling's center,
others hung in all four corners. Burning tripods stood at each of the
four walls.

'What kind of proposition?' Clodon squinted.

Thick rugs overlapped on the floor. Fat cushions lay about. There
were ornate chairs and a great bed, heaped with pillows and bolsters.
On small tables more lamps flickered.

'Just a moment. I'll show you.' The mortician pointed to the wall.
'Have you ever seen one of these?'

Clodon had thought it was an elaborately framed window — perhaps into another room. For lamps burned beyond it.

'It's a mirror,' the man said. 'Perhaps you've seen small ones traveling vendors sell in the provincial markets: pieces of polished metal in
which, for a few months, you can see your face, till they go dark with
tarnish. Seldom though will you find one this size. Stand in front of it,
and, with only the smallest distortion, it will show you something
few of us more than glimpse in a forest pool or in some street puddle
minutes after rain. I mean, of course, yourself. Here. Step up. Take a
look . . .'

Moving closer, Clodon stared into the metal that, in a moment, seemed a solid surface and, in another, something just not there. The figure inside, he only just comprehended, was he . . .

The man strode to the other side of the room.

'Now, let's see — ' He came back slowly.

When the second figure joined the first (and it *was* the man, Clodon saw), Clodon realized the first, indeed, showed not just him, but specifically how his eyes sat wide apart in his face, how his full mouth hung a little open, how he carried his shoulders sloped on broad collar bones — 'We'll just add this. Here.' The man held something, which he lifted — and placed around Clodon's neck. A metallic clink —

Surprised, Clodon looked away from the flickering metal to the man beside him. Something heavy and cold clung to his throat. Clodon reached up to pull it away.

The man took his wrist. 'It's an iron slave collar I've put on you.'

Surprised, Clodon raised his other hand.

'Wait — !' The man's voice was sharp, more commanding still; and the fumes below had not, after all, completely cleared. 'The lock is *broken* . . . !' he said with caressing reassurance. 'It will hold together while you wear it. But you can remove it any time you want. All you have to do is pull it apart. I promise you!'

Again Clodon raised his hands to tug at the metal; and the lock, indeed, clicked open. He felt it come apart. But the man's hands were there to snap it closed again.

In the mirror — and beside him — the man smiled.

'Look. At your reflection, now. There, turn yourself left and right. And watch.'

Clodon turned while he tried to keep looking.

'What do you see?'

'What do you mean?' Clodon was actually surprised there was only one voice, since, in the mirror, the lips moved too.

'There: what is it that looks out at you? In his iron collar, with the whip marks scarring his strong, brown body, surely that's no drunken country boy, in trouble because he's stolen some silly tax collector's supper. Look again. What do you see?'

Clodon said: 'I don't see any — '

'Don't you see a slave? And not just *any* slave, but an evil one — a slave who once rose up against his master, a slave who pulled down on his careless back all punishment and retribution, and who now carries the welts of his wickedness inscribed on his flesh like a message to all. Can't you see him? Can't you see a slave who has been marked, and in whose markings, there for all who can to read, lie his disdain for all authority, his contempt for all human law, and his loathing for the order of the nameless gods whom he would be the first to call chick and cabbage leaf, as he howls his laughter and disrespect!'

'I'm no slave — !' Clodon turned from the metal.

The man laughed and stepped back. 'I know that very well!' His voice, which had risen into a kind of chant, returned to the tones of conversation. 'But between you and me, we have all the pieces from which to *construct* such a slave. At least I believe we do. And such a slave, created of craft, artifice, and crime, may be more valuable, finally, than one formed only by the accidents of society and nature. Certainly he may well make more money.'

'What do I have to . . . ?' Clodon began. Then he said: 'I already told you, I don't *like* to — '

'Tell me,' the man said, interrupting. 'Have you ever pissed on anyone?'

Clodon said: 'Huh?'

'I said: have you ever pissed on another person?'

'No! *Why* would I — '

'Don't answer too quickly. Think back, through the whole of your life. There're not that many years in it to search over. So think. Ever, ever, ever, have you spilled urine on another human being?'

Frowning, Clodon moved his shoulders under the iron's weight. 'I guess . . . there was one time: when this old guy started hanging around our village. He wasn't from there. He was just a beggar. And he was always drunk. So once, when we found him, passed out behind the smithy, Imrog dared me to do it. He didn't think I would. But I did it. So he did it too! It was just a joke. That's all. We thought it was funny, right in the drunken old man's dirty beard and — '

But the man had raised his hand. 'Have you ever bullied someone into doing something he didn't want to do?'

'What — ?'

'What do I mean? Well, I suppose I mean . . .' Suddenly the man stepped, sharply, forward. His forearm came up, hard, under Clodon's chin. 'You're going to do what I say now, aren't you?' His voice was an intense whisper. 'You're *going* to do it!'

Clodon went back against the wall, swallowing, blinking. '*Hey* — !'

'Shut up!' Sharply — and lightly — with his free hand, the man slapped Clodon's cheek. 'You're going to do it?' He slapped him again. 'You're going to do it!'

'Hey, what are you — ?'

When Clodon raised a hand, the man knocked it, hard, away.

And slapped him, lightly, again. 'You're going to do it, now, aren't you?'

When Clodon tried to twist free, the forearm under his chin pushed his head back against the wall. 'All right! *Ow!* Hey — !'

'You're *going* to!'

While Clodon searched his confusion for the anger the slaps kept knocking aside, leaving only fear, the man suddenly stepped back. (They'd been standing belly to belly, thigh to thigh — which only registered when the bunched cloth of the man's tunic and the hard links of his belt pulled away.) Clodon said:

'Hey, *what* were you — ?'

'What I *mean*,' the man said, 'is, did you ever, with someone, say, smaller than you, younger than you perhaps, or not as sure of himself as you were, use the fact that surprise, intensity, and intimidation can effect the most amazing changes in what one person will do for another?'

'Why did you *do* that — ?'

'Only to demonstrate exactly what I was referring to — so that you, thinking back on your history, might recognize the action we're speaking of here.'

'You hurt my arm!' Clodon rubbed his wrist.

'Not that much. If you can feel it in the morning, I'll give you an extra coin. But tell me, did you — '

'Yeah!' Clodon said. 'Sure, with kids sometimes, when you're fooling with them — and they're trying to show you how big and bad they are. Sometimes you *have* to do that. Don't you? If they've got something you want, and they won't give it to you . . . something like that.'

'There,' the man said. 'I thought so. And now I'll ask you this. Have you ever tormented someone who couldn't fight back? Perhaps because you'd tied them up. Or because they were caught somewhere and couldn't get loose. Maybe you tickled them. Or perhaps you beat them — with a rope or a bit of leather. Oh, not hard — necessarily. I seem to remember earlier, when we were talking before, that you told me about one boy whom you once — '

'But that was just *fooling!*' Clodon insisted, at this point not sure which of the many things he'd told the man was being re-presented to him among all these flickering lights. 'I don't under — '

'Fooling? Very good! Because it's only another *sort* of fooling that I'm asking you to consider. Have you ever — ' the man interrupted himself again — 'though, on this point I don't even have to ask — in your anger, called someone humiliating and insulting names. Just from this afternoon I know the kind of language you use in your normal accounts. Certainly under the heat of injury, your invectives must grow even more colorful. For instance, try calling me a . . . sick piece of maggoty mule shit!'

Clodon paused. 'Is all this stuff — ' he frowned slowly — 'what you want me to do, to *you* . . . ?' He stepped away from the wall. (The man still smiled.) 'You *are* some kind of sick piece of shit . . .'

'There!' The man opened his hand and extended it toward Clodon. Somehow, he'd managed to get out another coin, without Clodon seeing from where. The dark disk lay on the dark palm. 'You see? My point is merely that there's nothing you'd be called on to do you haven't already done at one time or another — and done because you chose to do it. And when you were just fooling, at that. You've done very well, so far. Take your first pay.' The man flipped the coin, spinning, through the air.

Clodon reached out for it — and missed.

It fell to the rug between his feet. Because of the nap, it did not roll. Clodon looked up. 'You really want me to do stuff like that to . . . I don't know. You'd have to pay me a *lot* for it!'

'But I *don't* want you to do it to me,' the man said. 'At least not now. But many other people will. And they will pay you far more handsomely than you probably even imagine. My proposition for you tonight is this. Stay here this evening. Wear the collar. Tomorrow morning, return to the bridge. And do not remove it. Wear it there for . . . oh, only a single week. Night and day. You will be approached by people very differently, I can assure you, from the ones who have approached you up till now. You will do, I assure you equally, far better than you have done till now.'

'But people are going to think I'm some kind of slave — '

The man laughed. 'If you wear a slave collar; and if you carry the scars of a marked rebel; and if you stand out on the Bridge of Lost Desire — well, these, taken all together, become a kind of sign. Some who see it and come will be wearing collars themselves. Some who come to you will not. Mistaken for a *real* slave? I very much doubt it. But consider: if you *were* an actual slave, then somewhere you would have an actual master, am I right? And you would be *his* responsibility, no one else's — believe me, everyone, at least in that neighborhood, will leave you alone.'

'Well . . .' Clodon said. 'What about you?'

'I said my proposition is that you wear your collar — for I'm giving it to you, as of now — seven days. Work the bridge in it, making whatever you can. And I assure you you will make quite a lot. After a week, I will come down to see you. If you are still wearing it, I will come up to you — and pay you whatever you ask. If you have decided to discard it, well, then . . . I will smile, nod, and go on walking. And find someone else. We need never mention it again — if, indeed, we ever have anything further to do with one another.'

'But you really don't want to do anything *now?*' Somehow all of this was beginning to seem funny. 'Why not try me out — see how I am?'

'There are people who will truly appreciate your novice status in this profession; they are the ones whom you should go with while you're a novice. Myself, I know from experience I will enjoy it far more if you have had a week's practice.'

'Suppose they want me to do something I don't want to? I mean, going with men and doing that kind of thing just — '

'My country friend,' the man said, leaning forward, 'though the first who approach you will, most certainly, be men, there are just as many women in this rich, rich city who are seeking what you may now provide. Do your job well, with as much skill as you can bring to it, and before the week is out, I promise you, the reputation of a committed craftsman — if that's what you turn out to be — will spread far beyond that bit of stone that runs above the water. You will soon have your choice of whomever you want. You ask what happens if someone wishes you to do something that does not please you?' The man laughed. 'I would have thought you'd have already known the answer there. You simply say, "No." ' The man turned away and walked across the room. 'What all those signs mean, brought together and placed in the positions that we have discussed, as I'm sure you've now understood, is that you — ' He turned from a cabinet, where he had taken out two ceramic cups — 'are the Master.' He set them on a table. 'Now come. Let's have a drink. It will lighten all this heavy talk.'

It was cider, not beer. And this time — perhaps it was the amount he'd already drunk — Clodon didn't mind it. What Clodon wanted to talk more about was the women. 'You really think they'll *be* women — I don't mean at first, like you said. But after a while?'

'I know there'll be.' They sat on cushions across from each other, sipping strong drink. 'It makes a great deal of difference to you now. But I think shortly you'll find that it seems a less and less important distinction — assuming you take to your task. Here: say you blindfold someone. And they want to be beaten. They, of course, will want to be hit on the genitals. But you will strike them on the face, instead —gently when they expect to be hit roughly. And roughly when they expect to be hit gently. Ask them questions; and make your response of anger or approbation to their answers wholly random. In most cases that will excite far more than simply whips and chains. And always be sure to agree on some sign to let you know when the game is over: a word, a gesture — that need be all. Uttered by them or you, it simply means it's time to stop, put up the toys, settle accounts, and go home. But because you come to it with dispassion, you are not likely to let the heat of it all carry you away. You're a rough looking boy, even handsome, in a low, country-bred manner. Nor are you dull. If you can apply the brains you have to your job, you'll be able, with a bit of rope and a length of leather, to drive your clients — both the men *and* the women — to pleasure that others, with whole dungeons at their disposal, cannot achieve. What you embark on now is an admirable profession, and ought to have its own god of craft, however nameless, to oversee it. But because we do not have such a god, it must, in the end, be overseen by men and women, like me, like you . . .' Thus the conversation ran on through the night, while one lamp and then another guttered out. 'And remember — ' The man yawned, then recovered, looking down into his cup — 'there's nothing you need do really foreign to that nature you've already drawn for me in some detail.'

Clodon said: 'This is really something. Nobody at my home would believe it. You do this a lot? I mean . . . is this how you get people to do things for you . . . ?' He frowned. 'How many times *have* you done this? Before I mean. With others?'

The man mused. 'Let me see . . . was it a load of nine old broken collars that I purchased from that market harridan? I have two left. That means, over three years, you'll be the seventh.'

Clodon grinned. 'And it works?'

'As a matter of fact I've . . . never seen any of you again. Oh, in a week I'll certainly be on the bridge, looking. But you won't be there —or if you are, you'll have discarded — or sold — your collar days since. That's what experience has told me will happen. But I go on do-ing it. I suppose I shall keep on, until I succeed — or run out of col-lars . . . Oh, certainly I'll keep one for myself. Maybe, someday, I'll even learn why it is I fail. But, then, perhaps such failure can't be un-derstood.' He looked up, slowly, sleepily. 'Or perhaps that's what de-sire is about . . . ?'

Which to Clodon, just — at that hour — seemed even funnier.

He had no memory of the conversation halting or of settling down among the cushions to sleep.

Sometime later, though, the man was shaking his shoulder. 'I'm sorry — you have to go now.'

Clodon opened his eyes, unsure where he was. In the dark room there was the deepest blue around the door hanging. All but one lamp, in the corner, beneath its thread of smoke, were out. Clodon lifted his head from the cushion, shook it — and felt sick.

'You have to go now,' the man repeated. 'Here, get up. I've got money for you. But you have to go. Get up, now. Please. I'm sorry. But Father's returned from his trip — much earlier than I expected. He's outside now and will be upstairs shortly. He's much less tolerant about these things than my mother. Really. But you *must* be on your way!' The man tugged Clodon almost to his feet.

'All right. All . . . I'm going. All right, now. Don't *do* that — '

'Some money,' the man repeated. 'Take it now.'

'Huh?' Clodon said. 'What — ?'

It was a small purse. As Clodon got it in his fist, he could feel, through the leather, there were not a lot of coins in it — but more than he'd had on any day since he'd been in the city. 'Oh, yeah,' he said. 'All right, I mean . . .'

'And now you *have* to go! Just a moment — ' The man loped across the room, pushed back the door hanging, and looked out into the blue, then dropped it to hurry back. 'No, he's not up yet. Come. Let's go.' With a hand on Clodon's shoulder, he hurried the boy, who stumbled once on another cushion, forward.

'Wait a minute, now! Wait a minute, *will* you? Wait — '

Movement caught Clodon's eye to the left.

But it was his own figure, staggering, dark, on the metal.

Then they were outside and crossing between the shrubs and ivy. The paving slates were wet, as though it had rained. Or perhaps the pool had overflowed? Before he could see, the man pushed Clodon through another hanging.

'Hey, don't throw me down the stairs — !'

'Be quiet!' The man breathed heavily. 'I'm *not* throwing you down the stairs!' He sounded peevish. 'But you have to go. And go now!'

Clodon held on to the walls, the purse still in one fist. He put his foot down on the step below.

There was a sound behind them.

The man said: 'You simply *must* get out. Now. I told you, my father is back! I didn't expect him till this afternoon. But he's returned early — oh, it's not your concern! But those are his wagons outside.' Somewhere beyond the wall, it did sound like wagons; someone who could have been a driver called to someone else. 'Look. Go right down there!' The man pointed with a sharp gesture over Clodon's shoulder. 'You won't come out where we came in; but you turn straight to the left and keep on . . . oh, seven, eight blocks. You'll cross a big intersection. At this hour, you'll probably see the sun rising at the end. Go towards it. You'll hit the Pavē after another few streets — you'll recognize the paving stones. You take that right back to the bridge. Now, go! I'm *not* kidding!'

'All right . . . !' Clodon said thickly, and turned to start, unsteadily, down.

'I'll see you in a week back on the bridge!' Which, at this point, meant almost nothing to Clodon.

But he paused anyway, because he'd suddenly remembered where he was. He looked back over his shoulder. 'Do I have to go through all those *dead* people — ?'

'*Go!*' the man hissed.

Clodon started again. At the bottom, somehow he dropped the

purse. But, stooping, he got it up from the dusty floor; he stood, feeling all of last night's drink at once, and barrelled through the hanging out into gray morning. The street was wet in irregular patches. Perhaps it was not rain but fog. The sound of the wagons reached him again from around the building's corner. He wondered if he should go look. But he felt too queazy. He started off, left, down the street.

When he reached the intersection, there was no sun either way. It was too overcast to see the sunrise. Oh, it was a *little* lighter in that direction. So that was the direction Clodon walked in.

Once he stopped a woman with a water jar on her shoulder to ask directions to the Old Market. She pointed down a narrow street which made him think, for a while, he'd gotten completely turned around. But three minutes later he came out at the familiar mouth of the bridge.

He was halfway across when he remembered the collar. It was still closed on his neck. Suppose, he thought, the lock was *not* broken; and the man had fixed it to him permanently . . . In a moment's panic, he raised his hands to grasp it.

'Hey — ?'

Clodon hesitated at the woman's voice behind him, then turned.

He'd seen the pudgy barbarian prostitute there several times. Black triangles spread up across her pale brows, out to her temples.

'I got an old man down there,' she said, nodding over her shoulder. 'He wants to do something with you — the two of us together. He's got money. And a place. He's okay. I know. I've been with him a lot of times.'

Clodon looked beyond her shoulder. Several men stood or walked near the bridge's far end. He could not tell which one she meant. But the idea that the sexual traffic, which he'd always assumed was an afternoon or evening activity, had begun at this early hour made him frown.

'He told me to come talk to you,' she went on. 'I'm supposed to find out how much you'll take.' She wore a colorful piece of cloth around her bulging belly. Her breasts hung over it, wide, smudgy aureoles centered with nipples small as a man's. 'He told me to ask you,' she repeated. 'Don't worry. He's all right.'

'What does he want to do?' Clodon asked.

Though there was no one near them, she stepped closer and began to talk more softly.

When she had gone on a minute, Clodon suddenly said: 'No. No. I don't do that. You tell him I don't do that.'

'Why not?' she said. 'He'll pay you good.'

'No,' Clodon said. Then he said, 'No, don't tell him . . . Tell him I'm — busy. Tell him I'm supposed to meet somebody here. This morning. In a few minutes. That's all. So I can't go with you, see?'

She shrugged. 'I don't care.' She turned away. 'I'll tell him you're busy.'

On her wide, uninteresting feet, she started down the bridge.

Clodon started up toward the market.

Here, he thought, he'd not even been looking, and already one proposition had come along. There'd even been a woman involved with it. Not that he liked barbarian women. Fat or thin, he didn't find them attractive. The men who did — there were always enough of them around the bridge — he thought were strange.

Before he reached the end, a sort of tiredness rolled through Clodon's body that at first seemed part of the sickness left over from the drink. He leaned against the wall and raised his hands again to the iron around his neck. With the tiredness, came a heaviness to his arms. Fingers not quite touching it, he waited. I could take it off now, he thought. Stash it somewhere. Seven days from now I'll put it on again — if I still want to. Maybe that time I *can* get his purse.

But Clodon had a purse already. The man had given it to him. It was tucked under the leather he wore at his waist now. There'd be enough in it to eat for a couple of days, if he was careful.

There was nothing to fear from the collar. It had come open once last night . . .

Now Clodon thought about the woman with the water jar.

Then, he hadn't even realized he had it on! He'd just gone up to her, asked her directions as if he were any normal person. And as if he were any normal person, she had given them. Certainly she'd *seen* it.

Was it, perhaps, like his scars? You couldn't go round, all your life, never speaking to this one, not going here, not doing this, just because someone might have something to say about it. That's what he thought — though it wasn't always what he did. Still, most of the time people ignored them. Or at least pretended to. Perhaps it was the same with the iron.

And maybe a scarred slave — at least out here on the bridge — was a better person to be than a criminal.

The scars were permanent. There was something intriguing in wondering if, somehow, the collar *was*, now, permanent too.

A large market wagon was rolling by, its bed heaped with gray-green melons toward the front and yellow squash at the rear. Beside it, holding the halter to the pair of oxen, the driver walked, a tall, bearded bear of a fellow.

Clodon looked at him, because, he realized, the man was looking at him. Their eyes stayed together for three breaths, four breaths, five. That wasn't the usual sort who took an interest in Clodon. In a moment, anyway, he would look away; the cart would roll on.

What happened, however, was that suddenly the man shook the halter, clucked the beasts to a stop, and strode over. He was a good two heads taller than Clodon. 'You!' He spoke as though Clodon was someone he'd worked with for years and just run into after a month's absence. 'I got a room a few blocks away.' His direct and open tone made Clodon wonder a moment if this were really a sexual encounter. 'We can go there when I finish unloading these. How much will you charge me for an hour or so?'

'What do you want to do?' Clodon asked.

'You know.' The man pursed his lips. 'The usual.'

'I don't do,' Clodon said, 'the usual.'

The man said: 'I don't do the usual either. That's why I asked you. What do you say. How much?'

Clodon considered a moment. Then he said. 'No. I don't feel like it. Forget it. Not today.'

The man smiled and gave a kind of grunt. 'All right. Maybe another time, then.' He started back to his wagon, then turned again. 'Where can I get one of those?' He pointed with a thick thumb over his fist at Clodon's neck.

Surprised, Clodon shrugged.

'Where'd you get yours?' the man asked.

Clodon shrugged again. 'What's it to you?'

The man suddenly turned again, seized up the halter, and started his cart.

I am in another city, Clodon thought. What would it be like, he wondered, if I put a wing of paint on one eye as well? Perhaps, he thought, this is just a particularly busy time and I've never noticed. But how often have I been out on the bridge this early before? Ordi-

narily, a whole day's waiting and walking, when he was actually looking for it, got him three, maybe four propositions. These had both
come within minutes, when there weren't even that many people out.

He wished he didn't feel so ill. He had a headache now. How long,
he wondered, would it be before he said yes?

The third came before the hour was out. It was a pudgy, effeminate
man — though he was just as direct as the other two — who walked
up to Clodon, clasped his hands before him, and declared: 'My, aren't
you a fine looking gentleman! I assume you're sitting out here because you *mean* it? Tell me, how much would it cost me to — '

Clodon only half listened to the man's request. Halfway through
it, he said, 'Look. That's just play. I don't do that. I'm only into *serious*
things.'

'Are you, now?' The man raised an eyebrow. 'Well, perhaps you're a
little *too* serious for me then . . .' He paused, bit at his lower lip. 'I'd
pay you well for it.' Then he frowned. 'Will you tell me what it is you
do do?'

'I told you,' Clodon said. 'No! Now get out of my face!'

The man gave a small, conciliatory bow, then turned and hurried
down the walkway. How long, Clodon wondered, can I keep this up?
Yet there was a fascination with it. This new city that the mortician
had introduced him to — how, he wondered, did it fit in with the
other Kolhari that he knew? Who else lived in it? Could it be that just
by sitting here he would meet them all?

The man had said women dwelled here, too . . . ?

Might one of the inhabitants, Clodon wondered, be a strong, young,
dark-eyed creature with beautiful feet and cunning hands? Perhaps
an hour later, when he began to get hungry, it occurred to Clodon to
look in the purse and count exactly how much the man had given
him.

The purse contained nine iron coins.

Clodon wore the collar for three days.

He didn't eat very much during that time.

Never a particularly clean youth, he didn't wash either.

For the first two, he didn't leave the bridge at all.

As a kind of endurance test, he refused even to see if he could pull
the lock apart. When he took it off, he knew, it would come off for
good. That would be the end of it. But until then, it was, he realized,

fascinating to be something other than a common country criminal lost in the city's confusion.

Once he saw his barbarian friend. But apparently *he* wasn't speaking to Clodon any more.

But with a frequency that kept surprising him, through the day and evening, one and another person would stop to talk with him, to outline some odd and abhorrent want.

He felt very strange. It was as if the collar both trapped him and, at the same time, freed him into this odd world — freed him, at least, to stand at its edge and, as he listened to one request after another, to gaze out into it.

He said no to them all.

It was at the end of the second day he began to get the feeling the people he refused were actually taking something away from him. Each one, walking off when he told them, curtly, that, no, he didn't *do* that, left, he was sure, with a little more; and still a bit more. He slept under the bridge that night. And on the third day, he wandered off it in a kind of daze — actually surprised some barrier was not there to keep him to the place where collar and flogging marks, in combination, alone had the meaning they did.

Later he walked into a yard. There was a cistern in it. He went and sat on the wall awhile, staring down at the flagstones. Once a boy walked by, without really looking at him. Later the boy walked by two or three more times — no, Clodon realized, he *was* looking.

Not that it made any difference.

For a while he sat on the ground, his back against the cistern. Did he doze a bit?

Finally, growing truly tired, Clodon went over by one of the buildings, lay down, and slept for a few hours. Waking, he stretched out his arm, stretched out his leg — which cramped on him. Standing up, he limped back to the cistern, wondering how long the cramp would take to go away. Some women with a child between them walked by. Now he thought he saw the boy again, standing off in a doorway in one of the alleys. Perhaps because he'd slept some, or because of the cramp, or because he was no longer on the bridge — or because, being off it, he had not actually been approached for some hours — Clodon leaned his thighs against the cistern wall, not really looking over it.

Then, after a few moments, he raised his face — it was already evening. The moon was up. A thread of cloud lay across a sky that had deepened to indigo. Clodon lifted his hands to the collar, to hook his fingers over the iron.

He tugged.

With a click, the semi-circles of metal, on the old hinge, came apart in his fists. Clodon pulled the collar from under his hair and raised it to the sky, the curved jaws open in his hand to gulp a bite of blue.

Then he tossed it into the cistern.

It splashed — further down than he could have thought. The water was low.

Still, when you threw things into cisterns, here in the city (Clodon had already learned), old women passing hollered at you: 'That's water we have to drink, you know!' But there were no women.

Clodon turned and lowered himself to sit again on the wall.

Did the boy in the doorway walk by again? Maybe it was another boy, this time. But Clodon was thinking about other things. For the first time, in these last three days, Clodon had looked at the number of people who, indeed, crossed the bridge wearing slave collars. Without even seeing them before, he had just assumed that, on their way to the market for a master, they had been slaves — how stupid could you be? Just before he'd left, he'd seen one, a country fellow only a few years older than himself, who wore the iron on his neck and whose back was crossed with nine, ugly rigid welts. He'd walked by, paying no more attention to Clodon than Clodon once would have paid to him. Clodon tried to remember his image in the mirror. But it was very hard. So he sat a while.

Then he went back to the bridge.

It was a little later, in the moonlight, that the young people, in their tunics and sandals, came down to the Bridge of Lost Desire — and Clodon, turning to watch them, recognized the dark-eyed woman he'd seen six weeks before kneeling on the rock beneath, thinking they were about to come across.

He stopped walking, stopped breathing . . .

No, we have not tried to sketch out the whole of a life. (He saw the mortician pass two or three times again, too; but they didn't speak, or

— after the first time — even look at each other.) We've only tried to suggest a few fragments, some of which fit together one way, some another.

Only *one* more point, however, before we move, twenty-five years on, to Clodon in the Narnis inn yard.

After he left Kolhari, as we have said, his sense of his time in the city grew distorted. In the orgy with the two women at the shack above Vinelet, near-twenty years forward, he could never recall exactly when the fight with the boy and the beer pitcher had occurred. Had it come before the trip into town with the tall woman? Or had it come after? Was it part of the actual murder? Or was it some other skirmish? Similarly, though Clodon remembered, sometimes with great vividness, his encounter with the dark-eyed woman under the bridge and also his visit with the mortician, four months, six months, a year later (as his three months in Kolhari swelled into twelve), it would have been just as hard for him to say which of these came after which — and therefore which had more to do with his leaving.

Clodon was just as unsure about it — and worried about it just as much — as he was and did, years on, about the murder.

But fortunately we — as we do not with the murder — know.

In terms of what happened one afternoon twenty-five years later, this may be significant.

12. The eyes. The hands.

Funig said, 'That's her!' just as though the open window she stood at made it impossible to hear him, made it impossible to see his pointing and gesticulating. 'That's the one I told you about — the actress, with the mummers, who came with the man from — '

Clodon hit him in the side with his elbow:

'Go on, now!' Clodon whispered. 'Get out of here! Go look after your sister!'

And he thought:

No. No, she couldn't have the feet too . . .

And he smiled.

(Funig, after a moment, lurched off around the building corner.)

Smiling, Clodon stopped breathing.

Then, after a few seconds, he turned right — but only to heave the apple core into the bushes. Then he swung left and stalked into the grass, to step the blades with one foot down on top of the other, rubbing them back and forth, wiping his right foot, then his left, free of Krator's slop. Those eyes, he thought. Those hands . . . ! By all the nameless gods —

But, because he had looked away, had walked away, he *was* breathing again.

Is it only, he wondered, because I haven't yet seen her feet that I'm still here? That I haven't run from the inn yard like a rude boy? Look back at her —

Which is when she said: 'Will you come here?'

Clodon caught his breath. And looked back.

And pulled in more air.

And smiled.

Again.

'Please,' she said, leaning on the sill. 'Come . . . just for a moment?'

He started walking toward her, wondering if he might fall or stagger. A jay, silent, swooped between him and the window, bright as a shard of evening hurled across the day.

He *kept* breathing this time, while, at the sill, she filled up his eyes and he blinked. Would I dare, he wondered, lean in over beside her and peer down at them — just to see? What, with her, *would* I dare?

As he stepped up, she reached out and a little down — the window put her not a full head above him — and touched his ear, so that her foreknuckles lay against his beard. 'What's that?'

He swallowed, turning his head aside. Her fingers — the wonderful fingers — supported his lobe.

'It's . . .' he began, hoarsely. 'It's something I . . . well, the men wear it, you see. In the Menyat Canyon. Do you know where that is?' He glanced at her when she dropped her hand.

'I've heard of it,' she said.

'It . . . It's a . . .' knowing that there was a word for it, but losing articulation before her.

What it was was a peg of hard wood, carved with intricate designs and grooved around its middle. Sometime when he was older than twenty but not yet twenty-five, and living among outlaws at the foot of the Menyat, growing bored he'd asked a friend who wore one how to put it in. The peg itself they'd gotten carved by a taciturn geezer who wore three such in one ear and five in the other, with heavily tattooed cheeks and knees. Insertion had involved not just a needle through the lobe, as for some silly ring, but an awl driven through; then, over three weeks, it had to be stretched and stretched further, so that to wear one involved a month's pain and another's discomfort.

Today he never thought of it unless someone mentioned it.

She said: 'Then it's not Narnis work?'

Clodon shook his head.

'Oh. I thought you were from around here.' Her smile fell.

Clodon blinked and grew desperate. 'But I *am*! Born in Narnis, grew up here, I'll probably die here, too — in my own home village!' He reached up to scratch the ear, feeling the distended lobe and the textured wood as if for the first time. 'Of course I ran off a while when I was young. I lived for a year in the big city.'

'Kolhari?' Her smile had started to return.

He nodded. 'But that was a long time ago. I'm sure you know it better than I do.' (She nodded back.) 'Then, of course, I had to travel a bit. I was in the Menyat — where I got this.' He flipped the ear peg with his forefinger, feeling it wobble. 'For a while I went to — ' Daringly, he named his own town — 'where all I got was in trouble.' Clodon laughed sharply. 'Oh, they're small minded, petty people in that place. Not like Narnis, where the people have some breadth. I tell you, that's a good town to stay away from!'

'I've never even heard of it.' Her smile faltered again. 'I doubt I'll ever visit — unless my troupe decides to put it on the tour. I have to meet up with them in Yenla'h.'

'You're a fortunate woman to have missed the place. Yenla'h is much nicer. Oh, I've been as far south as Enoch and Adami. I've been as far north as Ellamon and Ka'hesh.' How surprising, he thought, that she listened and spoke like any other woman. 'But now I'm back in my own village, where I know every boulder and pebble around it, every tree and every twig on her, like I know the veins that cross the back of my own — '

'Wait,' she said. Her smile was back. 'Just a moment, will you?'

Then she was gone from the window —

— so suddenly he wondered, staring at the empty frame, if the whole conversation hadn't been something he'd imagined out of wanting it and not believing it could be.

He put his hands on the sill, stood on tip-toe, and leaned in to look down the hall. Though he'd been inside the place at least three times, he did not recognize the corridor. At least, he thought, while he strained to catch a glimpse of her, in five weeks I know Narnis well enough for anything she might want to find in it.

Old leather creaked.

As Clodon stood up, he saw her push out from the door-hanging and step, with bare, slender feet, to the dust. He was beyond the point where breath might stop now —

As she walked toward him, her toes reached forward like small, separate limbs on the ball of each foot.

— and his heart malletted behind both ears, till the left one — the one with the peg, the one she'd touched — ached. No, he didn't stop breathing. But as she paused before him, he lost most of one breath in awe of her.

'Do you think there's any chance that you . . . ?'

He forced his eyes up.

She was smiling.

He smiled. He breathed.

He said: 'What is it? You tell me, and I'll help — '

'Unless of course you're working now, and you don't have time — '

'What?' he blurted. It came out crassly, hoarsely, and made him blink. Then his eyes began to water. The belligerence that had been his life-long response to anything that annoyed, angered, or confused began to rise, tried to rise — 'What do you want — ?' and was struck down by something powerful as a fist. 'What do you want me to do? I'll . . . do it! Anything. That I can help you with. Please! You just tell me . . . !'

'Thank you!' There was some surprise in her voice. 'You see, I've just heard about the gorge. It's supposed to be very beautiful.' (Bluntly, blindly, Clodon nodded. He reached up to wipe his tearing eyes.) 'My traveling companion's off for the morning. So I thought I'd ask someone to point me in the right direction. Or, maybe — for a coin or two, certainly — to take me there.'

'I'll take you,' Clodon said. 'I'll take you there. I wouldn't take your money for it. But I'd certainly take you to see it. Yes, it's what everyone talks about!'

In the little more than a month he'd been there, Clodon had heard half a dozen mentions of the Narnis gorge with its high rocks and its crashing falls. He even knew approximately in what direction it was. He'd never actually been there, though. For all his travels, Clodon was not much of a sightseer. And since no one had noted it as a place to get drunk, it had not occurred to him to go.

'We'll walk right along up there,' he said. 'It isn't far at all.'

'You're sure I'm not taking you from something?' (The dark disks around her nipples were the same color as the shadowed skin setting off her eyes, making her breasts, suddenly, quite wonderful!) 'Really, if you just wanted to tell me where — '

'No,' he said. 'No. We'll go. You and me, together. I'm not doing anything. It would be nice. And easy — ' He wondered if he should excuse himself a minute, run around, and search up Funig to check on the directions. But Funig would only want to come too — certainly there was no way to keep him from coming back to leer and probably say something stupid, if he didn't simply confound Clodon's lies. 'We'll go right along, now. Up around this way.'

'Fine, then,' she said. Then she said, because he was still standing: 'Can we leave now?'

He started abruptly across the yard. She walked after him, taking long strides. He waited for her at the corner. She came up the dusty slope. 'How far is it?' she asked.

Clodon made a face. 'Not long. An hour. Maybe two — '

'They told me last night,' she said, 'that it wasn't more than half an hour's walk — '

'I was just thinking that the way a nice lady goes along — ' he gave her another silly grin — 'it might take a *little* longer!'

'Oh, I can stride out,' she said. 'Don't you worry!' They walked together up the path. 'What's your name?' she asked.

'Who?' he said. 'Me? My name is Clodon.'

'My name is Alharid,' she said.

Which sounded foreign and difficult and which, he realized, he'd lost as she'd said it — though he'd been sure, a moment back, that, whatever it was, he'd remember it till his death hour. 'What kind of name is that?'

'Alharid?' She smiled. 'Well, I don't really know. Just a name.'

'Say it again?' Clodon asked. 'It's a nice name . . . ?'

'Alharid. Some people have problems with it. But when you're in the theater, that makes it even more memorable to others. Can you say it?'

'Al — ' Clodon hesitated. 'No . . . I don't think I can. I'd get it wrong. And then you'd laugh at me.' But he didn't mind her laughter: indeed, he wanted her to smile and laugh as much as she might. 'Allary — '

'Alharid.'

'Ulrik — '

'Alharid?'

'Clodon!'

'Oh, you're doing it on purpose!' And she did think that was funny.

'But I really can't say it,' he told her. 'It sounds like a foreign name.'

'Not at all!' she said. 'At least it's not foreign where I come from.'

Clodon stopped and turned to orient himself — wondering if, from the little height they'd walked to, he might learn more. They were fifty feet from the inn and only a bit above it. By the back of the low stone building, in the shade, Funig sat against the wall, pawing something up out of a bowl. He'd gotten his breakfast from Jara and had snuck off to have it alone! There, he was up on one knee, squinting after them — set to run, now that Clodon had seen him.

Clodon looked at Alharid. 'That's my friend,' he said with a jerk of his head.

She raised her hand to wave.

'No, leave him alone!' Clodon all but reached out to pull her arm down. 'He's got things to do.' He turned and started up the road again.

'Oh.' She walked with him.

If, in a minute, Funig came lurching up behind them with an offer to share his pot, Clodon would tell him what he could do with it!

But a minute later, they were still alone.

Clodon said: 'Al . . . Alharid?' So much for friends, in these mean, small-minded towns.

'Yes?'

'Now I was wondering. About the man they said you came here with.'

'He's from Minogra,' Alharid said.

'Now that's a town I've never been in. But I hear it's not more than three, four days off.'

'I've only spent an afternoon there myself. It's a little clutch of buildings up on a cliffside — not much else.'

'Is he your fellow?'

'Him?' She put her hands against the dark skirt covering her thighs and bent forward to laugh, then threw back her head. 'Oh, no — he's a very proper country gentleman! He has a whole set of little fruit orchards there. And I'm sure at least one, if not three, mistresses, besides his very dour faced wife you couldn't tell from a house slave, the way he orders her about to bring him this and fetch him that! He's got eight grown children — and I don't think he's as old as you are!'

Clodon thought about saying he had a few himself. Then thought better. But she was going on:

'You can be sure: he'd rather take seven of the welts off your back and put them on his own, before he'd have anything carnal to do with a woman who mounts the mummer's platform in the markets of the great cities and sings and dances and plays her Highness the Empress one night, a prostitute the next, and an evil sorceress the night after. No.' She shook her head. 'He was nice enough to offer me a ride and what little protection he could as far as Narnis and the next town over. But he has his business. I have mine. And there we'll part company.' She glanced at him. 'He has his troubles with my name too.'

'The Empress,' he said. 'And a prostitute — and a sorceress? You're very young to be so many things.'

'Do you think so? How sweet! What age do you think I am?'

'Seventeen?' The woman under the bridge he'd always thought had been about twenty. 'Eighteen?'

'Oh, you're not sweet at all!' she declared. 'You're lying!'

Thinking he'd been found out, he tried to look sheepish.

'I'm a good deal closer to thirty than I am to twenty — and from the wrong direction, too. At least if you're in *my* line of work.'

Clodon was startled. He *had* thought she was twenty, or not much above. 'Well, you know,' he said. 'You get my age and all you youngsters start to look alike.

'Youngster?' She cocked her head. 'Then you *are* sweet after all, I suppose! And with no make-up on, either? But I'm not a little girl, though I'm endlessly flattered you think so.'

They were coming to the edge of the village proper. The prospect of an hour's walk beyond it through rocks and trees to an unknown end began to weigh on Clodon.

Off between two poorer shacks a boy was walking whom Clodon had seen before. Sometimes Funig had spoken to him — he was supposed to be a bad sort. His parents were dead, and he lived with his grandfather. He wouldn't stay on any job more than a few days; and the village rumor was that if he went on the way he was, he was not more than a year from a flogging.

'You stay here — ' Clodon said, suddenly, and hurried off after him. 'Hey — !'

The boy kept walking.

'Hey, you hear me talking to you?'

The boy glanced back, but kept going.

'Here, stop up a minute! I'm speaking to you.'

With a wary look, the boy halted.

Clodon came up to him, lowering his voice. 'How do I get to the gorge?'

The boy said: 'What?'

'The gorge. Which way is it?'

The boy said: 'Why?'

'Come on,' Clodon said, 'tell me! The lady there, she has to go. You know where it is?'

The boy moved one foot on the dirt and scowled, as if debating with himself whether to say.

'Come on, now!' Clodon said. 'You want me to take a hand to you?'

'Well, it isn't *that* way.' The boy nodded back toward where the woman stood.

Clodon put a fist on his hip. 'Then how *do* you go? You probably don't even know!'

'What if I didn't?'

Clodon grunted and raised his chin.

The boy said: 'You take the big path. It goes along to it.'

'What big path?'

'The *big* path,' the boy said. 'Down there.' He pointed through the country alley. 'When it splits, you go that way,' which was a jerk of his head to the left. 'Puts you right out at the bottom of Venn's Stair.'

'And that's it?' Whatever Venn's Stair was, Clodon just hoped it was where he wanted to go.

'You'll be right at it.' The boy looked Clodon up and down, as if getting ready to say something. But Clodon sucked his teeth, turned, and hurried back to Alharid — remembering, with irrelevant surprise, from years and years ago, a woman with a water jar on her shoulder who'd once given him directions in Kolhari. For all the disadvantages of city life, there was something to be said for a place where, when you asked someone something, they told you what you wanted to know without a lot of smart answers.

'What was *that* about?' Alharid asked.

'I just had some business with him.' Clodon gave a few small nods. He didn't want to go down that way if the boy was just standing and staring and glanced back to see if the boy had gone.

The boy *was* standing and staring.

Well, they could go down a little ways above and catch the same big path — if it was the one Clodon, now, was sure it was. 'Come on.' He started again.

She walked with him. 'I wasn't trying to eavesdrop,' she said. 'But I thought I heard him say it was *that* way . . . ?' She gave a very small incline to her head.

'It is,' he said. 'We'll go over there in a bit.' The path became steeper. 'You know, some things, local sights, you know? Because you live with them all your life, you never go see them. Now would you believe, I haven't been up to the gorge since I was his age.' He thumbed back to where the boy still watched. 'I hardly remember the way. They were supposed to be building a new road there, a few years back, so that people like you could go and see it any time they wanted.' All these stories, Clodon thought. Well, at least they filled the time. 'But I never even heard if they finished it or not. That's all I was asking about.'

'Oh,' she said.

He wondered if she believed any of them. 'We'll go by here.'

Beyond the next house the path aside sloped grandly down. In two minutes they came to a wide dirt road, which Clodon recognized as the one on which, a hundred yards back and around a bend, Teren was building his new house. At least the work site was behind them.

They turned along it.

The road sloped gently.

'It splits off up here,' he said. 'We have to keep an eye out for it.'

'All right.' She looked up at the trees on either side. 'It is a wonderful day, isn't it?'

He nodded. 'Yes. Are you from Kolhari?'

'I've lived there more of my life than not. But no, I wasn't born there — though, in Kolhari, that's true of half the people you see on the street. It's like every small town in Nevèrÿon, poured into one kettle and mixed about.'

He was afraid she'd start to ask him about his year there. So he said: 'Your traveling friend — someone told me, last night at the inn, he was talking about the Liberator, this Gorgik fellow? There was a great discussion.'

'Oh, was there now?' She shook her head a bit. 'When we were riding together, though I certainly tried, *I* couldn't get him to talk about anything! After a few stabs, I finally sat back and decided I'd best be the demure thing he'd be most comfortable with. Gorgik the Liberator? Now *that's* something I happen to know of. His loss. But isn't that the way with country gentlemen?'

'They were talking about him and his barbarian friend. I knew some barbarians when I was in Kolhari. But they weren't much for friendship.

'Well, why should they be, at least with us?'

He wasn't sure what she meant, so he said, '*Mmm.*'

'Really,' she went on, 'that's exactly what I mean. About the barbarian. That's news a year out of date! If he'd done more than grunt at me when his wagon wheel went over a rock, he would have known it and had something interesting to say to his tavern cronies when he got here. I went to bed early.' She frowned. 'And slept so *late* . . . !'

'What do you know about the Liberator?'

'Well, he's not fighting alongside his barbarian any more. They had a falling out.'

'That would be what I'd expect from the barbarians I knew, when I was in Kolhari.'

'His new lieutenant is a strange little one-eyed man. There're all sorts of tales. Some say it's magic; some say politics.'

'Have you ever seen him?'

'Which one? The Liberator? His lieutenant?'

'Either.'

'Oh, when our troupe plays the old Kolhari market, sometimes he walks through the square — '

'Off the Bridge of Lost Desire?' Clodon offered.

'That's the one. Our platform and wagons always were set up on the far side. Did you ever see us?'

Clodon snorted. 'I was there twenty-five years ago, little girl!' He'd never seen any mummers at all, though once someone had told him vaguely what they did.

'Well, then, you certainly wouldn't have seen *me* in the troupe! I didn't mount the boards for the first time till I was at *least* thirteen. Then, at seventeen I retired to be the loving wife of a man who didn't appreciate my talent at all. I made my triumphal return to the stage when I was twenty — don't ask me what happened to the children. You'll make me start to cry.'

Clodon laughed. 'You don't ask me about mine; I won't ask you about yours.' When he looked at her again, though, she was blinking at him seriously.

'Maybe,' she said, 'we're not such a nice pair after all.'

He frowned back. 'What about the Liberator?'

'Oh, the great Gorgik? He doesn't like the theater. I told you he walks about in the market. Now in between our skits, now from around the corner of one of the prop wagons, I've had him pointed out to me fifty times. And I've pointed him out at least to fifty others. Oh, he's a very impressive man to see. And to listen to, at least I've been told so. I've never heard him speak myself, but I've spoken to others who've heard him not an hour before telling me about it. They say he has a great and sincere desire for freedom for all Nevèrÿon's oppressed.'

'Oh, *I* know what kind of desire he has!'

'Well,' she said, 'there's *that* too. But then he's never made a secret of it.'

'How could he,' Clodon said, 'if he wears his collar right out for all to see?'

But she seemed to be thinking of something else. 'I've always wondered why he never stopped to watch us. No time for it, I suppose. Though, in at least a dozen of our entertainments, we've made him a character — now the hero, now the villain, depending on the temper of the times. But that's fame for you. Myself, if I were him, I'd want to see what people were saying about me. But he's a man with a mission. A man? He's practically a giant. He strides about, in his great iron collar — '

'With the welts of a rebellious slave across his back?'

Alharid frowned. 'No, actually.' She pursed her lips. 'He has a scar on his face — right down across one eye. A bit like yours, there. At least it's in the same place. But it's much bigger. Not that anyone could mistake the two of you for one another.' (The road had split. Without even a mention, Clodon had taken them off to the left, like one easy and familiar with this landscape a lifetime. Only why, he wondered, was the general slope down, rather than up?) 'He was a real slave himself, once. But you knew that.' (Clodon hadn't till now. It made it all seem odder.) 'It's how I think we all know he's sincere. But all his rebellion came only once he managed to get free: no, he avoided flogging while he was in servitude. There're as many among the more radical factions in this land who think that stands against him as there're those, among the conservatives, who find it a trait to praise. No.' With a considering expression, she shook her head slowly. 'He has no flogging marks. And that's the sort of thing I'd remember.'

'And why would somebody like you remember something like that?'

'It's the kind of thing one sees about a man. If you're me, at any rate. The fact is, for reasons I couldn't begin to tell — ' she looked at him with a sideways smile that was different, and more interesting, than any of her others — 'I've always had a fascination with men who rebelled enough to get themselves whipped for it. Doesn't *that* make me a silly woman, now!'

He looked at her, having, at this point, forgotten to smile.

'What kind of fascination . . . ?'

'Oh, what kind of fascination does a woman develop? I even married one, once. Eighteen welts across his back from three different whippings in three different towns. No, I'm not talking about the scoundrel I left the mummers for when I was seventeen — he *should* have been flogged! Both before he met me and, certainly, after. But this was in Sarness — much later. It didn't last very long. A disaster, really. They came and arrested him practically out from under me — I could still smell his sweat on the insides of my arms. Oh, I suppose I should have fought and screamed and bitten and tried to hold him to me. But it wouldn't have made much difference. I just stood there . . . and watched while they took him away. I guess my fascination doesn't really extend *that* far. It probably would have been lovely, though, if we'd just been friends for a while. Like you and me.'

Clodon had — almost — stopped breathing again. He said: 'I have a fascination with . . . women . . . with — ' He gulped in air, and looked at her; she looked at him with all seriousness, all smile gone; and suddenly it seemed so terribly important to say it, for he was sure he would never have another chance — 'who smile at me with eyes . . . like your eyes. Who have such hands as you have.' There, was that it? Turning his face forward, he realized he couldn't see the road at all in front of him. 'Who walk — ' He heard his voice catch roughly — 'with such feet as you walk with.' He slapped both hands against his face, pulling a breath between his palms, rubbing his eyes with horny fingers. And went on walking. 'And it's going to shake me apart, today, if it doesn't kill me before the night comes. Is that the kind of fascination . . . that you have? That you *could* have . . . for someone who had . . . ?' He tried to say it but it was something between a choking and a grunting and a gasp.

While he rubbed his eyes and kept walking, she didn't speak, so that, as when she'd vanished from the window, he began to wonder if, yet again, she were really there at all and this was only some fantasy that had, in his dotage, become *too* real.

'I'm an old man,' he said. 'An old, bad, dirty man. Sometimes rough men, old men, men with no breeding, like me, they'll talk about each other's foolishness over the girls, and they'll say, "Well, you know, he hadn't had a woman in a while," to explain why one of them did what they did. But they're fools and liars. I've had women, plenty of women, in all the ways a man can have them — but, when I see you — ' He took his hands, his ugly hands, the right one with its missing finger, away from his eyes, blinking the road back into tearing clarity —

She touched his shoulder . . . with her fingertips! And they moved in a way that told him she was walking with him, was listening to him, even though he couldn't look at her.

' — but when I see *you*,' he said, 'I know I've never had *any* woman before — not like you. I've never been nearer one than now, never glimpsed one from so close before, and certainly never spoken to any. I'm an ugly, dirty, bad old man, who's never had a woman — like you? But why should I even have to *say* that part? And it's the cruelest thing the nameless gods have ever done to me to make me say it now. To you. Like this. And look such a *fool* for it!'

They walked for a while. There was a roaring someplace. She said: 'Then why have you done it?' There was, at least, concern in her voice. 'What did you hope to do by . . . saying it?'

'I don't know,' he said. 'I don't know! Nothing! I don't know . . .'

They walked a little further. The air had grown damp around them. After a bit she said:

'No . . .' in such a way that he looked at her. 'No, that's not the kind of fascination *I* mean.'

He looked ahead again. Off through an arch of trees, water rushed. He glanced at her.

'For one thing,' she said, her smile coming back, 'I've *known* my share of criminal gentlemen. You say you haven't known very many like — well, me. But perhaps you're exaggerating for effect.' (He shook his head in wild denial.) 'Though, it's true, that's not the type I would have thought you. Oh, perhaps there's something about the way I'm taken with marked men that's a *little* like what you talk of; but, if only for that part, there's got to be something about it quite different.' She took her hand away. 'But I hope you're happier now that you've told me.'

He took a breath.

'And I don't think you're a fool. Who's going to think *anyone's* a fool for liking them? You shouldn't feel badly — '

'Oh, I don't!' he said. 'No, I don't at all — '

'I mean,' she said, 'it *is* the reason I called you over. I'm not going to play about that. I'm too old and you're too old. I like you. I hope that's not going to be too terrible for you. You're certainly better than my gentleman farmer. But, look, now — I just don't believe, at your age, you've *never* encountered some woman before who liked the fact that you had some spirit to you, that you'd been a few places and — let's say it out — had gotten your welts in the process!'

'I have!' Clodon swallowed. 'Only, I wasn't ready for that to be you,' he admitted. 'I wish we had a drink . . . !'

She laughed, like a traveler relaxing on hearing some local saw that, repeated a hundred, a thousand times, now identified which county they'd ended up in. 'Well, we don't. So we'll have to act like real ladies and gentlemen. Do you want to hold my hand? I'd like to hold yours.'

While he wondered how he was supposed to take hers up in his mutilated fist, she took his. He almost couldn't feel it. So delicate, it seemed the same temperature as the air.

She said: 'There!'

They stepped through the arch of leaves before the water cutting them off.

The last waterfall Clodon had seen was one he'd just come across in the forest, maybe three years back: it had been some fifteen or twenty feet high. And that's what he'd been expecting here. But the water before them was a mazy twenty, even thirty feet wide. It wound away up stream perhaps forty or fifty yards. Then, in a series of boulders, stone platforms, and rocky levels, it rose, and rose, and rose, in glassy sprays and crashes of white, which did not even reach the top of the rocks. Rather, higher than he'd ever imagined a mountain, much less a falls, the whole great scoop out of the stone turned aside and disappeared, while the rock face (a quarter of a mile? a half a mile off?) kept rising, still, to an edge of trees that looked, from this distance, thin as moss.

'The gorge . . . !' she whispered.

Clodon was so surprised that, until she said it, he was not really sure if this were their goal, or just some wonder encountered by the way.

He looked around. 'We can climb along some of it,' he told her.

A ledge had been cut directly into the stone of the shore that, level, led some feet above the rapids. Ahead, they could see it rise, in several sets of steps, at some places even cut into the wall to form a corridor with a ceiling and sided by squat stone columns.

'That must be what they call Venn's Stair,' she said.

He wondered how she knew so much about the place and he so little.

The promenade seemed to dwindle, till it was just a line high up the rocks that (a mile off?) disappeared behind the far wall of trees and soaring cliffs.

'How far does it go up?' she asked, dropping his hand and starting out along it. Clodon followed. 'Well, you know — ' He came up after her — 'it's been so long since I've been here. I don't really remember. Pretty far, I'd say . . .' He wondered if he should take her hand again. Steps ahead, she started up the second set of uneven, stone stairs, their crevices wedged with leaves.

Clodon said: 'I've . . . never been here before!'

Still climbing, she looked back at him with that particularly interesting smile. 'I didn't think you had.' She reached behind and gave his arm a squeeze. Clumsily he squeezed her hand back.

Then it didn't seem to matter if they held hands or not — since, as one swung by her skirted hip or the other raised to press the mossy stone, he could (as he mounted three steps behind her) watch.

They climbed a long while.

Distances were not so great as he'd thought.

But when they'd climbed along twenty minutes, over the low wall beside them they could see what looked like a stade of nothing, with a swirl of froth on green-black water at its bottom, and some water-slicked boulders, some rising spume. Across from them, flecked with trees and vegetation, red-brown rock leaned majestically away. Here and there it was cut with ledges that looked wholly unattainable — till you began to think about the steps they climbed now, which every once in a while became a damp corridor, with a low ceiling and a colonnade of squat columns, some wrapped as high as his shoulders with moss.

Between them, the gorge . . .

They'd gone around a curve so gentle Clodon had not even been aware of it; but the vista had changed completely, opening onto an even higher wedge of rock (the word suggesting something smaller than what was below, but they were looking at something half again as huge as what they'd already seen), down which white water fell, hundreds and hundreds of feet, the wind catching curls of it to blow out on the air.

Clodon said: 'I guess the steps end just ahead.'

Over the waist high wall beside them, where the curve was sharper, a tributary falls roared from a crevice fifty feet on and a little below, to drop and drop and drop, joining the main cascade, measureless rods down. The steps seemed to stop at some sort of observation place — seemed to; because when they reached it, what they actually did were swing around and continue along the side of the tributary's canyon.

The far wall here was only twenty feet away. Sky began maybe forty feet up. Again they were on a wide ledge. The water, which, just before, had rushed to spill a quarter of a mile through air, here had a surface so smooth it seemed not to move, save when a twig or a leaf shot along it. Through it, rocky ledges and outcropping were visible to a bed nine feet down. They wound their way, looking above, looking below. The light between the cliffs was luminous. The feat of the stairs' construction gave way for a few yards to something almost nat-

ural, before more steps swung around another bend in the crevice —
Things darkened about them.

They looked up. In that second the light returned.

'What *was* that?' Alharid asked.

And Clodon realized how much the water's roar had subsided. The last time she'd spoken, he hadn't been able to hear her.

'Isn't this incredible?' she said, a few steps further. She'd said it several times before.

Impressed with the first dozen views, it was beginning to pall for Clodon. But he was glad she still enjoyed it.

'Can you imagine,' she went on, 'someone in a tiny town like this, cutting steps through all that stone? And they don't even have a castle here. It must have taken a hundred years!'

Quite simply, Clodon could *not* imagine it; he'd given up trying before they'd turned into this grotto.

She frowned up. 'Do you think it was a bird? I mean, that shadow, just before?'

'It was a pretty big one, then.' Clodon looked at the leafy ledges of the rock walls, now on their side of the water, now on the other.

She took his hand. 'Maybe it was a cloud?'

'Then it was a pretty fast one.'

They started again. The ledge they walked was broad enough for them to go abreast. The water's surface, at its mossy line, was ten feet down.

The far wall sloped much lower here — but not the near one. Then, again suggesting unknowns of history and contrivance, the ledge went round another corner to reveal a bridge. It was wood. Clearly it marked the end of the stair. Once it may have been sturdy.

'I don't think there're enough people in Narnis to keep something like this in any kind of repair.' Alharid gave words to a thought that was only a vague discomfort for Clodon.

He put his foot out on it and leaned. 'It seems strong.' He pulled his foot back, then stamped. Nothing even shook. So he stepped out on it. 'Come on.'

She glanced up, took a great breath, and started after him.

On the other side, the road — for it was just a road now, as you might find through any stretch of country — moved away from the water into the trees. Yellowing leaves made the light a gold haze. They looked down a slope that lost itself among slim trunks.

Once the trees broke, and they looked out across a valley in which, somewhere, the falls must now be hidden. As they walked, Clodon wrinkled his nose. 'You know what I think it was we saw?' He sniffed. 'The thing that crossed the crevice above us?'

'What?'

'A dragon.'

'Oh, that's silly!' she declared. 'Narnis is *much* too far west of Ellamon for dragons!'

'All those ledges and cliffs and canyons — you saw them. That's dragon country.'

'Yes, but there *aren't* any dragons any more — *except* at Ellamon. And they're all in corrals.'

'Smell,' he said. 'Go on. Take a sniff.'

She wrinkled her nose, breathed in deeply. 'That's not dragons,' she said. 'It's just that funny stink cypress trees give off. When their cones drip.'

'Not the cypresses,' he said. 'The smell under them — as if the cypresses were trying to cover it.'

She frowned. She sniffed. 'I don't smell anything.'

'You ever *smell* a dragon before?'

She shrugged. 'Not really. Who ever gets close enough for that . . . ? I don't really think I'd want to.' Then she asked: 'Did you?'

'Wait here a minute.' Clodon pushed off into the underbrush beside the road. Once the branches eased up, then thickened again about him. A few feet on, there was a drop. He lowered himself to his knee, and leaned over. Down three or four feet was a slope of bare, white stone that extended out in a cliff that ran along, nine or ten feet wide. Beyond that was nothing but sky, cloud, and the valley's far mountain. Clodon sniffed again.

He ran his eye back along the ledge: grayish-green, oval, a little larger than good-sized apples, and slightly wrinkled like spoiled fruit, they lay in an uneven depression. He counted five, six, seven of the things!

'Come here!' he called over his shoulder. 'You can see! Here!'

'Where are you?'

He heard her pushing through leaves.

'Over here.'

'What did you find?'

'Look . . .'

She came up beside him, standing while he kneeled. 'Where . . . ?'

He pointed.

'I don't see any — '

'There. Those are the flying creature's eggs.' (Now she dropped beside him.) 'Told you I could smell them. The stink's dragon spoor. Put a lot of them together and it's something really fierce — even with no cypresses.'

Her arm was against his. So was her hip. The brush was thick enough that there was no way to be together and *not* be that close. She said, 'Oh . . .' with real surprise. 'Do you really think — ?'

When he glanced back at her, though, she was smiling again.

'No . . .' she said, suddenly, cajolingly. 'Those aren't real dragon eggs!'

'What are they, then?'

'I think they're dragonfruit.'

He said: 'Dragonfruit doesn't smell like that.'

'Neither do dragon eggs.'

'But the dragons who come to make their nests on the ledges around these parts do — you can believe that!'

'Well, I *did* see some dragonfruit trees a bit further down.' She sat back on her heels. 'And I know all about the way the children pick and dry them in the sun till they get them the proper color with the proper wrinkles, then try to fool you and each other and everybody else into thinking they're the real thing.'

'There aren't any dragonfruit trees *here*.' Clodon hadn't seen any at all. But then, he hadn't been looking for them. 'Besides, who would pick them and put them out there?'

'One of your local bad boys, here an hour before us. I bet the sullen one you got the directions from beat us here by a short cut, then rolled them along — just so you'd think what you're thinking!'

'It's a lot of trouble to go to for a prank.' Nor, he thought, was it the sort of prank that particular boy would play.

She said: 'It's a lot of trouble for someone to cut that ledge and all those steps and columns. But people do things like that.' She looked at him, put her hand on his shoulder, and leaned a little. 'You could just as easily say it was a lot of trouble for us to come all the way up here to get off from those nosy people in that silly little town.' She looked very serious. Then the seriousness gave way to a smile again. 'But we did it.'

He looked back. After moments, he said, a little wildly: 'I'd have to have a drink . . . !'

'Come,' she said, raising her other hand to his beard, touching a knuckle to his heavy under lip. 'Come. Out of these bushes, now!'

They didn't get all the way to the road. In the partial clearing half-way back, there were enough fallen leaves scattered so that when Clodon broke away three or four more shrubs and hurled them off, there was room to stretch out — almost comfortably. He lay on his back with his arms around her, kissing and kissing her hand. Then he kissed her feet. Then he just held them. Finally he lay down again and kissed her face.

She stroked him and kissed him back.

'Oh . . .' he said; 'Oh . . .' with each breath. And wondered if he were going to die right there. Then forgot death as if it were the smallest scar familiar on his body.

'See,' she said. 'Now you see? You *don't* need a drink!'

He said: 'Oh . . . !'

13.1 And Clodon was dreaming.

It was a clear, passionate, complex dream, vivid with voices and colors, actions and artifacts.

The voice said:

'Lust has made me a slave. But desire has set me free.'

The voice said:

'Freedom has let me lust. But I am a slave to desire.'

13.2 Clodon was peering into a cloud or a pool or a fog. A figure came forward, clearing as if lit by a thousand lamps. He was a ponderous man, sort of a giant, though there was more good humor about him than you might have expected.

He might even, Clodon thought, be a good man.

Clodon could see that now.

He wore an iron collar around his neck, like a slave. But on his heavy flanks, confounding all judgments, the ends of the welts showed rigid from where he'd been flogged — like a murderer, like a bandit, like someone with nothing but contempt for all the laws of humanity, with nothing but loathing for the order of the nameless gods.

The only thing unclear was which of the voices was his and which was Clodon's.

Slavery . . . lust . . . freedom . . . desire . . . ?
Even if it meant the death of him, Clodon couldn't remember
which of the words came first.

13.3 The voice said:
    'Desire has made me a slave. But lust has set me free.'
    The voice said:
    'I am a slave to freedom. But desire is slave to lust.'

14. He woke with leaves beating at his face, thinking, somehow, he
was beside rushing water. Only she was moving, shaking him — and
the sound was a kind of roaring, and also a honking, like a donkey in
a storm. She whispered: '. . . We have to go! We *must* . . . !' Then,
suddenly, he grabbed her, pushed to his knees, pulling at her, and got
his feet under him, to stagger through the brumbles. The leaves on all
the trees around roared and roared, loud as the falls so far down. The
branches dipped maniacally and rose and thundered around them.
He knocked back more branches and ran. Behind him, her arm tugging in his hand, she called, 'Clodon . . . !' and, for a moment, he was
sure they would break out from the brush and go right over a ledge
into the empty, empty air —
    They stumbled out on the road, though. He started to sprint along
it. Then, frowning, he looked back — to see *her* looking back.
    The trees, only in that one place, waved and clashed their branches.
The trumpeting honk trailed, so slowly, off, as if forced out by a pair
of lungs each big as a bullocks. 'Come . . . !' he shouted. And she
ran, catching herself against him. They hurried together across the
bridge and into the tributary crevice.
    Without slowing, they rushed above glassy water, now glancing
up at blue air and cloud, now down at their reflections.
    Ahead, the crevice opened up. The frothing falls spumed out into
the gorge, to join the greater cascade.
    'Oh, stop . . . !' She grabbed his shoulder and leaned her head
there, breathing hard. 'It isn't protected, once we're around the corner.
Do you think . . . ?'
    He took a breath, shook his head, and said: 'Dragonfruit . . . !'
    'It could fly right down at us,' she said, 'once we're out on the main
part of the stair!'

He looked up between the leaf-fringed walls. 'They don't *do* that,' he said. 'I don't think.'

'Don't you think we should wait . . . ?'

He sucked his teeth. 'Come *on*!'

She managed half a smile. 'Oh, you *are* a terrible man!'

He managed one back. 'Dragonfruit!'

They started, reached the corner — where they came out on it now, the gorge was enough to make him sit right down, there on the wet steps.

But they hurried, only lingering when they were in some corridor with the mossy columns squatting thickly between them and the sky.

'It was, really,' she said, when, an hour later, holding hands, they came down the last steps beside the broad river rushing away along the valley, 'kind of wonderful. I've never seen a dragon before. Not even at Ellamon. I've just heard about them.' Behind them the falls roared, louder than any beast. 'And don't say "dragonfruit" to me again!'

Before the arch of trees covering the big path, they both stopped.

'I . . .' he said. 'I had a dream. While we were sleeping. Up there.'

'Oh?' She stretched her arms over her head. 'And I *did* sleep wonderfully, too — until that . . . *thing* started to tear the forest down around us!'

'It was *just* a dragon.'

'It was *ten* dragons!' she said. 'All trying to kill each other. At once. I'm sure.'

'You *saw* it?'

'No,' she said, 'thank all the nameless gods!'

'Neither did I.' He made a face. 'But I smelled it. Probably wasn't a big one.'

'I'd always heard dragons weren't even supposed to *have* nests. I mean, the kind of nest they mother. They're just supposed to lay their eggs on a cliff somewhere, and — ' She flapped one hand — 'fly off and forget them. Leave them to the sun and the stars to hatch.'

'Well,' Clodon said, 'this one came back.' He repeated: 'I smelled it.'

'I smelled it too,' she said. 'At least when it woke us up.'

They turned under the trees back down the path toward Narnis.

Clodon said, again: 'I had a dream . . .'

She looked over at him.

In the late afternoon, there was a copper cast to the light slanting among the branches.

'It was about the Liberator,' he said. 'At least I think it was. Probably because we were talking about him, before . . .' But what could he tell her of such a dream? 'You say he doesn't work with the barbarian any more — that he has a one-eyed man for a lieutenant, these days? Now I could tell them that, back at the inn some night. That would get them to listen. Only, of course, if it came from me, someone would say: "How do *you* know? You've always been a liar and fool!" '

'Well,' she said, 'you could say you got it straight from someone who knows a lot more about it than *they* do. And it would be true, too. I follow what the Liberator does pretty closely. A lot do, these days. Some say they're only waiting to make him a minister.'

'Now if I said *that* in the tavern — ' Clodon spat — 'they'd only think it was more lies and rumors and gossip — and pay it no mind.' He thumbed his mustache for spit.

'Isn't that odd about little towns,' she said. 'One person's rumor they can take to heart and make a holy thing of it, while another's they just toss off and never heed it at all. And neither one has to be any truer than the other — or any falser.'

They walked a while.

Clodon said: 'There was a man, once — a long time back. During the year I lived in Kolhari.'

'Did you really live in Kolhari?' she asked. 'Vinelet, I'd believe — but Kolhari?'

'Oh, yes,' Clodon said. 'I certainly did. A whole year, too.' And he did not even know he was lying. 'He was an undertaker. Now he'd be one to wear the collar, like the Liberator does — if he dared. I met him on the Bridge of Lost Desire. I think he really wanted to show me something — something about myself. Said he wanted me to do a job.' Clodon humphed again. 'He talked about it as if it were learning a trade. Only I couldn't see it. Nor was I much for working, back then. But I really think he wanted to take everything mean, and bad, and wicked about me and turn it to some good purpose — at least as he saw it — so that others might get some pleasure from it.' Clodon laughed. 'He said it never worked. I didn't see it then, though it looks so clear to me now. I'm just not like them. That's all it is. I'm not like they are. And they're not like me — no matter how much he thought, perhaps, we were. Our basic natures, they're just different.' Did she understand, he wondered, at all? And why was he saying it? 'What *I* want to do, it's not much different from what we did. With maybe just a jug of beer along.'

'It *would* have been nice to have a little something to drink.' She nodded now. 'But I wouldn't have wanted to carry it up all those steps. Or run back down with it.'

'The ones who see themselves clear; who can look in a mirror and see who they are. They're lucky. And yet, when you *do* see what it is you want, it seems so . . .'

'Simple?' she asked.

He laughed a little without opening his mouth. 'Lucky . . . that's all!'

'Am I supposed to say at this point,' she asked, a bit guardedly, ' "You know, Clodon, you really *are* a good man?" ' She put her hands behind her now as they walked. 'The thing is, I really *have* known a fair number of your sort. If it's what you want to hear, and will make you happier for the day, I suppose I can say it.'

'Me?' Clodon said. 'A good man? Ha!' He walked a little slower. 'Sometimes, though, I wonder what I'd have to do to become one.'

'Now *that's* such an easy question!' she said. 'At least for me. Stay here in this little town. Work. And keep on working. Don't get drunk more than once a month. Get in the habit of speaking the truth — it's no less a habit than lying. Be kind to children and small animals. When you get some woman pregnant — and, drunk or not, you will — *don't* run off to another town the week you hear the news. Be as kind and considerate to her as you've been to me. And when the dragon beats her wings and honks, hold her, hold her in the dark, and tell her, "No, no, there's nothing to be afraid of! It'll be all right!" '

Clodon said: 'There really *isn't* much to be afraid of with dragons. Up close, they're all noise and bad smell. And there're not that many left.'

'Now you see?' she said. 'That's something, somewhere in your travels, you've actually learned. It's very valuable knowledge, too.'

Clodon drew himself up. 'Still,' he said, 'you're asking a lot of a man like me.'

'I wasn't asking anything,' she said. 'I was answering. But an answer doesn't mean much if you can't hear your own question.'

Clodon said: 'You know, right up ahead is where I work. Just around that bend is where Teren's building his new house. We'll walk by, and there they'll all be, digging away at his foundation. Now if he had any sense, he'd make me his foreman. I'd get the job done for him in half the time those lazy fools are taking. I've done that kind of work before, and I know what it's about — a good bit better than *he* does. And what'll they think of me in a minute, walking by with you?'

After three steps, she stopped.

'What . . . ?' he said.

'It occurs to me,' Alharid said, 'maybe to make things easier for me and easier for you, that I should go on by myself. You wait here a bit, then come after me. They're probably rumors enough already flying about the town. I'm sure at least two people saw us walking off. And that's all it takes. But still, it might help things out just a little if lots of people didn't see us together.'

'Oh,' he said. 'That's right . . .'

'How do I get back to the inn from here?'

'Follow this path right along. You'll see where they're working. A little while on, it swings around and goes by the tavern — only in the front. You won't miss it. We just took the back way.'

'Oh.' She lifted her head. 'Well, give me ten or fifteen minutes. Then you can come.' She leaned over, giving him a kiss; then she walked quickly away.

Standing, watching her, Clodon began to feel the ache of incompletion, of wanting, of anxiety — would she be staying at the inn that night? Would he have a chance to see her again, or even to say goodbye as she was leaving? Clodon, as we have written, had always lived with desire at a distance. But though he could be as proprietary, possessive, or jealous about a bed-mate as the next man, it would have taken a great deal more than one afternoon to make him feel he had any *right* to what had just happened up on the ridge above the gorge.

He stood, under the trees, fifteen minutes or more. While he stood, he thought: Narnis wasn't such a bad town. It had a gorge beside it — with dragons! And now and again interesting strangers, among them this astonishing woman, came through. He'd even saved her from the loud beast . . . He *was* getting older. Would it really be so bad to show up every day at Teren's foundation till the stone house rose above it? No, he didn't like work; but he wasn't afraid of it either.

And she might someday come back. After all, she liked his sort.

She had a fascination. Wouldn't she be surprised if, when she returned, he had a hut of his own, where he could ask her in and pour her a mug of beer, or cider if that's what she drank, or rum —

Yes, it *had* been fully fifteen minutes. And he was mortally thirsty. Maybe Teren would be buying his men an after-work beer. And if Clodon just tagged along . . .

He started up the road.

In a minute, he rounded the bend.

There they all were, digging like dung beetles.

Teren stood off at the side, looking down, rubbing his fingers against his short, black beard.

And there, with his bucket in his good hand, and starting up the ladder, was Funig. So, he'd come on up to be put to work after all!

'Hey, Funig!' Clodon called.

The boy looked up, saw him, and nodded, grinning.

Clodon walked between dug-up piles of earth to step over the handles of a wooden barrow, turned with its wheels in the air. 'I see you finally got *him* to bend his back!' he called to Teren. 'I didn't think he was going to get here at *all* today!'

Teren kept looking down. Then he said, 'There, that's enough,' to someone else, like something important was going on, down in the pit. He glanced at Clodon, then stepped away.

'Hey, Teren!' Clodon said. 'I just stopped by to tell you I think I'll be back here tomorrow.'

Teren's ragged vest didn't come all the way below his shoulder blades. 'Who says I want you?' Without turning back, Teren bent to pick up a hoe lying dangerously with its blade up; his kilt showed the crevice between his buttocks.

Clodon stuck a thumb beneath his own leather clout to tug it up a bit. 'Well, you need all the men you can get. Especially those who know this kind of work. You said that, yourself. This is quite a job — you're coming along well, too!'

Standing, Teren turned. 'Don't come here tomorrow, Clodon.' He let the hoe fall against a mound.

'You put the boy on, and he didn't come in till half the day was done.'

Funig was lurching over, the treachery of breakfast forgotten.

'But I'm not putting *you* on!'

'You're acting like this, just because I missed a day? Well, I drink too much, sometimes. It's hard for me, then, to get out and about. What man here can't you say that of? That's no news!'

What rumors, Clodon wondered, could have possibly started in so little time about him and a woman even less a part of Narnis than he? If it had been Jara he'd gone off with, he could see it.

'Hey, Clodon!' Funig said. 'You coming down to the inn after work? We can go off and — '

'You're not going anywhere with Clodon,' Teren said. 'If I see you with him, boy, I'll beat you. With my own fist. And you won't work for me or anyone else any more. And you'll get your first flogging for it. I'm not fooling.'

Funig protested: 'We're just going to talk — '

'You don't have anything to say to Clodon. And he doesn't have anything to say to you.' Teren looked like he was about to strike Funig. 'You hear me, now?'

Funig flinched. He glanced at Clodon, at Teren, then turned and lurched off between the piles.

'What's all this about?' Clodon's voice hung between mock openness and mock belligerence; he felt a growing anxiousness.

Teren's hard hand fell on Clodon's shoulder. 'I'm going to have a talk with you,' he said. 'And then I'm *not* going to talk to you any more!' He walked Clodon across the site.

Some of the others looked up.

Teren didn't stop until he was at the very edge, standing just at the big path's scooped out shoulder. 'When were you in Minogra?'

Clodon felt a kind of coldness at the small of his back. 'Minogra?' He shook his head. 'What is it? Where is it? I don't know anything about Minogra.'

'There's a man here, from Minogra, who stayed at the inn last night. He's traveling with the lady who just came by. Did you see her up the road?'

'What lady?' Clodon said. 'What man?'

That was stupid, Clodon thought. The boy he'd asked the directions from will tell him we were together. For all his bad ways, he was still Teren's cousin. Oh, he'd tell, all right!

'The man came by. He spent some time here at the site today. He was talking with me, you see. He said about six weeks back, there was a fellow at Minogra — had a gut on him. He'd been whipped, too. Had twelve welts across his back. I think it was twelve — you want to turn around and let me count them, one at a time?'

'So . . . ?' Clodon said. 'So there was a man there. So what?'

'He'd only been there a while. But they caught him thieving — the same kinds of things you and Funig have been pulling here.'

'Now you know Funig talks a lot of noise. But he's a fool, not a thief!'

'I'm talking about *you*, man!'

Clodon narrowed his eyes.

'They caught you. At Minogra. The bailiff had you for a whole day, but you broke loose and fled the place — before you could get your *next* whipping.'

'Now that's a rumor!' Clodon declared. 'That's all! It's just something somebody said. How's he supposed to know it was me?' A whole *day*? The bailiff hadn't been able to keep him an hour, before he'd got himself loose and gone! Oh, those old Minogra farmers could be liars! 'A stranger from another town comes by, and you're going to take a bit of gossip and throw it up to me like that, after I've worked for you here on your dirty dig? That's not right, Teren! That's not right! I wasn't anywhere near Minogra. I've never even heard of it! You're going to take his word over mine, just because I'm a marked man? Well, my marks say that I've paid up what I owe. That's what they say. You don't have to know much to read *that* from a flogged man's hide!'

'If you ran out on a flogging still owing, you can't talk about debts paid!'

Clodon pulled back, but Teren yanked him forward again by the shoulder.

'The man who escaped at Minogra,' Teren said, 'had a peg in his ear from the Menyat. He had a finger off his right hand. And he had a scar on his lower lip, and another through his eyebrow. I'm not a vicious man, Clodon. But if you show up tomorrow, the bailiff will be here ten minutes later. And if you go to the tavern tonight, bothering Funig or Jara, he'll be *there*. And if you stand around here for more than another three minutes, I'll send someone for him *now*!'

Clodon started.

But Teren pulled him forward once more. 'Do you hear what I'm saying? There's the path down to the highway. You keep on it. There's nobody in this town you need to say another word to. And *maybe*, if you leave tonight, I won't send anyone after you. Do you hear!'

Clodon stepped back again, yanking from Teren's grip.

He looked around at the dig.

He blinked at Teren, who was standing there, breathing quickly, with his eyes kind of slit.

Then Clodon turned and started down the road.

Perhaps, he thought, he could stop at the inn for a minute, and see Alharid, and tell her what had happened. But then, she was *with* the man from Minogra. And hadn't she said it? Her fascination didn't go that far.

Suddenly, Clodon turned off into the woods.

You just couldn't trust small-town folk like Teren, once they got righteous.

After only five weeks, too — oh, it wasn't fair to drive him out from such a town as Narnis!

Still, it *was* a better exit than he'd taken from Minogra.

But he'd only had an apple that morning. And not even a pitcher of beer to warm him on his way. (Funig would have managed to do *that* for him, he knew — if Teren had given him a chance!) 'Now, Funig,' Clodon muttered, ducking around one trunk and in between two others, 'you won't have to listen any more to *my* dangerous tales. Every night now you can hear them at the inn tell fine, upstanding stories of the Liberator — a year out of date! That's the sort you need! Tales you're too thick to understand anyway. . . .' He swung up an arm for the underbrush, lifted his leg for a log. Who did Teren think he was? If Clodon had been younger — or drunk — he might have thrown a punch at him. Now *that* would have been a proper goodbye! Oh, someday, Teren, you'll be driving your cart on a back road at evening between villages. And I'll be there. Then we'll have a very different little talk — before I push a blade up under your chin so hard it goes through your brain pan and out the top of your skull! Where will you and your fine stone house be, then? Still, for now, when village folk got on you like that, it was best to be shut of them, fast as you could, while their ears were hungry for the lies any stranger might tell. (A whole *day* — !) And through the woods it was shorter down to the north-south highway: he'd best be on it soon as he could, if he wanted to . . . You know what to read in the pause.

New York,
February 1987

The Tale of Gorgik

Because we must deal with the unknown, whose nature is by definition speculative and outside the flowing chain of language, whatever we make of it will be no more than probability and no less than error. The awareness of possible error in speculation and of a continued speculation regardless of error is an event in the history of modern rationalism whose importance, I think, cannot be overemphasized . . . Nevertheless, the subject of how and when we become certain that what we are doing is quite possibly wrong *but at least a beginning* has to be studied in its full historical and intellectual richness. — EDWARD SAID

Beginnings, Intention and Method

1

His mother from time to time claimed eastern connections with one of the great families of fisherwomen in the Ulvayn Islands: she had the eyes, but not the hair. His father was a sailor who, after a hip injury at sea, had fixed himself to the port of Kolhari, where he worked as a waterfront dispatcher for a wealthier importer. So Gorgik grew up in the greatest of Nevèrÿon ports, his youth along the docks substantially rougher than his parents would have liked and peppered with more trouble than they thought they could bear — though not so rough or troubled as some of his friends': he was neither killed by accidental deviltry nor arrested.

Childhood in Kolhari? Somehow, soldiers and sailors from the breadth of Nevèrÿon ambled and shouted all through it, up and down the Old Pavē; merchants and merchants' wives strolled on Black Avenue, so called for its topping that, on hot days, softened under the sandals; travelers and tradesmen met to chat in front of dockside inns — the Sump, the Kraken, the Dive; and among them all slipped the male and female slaves, those of aristocratic masters dressed more elegantly than many merchants, while others were so ragged and dirty their sex was indistinguishable, yet all with the hinged iron collars above fine or frayed shirt necks or bony shoulders, loose or tight around stringy or fleshy necks, and sometimes even hidden under jeweled pieces of damasked cloth set with beryls and tourmalines. Frequently this double memory returned to Gorgik: leaving a room where a lot of coins, some stacked, some scattered, lay on sheets of written-over parchment, to enter the storage room at the back of the warehouse his father worked in — but instead of bolts of hide and bales of hemp, he saw some two dozen, cross-legged on the gritty flooring, a few leaning against the earthen wall, three asleep in the corner, and one making water astraddle the trough that grooved the room's center. All were sullen, silent, naked — save the iron at their throats. As he walked through, none even looked at him. An hour, or two hours, or four hours later, he walked into that storage room again: empty. About the floor lay two dozen collars hinged open. From each a chain coiled the pitted grit to hang from a plank set in the wall to which the last, oversized links were pegged. The air was cool and fetid. In another room coins clinked. Had he been six? Or seven? Or five . . . ? On the street behind the dockside warehouses women made jewelry and men made baskets; for oiled iron boys sold baked sweet potatoes that in winter were flaky and cold on the outside with just a trace of warmth in the center and, in summer, hot on the first bite but with a hard wet knot in the middle; and mothers harangued their girls from raffia-curtained windows: 'Get in the house, get in the house, get in the house this instant! There's work to do!'

With spring came the red and unmentionable ships from the south. And the balls. (Most things dubbed unmentionable have usually been mentioned quite fully in certain back alleys, at certain low dives, beside certain cisterns, by low men — and women — who do not shun low language. There have always been some phenomena, however, which are so baffling that neither high language nor low seems able to deal with them. The primitive response to such phenomena is terror and the sophisticated one, ignoral. These ships produced their share of both, sold their cargo, and were not talked of.) The balls were small enough for a big man to hide one in his fist and made of some barely pliable blackish matter that juvenile dissection revealed hid a knuckle-sized bubble. With the balls came the rhyme that you bounced to on the stone flags around the neighborhood cistern:

> I went out to Babàra's Pit
> At the crescent moon's first dawning.
> But the Thanes of Garth had covered it,
> And no one found a place to sit,
> And Belham's key no longer fit,
> And all the soldiers fought a bit,
> And neither general cared a whit
> If any man of his was hit . . .

The rhyme went on as long as you could keep the little ball going, usually with a few repetitions, as many improvisations; and when you wanted to stop, you concluded:

. . . And the eagle sighed and the serpent cried
For all my lady's warning!

On *warning!* you slammed the ball hard as you could into the cistern's salt-stained wall. The black ball soared in sunlight. Boys and girls ran, pranced, squinted . . . Whoever caught it got next bounce.

Sometimes it was '. . . for all the Mad witch's warning . . .' which didn't fit the rhythm; sometimes it was '. . . for all Mad Olin's warning . . .' which did, but no one was sure what that meant. And anyone with an amphibrachic name was always in for ribbing. For one thing was certain: whoever'd done the warning had meant no good by it.

A number of balls went into cisterns. A number simply went wherever lost toys go. By autumn all were gone. (He was sad for that, too, because by many days' practice on the abandoned cistern down at the alley end behind the grain warehouse, he'd gotten so he could bounce the ball higher than any but the children half again his age.) The rhyme lingered in the heaped-over corners of memory's store, turned up, at longer and longer intervals, perhaps a moment before sleep on a winter evening, in a run along the walled bank of the Big Khora on some next-summer's afternoon.

A run in the streets of Kolhari? Those streets were loud with the profanity of a dozen languages. At the edges of the Spur, Gorgik learned that *voldreg* meant 'excrement-caked privates of a female camel,' which seemed to be the most common epithet in the glottal-rich speech of the dark-robed northern men, but if you used the word *ini*, which meant 'a white gilley-flower,' with these same men, you could get a smack for it. In the Alley of Gulls, inhabited mostly by southern folk, he heard the women, as they lugged their daubed baskets of water, dripping over the green-gray flags, talk of *nivu* this and *nivu* that, in their sibilant, lisping way and usually with a laugh. But when he asked Miese, the southern barbarian girl who carried vegetables and fish to the back door of the Kraken, what it meant, she told him — laughing — that it was not a word a man would want to know.

'Then it must have something to do with what happens to women every month, yes?' he'd asked with all the city-bred candor and sophistication of his (by now) fourteen years.

Miese tugged her basket higher on her hip: 'I should think a man would want to know about *that!*' She stepped up the stairs to shoulder through the leather curtain that, when the boards were removed for the day, became the Kraken's back door. 'No, it has nothing to do with a woman's monthly blood. You city people have the strangest ideas.' And she was gone inside.

He never did learn the meaning.

The lower end of New Pavē (so called somewhere between ten and ten thousand years) was one with the dockside. Along the upper end, where the road dipped down again to cross the Bridge of Lost Desire, male and female prostitutes loitered or drank in the streets or solicited along the bridge's walkways, many come from exotic places and many spawned by old Kolhari herself, most of them brown by birth and darkened more by summer, like the fine, respectable folk of the city (indeed, like himself), though here were a few with yellow hair, pale skin, gray eyes, and their own lisping language (like Meise) bespeaking barbaric origins.

And weren't there more of them up this year than last?

Some stood about all but naked, squinting in the sun, while some wore elaborate skirts and belts and necklaces, most of the women and half the men with dark wings of paint laid about their eyes, some sleepy and slow-moving, some with quick smiles and inquisitive comments to every passerby, with sudden laughter and as-sudden anger (when the words for women's genitals, men's excreta, and cooking implements, all combined in truly novel ways, would howl across the bridge: the curses of the day). Yet all of them had, once they began to talk to you, astonishingly similar stories, as if one tale of pain, impoverishment, and privation (or a single, dull, if over-violent, life) had been passed from one to the other, belonging really to none of them, but only held by each the length of time it took to tell it, the only variation, as this one or that one recounted it, in the name of this small town or that abusive relative, or perhaps the particular betrayal, theft, or outrage that meant they could not go home.

By the dusty yards and stone-walled warehouses where the great commercial caravans pulled up after their months out in the land, with their mules and horses and covered carriages and open carts and provision wagons, once Gorgik stopped to talk to a caravan guard who stood a bit away from some others — who were squatting at the corner over a game of bones.

Rubbing his sweating hands against his leather kilt, the man began to speak to Gorgik of bandits in the mountains and brigands in the deserts — till, in a swirl of dark brocade, with street dust rising about his sandals, a merchant with cheeks as wrinkled as prunes, long teeth stained brown and black, and a beard like little tufts of wool stuck all over his dark jaw, rushed forward waving both his fists about his shoulders. 'You . . . ! You . . . ! You'll never work for me again! The steward has told me all, all about your thievery and your lies! Oh, no — you'll not endanger *my* carriages with your cowardice and your conniving! Here —' From among his robes the old man pulled out a handful of coins and flung them so that gold and iron struck the guard's neck, chest, and hip. (As if the disks were hot from the smithy across the street, the guard flinched away.) 'That's half your pay! Take it and be happy for it — when you're not worth a single bit of iron!' And though the guard wore a knife at his hip (and that must have been *his* spear leaning on the wall behind them) and was younger, bigger, and certainly stronger than the enraged merchant, he went scrabbling for his coins in the street and, with only a snarl and a glare — not even a fully articulated curse — snatched up his spear and hurried off. Only when he was a block away did he look back. Once. That's when Gorgik saw that the other guards had stopped their gambling to stand and move a step nearer. Still muttering, the old man turned back among them (who, Gorgik realized, were still very much expecting their own full salaries). They followed the merchant back to the warehouse, leaving Gorgik in the street with half an adventure in his head, a tale yearning for completion.

Another time when he and some friends were playing near the docks, from beside a mound of barrels a woman called to them: 'Come here . . . you children!' She had a hard, lined face, was taller than his father, and her hair was shorter than his mother's. Walking up to her, they could see her hands and feet both were callused and cracked about their lighter edges. 'Where . . . ,' she asked, quiet, tentative, 'tell me . . . where do they hire the women to wash the clothes?'

He and his friends just looked.

'Where do they . . . hire the washerwomen?' Her speech was accented; her skin was that deep, deep brown, a shade or two darker than his own, so often called black. 'They hire women . . . somewhere near here, to wash the clothes. I heard it. Where is it? I need work. Where . . . where should I go?'

And he realized what halted and held back her words was fear — which is always difficult for children to understand in adults; especially in an adult as tall and as strong as this hard, handsome woman.

One of the older girls said: 'You don't want to do that. They only hire barbarian women to do that, up in the Spur.'

'But I need work,' she said. 'I need it . . . the Spur — where is that?'

One of the younger boys started to point. But, as if in an excess of nervousness or just high spirits, another suddenly shouted and at the same time flung his ball into the air. A moment later all of them were running and yelling to each other, now leaping across a coil of rope, now dodging around an overturned dingy. He looked back to see the woman calling after them — though, for the shouting, he could not hear — and turned, as a friend tagged him, around a corner into another alley, all the time wondering what she was crying, what more she wanted to tell, what else she wanted to ask . . . The rest of the afternoon, in the dockloaders' calls, just below his friends' shrieks between the warehouses, behind the echoes of his own shouts across the yard where he ran after the others, he seemed to hear her, hear the fragments of some endless want, fear, hope, and harassment . . .

And still another time, when he wandered into the yard, he saw the boy (a few years older than himself? an old-looking sixteen? a young-looking eighteen?) sitting on the abandoned cistern's wall.

Thin.

That's the first thing he thought, looking at those knobbly shoulders, those sharp knees. Gorgik walked nearer. The boy's skin had begun the same brown as his own. But it was as if some black wash of street dirt and gutter water had been splashed over him, heels to ears. The boy was not looking at him but stared at some spot on the flagstones a little ahead, so that it was easy to walk by and look at him more closely —

When he saw the iron collar around the boy's neck, Gorgik stopped — walking, thinking, breathing. There was a thud, thud, thud in his chest. For moments, he was dizzy. The shock was as intense as heat or cold.

When his vision cleared, the next thing Gorgik saw were the scars.

They were thick as his fingers and wormed around the boy's soiled flanks. Here the welts were brown, there darker than the surrounding skin — he knew what they were, though he had never seen anyone bearing them before. At least not from this close. They were from a flogging. In provincial villages, he knew, whipping was used to punish criminals. And, of course, slaves.

Wanting desperately to move away, he stood staring for seconds, minutes, hours at the boy — who still did not look at him. No. *Only* seconds, he realized when, a breath later, he was walking on. Reaching the other alley, he stopped. He took three more breaths. And a fourth. Then he looked back.

Under his matted hair, the slave still had not looked up.

Stepping close to the wall, Gorgik stood there a long time. Soon he had framed ten, twenty, fifty questions he wanted to ask. But each time he pictured himself going up to speak to the collared boy, his breath grew short and his heart pounded. Finally, after trying three times, he managed to saunter again across the yard — first behind the cistern: the boy's back was webbed with six welts that, even as Gorgik counted them with held breath, seemed like a hundred in their irruptions and intersections. After waiting almost three minutes, he crossed the yard again, walking in front of the boy this time — then crossed twice more, once in front and again in back. Then, all at once, he left hurriedly, fearing, even though the boy *still* had not looked, someone passing by one of the alley openings might have seen — though the slave himself (newly escaped? a mad one who'd wandered off from, or been abandoned by, his master?), immobile on the cistern wall, gazed only at the ground.

Half an hour later, Gorgik was back.

The boy sat on the flags now, eyes closed, head back against the cistern wall. What had begun as a series of silent questions had turned for Gorgik into an entire dialogue, with a hundred answers the boy had begun to give him, a hundred stories the boy had begun to tell him. Gorgik walked past, his own feet only inches from the foul toenails. He gazed at the iron collar, till, again, he was moving away. He left by the Alley of No Name, telling himself that, really, he'd spied enough on this pathetic creature.

The dialogue, however, did not end.

When he returned in the lowering light an hour on, the boy was gone from the wall. Seconds later, Gorgik saw him, on the other side of the yard, by one of the buildings, curled up with his back against the sandstone, asleep. Again Gorgik walked past him, at several distances, several times — one minute or five between each passage. But finally he settled himself against the far alley entrance to watch, while the tale the boy told him went on and on, stopping and starting, repeating and revising, sometimes whispered so faintly he could not catch the words, sometimes crisp and vivid as life or dream, so that the square before him, with its circular cistern and the few pots, mostly broken, beside it, grew indistinct beneath a sky whose deepening blue was paled by an ivory wash above the far building, as the moon's gibbous arc slid over it —

The slave stretched out a leg, pulled it back, then rubbed at his cheek with one hand.

The tale halted, hammered to silence by Gorgik's heart. While Gorgik had been talking to himself, he'd been thinking, really, how easy it would be, once the boy woke, to go up to him, to speak, to ask him where he was from, where he was going, to offer sympathy, maybe a promise to return with food or a coin, to inquire after the particulars of his servitude, to proffer friendship, interest, advice . . .

Across the yard the slave stretched out his other hand, made a fist. Then, not suddenly but over a period of ten or fifteen seconds, he rocked a few times and pushed himself up on one arm.

Contending fear and fascination bound Gorgik as strongly as they had the moment he'd first glimpsed the dirty fellow's collar. Gorgik pulled back into the doorway, then peered out again.

With a child between, two women ambled by and into the yard. Again Gorgik froze — though they paid no more attention to the boy lingering in the doorway than they did to the slave lounging by the wall. As the three of them strolled across the dust, the dirty youth stood, very slowly. He swayed. When he took a step, Gorgik saw that he limped — and a dozen tales in his head were catastrophically revised to accommodate it.

Walk out now and nod at him, smile at him, say something . . .

The two women and their child turned out of the yard down the Street of Small Fish.

The slave limped toward the cistern.

Gorgik stood paralysed in the alley door.

When the scarred youth reached the cistern's waist-high wall, he stopped, not really looking into it. Hair stuck out about his head, sharp in the moonlight. After a few moments, he lifted his face, as though the single thread of cloud across the indigo sky attracted him. He raised his hands to his neck, to hook his fingers over the collar. He tugged —

What occurred next was, in the moment it happened, wholly unclear to Gorgik, for the tale he was just then telling himself was of an escaped slave who, with his criminal markings and limping toward an abandoned cistern, had raised his face to the moon and, in a moment of rebellion, grasped his collar to yank futilely and hopelessly at the iron locked on his neck — the collar that forever and irrevocably marked him as a fugitive for the slavers who patrolled the land, searching out new laborers in the villages, mostly these days (so he'd heard) in the south . . .

The semicircles of metal, hinged at the back, came apart in the boy's fists, as though the lock had not been set, or was broken. Now the boy raised the metal to the moon, its curved jaws open in his hand like black mandibles on some fabled dragon or even some unknown sign Gorgik's father might mark down in the dockside warehouse.

The boy tossed the collar over the wall.

Only when the iron vanished below the stone (the splash was very soft — and a beat after he expected it) did Gorgik realize that the collar, broken, or not locked in the first place, had truly been removed. With no comprehension as to why, he was overcome by chills. They rolled over him, flank, thigh, and shoulder. His fingers against the doorway corner were sweaty on the stone. After five breaths with his mouth wide so as not to make a sound, questions began to pour through his mind: Was this some criminal only pretending to be a slave? Or was it a slave who, now that he'd freed himself from the iron, would pretend to be a criminal? Or was it just a young madman, whose tale in its broken, inarticulate complexities he could never hope to know? Or was there some limpid and logical answer to it that only seemed so complex because, till now, he'd never thought to ask the proper questions?

The boy turned and lowered himself to sit again on the stone.

Gorgik moved his hand, just a little, on the jamb.

Go, he thought. Speak to him. He may be older, but I'm still bigger than he, and stronger. What harm could it do me, if I just went up and asked him to tell me who he is, to give me whatever bit of his story . . . ? Chills irrupted again, while he searched among the tales he'd been telling himself for any right reason to fear — in the middle of what had every aspect of terror about it, save motivation.

For some reason he remembered the woman on the docks. Had her fear, in all its irrationality, been anything like this . . . ?

Five minutes later, he walked into the yard again — as he had already done a dozen times that day. The boy sat there, still not looking. Gorgik's own eyes fixed on the thin neck, below ear and black, spiking hair, where the collar had been. In the moonlight, now and again as he neared, with this step and with that, he could almost see the iron against the dirty brown, where a neck ligament was crossed by an irregular vein . . .

No, the collar was gone.

But even absent, it plummeted Gorgik into as much confusion as it had before, so that, as he passed, it was all he could do not to flinch away, like the guard before the merchant's coins, ears blocked by his own loud blood, all speech denied — and he was walking on, to the other side of the yard, down the alley, unable to remember the actual moment he'd passed the boy, who, he was sure, still had not looked up.

Gorgik was back at the yard with the sunrise.

The flogged boy was gone.

But as he wandered about, now glancing into the nearly empty cistern (he could make out nothing among the flashes on the black), now ambling off to examine this corner or that alley entrance, while dawn light slanted the western wall, all Gorgik was left with was a kind of hunger, a groping after some tale, some knowledge, some warm and material feeling against his body of what had escaped through silence.

Soon he returned to his house, where the dock water glittered down between the porch planks.

Kolhari was home to any and every adventurer — and to any and every adventure they were often so eager to tell. As Gorgik listened to this one and that, now from a tarry-armed sailor packing grain sacks at the docks, now from a heavy young market woman taking a break at the edge of the Spur, now to a tale of lust and loyalty, now to one of love and power, it was as if the ones he heard combined with the hunger left from the ones he'd missed, so that, in a week or a month, when he found himself reviewing them, he was not sure if the stories he had were dreams of his own or of the lives of others. Still, for all the tales, for all the dreaming, an adolescence spent roaming the city's boisterous back streets, its bustling avenues, taught Gorgik the double lesson that is, finally, all civilization can know:

The breadth of the world is vasty and wide; nevertheless movement from place to place in it is possible; the ways of humanity are various and complex — but nevertheless negotiable.

Five weeks before Gorgik turned sixteen, the Child Empress Ynelgo, whose coming was just and generous, seized power. On that blustery afternoon in the month of the Rat, soldiers shouted from every street corner that the city's name was now, in fact, Kolhari — as every beggar woman and ship's boy and tavern maid and grain vendor had been calling it time out of memory. (It was no longer Neveryóna — which is what the last, dragon-bred residents of the High Court of Eagles had officially, but ineffectually, renamed it twenty years before.) That night several wealthy importers were assassinated, their homes sacked, their employees murdered — among them Gorgik's father. The employees' families were taken as slaves.

While in another room his mother's sobbing turned suddenly to a scream, then abruptly ceased, Gorgik was dragged naked into the chilly street. He spent his next five years in a Nevèrÿon obsidian mine thirty miles inland at the foot of the Faltha Mountains.

Gorgik was tall, strong, big-boned, friendly, and clever. Cleverness and friendliness had kept him from death and arrest on the docks. In the mines, along with the fact that he had been taught enough rudiments of writing to put down names and record workloads, they eventually secured the slave a work-gang foremanship: which meant that, with only a little stealing, he could get enough food so that instead of the wiry muscles that tightened along the bony frames of most miners, his arms and thighs and neck and chest swelled, high-veined and heavy, on his already heavy bones. At twenty-one he was a towering, black-haired gorilla of a youth, eyes permanently reddened from rockdust, a scar from a pickax flung in a barracks brawl spilling one brown cheekbone. His hands were huge and rough-palmed, his foot soles like cracked leather.

He did not look a day more than fifteen years above his actual age.

2

The caravan of the Handmaid and Vizerine Myrgot, of the tan skin and tawny eyes, returning from the mountain hold of fabled Ellamon to the High Court of Eagles at Kolhari, made camp half a mile from the mines, beneath the Falthas' ragged and piney escarpments. In her youth, Myrgot had been called 'an interesting-looking girl'; today she was known as a bottomless well of cunning and vice.

It was spring and the Vizerine was bored.

She had volunteered for the Ellamon mission because life at the High Court, under the Child Empress Ynelgo, whose reign was peaceful and productive, had of late been also damnably dull. The journey itself had refreshed her. But within Ellamon's fabled walls, once she had spent the obligatory afternoon out at the dragon corrals in the mountain sun, squinting up to watch the swoopings and turnings of the great, winged creatures (about which had gathered all the fables), she found herself, in the midst of her politicking with the mountain lairds and burghers, having to suffer the attentions of provincial bores — who were worse, she decided after a week, than their cosmopolitan counterparts.

But the mission was done. She sighed.

Myrgot stood in her tent door; she looked up at the black Falthas clawing through evening clouds and wondered if she might see any of the dark and fabled beasts arch the sunset. But no, for when all the fables were done, dragons were pretty well restricted to a few hundred yards of soaring and at a loss for launching from anywhere other than their craggy ledges. She watched the women in red scarves go off among other tents. 'Jahor . . . ?'

The eunuch with the large nose stepped from behind her, turbaned and breeched in blue wool.

'I have dismissed my maids for the night. The mines are not far from here . . .' The Vizerine, known for her high-handed manners and low-minded pleasures, put her forearm across her breasts and kneaded her bare, bony elbow. 'Go to the mines, Jahor. Bring me back the foulest, filthiest, wretchedest pit slave from the deepest darkest hole. I wish to slake my passion in some vile, low way.' Her tongue, only a pink bud, moved along the tight line of her lips.

The eunuch touched the back of his fist to his forehead, nodded, bowed, backed away the three required steps, turned, and departed.

An hour later, the Vizerine was looking out through the seam in the canvas at the tent's corner.

The boy whom Jahor guided before him into the clearing limped a few steps forward, then turned his face up in the light drizzle, that had begun minutes back, opening and closing his mouth as if around a recently forgotten word. The pit slave's name was Noyeed. He was fourteen. He had lost an eye three months ago: the wound had never been dressed and had not really healed. He had a fever. He was shivering. Bleeding gums had left his mouth scabby. Dirt had made his flesh scaly. He had been at the mines one month and was not expected to last another. Seeing this as a reasonable excuse, seven men at the mines two nights before had abused the boy cruelly and repeatedly — hence his limp.

Jahor let him stand there, mouthing tiny drops that glittered on his crusted lips, and went into the tent. 'Madame, I — '

The Vizerine turned in the tent corner. 'I have changed my mind.' She frowned beneath the black hair (dyed now) braided in many loops across her forehead. From a tiny taboret, she picked up a thin-necked copper cruet and reached up between the brass chains to pour out half a cup more oil. The lamp flared. She replaced the cruet on the low table. 'Oh, Jahor, there must be *someone* there . . . you know what I like. Really, our tastes are not that different. Try again. Bring someone else.'

Jahor touched the back of his fist to his forehead, nodded his blue-bound head, and withdrew.

After returning Noyeed to his barracks, Jahor had no trouble with his next selection. When he had first come rattling the barred door of the guards' building, he had been testily sent on in among the slat-walled barracks, with a sleepy guard for guide, to seek out one of the gang foremen. In the foul sleeping quarters, the burly slave whom Jahor had shaken awake first cursed the eunuch like a dog; then, when he heard the Vizerine's request, laughed. The tall fellow had gotten up, taken Jahor to another, even fouler barracks, found Noyeed for him, and all in all seemed a congenial sort. With his scarred and puggish face and dirt-stiffened hair he was no one's handsome. But he was animally strong, of a piece, and had enough pit dirt ground into him to satisfy anyone's *nostalgie de la boue*, thought Jahor as the foreman lumbered off back to his own sleeping quarters.

When, for the second time that night, the guard unlocked the double catch at each side the plank across the barrack entrance, Jahor pushed inside, stepping from the rain and across the sill to flooring as muddy within as without. The guard stepped in behind, holding up the spitting pine torch: smoke licked the damp beams; vermin scurried in the light or dropped down, glittering, to the dirt. Jahor picked his way across muddy straw, went to the first heap curled away from him in thatch and shadow. He stopped, pulled aside frayed canvas.

The great head rolled up; red eyes blinked over a heavy arm. 'Oh . . . ,' the slave grunted. 'You again?'

'Come with me,' Jahor said. 'She wants *you* now.'

The reddened eyes narrowed; the slave pushed up on one great arm. His dark face crinkled around its scar. With his free hand he rubbed his great neck, the skin stretched between thick thumb and horny forefinger cracked and gray. 'She wants *me* to . . . ?' Again he frowned. Suddenly he went scrabbling in the straw beside him and a moment later turned back with the metal collar, hinged open, a semicircle of it in each huge hand. Once he shook his head, as if to rid it of sleep. Straw fell from his hair, slid across his bunched shoulder. Then he bent forward, raised the collar, and clacked it closed. Matted hair caught in the clasp at the back of his neck. Digging with one thick finger, he pulled it loose. 'There . . . ' He rose from his pallet to stand among the sleeping slaves, looking twice his size in the barracks shadow. His eyes caught the big-nosed eunuch's. He grinned, rubbed the metal ring with three fingers. 'Now they'll let me back in. Come on, then.'

So Gorgik came, with Jahor, to the Vizerine's tent.

And passed the night with Myrgot — who was forty-five and, in the narrowly restricted area she allowed for personal life, rather a romantic. The most passionate, not to say the most perverse, lovemaking (we are not speaking of foreplay), though it run the night's course, seldom takes more than twenty minutes from the hour. As boredom was Myrgot's problem and lust only its emblem, here and there through the morning hours the pit slave found himself disposed in conversation with the Vizerine. Since there is very little entertainment for pit slaves in an obsidian mine *except* conversation and tall-tale telling, when Gorgik began to see her true dilemma, he obliged her with stories of his life before, and at, the mines — a few of which tales were lies appropriated from other slaves, a few of which were embroideries on his own childhood experiences. But since entertainment was the desired effect, and temporariness seemed the evening's hallmark, there was no reason to shun prevarication. Five times during the night, he made jokes the Vizerine thought wickedly funny. Three times he made observations on the working of the human heart she thought profound. For the rest, he was deferential, anecdotal, as honest about his feelings as someone might be who sees no hope in his situation. Gorgik's main interest in the encounter was the story it would make at the next night's supper of gruel and cold pig fat, though that interest was somewhat tempered by the prospect of the ten-hour workday with no sleep to come. Without illusion that more gain than the tale would accrue, lying on his back on sweaty silk his own body had soiled, staring up at the dead lamps swaying under the striped canvas, sometimes dozing in the midst of his own ponderings while the Vizerine beside him gave her own opinions on this, that, or the other, he only hoped there would be no higher price.

When the slits between the tent lacings grew luminous, the Vizerine suddenly sat up in a rustle of silks and a whisper of furs whose splendor had by now become part of the glister of Gorgik's fatigue. She called sharply for Jahor, then bade Gorgik rise and stand outside.

Outside Gorgik stood, tired, lightheaded, and naked in the moist grass, already worn here and there to the earth with the previous goings and comings of the caravan personnel. He looked at the tents, at the black mountains beyond them, at the cloudless sky already coppered one side along the pinetops: I could run, he thought; and if I ran, yes, I would stumble into slavers' hands within the day; and I'm too tired anyway. But I *could* run. I . . .

Inside, Myrgot, with sweaty silk bunched in her fists beneath her chin, head bent and rocking slowly, considered. 'You know, Jahor,' she said, her voice quiet, because it was morning and if you have lived most of your life in a castle with many other people you are quiet in the morning; 'that man is wasted in the mines.' The voice had been roughened by excess. 'I say man; he looks like a man; but he's really just a boy — oh, I don't mean he's a genius or anything. But he can speak two languages passably, and can practically read in one of them. For him to be sunk in an obsidian pit is ridiculous! And do you know . . . I'm the only woman he's ever had?'

Outside, Gorgik, still standing, eyes half closed, was still thinking: yes, *perhaps* I could . . . when Jahor came for him.

'Come with me.'

'Back to the pit?' Gorgik snorted something that general good nature made come out half a laugh.

'No,' Jahor said briskly and quietly in a way that made the slave frown. 'To my tent.'

Gorgik stayed in the large-nosed eunuch's tent all morning, on sheets and coverlets not so fine as the Vizerine's but fine enough; and the tent's furnishings — little chairs, low tables, shelves, compartmented chests, and numberless bronze and ceramic figurines set all over — were far more opulent than Myrgot's austere appointments. With forty minutes this hour and forty minutes that, Jahor found the slave gruff, friendly — and about as pleasant as an exhausted miner can be at four, five, or six in the morning. He corroborated the Vizerine's assessment — and Jahor had done things very much like this many, many times. At one point the eunuch rose from the bed, bound himself about with blue wool, turned to excuse himself a moment — unnecessarily, because Gorgik had fallen immediately to sleep — and went back to the Vizerine's tent.

Exactly what transpired there, Gorgik never learned. One subject, from time to time in the discussion, however, would no doubt have surprised, if not shocked him. When the Vizerine had been much younger, she herself had been taken a slave for three weeks and forced to perform services arduous and demeaning for a provincial potentate — who bore such a resemblance to her present cook at Court that it all but kept her out of the kitchen. She had been a slave *only* three weeks: an army had come, fire-arrows had lanced through the narrow stone windows, and the potentate's ill-shaved head was hacked off and tossed in the firelight from spear to spear by several incredibly dirty, incredibly tattooed soldiers so vicious and shrill that she finally decided (from what they later did to two women of the potentate's entourage in front of everyone) they were insane. The soldiers' chief, however, was in alliance with her uncle; and she had been returned to him comparatively unharmed. Still, the whole experience had been enough to make her decide that the institution of slavery was totally distasteful and so was the institution of war — that, indeed, the only excuse for the latter was the termination of the former. Such experiences, among an aristocracy deposed by the dragon for twenty years and only recently returned to power, were actually rather common, even if the ideas taken from them were not. The present government did not as an official policy oppose slavery, but it did not go out of its way to support it either; and the Child Empress herself, whose reign was proud and prudent, had set a tradition that no slaves were used at Court.

From dreams of hunger and pains in his gut and groin, where a boy with clotted mouth, scaly hands, half his face in darkness, and his flank wrapped round with whip welts tried to tell him something he could not understand, but which seemed desperately important that he knew, Gorgik woke with the sun in his eyes. The tent was being taken down from over him. A blue-turbaned head blocked the light. 'Oh, you *are* awake . . . ! Then you'd better come with me.' With the noise of the decamping caravan around them Jahor took Gorgik to see the Vizerine. Bluntly she informed him, while ox drivers, yellow-turbaned secretaries, red-scarved maids, and harnessed porters came in and out of the tent, lifting, carrying, unlacing throughout the interview, that she was taking him to Kolhari under her protection. He had been purchased from the mines — take off that collar and put it somewhere. At least by day. She would trust him never to speak to her unless she spoke to him first: he was to understand that if she suspected her decision were a mistake, she could and would make his life far more miserable than it had ever been in the mines. Gorgik was at first not so much astonished as uncomprehending. Then, when astonishment, with comprehension, formed, he began to babble his inarticulate thanks — till, of a sudden, he became confused again and disbelieving and so, as suddenly, stopped. (Myrgot merely assumed he had realized that even gratitude is best displayed in moderation, which she took as another sign of his high character and her right choice.) Then men were taking the tent down from around them, too. With narrowed eyes, Gorgik looked at the thin woman in the green shift and sudden sun, sitting at a table from which women in red scarves were already removing caskets, things rolled and tied in ribbons, instruments of glass and bronze. Was she suddenly smaller? The thin braids, looped bright black about her head, looked artificial, almost like a wig. (He knew they weren't.) Her dress seemed made for a woman fleshier, broader. She looked at him, the skin near her eyes wrinkled in the bright morning, her neck a little loose, the veins on the backs of her hands as high from age as those on his from labor. What he did realize, as she blinked in the full sunlight, was that he must suddenly look as different to her as she now looked to him.

Jahor touched Gorgik's arm, led him away.

Gorgik had at least ascertained that his new and precarious position meant keeping silent. The caravan steward put him to work grooming oxen by day — which he liked. The next night he spent in the Vizerine's tent. And dreams of the mutilated child woke him with blocked throat and wide eyes only half a dozen times. And Noyeed was probably dead by now anyway, as Gorgik had watched dozens of other slaves die in those suddenly fading years.

Once Myrgot was sure that, during the day, Gorgik could keep himself to himself, she became quite lavish with gifts and clothing, jewels, and trinkets. (Though she herself never wore ornaments when traveling, she carried trunks of the things in her train.) Jahor — in whose tent from time to time Gorgik spent a morning or afternoon — advised him of the Vizerine's moods, of when he should come to her smelling of oxen and wearing the grimy leather-belted rag — with his slave collar — that was all he had taken from the mines. Or when, as happened quite soon, he should do better to arrive freshly washed, his beard shaved, disporting her various gifts. More important, he was advised when he should be prepared to make love, and when he should be ready simply to tell tales or, as it soon came, just to listen. And Gorgik learned that most valuable of lessons without which no social progress is possible: if you are to stay in the good graces of the powerful, you had best, however unobtrusively, please the servants of the powerful.

Next morning the talk through the whole caravan was: 'Kolhari by noon!'

By nine, winding off between fields and cypress glades, a silver thread had widened into a reed-bordered river down below the bank of the caravan road. The Kohra, one groom told him; which made

Gorgik start. He had known the Big Kohra and the Kohra Spur as two walled and garbage-clotted canals, moving sluggishly into the harbor from beneath a big and a little rock-walled bridge at the upper end of New Pavē. The hovels and filthy alleys in the city between (also called the Spur) were home to thieves, pickpockets, murderers and worse, he'd always been told.

Here, on this stretch of the river, were great, high houses, of two and even three stories, widely spaced and frequently gated. Where were they now? Why, this *was* Kolhari — at least the precinct. They were passing through the suburb of Neveryóna (which so recently had named the entire port) where the oldest and richest of the city's aristocracy dwelt. Not far in that direction was the suburb of Sallese, where the rich merchants and importers had their homes: though with less land and no prospect on the river, many of the actual houses were far more elegant. This last was in conversation with a stocky woman — one of the red-scarved maids — who frequently took off her sandals, hiked up her skirts, and walked among the ox drivers, joking with them in the roughest language. In the midst of her description, Gorgik was surprised by a sudden and startling memory: playing at the edge of a statue-ringed rock pool in the garden of his father's employer on some rare trip to Sallese as a child. With the memory came the realization that he had not the faintest idea how to get from these wealthy environs to the waterfront neighborhood that was *his* Kolhari. Minutes later, as the logical solution (follow the Khora) came, the caravan began to swing off the river road.

First in an overheard conversation among the caravan steward and some grooms, then in another between the chief porter and the matron of attendent women, Gorgik heard: '. . . the High Court . . . ,' '. . . the Court . . . ,' and '. . . the High Court of Eagles . . . ,' and one black and sweaty-armed driver, whose beast was halted on the road with a cartwheel run into a ditch, wrestled and cursed his heavy-lidded charge as Gorgik walked past. 'By the child Empress, whose reign is good and gracious, I'll break your fleabitten neck! So close to home, and you run off the path!'

An hour on the new road, which wound back and forth between the glades of cypress, and Gorgik was not sure if the Khora was to his right or left.

But ahead was a wall, with guard houses left and right of a gate over which a chipped and rough-carved eagle spread her man-length wings. Soldiers pulled away the massive planks (with their dozen barred insets), then stood back, joking with one another, as the carts rolled through.

Was *that* great building beside the lake the High Court?

No, merely one of the outbuildings. Look there, above that hedge of trees —

'There . . . ?'

He hadn't seen it because it was too big. And when he did — rising and rising above the evergreens — for a dozen seconds he tried to shake loose from his mind the idea that he was looking at some natural object, like the Falthas themselves. Oh, yes, cut into here, leveled off there — but building upon building, wing upon wing, more a city than a single edifice, that great pile (he kept trying to separate it into different buildings, but it all seemed, despite its many levels, and its outcroppings, and its abutments, one) could not have been *built* . . . ?

He kept wishing the caravan would halt so he could look at it all. But the road was carpeted with needles now, and evergreens swatted half-bare branches across the towers, the clouds, the sky. Then, for a few moments, a gray wall was coming toward him, was towering over him, was about to fall on him in some infinitely delayed topple —

Jahor was calling.

Gorgik looked down from the parapet.

The eunuch motioned him to follow the dozen women who had separated from the caravan — among them the Vizerine: a tiny door swallowed them one and another. Gorgik had to duck.

As conversation babbled along the corridor, past more soldiers standing in their separate niches ('. . . home at last . . . ,' '. . . what an exhausting trip . . . ,' '. . . here at home in Kolhari . . . ,' '. . . when one returns home to the High Court . . . ,' '. . . only in Kolhari . . .'), Gorgik realized that, somehow, all along he had been expecting to come to his childhood home; and that, rather than coming home at all, he had no idea *where* he was.

Gorgik spent five months at the High Court of the Child Empress Ynelgo. The Vizerine put him in a small, low-ceilinged room, with a slit window, just behind her own chambers. The stones of the floor and walls were out of line and missing mortar, as though pressure from the rock above, below, and around it had compacted the little space all out of shape. By the end of the first month, both the Vizerine and her steward had almost lost interest in him. But several times before her interest waned, she had presented him at various private suppers of seven to fourteen guests in the several dining rooms of her suite, all with beamed ceilings and tapestried walls, some with wide windows opening out on sections of roof, some windowless with whole walls of numberless lamps and ingenious flues to suck off the fumes. Here he met some of her court friends, a number of whom found him interesting, and three of whom actually befriended him. At one such supper he talked too much. At two more he was too silent. At the other six, however, he acquitted himself well, for seven to fourteen is the number a mine slave usually dines with, and he was comfortable with the basic structures of communication by which such a group (whether seated on logs and rocks, or cushions and couches) comports itself at meals, if not with the forms of politeness this particular group's expression of those structures had settled on.

But those could be learned.

He learned them.

Gorgik had immediately seen there was no way to compete with the aristocrats in sophistication: he intuited that they would only be offended or, worse, bored if he tried. What interested them in him was his difference from them. And to their credit (or the credit of the Vizerine's wise selection of supper guests) for the sake of this interest and affection for the Vizerine they made allowances, in ways he was only to appreciate years later, when he drank too much, or expressed like or dislike for one of their number not present a little too freely, or when his language became too hot on whatever topic was about — most of the time to accuse them of nonsense or of playing with him, coupled with good-natured but firm threats of what he would do to them were they on his territory rather than he on theirs. *Their* language, polished and mellifluous, flowed, between bouts of laughter in which his indelicacies were generously absorbed and forgiven (if not forgotten), over subjects ranging from the scandalous to the scabrous: when Gorgik could follow it, it often made his mouth drop, or at least his teeth open behind his lips. *His* language, blunt and blistered with scatalogs that frequently upped the odd aristocratic eyebrow, adhered finally to a very narrow range: the fights, feuds, and scrabblings for tiny honors, petty dignities, and minuscule assertions of rights among slaves and thieves, dock-beggars and prostitutes, sailors and barmaids and more slaves — people, in short, with no power beyond their voices, fingers, or feet — a subject rendered acceptable to the fine folk of the court only by his basic anecdotal talent and the topic's novelty in a setting where boredom was the greatest affliction.

Gorgik did not find the social strictures on his relations with the Vizerine demeaning. The Vizerine worked — the sort of work only those in art or government can know, where the hours were seldom defined and real tasks were seldom put in simple terms (while false tasks *always* were). Conferences and consultations made up her day. At least two meals out of every three were spent with some ambassador, governor, or petitioner, if not at some affair of state. To do her credit, in that first month, we can thus account for all twenty-two evening meals Myrgot did not share with her slave.

Had her slave, indeed, spent his past five years as, say, a free, clever, and curious apprentice to a well-off potter down in the port, he might have harbored some image of a totally leisured and totally capricious aristocracy, for which there were certainly enough emblems around him now, but which emblems, had he proceeded on them, as certainly would have gotten him into trouble. Gorgik, however, had passed so much of his life at drudgeries he knew would, foreman or no, probably kill him in another decade and certainly in two, he was too dazzled by his own, unexpected freedom from such drudgeries to question how others drudged. To pass the Vizerine's open door and see Myrgot at her desk, head bent over a map, a pair of compasses in one hand and a straight edge in the other (which, to that clever, curious, and ambitious apprentice, would have signed work), and then to pass the same door later and see her standing beside her desk, looking vacantly toward some cloud passing by the high, beveled window (which, to the same apprentice, would have signed a leisure that could reasonably be intruded upon, thus making her order never to intrude appear, for a lover at any rate, patently unreasonable), were states he simply did not distinguish: their textures were both so rich, so complex, and so unusual to him that he read no structure of meaning in either, much less did he read the meaning of those structures somehow as opposition. In obeying the Vizerine's restriction, and not intruding on either situation, his reasons were closer to something aesthetic than practical. Gorgik was acting on that disposition for which the apprentice would have despised him as the slave he was: he knew his place. Yet that apprentice's valuation would have been too coarse, for the truth is that in such society, Gorgik — no more than a potter's boy — *had* no place . . . if we use 'to have' other than in that mythical and mystifying sense in which both a slave *has* a master and good people *have* certain rights, but rather in the sense of possession that implies some way (either through power or convention) of enforcing that possession, if not to the necessary extent, at least to a visible one. Had Gorgik suddenly developed a disposition to intrude, from some rage grown either in whim or reason, he *would* have intruded on either situation — a disposition that his aristocratic supper companions would have found more sympathetic than the apprentice's presumptions, assumptions, and distinctions all to no use. Our potter's boy would no doubt have gotten himself turned out of the castle, thrown into one of the High Court's lower dungeons, or killed — for these were brutal and barbaric times, and the Vizerine was frequently known to be both violent and vicious. Had Gorgik intruded, yes, the aristocrats would have been in far greater sympathy with him — as they turned him out, threw him into a dungeon, or killed him. No doubt this means the distinction is of little use. But we are trying to map the borders of the disposition that was, indeed, the case. Gorgik, who had survived on the waterfront and survived in the mine, survived at the High Court of Eagles. To do it, he had to learn a great deal.

Not allowed to approach the Vizerine and constrained to wait till she approached him, he learned, among the first lessons, that there was hardly one person at court who was not, practically speaking, in a similar position with at least one other person — if not whole groups. Thus Lord Vanar (who shared Jahor's tastes and gave Gorgik several large rocks with gems embedded in them that lay in the corners of his room, gathering dust) and the Baron Inige (who did not, but who once took him hunting in the royal preserves and talked endlessly about flowers throughout the breadth of Nevèrÿon — and from whom Gorgik now learned that an *ini*, which brought back a torrent of memories from his dockside adolescence, was deadly poison) would never attend the same function, though both must always be invited. The Thane of Sallese could be invited to the same gathering as Lord Ekoris *unless* the Countess Esulla was to be present —

however, in such cases Curly (the Baron Inige's nickname) would be excused. No one known as a friend of Lord Aldamir (who had not been at Court now for many years, though everyone seemed to remember him with fondness) should be seated next to, or across from, any relative, unto the second cousins, of the Baronine Jeu-Forsi . . . Ah, but with perhaps half a dozen insistently minor exceptions, commented the elderly Princess Grutn, putting one arm back over the tasseled cushion and moving nuts about on her palm with her heavily ringed thumb.

But they were not minor at *all*, laughed Curly, sitting forward on his couch, joining his hands with a smile as excited as if he had just discovered a new toadstool.

But they *were* minor, insisted the princess, letting the nuts fall back to the silver tray and picking up her chased-silver goblet to brood moodily on its wine. Why, several people had commented to her only within the last month that perhaps the Baron had regrettably lost sight of *just* how minor those exceptions were.

'Sometimes I wonder if the main sign of the power of our most charming cousin, whose reign is courteous and courageous, is that, for her sake, all these amenities, both minor and major, are forgotten for a gathering she will attend!' Inige laughed.

And Gorgik, sitting on the floor, picked his teeth with a silver knife whose blade was shorter than his little finger and listened — not with the avidity of a social adventurer storing information for future dealings with the great, but with the relaxed attention of an aesthete hearing for the first time a difficult poem, which he already knows from the artist's previous work will require many exposures before its meanings clear.

Our young potter's boy would have brought with him to these same suppers a ready-made image of the pyramid of power, and no doubt in the light of these arcane informations tried to map the whole volume of that pyramid on to a single line, with every thane and duchess in place, each above this one and below that one, the whole forming a cord that could be negotiated knot by knot, a path that presumably ended at some *one* — perhaps the Child Empress Ynelgo herself. Gorgik, because he brought to the supper rooms no such preconceptions, soon learned, between evenings with the Vizerine, dawn rides with the Baron, afternoon gatherings in the Old Hall, arranged by the young earls Jue-Grutn (not to be confused with the two older men who bore the same title, the bearded one of which was said to be either insane, a sorcerer, or both), or simply from gatherings overseen and overheard in his wanderings through the chains of rooms which formed the Middle Style of the castle, that the hierarchy of prestige branched; that the branches interwove; and that the interweavings in several places formed perfectly closed, if inexplicable, loops; as well, he observed that the presence of this earl or that thane (not to mention this steward or that attendant maid) could throw a whole subsection of the system into a different linking altogether.

Jahor, especially during the first weeks, took many walks with Gorgik through the castle. The eunuch steward was hugely rich in information about the architecture itself. The building still mystified the ex-miner. The oldest wings, like the Old Hall, were vast, cavernous spaces, with open roofs and water conduits grooved into the floor. Dozens of small, lightless cells opened off them, the upper ones reached by wooden ladders, stone steps, or sometimes mere mounds of earth heaped against the wall. Years ago, Jahor explained, these dusty, dank cavelets, smaller even than Gorgik's present room, had actually been the dwelling places of great kings, queens, and courtiers. From time to time they had housed officers of the army — and, during the several occupations, common soldiers. That little door up there, sealed over with stone and no steps to it? Why, that was where Mad Queen Olin had been walled up after she had presided at a banquet in this very hall, at which she served her own twin sons, their flesh roasted, their organs pickled. Halfway through the meal, a storm had burst over the castle, and rain had poured through the broad roof opening, while lightning fluttered and flickered its pale whips; but Olin forbade her guests to rise from the table before the feast was consumed. It's still debatable, quipped the eunuch, whether they entombed her because of the supper or the soaking. (*Olin*, thought Gorgik. *Olin's warning* . . . ? But Jahor was both talking and walking on.) Today, except for the Old Hall that was kept in some use, these ancient echoing wells were deserted, the cells were empty, or at best used to store objects that had grown useless, if not meaningless, with rust, dust, and time. About fifteen or fifty years ago, some particularly clever artisan — the same who laid out the New Pavē down in the port, Jahor explained, waking Gorgik's wandering attention again — had come up with the idea of the corridor (as well as the coin-press). At least half the castle had been built since then (and most of Nevèrÿon's money minted); for at least half the castle had its meeting rooms and storerooms, its kitchens and its living quarters, laid out along corridors. There were six whole many-storied wings of them. In the third floor of one of the newest, the Vizerine had her suite; in the second and third floor of one of the oldest, most business of state was carried on around the throne room of the Child Empress. For the rest, the castle was built in that strange and disconcerting method known as the Middle Style, in which rooms, on two sides, three sides, four sides, and sometimes with steps going up or down, opened on to other rooms; which opened on to others — big rooms, little rooms, some empty, some lavishly appointed, many without windows, some incredibly musty; and frequently two or three perfectly dark ones, which had to be traversed with torch and taper, lying between two that were in current, active use, a vast and hopeless hive.

Did Jahor actually know his way around the entire edifice?

No one knew his way around the *entire* court. Indeed, though his mistress went occasionally, Jahor had never been anywhere near the Empress's suite or the throne room. He knew the location of the wing only by report.

What about the Child Empress herself? Did she know all of it?

Oh, especially not the Child Empress herself, Jahor explained, an irony that our potter's boy might have questioned, but which was just another strangeness to the ex-pit slave.

But it was after this conversation that Jahor's company too began to fall off.

Gorgik's aristocratic friends had a particularly upsetting habit: one day they would be perfectly friendly, if not downright intimate; the next afternoon, if they were walking with some companion unknown to Gorgik, they would pass him in some rocky corridor and not even deign recognition — even if he smiled, raised his hand, or started to speak. Such snubs and slights would have provoked our potter, however stoically he forebore, to who-knows-what final outburst, ultimate indelicacy, or denouncement of the whole, undemocratic sham. But though Gorgik saw quite well he was the butt of such behavior more than they, he saw too that they treated him thus not because he was different so much as because that was the way they treated each other. The social hierarchy and patterns of deference to be learned here were as complex as those that had to be mastered — even by a foreman — on moving into a new slave barracks in the mine. (Poor potter! With all his simplistic assumptions about the lives of aristocrats, he would have had just as many about the lives of slaves.) Indeed, among slaves Gorgik knew what generated such complexity: servitude itself. The only question he could not answer here was: what were all *these* elegant lords and ladies slaves to? In this, of course, the potter would have had the advantage of knowledge. The answer was simple: power, pure, raw and obsessive. But in his ignorance, young Gorgik was again closer to the lords and ladies around him than an equally young potter's boy would have been. For it is precisely at its center that one loses the clear vision of what surrounds, what controls and contours every utterance, decides and develops every action, as the bird has no clear concept of air, though it support her every turn, or the fish no true vision of water, though it blur all she sees. A goodly, if not frightening, number of these same lords and ladies dwelling at the Court had as little idea of what shaped their every willed decision, conventional observance, and sheer, unthinking habit as did Gorgik — whereas the potter's boy Gorgik might have been, had the play of power five years before gone differently in these same halls and hives, would not even have had to ask.

For all the temperamental similarities we have drawn, Gorgik was not (nor should we be) under any illusion that either the lords, or their servants, accepted him as one of their own. But he had conversation; he had companionship — for some periods extremely warm companionship — from women and men who valued him for much the same reason as the Vizerine had. He was given frequent gifts. From time to time people in rooms he was not in and never visited suggested to one another that they look out for the gruff youngster in the little room on the third floor, see that he was fed, or that he was not left too much alone. (And certainly a few times when such conversations might have helped, they never occurred.) But, stripped to nothing but his history, Gorgik began to learn that even such a history — on the docks and in the mines — as it set him apart in experience from these others, was in some small way the equivalent of an aristocracy in itself: those who met him here at Court either did not bother him about it, or they respected it and made allowances for his eccentricities because of it — which is, after all, all their own aristocratic privileges gained them from one another.

Once he went five days in the castle without eating. When Gorgik did not have an invitation to some countess's or prince's dinner or luncheon, he went to the Vizerine's kitchen — Jahor had left standing instructions there that he was to be fed. But the Vizerine, with most of her suite, was away on another mission. And since the Vizerine's cooks had gone with the caravan, her kitchen had been shut down.

One evening the little Princess Elyne took both Gorgik's great dark hands in her small, brown ones and exclaimed as the other guests departed around them: 'But I have had to cancel the little get-together that I'd asked you to tomorrow. It's too terrible! I must go visit my uncle, the count, who will not be put off another — ' Here she stopped, pulled one of her hands away and put it over her mouth. 'But I *am* too terrible. For I'm lying dreadfully, and you probably know it! Tomorrow I must go home to my own horrid old castle, and I loathe it, loathe it there! Ah, you *did* know it, but you're too polite to say anything.' Gorgik, who'd known no such thing, laughed. 'So,' went on the little Princess, 'that is why I must cancel the party. You see, I have reasons. You *do* understand . . . ?' Gorgik, who was vaguely drunk, laughed again, shook his head, raised his hand when the princess began to make more excuses, and, still laughing, turned, and found his way back to his room.

The next day, as had happened before, no other invitations came; and because the Vizerine's kitchen was closed, he did not eat. The day after, there were still no invitations. He scoured as much of the castle as he dared for Curly; and became suddenly aware how little of the castle he felt comfortable wandering in. The third day? Well, the first two days of a fast are the most difficult — though Gorgik had no thoughts of fasting. He was not above begging, but he could not see how to beg here from someone he hadn't been introduced to. Steal? Yes, there were other suites, other kitchens. (Ah, it was now the fourth day; and other than a little lightheaded, his actual appetite seemed to have died somewhere inside him.) Steal food . . . ? He sat on the edge of his raised pallet, his fists a great, horny knot of interlocked knuckle and thickened nail, pendant between his knees. How many times had these lords and ladies praised his straightforwardness, his honesty? He had been stripped to nothing but his history, and now that history included their evaluations of him. Though, both on the docks and in the mines, no month had gone by since age six when he had not pilfered *something*, he'd stolen nothing here, and somehow he knew that to steal — here — meant losing part of this new history: and, in this mildly euphoric state, that new history seemed much too valuable — because it was associated with real learning (rather than with ill-applied judgements, which is what it would have meant for our young potter; and our young potter, though he had never stolen more than the odd cup from his master's shelf of seconds, would certainly have stolen now).

Gorgik had no idea how long it took to starve to death. But he had seen ill-fed men, worked fourteen hours a day, thrown into solitary confinement without food for three days, only to die within a week after their release. (And had once, in his first six months at the mines, been so confined himself; and had survived.) That a well-fed woman or man of total leisure (and leisure is all Gorgik had known now for close to a half a year) might go more than a month with astonishing ease on nothing but water never occurred to him. On the fifth day he was still lightheaded, not hungry, and extremely worried over the possibility that this sensation itself was the beginning of starvation.

In his sandals with the brass buckles, and a red smock which hung to mid-thigh (it should have been worn with an ornamental collar he did not bother to put on, and should have been belted with a woven sash of scarlet and gold, wrapped three times around the waist with the tassels hanging to the floor; but absently he had wrapped round it the old leather strap he'd used to girdle his loin rag in the mines), he left his room on the evening of the fifth day and again began to wander the castle. This time, perhaps because of the lightheadedness, he entered a hallway he had never entered before — and immediately found himself in a circular stone stairwell. On a whim, he went up instead of down. After two circuits the stairwell opened on another hallway — no, it was a roofed colonnade: through the arches, the further crenellations and parapets of the castle interrupted a night misted by moonlight while the moon itself was somewhere out of sight.

At the colonnade's end, another stairwell took him back down among cool rocks. About to leave the stair at one exit because there was a faint glimmer of lamps somewhere off in the distance, he realized that what he'd taken for a buzzing in his own ears was really — blurred by echoing stones — conversation and music from below. Wondering if perhaps some catered gathering large enough to absorb him were going on, with one hand on the wall, he descended the spiral of stone.

In the vestibule at the bottom hung a bronze lamp. But the vestibule's hangings were so drear the tiny chamber still looked black. The attention of the guard in the archway was all on the sumptuous bright crowds within. When, after half a dozen heartbeats' hesitation, Gorgik walked out into the hall, he was not detained.

Were there a hundred people in this brilliant room? Passing among them, he saw the Baron Curly; and the Countess Esulla; and over there the elderly Princess Grutn was talking with a dour, older gentleman (the Earl Jue-Grutn); and that was Lord Vanar! On the great table running the whole side of the room sat tall decanters of wine, wide bowls of fruit, platters of jellied welkin, circular loaves of hard bread and rounds of soft cheese. Gorgik knew that if he gorged he would be ill; and that, even if he ate prudently, within an hour of his first bite, his bowels would void themselves of five days' bile — in short, he knew what a man who had lived near hunger for five years needed to know of hunger to survive. Nevertheless, he made slow circuit after slow circuit of the hall. Each time he passed the table, he took a fruit or a piece of bread. On the seventh round, because the food whipped up an astonishing thirst, he poured himself a goblet of cider: three sips and it went to his head like a torrent reversing itself to crash back up the rocks. He wondered if he would be sick. The music was reeds and drums. The musicians, in great headdresses of gilded feathers and little else, wandered through the crowd, somehow managing to keep their insistent rhythms and reedy whines together. It was on the ninth round, with the goblet still in his hand and his belly like a small, swollen bag swinging back and forth uneasily inside him, that a thin girl with a brown, wide face and a sleeveless white shift, high on her neck and down to the floor, said: 'Sir, you are not dressed for this party!' Which was true.

Her rough hair was braided around her head, so tight you could see her scalp between the spiralling tiers.

Gorgik smiled and dropped his head just a little, because that was usually the way to talk to aristocrats. 'I'm not really a guest. I am a most presumptuous interloper here — a hungry man.' While he kept his smile, his stomach suddenly cramped, then, very slowly, unknotted.

The girl's sleeves, high off her bare, brown shoulders, were circled with tiny diamonds. Around her forehead ran the thinnest of silver wires, set every inch with small, bright stones. 'You are from the mines, aren't you — the Vizerine's favorite and the pet of Lord Aldamir's circle.'

'I have never met Lord Aldamir,' Gorgik said. 'Though everyone I have known here at Court speaks of him with regard.'

To which the girl looked absolutely blank for another moment. Then she laughed a — high and childish laugh that had in it an hysteric edge he had not heard before in any of his courtier acquaintances' merriment. 'The Empress Ynelgo would certainly not have you put out just because your clothes are poor. Though, really, if you were going to come, you might have shown *some* consideration.'

'The Empress's reign is just and generous,' Gorgik said, because that's what people always said at any mention of the Empress. 'This will probably sound strange to such a wellbred little slip of a thing like yourself, but do you know that for the last five days I have not — ' Someone touched his arm.

He glanced back to see Curly beside him.

'Your Highness,' said the Baron, 'have you been introduced to Gorgik yet? May I have the honor of presenting him to you? Gorgik, I present you to Her Majesty, the Child Empress Ynelgo.'

Gorgik just remembered to press the back of his fist to his forehead. 'Your Highness, I didn't know — '

'Curly,' the Child Empress said, 'really, we've already met. But then, I can't really call you Curly in front of him, now, can I?'

'You might as well, Your Highness. He does.'

'Ah, I see. Of course, I've heard a great deal about Gorgik already. Is it presumptuous to assume that you — ' Her large eyes, close to the surface of her dark brown face (like so many of the Nevèrÿon aristocrats), came to Gorgik's — 'have heard a great deal about me?' Then she laughed again, emerging from it with: 'Curly . . . !' The sharpness clearly surprised the Baron as well.

'Your Highness.' The Baron touched his fist to his forehead and, to Gorgik's distress, backed away.

The Empress looked again at Gorgik with an expression intense enough to make him start back. She said: 'Let me tell you what the most beautiful and distressing section of Nevèrÿon's empire is, Gorgik. It is the province of Garth — especially the forests around the Vygernangx Monastery. I was kept there as a child, before I was made Empress. They say the elder gods dwell somewhere in the ruins on which it was built — and they are much older than the monastery.' She began to talk of Nevèrÿon's craftsmenlike gods and general religion, a conversation which need not be recounted, both because Gorgik did not understand the fine points of such theological distinctions, and also because the true religion, or metaphysics, of a culture is another surround, both of that culture's slaves and of its lords: to specify it, even here, as different from our own would be to suggest, however much we tried to avoid it, that it occupied a different relation to its culture from that which ours does to ours — if only by those specified differences. (We are never out of metaphysics, even when we think we are critiquing someone else's.) Therefore it is a topic about which, by and large, we may be silent. After a while of such talk, she said: 'The lands there in the Garth are lush and lovely. I long to visit them again. But our nameless gods prevent me. Still, even today, there is more trouble from that little spit of land than any corner of the empire.'

'I will remember what you have told me, Your Highness,' Gorgik said, because he could think of no other rejoinder.

'It would be very well if you did.' The Child Empress blinked. Suddenly she looked left, then right, bit her lip in a most unimperial way, and walked quickly across the room. Threads of silver in the white shift glimmered.

'Isn't the Empress charming,' Curly said, at Gorgik's shoulder once more; with his hand on Gorgik's arm, he was leading him away.

'Eh . . . yes. She . . . the Empress is charming,' Gorgik said, because he had learned in the last months that when something must be said to fill the silence, but no one knows what, repetition of something said before will usually at least effect a delay.

'The Empress is perfectly charming,' Curly went on as they walked. 'The Empress is more charming than I've ever seen her before. Really, she is the most charming person in the entire court . . .'

Somewhere in the middle of this, Gorgik realized the Baron had no more idea what to say than he did. They reached the door. The Baron lowered his voice and his largish larynx rose behind his embroidered collar. 'You have received the Empress's favor. Anything else the evening might offer you would undoubtedly be an anticlimax. Gorgik, you would be wise to retire from the party . . .' Then, in an even lower voice: 'When I tell you, look to your left. You will see a gentleman in red look away from you just as you look at him . . . All right: now.'

Gorgik looked. Across the hall, talking to a glittering group, an older man with a brown, bony face, grizzled white hair, a red cloak, and a heavy copper chestpiece over his tunic, turned back to his conversation with two jeweled women.

'Do you know who that is?'

Gorgik shook his head.

'That is Krodar. Please. Look away from him now. I should not need to tell you that Nevèrÿon is *his* Empire; his soldiers put the Empress on the throne; his forces have kept her there. More to the point, his forces threw down the previous and unmentionable residents of the High Court of Eagles. The power of the Child Empress Ynelgo is Krodar's power. While the Child Empress favored you with a smile and a moment's conversation, Krodar cast in your direction a frown which few in this company failed to notice.' The Baron sighed. 'So you see, your position here is completely changed.'

'But how — ? Of course I shall leave, but . . .' Feeling a sudden ominousness, Gorgik frowned, lightheaded and bewildered. 'I mean, I don't want anything from the Empress.'

'There is no one in this room who does not want *something* from the Empress — including myself. For that reason alone, no one here would believe you — including myself.'

'But —'

'You came to court with the favor of the Vizerine. Everyone knows — or thinks they know — that such favor from Myrgot is only favor of the flesh, which they can gossip about, find amusing, and therefore tolerate. Most do not realize that Myrgot decides when to let such news of her favor enter the circuit of gossip — and that, in your case, such decision was made well after your flesh ceased to interest her; and in such ways the rumor can be, and has been, put to use.' The Baron's larynx bounded in his neck. 'But no one ever knows precisely what the Empress's favor means. No one is ever quite sure what use either she or you will make of it. Therefore, it is much more dangerous to have. And there is Krodar's disfavor to consider. For Krodar is the Empress's minister — her chief steward if you will. Can you imagine how difficult your life would have been here at court if you had, say, the Vizerine's favor but Jahor's enmity?'

Gorgik nodded, now lightheaded and ill. 'Should I go to Krodar then and show him he has nothing to fear from — '

'Krodar holds all the power of this Empire in his hands. He is not "afraid" of anyone. My friend — ' the Baron put his pale hand up on Gorgik's thick shoulder and leaned close — 'when you entered this game, you entered on the next-to-the-highest level possible and under the tutelage of one of its best players. You know that the Vizerine is not at court and is not expected till tomorrow. Remember: so do the people who planned this party. There are many individual men and women in this very room, wearing enough jewelry tonight to buy a year's produce of the mine you once worked in, who have struggled half their lives or more to arrive at a level in the play far below the one you began at. You were allowed to stay on that level because you had nothing and convinced those of us who met you that you wanted nothing. Indeed, for us, you were a relief from such murderous games.'

'I was a miner, working sixteen hours a day in a pit that would have killed me in ten years. I'm now . . . favored at the High Court of Eagles. What else *would* I want?'

'But you see, you have just moved from the next-to-highest level of play to the *very* highest. You come into a party to which you — and your protectoress — were specifically *not* invited, dressed like a barbarian; and in five minutes you won a word from the Empress herself. Do you know that by fifteen minutes' proper conversation with the proper people, who are here tonight, you could parley that into a governorship of a fairly valuable, if outlying, province — more, if you were skillful. I do not intend to introduce you to those people, because just as easily you could win your death from someone both desperate for, and deserving of, the same position who merely lacked that all-important credential: a word from Her Majesty. The Empress knows all this. So does Krodar. That indeed may be why he frowned.'

'But *you* spoke with — '

'Friend, I may speak with the Empress any time I wish. She is my second cousin once removed. When she was nine and I was twenty-three we spent eight months together in the same dungeon cell, while our execution was put off day by day by day — but that was when she was still a princess. The Empress may *not* speak to me any time she wishes, or she risks endangering the subtle balance of power between my forces at Yenla'h and hers at Vinelet — should the wrong thane or princeling misconstrue her friendliness as a sign of military weakness and move his forces accordingly. My approaches to her, you see, are only considered nepotistic fawning. Hers to me are considered something else again. Gorgik, you have amused me. You have even tolerated my enthusiasm for botany. I don't want to hear that your corpse was pulled out of a sewage trough or, worse, was found floating somewhere in the Khora down at the port. And the excuse for such an outrage need easily be no more than Krodar's frown — if not the Empress's smile.'

Gorgik stepped back, because his gut suddenly knotted. He began to sweat. But the Baron's thin fingers dug his shoulder, pulling him forward:

'Do you understand? Do you understand that, minutes ago, you had nothing anyone here *could* have wanted? Do you understand that now you have what a third of us in this room have at least once committed murder for and the other two-thirds done far worse to obtain —' an unsolicited word from the Empress?'

Gorgik swayed. 'Curly, I'm sick. I want a loaf of bread and a bottle of — '

'There is a decanter.' The Baron frowned. 'There is a loaf.' He looked around. They were standing by the table end. 'And there is the door.' The Baron shrugged. 'Take the first two and use the last.'

Gorgik took a breath which made the cloth of his tunic slide on his wet back. With a lurching motion, he picked up a loaf in one hand and a decanter in the other and lumbered through the arch.

A young duchess, who had been standing only a few feet away, turned to Inige. 'Do you know, if I'm not mistaken, I believe I just saw your inelegantly dressed companion, who, only a moment ago, was conferring with Her Highness, do the *strangest* thing — '

'And do *you* know,' said the Baron, taking her arm, 'that two months by, when I was in the Zenari provinces, I saw the most remarkable species of schist moss with a most uncharacteristic blossom. Let me tell you . . .' and he led her across the room.

Gorgik lurched through the drear vestibule, once more unhindered by the guard; once he stopped to grasp the hangings, which released dust dragons to coil down about the decanter hooked to his thumb and his dribbling arm; he plunged into the stairwell.

He climbed.

Each time he came around the narrow circle, a sharp breeze caught him on the right side. Suddenly he stopped, dropped his head, and, still holding the decanter by his thumb, leaned his forearm high on the wall (the decanter clicked the stone) and vomited. And vomited again. And once again. Then, while his belly clamped once more, suddenly and surprisingly, his gut gave up its runny freight, which slid down both legs to puddle under his heels. Splattered and befouled, his inner thighs wet, his chin dripping, he began to shiver; the breeze scoured his right flank. Bread and bottle away from his sides, he climbed, pausing now and again to scrape off his sandal soles on the bowed steps' edges, his skin crinkling with gooseflesh, teeth clattering.

The wide brass basin clattered and clinked in its ring. He finished washing himself, let the rag drop on the basin edge (weighted on one side, it ceased its tinny rocking), turned on the wet stones, stepped to his pallet, and stretched out naked. The fur throw dampened beneath his hair, his cheek, his heavy legs, his shoulders. Each knob of bone on each other knob felt awash at his body's joints. Belly and gut were still liquefactious. Any movement might restart the shivering and the teeth chattering for ten, twenty seconds, a minute, or more. He turned on his back.

And shivered awhile.

From time to time he reached from the bed to tear off a small piece from the loaf on the floor, sometimes dipping its edge in the chased silver beaker that, with every third dip, threatened to overturn on the tiles. While he lay, listening to the nighthawks cooing beyond the hangings at his narrow window, he thought: about where he'd first learned what happened to the body during days without food. After the fight that had gained him his scar, he'd been put in the solitary cell, foodless, for three days. Afterward, an old slave whose name for the life of him he could not remember had taken him back to the barracks, told him the symptoms to expect, and snored by his side for three nights. Only a rich man who'd had no experience of prison at all could have seriously considered his current situation at the palace its equal. Still, minutes at a time, Gorgik could entertain the notion that the only difference between then and now was that — now — he was a little sicker, a little lonelier, and was in a situation where he had been forced, for reasons that baffled him, to pretend to be well and happy. Also, for five years he had done ten to eighteen hours a day hard labor. For almost five months now he had done nothing. In some ways his present illness merely seemed an extension of a feeling he'd had frequently of late: that his entire body was in a singular state of confusion about how to react to anything and that this confusion had nothing to do with his mind. And yet his mind found the situation confusing enough. For a while Gorgik thought about his parents. His father was dead — he'd watched that murder happen. His mother was . . . dead. He had heard enough to know any other assumption was as improbable as his arrival here at the High Court. These crimes had been committed at the ascent of the Child Empress, and her entourage, including the Vizerine, Curly, the princesses Elyne and Grutn, and Jahor. That was why he, Gorgik, had been taken a slave. Perhaps, here at court, he had even met the person who had given the order that, in the carrying out, had caused Gorgik's own life to veer as sharply from waterfront dock rat as it had recently veered away from pit slave.

Gorgik — he had not shivered for the last few minutes now — smiled wryly in the dark. Curly? The Vizerine? Krodar? It was not a new thought. Had he been insensitive enough never to have entertained it before, it might have infused him, in his weakness, with a new sense of power or purpose. He might even have experienced in his sickness an urge to revenge. But months ago he had, for good or bad, dismissed it as a useless one. Now, when it might, in its awkward way, have been some bitter solace, he found he could not keep it in the foreground of consciousness. It simply coiled away till it fragmented, the fragments dissolving into myriad flickers. But he was, for all his unfocused thought, learning — still learning. He was learning that power — the great power that shattered lives and twisted the course of the nation — was like a fog over a meadow at evening. From any distance, it seemed to have a shape, a substance, a color, an edge. Yet, as you approached it, it seemed to recede before you. Finally, when common sense said you were at its very center, it still seemed just as far away; only by this time it was on all sides, obscuring any vision of the world beyond it. He lay on damp fur and remembered walking through such a foggy field in a line with other slaves, chains heavy from his neck before and behind. Wet grass had whipped his legs. Twigs and pebbles had bitten through the mud caking his feet. Then the vision flickered, fragmented, drifted. Lord Aldamir . . . ? Surfacing among all the names and titles with which his last months had been filled, this one now: was this phenomenon he had noted the reason why such men, who were truly concerned with the workings of power, chose to stay away from its center, so that they might never lose sight of power's contours? Then that thought fragmented in a sudden bout of chills.

Toward dawn, footsteps in the corridor outside woke him. There, people were grunting with heavy trunks. People were passing, were talking less quietly than they might. He lay, feeling much better than when he had drifted to sleep, listening to the return of the Vizerine's suite. To date Gorgik had not violated the Vizerine's stricture on their intercourse. But shortly he rose, dressed, and went to Jahor's rooms to request an audience. Why? the eunuch asked, looking stern.

Gorgik told him, and told him also his plan.

The large-nosed eunuch nodded. Yes, that was probably very wise. But why didn't Gorgik go first to the Vizerine's kitchen and take a reasonable breakfast?

Gorgik was sitting on the corner of a large wood table, eating a bowl of gruel from the fat cook, whose hairy belly pushed over the top of his stained apron (already sweatblotched at the thighs from stoking the week-cold hearth), and joking with the sleepy kitchen girl, when Jahor stepped through the door: 'The Vizerine will see you now.'

'So,' said Myrgot, one elbow on the parchment-strewn desk, running a thumb, on which she had already replaced the heavy rings of court, over her forehead — a gesture Gorgik knew meant she was tired, 'you had a word last night with our most grave and gracious Empress.'

Which took Gorgik aback. He had not even mentioned that to Jahor. 'Curly left a message that greeted me at the door,' the Vizerine explained. 'Tell me what she said: everything. If you can remember it word for word, so much the better.'

'She said she had heard of me. And that she would not have me put out of the party because my clothes were poor — '

Myrgot grunted. 'Well, it's true. I have not been as munificent with you of late as I might have been — '

'My Lady, I make no accusation. I only tell you what she — '

The Vizerine reached across the desk, took Gorgik's great wrist. 'I know you don't.' She stood, still holding his arm, and came around to the side, where, as he had done in the kitchen a little while before, she sat down on the desk's corner. 'Though any six of my former lovers — not to mention the present one — would have meant it as an accusation in the same situation. No, the accusation comes from our just and generous ruler herself.' She patted his hand, then dropped it. 'Go on.'

'She nodded Curly — the Baron Inige, I mean — away. She spoke of religion. Then she said that the most beautiful and distressing section of Nevèrÿon's empire is the province of Garth, especially the forests around some monastery — '

'The Vygernangx.'

'Yes. She said she was kept there as a girl before she was Empress. Curly told me later about when the two of them were in prison — '

'I know all about that time. I was in a cell only two away from theirs. Go on with what she said.'

'She said that the elder gods dwell there, and that they are even older than the monastery. She spoke of our nameless gods. She said that the lands were lush and lovely and that she longed to revisit them. But that even today there was more trouble from that little bit of land than from any other place in Nevèrÿon.'

'And while she spoke with you thus, Krodar cast you a dark look . . . ?' The Vizerine dropped both hands to the desk. She sighed. 'Do you know the Garth Peninsula?'

Gorgik shook his head.

'A brutish, uncivilized place — though the scenery is pretty enough. Every other old hovel one comes across houses a witch or a wizard; not to mention the occasional mad priest. And then, a few miles to the south, it is no longer forest but jungle; and there are nothing but barbarian tribes. And the amount of worry it causes is absolutely staggering!' She sighed again. 'Of course, you know, Gorgik, that the Empress associates you with me. So any word spoken to you — or even a look cast your way — may be read in some way as a message intended for Myrgot.'

'Then I hope I have not brought Myrgot an unhappy one.'

'It's not a good one.' The Vizerine sighed, leaned back a little on the desk, placing one fingertip on the shale of parchment. 'For the Empress to declare the elder gods are older than the monastery is to concede me a theological point that I support and that, till now, she has opposed. Over this point, many people have died. For her to say she wishes to go there is tantamount to declaring war on Lord Al-damir, in whose circle you and I both move, and who keeps his center of power there. For her to choose *you* to deliver this message is . . . But I shouldn't trouble you with the details of that meaning.'

'Yes, My Lady. There is no need. My Lady — ?'

The Vizerine raised her eyebrow.

'I *asked* to come and speak to you. Because I cannot stay here at Court any longer. What can I do to help you in the outside world? Can I be a messenger for you? Can I work some bit of your land? Within the castle here there is nothing for me.'

The Vizerine was silent long enough for Gorgik to suspect she disapproved of his request. 'Of course you're right,' she said at last, so that he was surprised and relieved. 'No, you can't stay on here. Especially after last night. I suppose I could always return you to the mines . . . no, that is a tasteless joke. Forgive me.'

'There is nothing to forgive, My Lady,' though Gorgik's heart had suddenly started. While it slowed, he ventured: 'Any post you can put me to, I would happily fill.'

After another few moments, the Vizerine said: 'Go now. I will send for you in an hour. By then we shall have decided what to do with you.'

'You know, Jahor — ' The Vizerine stood by the window, looking between the bars at the rain, at further battlements beyond the veils of water, the dripping mansards and streaming crenellations — 'he really is an exceptional man. After five months, he wishes to leave the castle. Think how many of the finest sons and daughters of pro-vincial noblemen who, once presented here, become parasites and hangers-on for five *years* or more — before they finally reach such a propitious decision as he has.' Rain gathered on the bars and dripped, wetting inches of the beveled sill.

Jahor sat in the Vizerine's great curved-back chair, rather slump-shouldered and, for all his greater bulk, filling it noticeably less well than she. 'He was wasted in the mines, My Lady. He is wasted at the castle. Only consider, My Lady, what *is* such a man fit for? First, childhood as a portside ragamuffin, then his youth as a mine slave, followed by a few months skulking in the shadows at the Court of Eagles — where, apparently, he still has not been able to keep out of sight. That is an erratic education to say the least. I can think of no place where he could put it to use. Return him to the mines now, My Lady. Not as a slave, if that troubles you. Free him and make him a guard. That's still more than he might ever have hoped for six months back.'

The bars dripped.

Myrgot pondered.

Jahor picked up a carefully crafted astrolabe from the desk, ran a long forenail over its calibrations, then rubbed his thumb across the curlicues of the rhet.

The Vizerine said: 'No. I do not think that I will do that, Jahor. It is too close to slavery.' She turned from the window and thought about her cook. 'I shall do something else with him.'

'*I* would put him back in the mines without his freedom,' Jahor said sullenly. 'But then, My Lady is almost as generous as the Empress herself. And as just.'

The Vizerine raised an eyebrow at what she considered an ill-put compliment. But then, of course, Jahor did not know the Empress's most recent message that Gorgik had so dutifully delivered. 'No. I have another idea for him . . .'

'To the mines with him, My Lady, and you will save yourself much trouble, if not grief.'

Had Gorgik known of the argument that was progressing in the Vizerine's chamber, he would most probably have misassigned the positions of the respective advocates — perhaps the strongest sign of his unfitness for court life.

Though it does not explain the actual assignment of the positions themselves, there was a simple reason for the tones of voice in which the respective positions were argued: for the last three weeks the Vizerine's lover had been a lithe seventeen-year-old barbarian with bitten nails and mad blue eyes, who would, someday, inherit the title of

Suzeraine of Strethi — though the land his parents owned, near the marshy Avila, was little more than a sizable farm. And the youth, for all his coming title, was — in his manners and bearing — little more than a barbarian farmer's son. His passion was for horses, which he rode superbly. Indeed, he had careered, naked, on a black mount, about the Vizerine's caravan for an hour one moonlit night when, two months before, she had been to visit the Avila province to meet with its reigning families anent taxes. She had sent Jahor to ascertain how she might meet this yellow-haired youth. A guest of his parents one evening, she discovered that they were quite anxious for him to go to court and that for one so young he had an impressive list of illegitimate children throughout the surrounding neighborhoods and was something of a bane to his kin. She had agreed to take him with her; and had kept her agreement. But the relationship was of a volatile and explosive sort that made her, from time to time, look back with fondness on the weeks with Gorgik. Four times now the suzeraine-apparent had run up atrocious debts gambling with the servants; twice he had tried to blackmail her; and he had been unfaithful to her with at least three palace serving women, and what's more they were *not* of Lord Aldamir's circle. The night before the Vizerine had departed on this her most recent mission — to get away from the child? but no — they had gotten into an incredible argument over a white gold chain which had ended with his declaring he would never let her withered lips and wrinkled paws defile his strong, bronzed body again. But just last night, however, hours before her return, he had ridden out to meet her caravan, charged into her tent, and declared he could not live without her caress another moment. In short, that small sector of Myrgot's life she set aside for personal involvement was currently full to overflowing. (Jahor, currently, had no lover at all, nor was he overfond of the Vizerine's.)

The Vizerine, in deference to the vaguest of promises to his barbaric parents, had been desultorily attempting to secure a small commission for the blond boy with some garrison in a safer part of the Empire. She knew he was too young for such a post, and of an impossible temperament to fill it, even were he half a dozen years older; also, there was really no way, in those days, to ascertain if any part of the Empire would remain safe. In any open combat, the little fool — for he was a fool, she did not delude herself about that — would probably be killed, and more than likely get any man under him killed as well — if his men did not turn and kill him first. (She had known such things to happen. Barbarians in positions of power were not popular with the people.) This young, unlettered chief's son was the sort who, for all his barbaric good looks, fiery temperament, and coming inheritance, one either loved or despised. And she had discovered, upon making inquiries into the gambling affair, much to her surprise, that no one in court other than herself seemed to love him. Well, she still did not want him to leave the court . . . not just now. She had only put any effort toward obtaining his commission at those moments when she had been most aware that soon she must want him as far away as possible.

The commission had arrived while she had been away; it was on her desk now.

No, after his marvelous ride last night to meet her, she did *not* want him to leave . . . *just yet*. But she was experienced enough to know the wishes that he would, with such as he, must come again. As would other commissions.

'Gorgik,' she said, when Jahor had led him in and retired, 'I am going to put you for six weeks with Master Narbu. He trains all of Curly's personal guards and has instructed many of the finest generals of this Empire in the arts of war. Most of the young men there will be two or three years younger than you, but that may easily, at your age, be as much an advantage as a hindrance. At the end of that time, you will be put in charge of a small garrison near the edge of K'haki desert — north of the Falthas. At the termination of your commission you will have the freedom in fact that, as of this morning, you now have on paper. I hope you will distinguish yourself in the name of the Empress, whose reign is wise and wondrous.' She smiled. 'Will you agree that this now terminates any and all of our mutual obligations?'

'You are very generous, My Lady,' Gorgik said, almost as flabbergasted as when he'd discovered himself purchased from the mines.

'Our Empress is just and generous,' the Vizerine said, almost as if correcting him. 'I am merely soft-hearted.' Her hand had strayed to the astrolabe. Suddenly she picked up the verdigrised disk, turned it over, frowned at it. 'Here, take this. Go on. Take it, keep it; and take with it one final piece of advice. It's heartfelt advice, my young friend. I want you always to remember the Empress's words to you last night.

Do you promise? Good — and as you value your freedom and your life, never set foot on the Garth Peninsula. And if the Vygernangx Monastery ever thrusts so much as the tiny tip of one tower over the treetops within the circle of your vision, you will turn yourself directly around and ride, run, crawl away as fast and as far as you can go. Now take it — take it, go on. And go.'

With the Vizerine's astrolabe in his hand, Gorgik touched his forehead and backed, frowning, from the chamber.

'My Lady, his education is already erratic enough. By making him an officer, you do not bring it to heel. It will only give him presumptions, which will bring him grief and you embarrassment.'

'Perhaps, Jahor. Then again, perhaps not. We shall see.'

Outside the window, the rains, after having let up for the space of an hour's sunlight, blew violently again, clouding the far towers and splattering all the way in to the edge of the stone sill, running down the inner wall to the floor.

'My Lady, wasn't there an astrolabe here on your desk earlier this morning . . . ?'

'Was there now . . . ? Ah yes. My pesky little blue-eyed devil was in here only moments ago, picking at it. No doubt he pocketed it on his way down to the stables. Really, Jahor, I *must* do something about that gold-haired little tyrant. He is a true barbarian and has become the bane of my life!

Six weeks is long enough for a man to learn to enjoy himself on a horse; it is not long enough to learn to ride.

Six weeks is long enough for a man to learn the rules and forms of fencing; it is not long enough to become a swordsman.

Master Narbu, born a slave himself to a high household in the foothills of the Falthas not far from fabled Ellamon, had as a child shown some animal grace that his baronial owner thought best turned to weapon wielding — from a sort of retrograde, baronial caprice. Naturally slaves were not encouraged to excel in arms. Narbu had taken the opportunity to practice — from a retrograde despair at servitude — constantly, continuously, dawn, noon, night, and any spare moment between. At first the hope had been, naturally and secretly and obviously to any but such a capricious master, for escape. Skill had become craft and craft had become art; and developing along was an impassioned love for weaponry itself. The Baron displayed the young slave's skill to friends; mock contests were arranged; then real contests — with other slaves, with freemen. Lords of the realm proud of their own skills challenged him; two lords of the realm died. And Narbu found himself in this paradoxical position: his license to sink sword blade into an aristocratic gut was only vouchsafed by the protection of an aristocrat. During several provincial skirmishes, Narbu fought valiantly beside his master. In several others, his master rented him out as a mercenary — by now his reputation (though he was not out of his twenties) was such that he was being urged, pressed, forced to learn the larger organizational skills and strategies that make war possible. One cannot truly trace the course of a life in a thousand pages. Let us have the reticence here not to attempt it in a thousand words. Twenty years later, during one of the many battles that resulted in the ascension of the present Child Empress Ynelgo to the Throne of Eagles, Narbu (now forty-four) and his master had been lucky enough to be on the winning side — though his master had been killed. But Narbu had distinguished himself. As a reward — for the Empress was brave and benevolent — Narbu was given his freedom and offered a position as instructor of the Empress's own guard, a job which involved training the sons of favored aristocrats in the finer (and grosser) points of battle. (Two of Narbu's earliest instructors had been daughters of the mysterious Western Crevasse, and much of his early finesse had been gained from these masked women with their strange and strangely sinister blades. Twice he had fought with such women; and once against them. But they did not usually venture in large groups too far from their own lands. Still, he had always suspected that Nevèrÿon, with its strictly male armies, was over-compensating for something.) In his position as royal master at arms, he found himself developing a rich and ritual tirade against his new pupils: they were soft, or when they were hard they had no discipline, or, when they had discipline, had no heart. What training they'd gotten must all be undone before they could really begin; aristocrats could never make good soldiers anyway; what was needed was good common stock. Though Master Narbu *was* common stock, had fought common stock, and been taught by common stock, Gorgik was the first man of common stock Master Narbu, in six years, had ever been paid to teach. And the good master now discovered that, as a teacher, somehow he had never developed a language to instruct any other than aristocrats — however badly trained, undisciplined, or heartless they were. As well, he found himself actually resenting this great-muscled, affable, quiet, giant of a youth. First, Gorgik's physique was not the sort (as Narbu was quick to point out to him) that naturally lent itself to horsemanship or any but gross combative skills. Besides, the rumor had gone the rounds that the youth had been put under Narbu's tutelage not even because of his exceptional strength, but because he was some high Court lady's catamite. But one morning Master Narbu woke, frowned at some sound outside, and sat up on his pallet. Through the bars on his window, he looked out across the yard where the training dummies and exercise forms stood in moonlight — it was over an hour to sunup. On the porch of the student barracks, beneath the frayed thatch, a great form, naked and crossed with shadow from the nearest porch poles, moved and turned and moved.

The new pupil was practicing. First he would try a few swings with the light wooden sword to develop form, moving slowly, returning to starting position, hefting the blade again. And going through the swing, parry, recovery . . . a little too self-consciously; and the arm not fully extended at the peak of the swing, the blade a little too high . . . Narbu frowned. The new student put down the wooden blade against the barracks wall, picked up the treble-weight iron blade used to improve strength: swing, parry, recovery; again, swing, parry — the student halted, stepped back, began again. Good. He'd remembered the extension this time. Better, Narbu reflected. Better . . . but not excellent. Of course, for the weighted blade, it was better than most of the youths — with those great sacks of muscle about his bones, really not so surprising . . . No, he didn't let the blade sag. But what was he doing up this early anyway . . . ?

Then Narbu saw something.

Narbu squinted a little to make sure he saw it.

What he saw was something he could not have named himself, either to baron or commoner. Indeed, we may have trouble describing it: he saw a concentration in this extremely strong, naked young man's practicing that, by so many little twists and sets of the body, flicks of the eye, bearings of the arms and hips, signed its origins in inspiration. He saw something that much resembled not a younger Narbu, but something that had been part of the younger Narbu and which, when he recognized it now, he realized was all-important. The others, Narbu thought (and his lips, set about with gray stubble, shaped the words), were too pampered, too soft . . . *how* many hours before sunrise? Not those others, no, not on your . . . that one, yes, *was* good common stock.

Narbu lay back down.

No, this common, one-time mercenary slave still did not know how to speak to a common, one-time pit slave as a teacher; and no, six weeks were not enough. But now, in the practice sessions, and sometimes in the rest periods during and after them, Narbu began to say things to the tall, scarfaced youth: 'In rocky terrain, look for a rider who holds one rein up near his beast's ear, with his thumb tucked well down; he'll be a Narnisman and the one to show you how to coax most from your mount in the mountains. Stick by him and watch him fast . . .' And: 'The best men with throwing weapons I've ever seen are the desert Adami: shy men, with little brass wires sewn up around the backs of their ears. You'll be lucky if you have a few in your garrison. Get one of them to practice with you, and you might learn something . . .' Or: 'When you requisition cart oxen in the Avila swamplands, if you get them from the Men of the Hide Shields, you must get one of them to drive, for it will be a good beast, but nervous. If you get a beast from the Men of the Palm Fiber Shields, then anyone in your garrison can drive it — they train them differently, but just how I am not sure.' Narbu said these things and many others. His saws cut through to where and how and what one might need to learn beyond those six weeks. They came out in no organized manner. But there were many of them. Gorgik remembered many; and he forgot many. Some of those he forgot would have saved him much time and trouble in the coming years. Some that he remembered he never got an opportunity to use. But even more than the practice and the instruction (and because Gorgik practiced most, at the end of the six weeks he was easily the best in his class), this was the education he took with him. And Myrgot was away from the castle when his commission began . . .

3

There was an oxcart ride along a narrow road with mountains looking over the trees to the left. With six other young officers, he forded an icy stream, up to his waist in foam; a horse ride over bare rocks, around steep slopes of slate . . . ahead were the little tongues of army campfires, alick on the blue, with the desert below white as milk in a quarter light.

Gorgik took on his garrison with an advantage over most: five years' experience in the mines as a foreman over fifty slaves.

His garrison contained only twenty-nine.

Nor were they despairing, unskilled, and purchased for life — though, over the next few years, from time to time Gorgik wondered just how much difference that made in the daily texture of their lives, for guards' lives were rough in those days. Over those same years, Gorgik became a good officer. He gained the affection of his men, mainly by keeping them alive in an epoch in which one of the horrors of war was that every time more than ten garrisons were brought together, twenty percent were lost through communicable diseases having nothing to do with battle (and much of the knowledge for this could be traced back to some of Master Narbu's more eccentric saws concerning various herbs, moldy fruit rinds, and moss — and not a few of Baron Curly's observations on botany that Gorgik found himself now and again recalling to great effect). As regards the army itself, Gorgik was a man recently enough blessed with an unexpected hope of life that all this human energy expended to create an institution solely bent on smashing that hope seemed arbitrary and absurd enough to marshal all his intelligence toward surviving it. He saw battle as a test to be endured, with true freedom as prize. He had experienced leading of a sort before, and he led well. But the personalities of his men — both their blustering camaraderie (which seemed a pale and farcical shadow of the brutal and destructive mayhem that, from time to time, had broken out in the slave quarters at the mines, always leaving one or two dead) and the constant resignation to danger and death (that any sane slave would have been trying his utmost to avoid) — confused him (and confusion he had traditionally dealt with by silence) and depressed him (and depression, frankly, he had never really had time to deal with, nor did he really here, so that its effects, finally, were basically just more anecdotes for later years on the stupidity of the military mind).

He knew all his men, and had a far easier relationship with them than most officers of that day. But only a very few did he ever consider friends, and then not for long. A frequent occurrence: some young recruit would take the easiness of some late-night campfire talk, or the revelations that occurred on a foggy morning hike, as a sign of lasting intimacy, only to find himself reprimanded — and, in three cases over the two years, struck to the ground for the presumption: for these were basic and brutal times — in a manner that recalled nothing so much (at least to Gorgik, eternally frustrated by having to give out these reprimands) as the snubs he had received in the halls of the High Court of Eagles the mornings after some particularly revelatory exchange with some count or princess.

Couldn't these imbeciles learn?

He had.

The ones who stayed in his garrison did. And respected him for the lesson — loved him, some of them would even have said in the drunken evenings that, during some lax period that, now at a village tavern, now at a mountain campsite where rum had been impounded from a passing caravan, still punctuated a guard's life. Gorgik laughed at this. His own silent appraisal of the situation had been, from the beginning: I may die; they may die; but if there is any way their death can delay mine, let theirs come down.

Yet within this strictly selfish ethical matrix, he was able to display enough lineaments both of reason and bravery to satisfy those above him in rank and those below — till, from time to time, especially in the face of rank cowardice (which he always tried to construe — and usually succeeded — as rank stupidity) in others, he could convince himself there might be something to the whole idea. 'Might' — for survival's sake he never allowed it to go any further.

He survived.

But such survival was a lonely business. After six months, out of loneliness, he hired a scribe to help him with some of the newer writing methods that had recently come to the land and composed a long letter to the Vizerine: inelegant, rambling, uncomfortable with its own discourse, wisely it touched neither on his affection for her nor his debt to her, but rather turned about what he had learned, had seen, had felt: the oddly depressed atmosphere of the marketplace in the town they had passed through the day before; the hectic nature of the smuggling in that small port where, for two weeks now, they had been garrisoned; the anxious gossip of the soldiers and prostitutes about the proposed public building scheduled to replace a section of slumlike huts in a city to the north; the brazen look to the sky from a southern mountain path that he and his men had wandered on for two hours in the evening before stopping to camp.

At the High Court the Vizerine read his letter — several times, and with a fondness that, now all pretence at the erotic was gone, grew, rather than diminished, in directions it would have been hard for grosser souls to follow, much less appreciate. His letter contained this paragraph:

'Rumors came down among the lieutenants last week that all the garrisons hereabout were to go south for the Garth in a month. I drank beer with the Major, diced him for his bone-handled knives and won. Two garrisons were to go to the Able-aini, in the swamps west of the Falthas — a thankless position, putting down small squabbles for ungrateful lords, he assured me, more dangerous and less interesting than the south. I gave him back his knives. He scratched his gray beard in which one or two rough, rusty hairs still twist, and gave me his promise of the swamp post, thinking me mad.'

The Vizerine read it, at dawn, standing by the barred windows (dripping with light rain as they had dripped on the morning of her last interview with Gorgik, half a year before), remembered him, looked back toward her desk where once a bronze astrolabe had lain among the parchments. A lamp flame wavered, threatened to go out, and steadied. She smiled.

Toward the end of Gorgik's three years (the occasional, unmistakably royal messenger who would come to his tent to deliver Myrgot's brief and very formal acknowledgements did not hurt his reputation among his troops), when his garrison was moving back and forth at bi-weekly intervals from the desert skirmishes near the Venarra Canyon to the comparatively calm hold of fabled Ellamon high in the Faltha range (where, like all tourists, Gorgik and his men went out to observe, from the white lime slopes, across the crags to the far corrals, the fabled, flying beasts that scarred the evening with their exercises), he discovered that some of his men had been smuggling purses of salt from the desert to the mountains. He made no great issue of it; but he called in the man whom he suspected to be second in charge of the smuggling operation and told him he wished a share — a modest share — of the profits. With that share, many miles to the south, he purchased three extra carts, and four extra oxen to pull them; and with a daring that astonished his men (for the empress's customs inspectors were neither easy nor forgiving) on his last trek, a week before his discharge, he brought three whole cartfuls of contraband salt, which he got through by turning off the main road, whereupon they were shortly met by what was obviously a ragged, private guard at the edge of private lands.

'Common soldiers may not trespass on the Hold of the Princess Elyne — !'

'Conduct me to her Highness!' Gorgik announced, holding his hand up to halt his men.

After dark, he returned to them (with a memory of high fires in the dank, roofless hall; and the happy princess with her heavy, jeweled robes and her hair greasy and her fingers thin and grubbier than his own, taking his hard, cracked hands in hers and saying: 'Oh, but you see what I've come home to? A bunch of hereditary heathens who think I am a goddess, and cannot make proper conversation for five minutes! No, no, tell me again of the Vizerine's last letter. I don't care if you've told me twice before. Tell me *again*, for it's been over a year since I've heard anything at all from Court. And I long for their company; I long for it. All my stay there taught me was to be dissatisfied with *this* ancient, moldy pile. No, sit there, on that bench, and I will sit beside you and have them bring us more bread and cider and meat. And you shall simply tell me again, friend Gorgik . . .') with leave for his men and his carts to pass through her lands; and thus he avoided the inspectors.

A month after he left the army, some friendlier men of an intricately tattooed and scarred desert tribe gave him some exquisitely worked copper vases. Provincial burghers in the Argini bought them from him for a price five times what he recalled, from his youth in the port, such work was worth in civilized cities. From the mountain women of Ka'hesh (well below Ellamon) he purchased a load of the brown berry leaves that, when smoked, put one in a state more relaxed than beer — he was now almost a year beyond his release from the army — and transported it all the way to the Port of Sarness, where, in small quantities, he sold it to sailors on outgoing merchant ships. While he was there, a man whom he had paid to help him told him of a warehouse whose back window was loose in which were stored great numbers of . . . But we could fill pages; let us compress both time and the word.

The basic education of Gorgik had been laid. All that followed — the months he reentered a private service as a mercenary officer again, then as a gamekeeper to a provincial count, then as paid slave-overseer to the same count's treecutters, then as bargeman on the river that ran through that count's land, again as a smuggler in Vinelet, the port at the estuary of that river, then as a mercenary again, then as a private caravan guard — all of these merely developed motifs we have already sounded. Gorgik, at thirty-six, was tall and great-muscled, with rough, thinning hair and a face (with its great scar) that looked no more than half a dozen years older than it had at twenty-one, a man comfortable with horse and sword, at home with slaves, thieves, soldiers, prostitutes, merchants, counts, and princesses; a man who was — in his way and for his epoch — the optimum product of his civilization. The slave mine, the Court, the army, the great ports and mountain holds, desert, field, and forest: each of his civilization's institutions had contributed to creating this scar-faced giant, who wore thick furs in cold weather and in the heat went naked (save for a layered disk of metal, with arcane etchings and cutouts upon it — an astrolabe — chained around his veined and heavy neck, whatever the month), an easy man in company yet able to hold his silence. Often, at dawn in the mountains or in evenings on the desert, he wondered what terribly important aspects there were to his civilization in excess of a proper ability, at the proper time, to tell the proper tale. But for the civilization in which he lived, this dark giant, soldier, and adventurer, with desires we've not yet named and dreams we've hardly mentioned, who could speak equally of and to barbarian tavern maids and High Court ladies, flogged slaves lost in the cities and provincial nobles at ease on their country estates, he was a civilized man.

— New York
October 1976

Appendix:
Closures and Openings

It is easy to see why Pasolini's arguments could have been so easily dismissed. He himself, only half jokingly, asked: 'What horrible sins are crouching in my philosophy?' and named the 'monstrous' juxtaposition of irrationalism and pragmatism, religion and action, and other 'fascist' aspects of our civilization . . . Let me suggest, however, that an unconventional, less literal or narrow reading of Pasolini's pronouncements (for such they undoubtedly were), one that would accept his provocations and work on the contradictions of his 'heretical empiricism,' could be helpful in resisting, if not countering, the more subtle seduction of a logico-semiotic humanism — TERESA DE LAURETIS

Alice Doesn't — Feminism, Semiotics, Cinema

1. Compositional elegance would certainly have us place here K. Leslie Steiner's translation of the c. 900 word Culhar' Fragment (also known as the Missolonghi Codex), that most ancient of ancient texts on which the stories in this series are all, in part or in whole, based — as well, perhaps, as include select samples of her three hundred pages of commentary, which make the various essays in which those comments first appeared and finally the book in which, in 1977, those essays were collected a work of genius and her own. (It was in their separate journal appearances, between 1972 and 1976, that they first excited us to fiction.) Professor Steiner was willing. But anguished over — and afflicted with a sadly inflated notion of — Nevèrÿon's commercial possibilities, her university publisher would not grant reprint rights for any affordable fee. Because the correspondence reached such heat, we have been advised for legal reason not even to mention the book's title! I can only exhort readers to go, find, and lovingly peruse that wonder-filled volume. All I can offer in the stead

of that absent text is these work-notes, marginal comments, and reminiscences.

2. I had every intention of making 'The Tale of Plagues and Carnivals' a farewell to my nearly ten-year sojourn in Nevèrÿon. The serial form, however, admits to certain speculations, elaborations, exfoliations. What origins, then, can we construct?

3. From the time I became aware that the Nevèrÿon tales would become a series — from the time I became aware of a certain dissatisfaction with the idea that a sequence of encounters with a set of socially central institutions was constitutive of the 'civilized' subject ('The Tale of Gorgik') and turned back to critique that notion with the idea that a sequence of far more subjective encounters with some far more marginal institutions could be equally constitutive ('The Tale of Old Venn') — I more or less thought of these stories as a Child's Garden of Semiotics.

The five stories of volume one (*Tales of Nevèrÿon*) struggle through the classical notion of the sign (stoically divided into a signifier and signified), positted by the pre-Socratic Greeks and persistent up through Saussure and Pierce, and the conservative notion of social relations that this 'classical' sign stabilizes. Under such a program, semiotics becomes the study of the way in which signs are *organized*.

The sixth tale, the novel that fills most of the second volume (*Neveryóna, or: The Tale of Signs and Cities*), struggles toward a somewhat richer view of the sign, shattering it into sign consumption/transformation/production (or *semiosis* — more usually defined as 'sign interpretation'), sign function, and sign vehicle — the schema that distinguishes Umberto Eco's semiotics as he adumbrated it in *Opera Aperta* (Milano: Bompiani, 1962) and the early essays in *The Role of the Reader* (Bloomington: Indiana University Press, 1984), expressed it in *A Theory of Semiotics* (Bloomington: Indiana University Press, 1976), and (subsequently) critiqued it from a historical perspective in *Semiotics and the Philosophy of Language* (Bloomington: Indiana University Press, 1984). This is certainly the most impressive account of semiosis that allows sign systems to evolve, generate new signs, critique themselves, and generally to change. In such a view, semiotics becomes the study of the way in which signs are *generated*.

In the third and fourth volumes (*Flight from Nevèrÿon*, as well as in this, I hope, final book), the tales move away from semiotics to a more general semiology, as Roland Barthes described it in his 'Inaugural Lecture' for the Chair of Literary Semiology at the College de France, January 7, 1977: for Barthes, semiology was 'the labor that collects the impurities of language, the wastes of linguistics, the immediate corruption of any message: nothing less than the desires, fears, expressions, intimidations, advances, blandishments, protests, excuses, aggressions, and melodies of which active language is made.' This idea of semiology as the excess, the leftover, the supplement of linguistics brings us round to Jacques Derrida's logic of the supplement, without which semiology and, indeed, poststructuralism in general would be hugely impoverished.

Language in its classical model begins as the grunt spilling out alongside gesture, the excess of indication, the supplement to ostension, the verbal signifier denoting reference. But eventually the grunt, the excess, the supplement recomplicates into meaning, a system so rich it reverses the hierarchy at precisely the point the grunt becomes a spillage, an excess, a supplement to emotion, need, desire (i.e., becomes itself a gesture indicating something otherwise unseeable, that is: at the first infant's cry). In its recomplication it becomes a system able to create and to control meaning on its own, developing in the process its own spillage, excess, supplement — writing — which begins to recomplicate all over again, again upsetting the power hierarchy, contouring it not to its former value but toward a new one. Through its richnesses, meaning has become power . . .

4. In the traditional paraliterary story/novel series, each new tale critiques the tale (or tales) before it. Is it belaboring the obvious to point out that, in the Nevèrÿon series, earlier tales (e.g., 'The Tale of Old Venn' and *Neveryóna*) dramatically critique later ones (e.g., 'The Tale of Plagues and Carnivals') as well . . . ?

I had every intention of making 'The Game of Time and Pain' a farewell to my sojourn in Nevèrÿon . . . But why must all assertions such as this end, from now on, with a pause?

5. The Nevèrÿon series takes place at the edge of the shadow of the late French psychiatrist Jacques Lacan, from the slaves who have va-

cated the collars in the first pages of the first tale (gone to what manu-
missions, executions, or other collars, the child Gorgik never knows,
though the rest of his life can be looked at as an attempt to find out)
to the series of vanished authorities and their empty citadels, such as
Lord Aldamir and his castle: the Dead father, the Absent father, the
Name of the Law.

At the same time, I have tried to keep a sharp vigil against the
muddling results of an essentialist sexuality. As the late Michel Foucault warned us so pointedly in a lecture at Stanford a few years back:
'We must get rid of the Freudian schema . . . the schema of the inte-
riorization of the law through the medium of sex.' Deeply I feel that
in our current social system, almost all claims of such an interioriza-
tion are, today, signs of potential terrorism, wherever they are made,
even by groups as seemingly diverse as orthodox and radical psychia-
try or the Moral Majority or feminist critics against pornography.

The material power of the present father is the material power of
any coercive aggressive individual, male or female, armed or unarmed.
But it is only the power to coerce in excess of immediate bodily force
— the power of the 'absent father' — that constitutes authority in our
patriarchal culture as a day-to-day social reality. And it is our habit-
ual insistence on reading all such absent-but-functioning authority
as male (even when, as in the case of the 'absent father,' gender is, indeed, materially absent) and at work, usually, on a feminine ground
of 'the natural' (e.g., where 'the natural' is a fragment of effective social functioning that is seen as somehow 'normal' [instead of tediously
learned and internalized], 'a-historical' [instead of insistently socially
constituted], or a product of 'the better side of human nature' [instead
of the intersection of a series of repressions], and thus essentially
feminine [instead of masculine, as it would be cognized were it seen
as a product of these now bracketed modes]) that stabilizes the socio-
economic realities of patriarchal society. Social power-relations, from
the way embarking passengers wait at a subway-car door for the
former passengers to leave the train, to the way a prisoner receives a
sentence of incarceration or death from a judge, are very much a language. They involve understood meanings, always more or less accepted, always more or less challenged, always in excess of bodily
coercion — in excess of striking body and rebounding body, i.e. of

classical mechanics — that contour appropriate *or* inappropriate behavior. But as long as power, whether it goes with or against the law, is named male, the law itself will *be* male — even if justice is a woman blinded by men, with both her hands occupied maintaining a passive and impossibly difficult balancing act.

As language comes from all that is in excess of gesture (unto containing gesture), so social power/authority comes from all that is in excess of mechanical coercion (unto containing mechanical coercion).

The unconscious is structured, declared Lacan so famously in *Ecrits*, as a language.

Well, so is social power/authority.

Indeed, the totality of social power/authority as it is interiorized for better or for worse by each individual may just *be* the structure of the unconscious.

Do I believe, then, Michael Ryan's assertion with which I opened the third volume, i.e., that the impossibility of individuating meanings at the level of the word, which Derrida has so powerfully demonstrated (or at the level of the sentence, which Quine has demonstrated with equal power, though with less fanfare; or at the level of any operationally rich, axiomatic system, which was Gödel's originary contribution — Derrida took the term 'undecidability' from Gödel), is a *material* force?

Frankly, I don't know.

But I think the possibility must be seriously considered by anyone interested in either language or power, not to mention their frighteningly elusive, always allusive, and often illusive relations.

6. Lacan, and at this point Lacan's commentators even more so, have led us back to a careful reconsideration of Freud's texts with a focus on language. (Our focus? Freud's? The text's? Often it is as intriguingly undecidable as the terminal prepositional phrase's antecedent in the previous sentence.) These rereadings have been scrupulously clarifying, profoundly exciting.

The objection to Freud, however, remains. I do not, of course, mean the problem of 'vulgar Freudianism,' where metonymies are interpreted as metaphors for their originary terms and situations. The valid Freudian enterprise is rather to discern the several social and psychological systems (clearly distinguishing which is which) by which metonymies exfoliate. And Freud's discovery of the force of sex as it worked among the psychological systems was a great one. The problem was, however, not that Freud paid too much attention to sex, but that — paradoxically — he paid too little attention to it. The nature of his inattention manifested itself as a series of metaphors that exhausted sex by purely social analogues. In the Oedipus Complex, for example, infantile sexuality becomes wholly entailed with the *emotions* of jealousy, aggression, and fear, which, after puberty, sexual feelings can, indeed, sometimes evoke when frustrated — though by no means necessarily so. Since sex is *not* an emotion, but an appetite, this entailment wreaks untold confusions in a theory that is supposed to be dealing with 'drives': in short, Freud does not deal with sex as an autonomous function that may (or may not) have its own working rules apart from the shifting emotional calculus in which it is embedded: and he deals with a negative irritant that can only be satisfied (however pleasurably) by a counter irritant as if it were a positive energy. At some point in any detailed analysis that goes on long enough, this must cause errors.

The objection to Lacan — a paradox that mirrors our objection to Freud — is that *he* does not pay enough attention to language. I am not talking of Lacan's famously recomplicated and allusive style. Rather, in the range of his theoretical elaboration there is little to suggest that, for all his brilliant speculation on the way language works [in] the mind, he entertains any grasp of the primary function of language, not only in the function and field of psychoanalysis, but in the general cultural scheme of things.

Language is first and foremost a *stabilizer* of behavior, thought, and feeling, of human responses and reactions — both for groups and for individuals. Its aid in intellectual analysis and communication are (one) secondary and (two) wholly entailed with its function as a stabilizing system. (It is precisely by its ability to stabilize reactions at the level of the signified that language creates — or 'introduces the subject into' — the Symbolic.) Language by itself can call up sexual responses in the absence of a sexual object — and, sometimes, repress sexual responses in the presence of one. Given the tasks we humans find, fixate on, and imagine, again and again our responses must achieve a variety, complexity, and accuracy surpassing those of other species by enormous factors. If there were not an extensive stabilizing system, that variety, complexity, and accuracy could never be achieved.

The masculinist bias in the language of patriarchal society and culture in general, and in psychoanalytic terminology in particular, from 'phallus,' 'castration,' and 'There is only one libido, and it is male,' to 'absent father' and the exemplary 'he,' is not the producer of the problem. But it most definitely stabilizes responses and patterns of response *to* the problem — responses now of individuals, now of groups.

A European study of the 1970s has shown that Italian mothers who breast-feed their infants wean their girl children 40 percent earlier, on the average, than they wean their sons. An American study of the same decade has shown that the average white-collar American father physically handles his under-a-year-old infant of either sex less than five *seconds* a day. Male children under five receive on the average more than five times the amount of physical contact, both from their parents and other adults of both sexes, than do female children of the same age. Infants handled primarily by one adult for their first eighteen months tend to be frightened of strangers and less secure as children than infants handled consistently by two or more adults for their first eighteen months. These and a host of like facts may just *be* among the strongest empirical causes for 'patriarchal culture.' As one collects more and more of them, one begins to read from them a relative brutalization of the female body and the female psyche in infancy and early childhood that manifests itself in any general collection of male and female adults in terms of adult physicality, attitude, and behavior; and they may directly or indirectly control both the Imaginary and the Symbolic orders well before the infant grows into her or his *stade du miroir* — that is, before the phallus (as opposed to the female genitalia or the male genitalia) is perceived as a signifier or anything else.

Language is a stabilizer among our responses to the world and to our problems in it. When the stabilizing system is so powerful and important as to make our responses as we recognize them, for all practical purposes (whether they are good responses or bad ones), possible, it is tempting to view the stabilizing system itself as causative of the responses if the responses are judged good, and causative of the problems themselves if the responses are judged bad (i.e. if the responses exacerbate the problems or just allow them to continue). But with the concept of stabilization of response, we can accept the overlap in both these cases while still avoiding its seductive confusions.

To make real changes in patriarchal society and culture will require complex, intricate, and accurate behavior. And things *can* be done about the empirical problems if our responses are stabilized by language.

Our earliest and originary Judeo-Christian myth tells us that Adam alone had the right to name — that is, he had the triple right, first, to divide up the world into the semantic units most useful for him, second, to organize those units into the fictions that would stabilize what was most useful to him to have stable, and, third, to exclude from language whatever was most convenient for him to leave unspoken. If we want a world where not only freedom of speech, but freedom of social determination exists for both sexes, women must seize this triple right to name, seize it violently and hold to it tenaciously; and they must use it for something more than simply retelling *his* old tales. For those tales were what stabilized patriarchal society in the first place. But only if they seize and use this right will they be able to stabilize reactions in both men and women at a fine enough precision to bring about the desired revolution in patriarchal society and culture. If women commit this seizure, that revolution, however painful, may still be a comparatively peaceful one.

If they do not, it will be a bloody one. For, once again, language is *not* the problem — only a tool to help with solutions.

But at this point the historical battle to name the law and to effect its constitution within an always-to-be-created society and culture — already a whit less patriarchal for sustaining the conflict even the length of time it takes to name it — has always-already begun. And certainly nothing I, a man, have written, write here, or could possibly write represents or expresses its origins.

7. If, as it turns to examine the interplay between the healthy and the pathological, psychoanalysis would untangle specific failures of the stabilizing system, or would examine ways in which the stabilizing system itself is unstable or, indeed, would explore response patterns stabilized in undesirable ways, all well and good. But it must be

prepared to find destabilizing systems, counter-stabilizing systems, and reactions and responses simply too great to be stabilized by the systems available (reactions both social and psychological), many if not most of them nonlinguistic. But only with its object so clarified can psychoanalysis proceed on any front with any lasting efficacy.

8. The excerpt from Ryan's preface that introduces volume three ends with a footnote commending the reader to a number of articles by Gayatri Chakravorty Spivak (from whose introduction to her translation of Derrida's *Of Grammatology* I took the motto for the first volume of these tales), among them: '*Il faut en s'en prenant à elles*,' in *Les fins de l' homme* (Paris, 1981); 'Revolutions that as Yet Have No Model: Derrida's "Limited Inc." ' *Diacritics* 10, no. 4 (Winter 1980); 'Finding Feminist Readings: Dante and Yeats,' *Social Texts* 3 (Fall 1980); 'Unmaking and Making in *To the Lighthouse*,' in *Women and Language in Literature and Society* (New York, 1980); 'Three Feminist Readings: McCullers, Drabble, Habermas,' *Union Seminary Quarterly Review* 35, nos. 1 and 2 (Fall-Winter 1979–80); 'Explanation and Culture: Marginalia,' *Humanities in Society* 2, no. 3 (Summer 1979); 'Displacement and the Discourse of Women,' in *Displacement: Derrida and After*, edited by Mark Krupnick, Indiana University Press (1983); 'Sex and History in *The Prelude* (1805): Books 9–13,' in *Texas Studies in Language and Literature;* 'Reading the World: Literary Studies in the 80s,' in *College English;* and 'French Feminism in an International Frame,' *Yale French Studies.*

Let me iterate Ryan's commendation.

In a sense, modern philosophy is a series of introductions to introductions to introductions, the movement between them controlled by the pro-te$\frac{c}{x}$tive play of forces about desire.

9. Early on, it occurred to me that the relationship of the Nevèrÿon series to semiotics/semiology might be, for better or for worse, much like that of Van Vogt's Null-A series to General Semantics.

I have tried to leave the odd sign of this in the text.

10. Davenport plumbs *Pausanias* (Volume II, Penguin edition, pp. 355–364?) for souvenirs of Elis and its resident Skeptic; Mabbott (or Julian Symons? That's where I found it) for young Poe's bogus Rus-

sian romp; perhaps Maurois for Hugo's visit, from his exile in Jersey, to Guernsey. But that's very different from the historical enterprise of Nevèrÿon; different from the way I comb Braudel, or, for that matter, the *Native*'s D'Eramo.

11. But origins are always constructs, always contouring ideological agendas.

What other kinds of origins, then, am I drawn to discuss?

What other kinds of origins am I drawn to exclude?

12. Childhood readings of Robert E. Howard, descriptions by various friends over the years of Leiber's Fafhrd and the Gray Mouser, Moore's Jeryl, Moorcock's Elric? Finally, I suppose, Russ's *Alyx* series and the introduction for its initial volume assemblage: but those are public precursors for any reader to infer.

I can remember others.

The first Nevèrÿon story, for example, was never finished, never titled; its two fragments, as far as I know, were lost.

In London in 1973, while I was completing the first draft of *Triton* and 'Shadows,' waiting for my daughter to get born, this image struck:

To a sequestered corral, somewhere near the mountain hold of fabled Ellamon, delinquent girls were sent for incarceration from all over the prehistoric land. There they were put to work as grooms and riders for a breed of flying dragon, local to the mountains, which, for some generations now, had been under Imperial protection.

I made two written starts into this imaginary visitation, both of which I thought might become one tale.

One ran to perhaps a dozen typewritten pages:

In a wagon caravan also carrying goods and stores for the mountain hold, a girl of fifteen was being transported from a primitive city, where she'd been convicted of stealing some coins, to the mountain reformatory. Her overseer was a foreign, Amazon-like woman named Raven, who wore a black rag mask across her eyes and who was to work as a guard at the prison once she had delivered her charge.

In the midst of the caravan journey through the forested slopes, bandits attacked the wagons, and, with bow and arrow, Raven killed their chief. (She was a crack shot.) During the attack, she gave the girl some orders, but, more hypnotized than frightened by the violence, the girl did not respond. She was so unused to taking orders, especially from another woman, that it didn't occur to her to obey — even to save her life and the lives of the others around her. Raven was not so much angered or bewildered by the girl's paralysis as amused. She speculated that a time in the reformatory with other young women criminals might do the girl good. The bandits were driven off, but, as the caravan resumed its journey, the girl, who'd always thought of herself as an adventurous, dangerous, and independent sort, was both fascinated and repelled by this foreign woman who killed men for rational reasons.

The other, six-page fragment, written perhaps three weeks earlier, detailed an incident that occurred some weeks later, with the girl now having become an inmate at the dragon corral and Raven having taken up her job among the guards:

The corral had something of a reputation throughout that primitive land, and from time to time men tried to break into it in hope of the sex to be had there from the young criminals. Led by an older inmate, a young woman possibly psychotic, a group of girls (including the newcomer) had captured such an interloper that morning. Binding his hands behind him, they hung him from a wooden rack (was it built for the purpose . . . ?) by one leg.

Over a day and night, the delinquents tortured, maimed, and — finally — killed him.

Was there some question as to whether the man was a willing victim, who'd let himself be captured and bound, under the impression that the delinquent girls, after they had 'enjoyed' him, would set him free . . . ?

Raven learned from the other guards that such male invasions happened two or three times a year — and always with the same end. When men penetrated the mountain reformatory, the more experienced women who guarded the youngsters looked the other way and let them do as they would. At first, when Raven (like the young man) thought the girls would 'enjoy' him and let him go, she'd even allowed some of the girls to sneak off to take part. Later, when she accidentally came upon the actual torture, however, she was deeply troubled — particularly by the participation of the girl she'd brought to the compound. While Raven could conceive of killing men (or women) for reasons of self-defense, this Dionysiac slaughter was, to her, deranged — though, unsettlingly, on discovering it, she could not bring herself to step in and stop it, almost as if she suffered from the same paralysis as had her young charge earlier.

That evening Raven decided she would not remain there as a guard but would leave the dragon corral the next morning and go elsewhere . . .

A third, unwritten scene was probably why the fragments never joined in a single tale. For the strongest of my initial visions was that, at the story's end, the newly imprisoned girl would ride gloriously through the air on the back of a flying dragon —

I begin, a sentence lover, an SF writer; which means I am stuck, willy-nilly, with a certain grammar, a certain logic. It seemed important that my young prisoner not escape (or die!) at the (potential) story's end. ('Escape' was something only Raven, by her decision, was free to do.) But the notion of all these young criminals, grooming and riding their own means to freedom but never actually *using* them, no matter what limitations they'd internalized through whatever social pressures, no matter how terrible the jungle or rock or desert they might have to struggle in when their dragons landed, seemed an oddity that, finally, meant there *was* no story.

Similarly, Raven's inability to bring herself to stop the slaughter of the young man seemed as unbelievable as the girl's inability to do anything to help when the caravan was attacked.

Both finally lacked what T. S. Eliot's generation called 'objective correlatives,' and mine, 'psychological veracity.'

These two moments of feminine paralysis on which everything hinged were 'literature' in its most degraded sense. Neither reflected in any interesting way anything I'd known of women or men in any real situation of material pressure, and both reflected all too much the psychological clichés for heroines of fifties' action-adventure movies.

I felt, and still feel, that it is important for fantasy to have a grasp of the *complexity* of fact, if not of factual content.

So the tale was put aside.

In December 1974, just before Christmas, after a stay of almost two years to the day, I returned from London to New York. When various papers were sent after me, the fragments were not among them.

I haven't seen them since.

The *Hanged Man* from the FitzGerald *Tarot*, drawn over '67 and '68; copyright '69

In some parallel world that tale may have been written, with all its excesses, unbelievabilities, and contradictions — the distortions that would make it 'work' committed largely on the personality of the foreign guard, on her young charges.

It's not my world.

Nevertheless, it remains in memory as one lost origin of Nevèrÿon: those two fragments, with the unwritten third, were the logical and grammatical violences against the real, torn apart, recast, recontoured, critiqued, reformed, elaborated in all their various atomika, and their atomika rejoined as this set of intricate lies that have tethered me to this odd structure, the Nevèrÿon series (built for what purpose . . . ?), a decade now.

13. 'The history of thought is the history of its models,' Fredric Jameson writes in the opening of his preface to *The Prison House of Language.*

14. The problem as some feminists have articulated it (most recently and brilliantly, Teresa de Lauretis, in *Alice Doesn't — Feminism, Semiotics, Cinema* Indiana University Press, 1984), is the exclusion of woman as 'historical subject' from an overwhelmingly male discourse. This exclusion has been effected by yet another logical contradiction of man: historically, woman has been projected again and again as the subject side of man (i.e., as nature, mystery, the unknown, the site of absence of the social constraints on which all society is grounded, the site of uncontrolled desire) and at once the object of man (sign of male social position, a source of cheap or unpaid labor, the desired object, and the unitary exchange commodity that at once binds, coheres, and generates patriarchal society-as-a-collection-of-bodies).

I would suggest that, theoretically, this 'exclusion of woman as historical subject' is a false problem (i.e., a misreading); I would further suggest that, within patriarchal society, the notion of 'historical subjects' itself stabilizes the contradiction and thus encourages the exclusion. The real problem, as I see it, is not the apparent contradiction between woman as subject and woman as object and the exclusion it seems to achieve. It is rather the obvious complicity between the denial, first, of woman as historical object and the denial, second, of woman as transhistorical subject: these twin denials, which have nothing contradictory about them, are the real mechanism for the exclusion of women from a cultural discourse, which, by that exclusion, stabilizes their social, psychological, and sexual exploitation — an exploitation largely carried out in over-whelmingly economic terms. I truly believe that, restated in this wise, the theoretical side of the problem is solved much the way the goose is gotten out of the bottle in the famous Zen koan. What is left for theory in practical terms, after this theoretical revision, is the specific assertion of women as historical object (research, history, speculation on where women have been and what they have done) and the assertion of the historical constitution of women as transhistorical subject (how has it been brought about). Lacan and Foucault both would seem to agree that this is identical with the constitution of 'man' as transhistorical subject. Certainly there must be an overlap: men and women are less than a chromosome apart. But the very existence of a feminist critique, totally aside from any rightness or wrongness of any of its elements, means that identity does not cover the case.

What the pursuit of the false problem has unearthed that is valid nevertheless can be easily represented under the theoretical rubrics of the constitution of woman as transhistorical subject and woman as historical object.

But the truth embodied in the ideological strategy as I have outlined it should be as axiomatic for the poststructuralists as the Saussurian postulate, 'The sign is arbitrary,' was axiomatic for the structuralist enterprise against which the array of poststructuralist positions arose in dialogue: 'The subject *is* transhistorical.' For that is only another way of saying that the subject is fallible: it can, and will, make mistakes.

The transhistoricity of the subject is, of course, an illusion; but it is an inescapable illusion, without which there *is* no subject. (It is, indeed, the ego's belief in itself.) To offer perhaps a somewhat strained analogy: cinema is an illusion constituted of successive frames of light projected on a screen. But without the light or a screen, there is no cinema — no illusion. The subject is a similar illusion, constituted of a sequence of historical responses projected within the sentient body. But without either history or the sentient body, there is no subject — no illusion. Needless to say, the relation between 'successive' historical responses is far more complex than that between the frames of a film; and at that syntactic level of complexity of relation and at the neurological level of complexity of the body in which these relations register, we have a human system quite complex enough for, and capable of, true freedom. (Determinism or indeterminism? No, *that* is not where the 'illusion' lies.) The historical question is, then, what makes women (or men) experience themselves as transhistorical at *one* point in history; what makes them experience themselves as transhistorical at *another* point. And the structure of oppression is as constitutive of that illusion as the organization of strengths. Historically, these things change for women, for men.

To assert that the subject is always transhistorical (and thus an illusion) is in no way one with the assertion that the historical process of the subject's constitution must (therefore) remain totally opaque and beyond all research and theory. It is simply to say that researchers and theoreticians alike must be careful — and on the watch for errors.

Nor do I mean that progress cannot (or has not) been made under the theoretical program of 'historical subjects' — which, in this society, are traditionally male — and its inescapable implication of a transhistorical object, always desired (by whom?), always absent (from what?), an eternally missing factor from the male dominated version of history save as the signifier of desire — the phallus, which woman (supposedly) *is*, but by which she is, the moment she threatens to appear in the Imaginary, displaced by and replaced with a male image, which results in her repression from the Symbolic order through a conspiracy of signs suspiciously similar to, if not identical with, the program by which her productions in society (Imaginary, Symbolic, and — *pace* Lacan — political), as well as all their rewards, are appropriated by, revalued by, and renamed by men, a program both men and women can recognize as exploitative and oppressive. I mean, rather, that such a verbal theoretical expression centering around the retrieval of 'historical subjects' does not *stabilize* the progress made under its rubric. The progress is made — but it tends to be forgotten very quickly, because it is already infiltrated by, and therefore soon dispersed by, the subject myths of patriarchal history with which, unless it remains insistently and programmatically critical of the theory that stabilizes them, it is so intimately entailed.

Counterstabilization, at this point, is necessary.

15. 'What is the Modular Calculus?' a reader writes.

The modular calculus began as a science fictional notion that turns out to be somewhat related to the famous Finagle Factor (that illusive constant sought by all researchers, by which the wrong answer is adjusted to get the right one).

Quine has talked about 'fitting grammars' and 'guiding grammars.' In more informal terms, there can be perfectly accurate descriptions of systems, of situations, or even of machines, which, while they tell us what these systems, situations, and machines look like, how they move, how they function (that is, tell us how they *might* work) nevertheless do not indicate how they *do* work. Similarly, there are explanations that tell us, accurately and precisely, how something actually does work, so that we can both recognize and (potentially) construct an object that works in the same way — though often those explanations will not let us recognize the initial object from which the grammar was derived (it doesn't necessarily tell us whether it was a green one or a red one, if its being green or red is not part of its workings) should we stumble over it in life. The first is, more or less, a fitting grammar. The second is, more or less, a guiding grammar. (And a description rich in *both* fitting and guiding elements is what anthropologist Clifford Geertz calls a 'thick description.')

The modular calculus is an algorithm or set of algorithms (a set of fixed operations) that can be applied to any fitting grammar to adjust it into a guiding grammar.

A limit case, however, strongly suggests such an algorithm is a total fantasy:

'There is a large red box with a button on one end and a light on the other. When you press the button, sometimes the light goes on; sometimes it does not.' The description might go on to include a *possible* circuit that would cause the described switch-and-light operations to occur. There is our fitting grammatical description of an object.

The modular calculus, if such a thing existed, would be a fixed set of algorithms one could apply to this description that would then produce a template of the actual circuitry inside the box, i.e. would give the guiding grammar for the situation.

Well, since there are an infinite number of 'circuits' that could bring about these results, some involving mechanical means, some involving electrical means, some involving electronic means, and many, many, many involving combinations of two or all three, obviously no algorithm could specify which *particular* circuit was *necessarily* inside the box from only our guiding description.

We can push our limit case a step further. 'There is a large black box with a button on one end and a light on the other end. When the button is pushed, the light does not go on.'

The modular calculus would, again, allow us to know from only this much what is in the box.

Since this box may contain nothing, or, indeed, any broken circuit ever envisioned, or any number of working circuits that just do other things, or a donkey, or a set of the *Encyclopaedia Britannica*, the modular calculus seems again reduced to a fantasy at one with a magic that not only lets you see through walls but also assures that you will understand what you see when you do.

If we allow a certain critical margin into the notion of the modular calculus, however, at least we move back to the realm of science fiction:

Clearly descriptions that grow richer in certain directions move closer to accurate functional explanation; certain descriptions as they become enriched in certain ways take on explanatory force. Also, certain descriptions seem to take on explanatory force that they then don't live up to. Others suggest explanations that turn out simply to be wrong.

Might there be an algorithm or set of algorithms that would tell us how close or how far a given description is from explanation, or that would tell us, from a given description, what kind of explanations may eventually be possible from it, or where the description might be further enriched to achieve explanation? For a limited set of situations, such algorithms might be developed and generalized.

In short, the problem of the modular calculus is: How do we know when we have a model of a situation; and how do we tell what kind of model it is?

16. Clearly the Nevèrÿon series is a model of late twentieth-century (mostly urban) America. The question is, of course: What kind of model is it?

This is not the same question as: Is it accurate or is it inaccurate? Rather: What sort of relation does it bear to the thing modeled?

Rich, eristic, and contestatory (as *well* as documentary), I hope.

17. 'Master, save thyself,' the well-traveled merchant who had been to Asia and Portugal told his younger brother, the London saddler

and narrator of Daniel Defoe's *Journal of the Plague Years* (1722), before going off to join his wife and two children whom he had already evacuated to Bedfordshire.

Yet that strangely faceless, bachelor tradesman (Henry Foe, uncle of Daniel, thirty-five when the Great Plague struck London in 1665 . . . ? Daniel himself was five in the year of the plague and 'invented' his well-researched memoir only after news of Marseille's plague of 1720 reached London and he was over sixty) stayed on in the city, despite his older brother's advice, out of a combination of self-interest, acedia, and an odd set of religious scruples (that we, certainly, read as a rationalization, or at any rate a stabilization, of the first two motives): while absently turning through his Bible, his finger fell on the Ninety-first Psalm: '. . . there shall no evil befall thee; neither shall any plague come nigh thy dwelling.' I say odd, because it makes him cleave to a kind of theological determinism (God has ordained all things) that is one with the Asian religion he has been decrying in the account of his brother only a page or so before.

18. All novelistic narrative, at least from the Richardson/Fielding dialogue on, takes place more or less against the following grid: Imagine an equal number of male and female characters. Now divide both into upper class, middle class, and working class, an equal number of males and females in each. Now, for each class and sex, divide your characters into children, adults, and oldsters. For the more modern tale-teller, the grid can be refined even more. Split each of the resultant groups into equal numbers of heterosexuals and homosexuals. If working class, middle class, and upper class is too gross a division, we can add students, teachers, blue-collar, white-collar, management, manual, service workers, civil servants, and artists, at all levels. A major division must be made along racial lines: for the United States, white, black, Amerindian, Oriental, and Hispanic, with most certainly intermediate groups between all of them. If, similarly, youth, maturity, and age seems too gross a set of divisions, they can be further shattered into children, adolescents, young adults, middle-agers, elderly, and aged. But this chart, this grid must eventually specify every possible racial/social/age/gender/sexual type, all of which become ideally equal through their ideal accessibility on this fictive grid.

Like the novel itself, this chart has nothing to do with the statistical prevalence of any one group in our society. (The Victorian novel would lead one to believe that most middle-class unmarried women worked as governesses, while at the same time there were almost no prostitutes in London — whereas in fact there were remarkably few such governesses [probably under two hundred in any one year] and possibly in excess of eighty thousand prostitutes in the city.] It is an ideal chart of possibilities.

Immediately on this imaginary chart we must be able to locate the sixty-four-year-old upper-class homosexual Hispanic woman comic-book artist as easily as the twenty-eight-year-old heterosexual lower-middle-class white male private detective.

Next, we must consider a set of novelistic relations: Friendship; sexual love; enmity; economic antagonism; religious approval; etc. Another generation of the grid must be set up where any and all the 'characters' can relate to any and all of the others [including characters of their own type] by any one of the possible novelistic relations.

This, of course, only gives us beginning points and end points in possible two-character subplots.

Given any two characters, in any relation, that relation must be seen as having the potential to change into any other. Again, the modern storyteller may always want to complicate this grid further by considering also possible relations between three, or even more, characters, that, in the course of the story, change not between two states, but move through three or more . . .

That we can, however mistily, conceive of this grid (and I was twenty when I first began to contemplate its multiple intricacies), even as we acknowledge the impossibility of ever completing it in the abstract, much less of actually writing the Great Novel that portrays, with insight, accuracy, and invention, examples of all that grid's combinations and developments, that conception nevertheless allows us to make some purely qualitative observations about the wealth of bourgeois fictions that take place against it, whether the individual novel privileges a single aging working-class man fishing alone off Cuba in his boat, who barely relates now and again to a young, working-class boy, as in Hemingway's *Old Man and the Sea*, or a single elderly working-class woman fishing alone through an absolute chaos of social interrelationships in Canada, as in Sheila Watson's *The Double Hook*.

This grid — as various novelists begin to impose on it their various economies, for their various conscious and unconscious reasons, picking out this character for a hero, that relationship for development, condensing some while blithely ignoring these, those, and the others — supplies us with the ideological contours of the individual novel as it is foregrounded against any historical or statistical grouping of texts. ('Why, through the range of post-World War II American fiction, are friendships between women almost entirely absent until the 1960s?') Yet it also allows us to bracket that ideological weight momentarily because we can at least be secure that every novel has one. ('Because the return of the male work force from the army made possible the destruction of female solidarity in an economy in which driving women out of work and replacing them with male veterans could be fairly easily stabilized by continuing and developing only slightly a preexistent narrative/language tradition.' This is an ugly, wholly criticizable, but historically accurate answer — at least in terms of a fitting grammar.)

This grid is what allows us to ask of any fiction: Precisely what does it have to say in excess of its ideological reduction? What does it say in excess of the location of its elements on this grid and the subsequent revelation of vast and overdetermined absences? The deconstructionists have led off this set of new readings and most energetically by asking of certain texts: 'What do they have to say that specifically undermines and subverts their own ideological array?' As energetic as the deconstructionist foray has been, we must remember that there are still going to be many texts for which we can expect the answer: 'Not much.'

19. Guy Davenport's fictions have given me more pleasure than those of any single writer I've read in the past three years. Initially I respond to them with complete emotional bewilderment as to why anyone could *want* to write the particular tales he does — why anyone would use what of the method as I can divine beneath his web of allusions and reconstructions. (Is it disingenuous of me to say I find tales such as 'Apples and Pears' and 'O *Gadjo Niglo*' most interesting when they are at their least homoerotic? Probably. What happens when '*Het Erewhonisch Sketsboek*' reaches the 18th Brumaire?) Within what describes for me, then, an arena of almost total dispassion, Davenport brings me again and again to breath-lost awe at the beauties he manages to construct in that lucid, glimmering language field.

'Robot'
'Dawn in Erewhon'
'The Death of Picasso'
These stories (with the greatest 'content,' and thus the greatest accessibility for the reader beginning to enter Davenport's worlds) are among the most carefully constructed art works I know. (In 'On Some Lines of Virgil' I only wish Jonquille could have been anchored to parents, home, landscape, and material life with the same precise, lush, and vivid calculus of writerly invention he lavishes so effortlessly on his boys; but it is an old complaint, an old exclusion.) In my personal pantheon they rank with 'To Here and the Easle,' *La Princesse de Cleves*, 'The Graveyard Heart,' 'The Dead,' 'The Second Inquisition,' 'The Metamorphosis,' *Le Bal du Compte d'Orgel*, 'The Asian Shore,' or *Nightwood*. Yet, where one goes after that, amidst Davenport's constructions, delineates where the *unique* pleasure of his envisionings will be found.

The effect for me is totally aesthetic and awesomely pleasurable — or, as I have taken to saying somewhat glibly to my friends: Davenport's tales are rich in everything I personally love about fiction, and almost wholly devoid of what in fiction, today, bores me.

Frankly, I cannot imagine anyone having that initial response of emotional bewilderment to the impetus behind *any* of the Nevèrÿon tales, whatever one thinks of their execution. (In at least one very important sense, its rhetorical urgencies make 'The Tale of Plagues and Carnivals' the *least* experimental of the series.) Yet I can imagine a hugely changed world, not a hundred years away, but only ten or twenty hence, where that, indeed, would be precisely the response of the common reader to these stories. That world would be, in many ways, the world I conceive of as a Utopia. In short, I suppose, I write yearning for a world in which all these stories might be *merely* 'beautiful.'

20. 'What are "Some Informal Remarks toward the Modular Calculus?" ' another reader writes.

They are a model of a system.

'Some Informal Remarks toward the Modular Calculus' includes, as Part One, the science fiction novel *Triton* and, as Part Two, 'Appendix B' to that novel, 'Ashima Slade and the Harbin-Y Lectures.' From its position in that book, it is undecidable whether 'Appendix

A: From the Triton Journal' is or is not a part of Part One. The 'Informal Remarks' do *not* include the first five tales in the Nevèrÿon series. The 'Appendix' to the first five tales, however, forms Part Three of the 'Informal Remarks.' The novel *Neveryóna, or: the Tale of Signs and Cities* is Part Four of the 'Informal Remarks.' From their position in that book it is undecidable whether or not 'Appendix A: The Culhar' Correspondence' *or* 'Appendix B: Acknowledgments' is or is not part of Part Four. The first two tales of volume three are *not* part of the 'Informal Remarks.' The third tale in *Flight from Nevèrÿon*, 'The Tale of Plagues and Carnivals,' constitutes Part Five of the 'Informal Remarks.' But from their position, it is undecidable whether anything that follows, in volume four (up to and including these notes) is or is not a part. But it would seem that any rich system tends to function through an interchange between what is inside the system and what is outside the system (with what is outside frequently fueling the system proper): and there are always certain elements, such as this appendix, which are undecidable as to whether they are inside or outside — often, though not always, those parts that encourage definition and revision.

ABOUT THE AUTHOR

Samuel R. Delany was born and grew up in New York City's Harlem. His first science fiction novel, published when he was twenty, was *The Jewels of Aptor* (1962). His most recent is *They Fly At Çiron* (1993). Since 1988 Mr. Delany has been a professor of comparative literature at the University of Massachusetts at Amherst.